AN EXPERT IN MURDER

An Expert in Murder

A New Mystery
Featuring Josephine Tey

NICOLA UPSON

HARPER

An Imprint of HarperCollins*Publishers*
www.harpercollins.com

HarperCollins books may be purchased for educational, business, or sales promotional use. For information, please write: Special Markets Department, HarperCollins Publishers, 10 East 53rd Street, New York, NY, 10022.

Extracts from *Richard of Bordeaux* (Gollancz) and *The Privateer* (Peter Davies) by Gordon Daviot [Josephine Tey] reproduced by kind permission of David Higham Associates.

First published in a different form in the United Kingdom in 2008 by Faber and Faber Ltd.

FIRST EDITION

Library of Congress Cataloging-in-Publication Data is available upon request.

ISBN: 978-0-06-145153-9

08 09 10 11 12 OFF/RRD 10 9 8 7 6 5 4 3 2 1

*To Phyllis and to Irene, for their wisdom
and belief, with love from us both*

AN EXPERT IN MURDER

Night was falling when at last he sat down, ready to write. Looking out over the garden, he watched as the louring, grey skies were replaced – inch by inch – with a blackness that wrapped itself like a shroud around the bushes at the limits of his view. Winter had played its customary trick, weaving the landscape together in a cloth of muted colours and bringing a spent uniformity to all he could see. The cold had deadened the richness of the world. In the morning, there would be a covering of frost on the window ledge.

Impatient now to hand over his past, he poured the last inch of warmth from the whisky bottle on the desk and drained his glass before reaching for a sheet of notepaper. It was, he thought with satisfaction, an original sort of bequest. As if in deference to the significance of the moment, the house – usually so alive with faint but familiar sounds – fell silent as he picked up the slim, brown volume that lay on the table in front of him. He flicked through its pages until he came to the section he wished to use; the phrase had always struck him as peculiarly apt, and never more so than now. With a bitter smile, which came half from regret and half from res-ignation, he picked up the pen and began, his lips forming the words in perfect unison with the ink on the page. 'To become an expert in murder', he wrote, 'cannot be so difficult.'

One

Had she been superstitious, Josephine Tey might have realised the odds were against her when she found that her train, the early-morning express from the Highlands, was running an hour and a half late. At six o'clock, when she walked down the steps to the south-bound platform, she expected to find the air of excitement which always accompanies the muddled loading of people and suitcases onto a departing train. Instead, she was met by a testament to the long wait ahead: the carriages were in darkness; the engine itself gravely silent; and a mountain of luggage built steadily along the cold, grey strand of platform. But like most people of her generation, who had lived through war and loss, Josephine had acquired a sense of perspective, and the train's mechanical failure foretold nothing more sinister to her than a tiresome wait in the station's buffet. In fact, although this was the day of the first murder, nothing would disturb her peace of mind until the following morning.

By the time she had drained three cups of bland coffee, the train appeared to be ready for its journey. She left the buffet's crowded warmth and prepared to board, stopping on the way to buy a copy of yesterday's *Times* and a bar of Fry's chocolate from the small news kiosk next to the platform. As she took her seat, she could not help but feel a rush of excitement in spite of the delay: in a matter of hours, she would be in London.

The ornate station clock declared that it was a quarter past eight when the train finally left the mouth of the station and moved slowly out into the countryside. Josephine settled back into her seat and allowed the gentle thrum of the wheels to soothe away any lingering frustrations of the morning. Removing her gloves and taking out a handkerchief, she cleared a small port-hole in the misted window and watched as the strengthening light took some of the tiredness from the cold March day. On the whole, winter had been kind. There had, thank God, been no repeat of the snow wreaths and roaring winds which had brought the Highland railway to a sudden standstill the year before, leaving her and many others stranded in waiting rooms overnight. Engines with snow ploughs attached had been sent to force a passage through, and she would never forget the sight of them charging the drifts at full speed, shooting huge blocks of snow forty feet into the air.

Shivering at the memory of it, she unfolded her newspaper and turned to the review pages, where she was surprised to find that the Crime Book Society's selection was 'a hair-raising yarn' called *Mr Munt Carries On*. They couldn't have read the book, she thought, since she had tried it herself and considered Mr Munt to have carried on for far too long to be worth seven and six of anybody's money. When she arrived at the theatre section, which she had purposely saved until last, she smiled to herself at the news that *Richard of Bordeaux* – her own play and now London's longest run – was about to enter its final week.

As the train moved south, effortlessly eating into four hundred miles or so of open fields and closed communities, she noticed that spring had come early to England – as quick to grace the gentle countryside as it had been to enhance the drama of the hills against a Highland sky. There was something very precious about the way that rail travel allowed you to see the landscape, she thought. It had an expansiveness about it that the close confinement of a motor car simply could not match and she had loved it since, as a young woman, she had spent her holidays travelling every inch of the single-track line that shadowed the turf from Inverness to Tain. Even now, more than twenty years later, she could never leave Scotland by train without remembering the summer of her seventeenth birthday, when she and her lover – in defiance of the terrible weather – had explored the Highlands by rail, taking a different route from Daviot Station every morning. When war broke out, a year later almost to the day, the world changed forever but – for her at least – that particular bond to a different age had stayed the same, and perhaps always would.

This link with the past was becoming harder to hold on to, though, as she found herself unexpectedly in the public eye. She had had thirteen months and four hundred and sixty performances to get used to being the author of the most popular play in London, but fame still tasted strange to her. *Richard of Bordeaux* had brought success, but success brought a relinquishing of privacy which, though necessary, was not easily or willingly given. Every time she journeyed south, she felt torn between the celebrity that awaited her in London and the ties which kept her in Inverness – and knew she was not truly comfortable with either. But during the miles in between, for a few precious hours, she could still remember how it had felt to be seventeen and sure of what you wanted.

Today, though, anonymity vanished even earlier than expected when a pleasant-looking young woman boarded the train at Berwick-upon-Tweed and slid back the door to Josephine's carriage. She struggled apologetically with her luggage, but a gentleman quickly stood to help her wrestle a large, beautifully embroidered travelling bag into the overhead luggage rack, and she smiled gratefully at him when he offered up his window seat. As the girl settled herself in, Josephine gazed at her in fascination, but it was not so much her features that drew attention as the remarkable hat that framed them – a cloche, made of fine black straw, which was accentuated on one side by a curled white ostrich feather, flecked with beige and brown and attached by a long, black-tipped hatpin. It was hardly the sort of thing that Josephine would ever wear herself, and it made her own plain velvet seem bland in comparison, but she admired its delicate beauty nonetheless.

The young woman nodded brightly at her and Josephine returned to her paper but, as she scanned the racing pages, she was uncomfortably conscious of being watched. When she looked up, the girl turned hurriedly back to her magazine, acutely embarrassed at having been caught, and began to study its pages with

5

exaggerated interest. Aware that the journey would be more relaxed for both of them if she smoothed the moment over, Josephine broke the ice. 'You know, I often think that for all the nonsense these racing pundits talk, I could get a job doing it myself,' she said.

The girl laughed, delighted to have a chance at conversation. 'As long as it doesn't take you away from the stage,' she replied, and – as she noticed Josephine's surprise – looked aghast at her own familiarity. 'I'm sorry to disturb you,' she continued, 'and I really don't want to be a nuisance, but I've just got to say something. It is you, isn't it? I recognised you straight away from that lovely article. What a wonderful coincidence!'

Josephine forced a smile and quietly cursed the publicity photograph that had appeared in one of the more obscure theatrical journals, confirming to its handful of readers that Gordon Daviot – the name she wrote under – was certainly not hers by birth. 'How observant of you,' she said, embarrassed to see that the other occupants of the carriage were taking a new interest in their travelling companion. 'That came out a year ago – I'm surprised you remember it.'

'That's the coincidence – I read it again just the other day when I found out I was coming down to see *Richard* in its final week, and I've got it with me now.' She pointed towards her bag as proof of the happy accident. 'Listen, I hope you won't think I'm just saying this because it's you, but I do love that play. I've been so many times already and I *will* miss it when it's gone.' She paused, absent-mindedly curling a lock of brown hair round her finger as she looked out of the window. 'I suppose most people would think it silly to get as engrossed in theatre as I do, or to put such value on stories that other people make up, but for me it's much more than a play.' She looked back at Josephine. 'I shouldn't be talking to you like this when we've only just met and you want to read your paper, but I must thank you now I've got the chance. My father died last year, and it's all been so miserable for my mother and me, and sometimes your play got me through. It was the only thing I could lose myself in.'

Touched, Josephine folded away her newspaper. 'It's not silly,' she said. 'If you took any notice of people who think it is, there'd be no pleasure in the world. I'm sorry to hear about your father, though. Was his death very sudden?'

'Oh no, he'd been ill for a long time. He was in the army, you see, and he never recovered from the war.' She smiled ruefully. 'And sometimes I think my mother will never recover from my father. She was devastated when we lost him – we both were – but she's been better lately. And we work together, so at least I've been able to keep an eye on her.'

'What do you do?' Josephine asked, genuinely curious.

The girl raised her eyes, and this time her smile was warm and conspiratorial. 'Can't you guess? We're in hats.' She held out her hand. 'I'm Elspeth, by the way. Elspeth Simmons.'

'Call me Josephine. It's beautiful, you know – your hat.' Elspeth blushed and started to protest, but Josephine interrupted her. 'No, honestly – if I've got to sit here and take compliments, then you must have your share. You've got a real talent – it must run in the family.'

'Perhaps, but I wouldn't really know – I'm adopted, you see,' Elspeth explained candidly. 'They took me on when I was a baby. You're right – my adoptive mother taught me everything, but we're not very much alike, although we get on tremendously well. All this play business drives her up the wall – she hates the theatre, apart from a bit of variety at Christmas, so I usually go with my uncle. When I tell her how pleased I am to have met you, she probably won't even know what I'm talking about. Still,' she added, a little wistfully, 'I like to think my original parents had some theatrical blood in them somewhere.'

Looking again at the memorable hat, Josephine guessed that Elspeth's adoptive mother was not without her own sense of the dramatic. Although by now the girl had lost much of her initial shyness and was talking eagerly about the theatre, Josephine could not resent the loss of her cherished peace and quiet. Rather, she felt a growing admiration for Elspeth's spirit and lack of self-pity. Her conversation did not entirely mask the series of tough blows that life had dealt her: abandoned as a baby, then claimed again only to have her second chance at happiness destroyed by a conflict which she was of no age to understand – if such an age existed. Thousands like Elspeth there might have been, but the sharing of tragedy – even on such a scale – did not make the personal cost any easier to bear for each individual it touched. Josephine knew that as well as anyone. Twenty years after it started, the war had reinvented its suffering for a second generation in the form of inescapable confinement with the sick and wounded, and an eventual loss whose pain was the more sharply felt for its delay. After her father's long illness, then his death, who could blame Elspeth for taking refuge in the less demanding emotions of the stage, or for contemplating another, more glamorous, identity? It was not so different to what she herself had done and – in the face of her own father's fragile health – what she continued to do.

'I hope you won't think it rude of me to ask,' Elspeth continued, 'but will you be sad when your play ends?'

Josephine had asked herself the same thing when she saw the press notice earlier. The answer had not required much soul-searching, although it would have been churlish to show the true extent of her relief. 'No, not really,' she said. 'It's going on tour, after all, and it's lovely to think that people all over the country will see it. I do have another play or two on the go, and my publisher wants a second mystery story at some point, so there's plenty to keep me busy.' She did not admit it to Elspeth, but there was another reason why her heart was no longer in the play that had made her name: that business last year with Elliott Vintner had soured the whole experience for her. The voice of reason inside her head told her time and time again that she was not to blame for the court case or its repercussions, but the thought that a man had taken his own life because of her success filled her with a coldness that no amount of rational argument could eradicate.

Fortunately, before Josephine could go further down that road, a restaurant attendant passed through the carriages to announce the next sitting for lunch. 'Let's go and have something to eat,' she suggested to Elspeth, conscious that the young woman's enthusiasm for her work was beginning to wear a little thin with everyone else in the compartment. 'It's been a long morning.'

The train's delay had created a healthy appetite in its passengers. The dining car was almost full when they arrived, but a waiter showed them to the last vacant table. 'Gosh – how lovely,' said Elspeth, looking round at the bronze lamps, plush carpets and walnut veneer panelling, 'I don't think I've ever eaten anywhere as luxurious as this before.' She removed her hat, then looked round anxiously for somewhere to put it before the waiter came to her rescue and took it from her with a wink. 'I'm not used to first class,' she admitted, picking up a silver butter knife to admire the railway crest on the handle. 'The ticket was a present. Will you order for us – I'm sure it's all delicious.'

Josephine smiled at her. 'To be honest,' she said, 'Inverness isn't exactly overrun with top restaurants so I think we should just treat it as a posh café and have what we like. I'm going for the sole – how about you?' Elspeth studied the menu and, when the waiter arrived, chose a no-nonsense steak and kidney pudding. 'A glass of wine, miss?' he asked.

'I'd love one, but I wouldn't know where to start,' Elspeth said, looking at Josephine.

'The Burgundy would go well with your lunch, so let's both have that,' she said and watched, amused, as the waiter unfolded Elspeth's napkin and slid a silver vase of flowers closer to her with another wink that brought a flush to her cheeks.

'I'd love to know more about the cast,' Elspeth said, as their drinks arrived. 'Tell me – are John Terry and Lydia Beaumont as close off stage as they are on? I won't tell anyone if it's a secret, but they make such a good couple as Richard and Anne.'

Josephine smiled to herself, imagining how pleased Terry would be to perpetuate the rumour of a romance with his glamorous leading lady, but she had to crush Elspeth's hopes. 'No, they're both . . . well, they're just good friends,' she said. 'I suppose it would be difficult to work together if they were involved and they've got another joint project lined up with my next play.'

'Am I allowed to ask what it is?'

'Of course you are. It's a play about Mary Queen of Scots. In fact, I wrote it for Lydia. She's always wanted to play her.'

'How special to have a play written for you! She must be so pleased. I can't wait to see her in it.'

'You'll see her sooner than that, actually. She should be meeting me at King's Cross if this train arrives before she has to be at the theatre,' Josephine explained, tucking in to her meal and encouraging Elspeth to do the same. 'I'll introduce you if you'd like to meet her.'

'Oh, that would be wonderful. You know, I can't wait to tell Uncle Frank about all this. He's seen *Richard* almost as many times as I have.'

'Is that who you're staying with?'

'Yes, I always do when I'm in London. He and my Aunty Betty have a shop in Hammersmith – shoes and knitwear, that sort of thing.'

'Do you come down often?'

'About once a month. I bring the hats and help out in the shop a bit. It's a family business, so we all chip in. But Uncle Frank's passionate about theatre. He collects memorabilia and drives Aunty Betty mad because there's only a small flat above the shop and he packs it with stuff. When I'm down, we spend as much time as we can in the West End. He'll be so thrilled when I tell him about my journey. I don't suppose you could sign a copy of the programme for him and leave it at stage door, could you? Would it be too much trouble?'

'Of course not, and I'll sign your magazine as well if you like.' She thought for a moment, then said: 'Do you have your tickets for the show yet? I've got some reserved for the week and you'd be most welcome to join me one evening.' It was unlike her to encourage intimacy in this way but, for some reason, she felt protective towards the young woman in front of her. Much to her surprise, the response to her question was a pink tide which began at Elspeth's neck and rose slowly upwards.

'Actually, I'm going with someone tomorrow night and he's got us top price seats,' she explained. 'We've been out a few times and he's lovely. It's his first job in theatre and he doesn't get much time off, so I suppose the last thing he needs is to sit through it all again,' she added, and instantly looked horrified. 'Not that he doesn't love the play, of course, it's just . . .'

She tailed off, at a loss as to how to redeem herself, and Josephine came to her rescue. 'Please don't worry – if I could choose between another night with *Richard* and a good dinner at the Cowdray Club, there'd really be no contest. You can have too much of a good thing. No matter how entertaining it is for the audience, it's a bit of a busman's holiday if you work there – he must be very keen on you to go at all.'

As Elspeth blushed again and excused herself for a moment, Josephine asked for the bill. She looked on, amused, as the waiter transferred his attentions from Elspeth to another table, where he spent more time than was strictly necessary polishing a crystal glass for a young woman dining alone. This girl was more receptive, and she watched while the couple circled round each other, wondering what the outcome would be. When Elspeth reappeared, Josephine shook off her insistence that the bill should be halved and they headed back to their compartment.

At last, the carriages began snaking through the outskirts of the capital. How England's cities were changing, Josephine thought, looking out at the small, modern houses and giant cinemas which seemed to have sprung up everywhere. As the train slowed its speed still further and ran into a deep cutting, the dwindling daylight vanished altogether. When it returned, it gave form to the dark bulk of St Pancras and the Midland Grand, an edifice which would have looked more at home in a gothic tale of terror than it did next to the ordinary contours of King's Cross. Josephine had heard that engine drivers on this route took a pride in the journey, racing against the timetable and each other to achieve speeds of more than ninety miles an hour, and she was not the only passenger on board to offer up a silent prayer of thanks to the competitive nature which had brought the train to its destination less than an hour behind schedule.

*

Stamping her feet against the coldness of the day, Lydia Beaumont was nevertheless in a remarkably good mood. Ever the actress, she always felt an affinity with the transience and variety of somewhere like King's Cross: the wandering population of travellers and street traders had an anonymity which intrigued her and a colour which appealed to her weakness for showmanship and talent for mimicry.

The other reason for Lydia's unshakeable good humour was standing beside her. She and Marta Fox were, to paraphrase her character in the play, still at the stage in their relationship where the heavens could collapse without undue damage to either of them. By March, it was not uncommon for the year to have offered Lydia at least three different versions of the love of her life, but Marta had survived to enter victoriously into a fourth month of tenure. By Lydia's own admission, this was a relationship of some permanence.

From the approaching train, Josephine spotted her friend and felt the same mixture of admiration and apprehension that always accompanied their meetings: admiration for her graceful charm and childlike mischief, for the humour which was always in her eyes and never far from the corners of her mouth; apprehension because, if she were honest, Josephine was almost as uncomfortable with the celebrity of others as she was with her own. With Lydia, though, there had been a mutual appreciation from the outset – a genuine trust stemming from their shared frankness and hatred of vanity in all its guises – and Josephine had come to value the friendship greatly, whilst marvelling that it should be hers. From force of habit, she cast an appraising eye over the woman who stood next to Lydia on the platform and was pleased to note that her own first impressions tallied with the description that her friend's letters had carried to Inverness. Even from a distance, there was an air of calm about her, a quiet containment in the resolute stance that held its own beauty. If Marta proved as strong as she seemed, she could be just the antidote Lydia needed to the fickleness which was an inevitable part of her life in the theatre.

Elspeth was so excited at the sight of Anne of Bohemia alive and well less than fifty yards away that Josephine's gentle wave of greeting could hardly be seen from the platform. Keen to leave the train and meet Lydia, the girl reached up to drag her bag down from the luggage rack but, in her haste, forgot that she had opened it earlier to find the magazine for Josephine to sign. When its contents spilled out onto the floor, she looked mortified and Josephine – whose instinct towards amusement was overcome by her sympathy for Elspeth's vulnerability – came quickly to her aid. As the two scrabbled on the floor for stray sweets and loose change, they looked at each other through the legs of the other passengers, and laughter soon won out. Standing back against the window to allow everyone else to gather their belongings, they took a minute to compose themselves sufficiently to leave the compartment. What sort of scene they were creating for those on the platform, Josephine could hardly imagine.

'Here she is at last,' said Lydia, pointing towards the carriage window. 'My God, dear, have you seen that hat?' Marta took one look and muttered something about getting them a place in the queue for taxis. 'We'll be with you in a jiffy,' Lydia called after her.

When she turned back to the train, Josephine was on her way over with the companion who had made such an impression on the train's arrival. Had she not known her, Lydia would never have guessed that this quiet Scottish woman, dressed simply in a dark suit and pearls, was the author of the biggest hit in the West End. Nothing about Josephine had changed since Lydia first became aware of her as a shadowy presence in the stalls during rehearsals. She still looked more like a school teacher or one of those solitary women you saw writing letters in the corner of a hotel lounge. It had been hard to get to know her, as she discouraged intimacy and rarely gave her confidence to anyone, but the effort had been worthwhile. Josephine was thoughtful and sensitive, interested in everything and possessed of a puckish, sarcastic wit that was as evident in her conversation as it was in her work.

Greeting Lydia with a hug, Josephine introduced the girl as a friend she had met on the journey down. The actress, always gracious when faced with her public, went through the routine of conversation and autographs that had become second nature to her, whilst managing to make Elspeth feel that she was the first person ever to mention the poignancy of the death scene. After a politely timed exchange of charm and admiration, she remembered Marta and the waiting taxi. 'Come on, we must get you safely to that madhouse you're staying in,' she said to Josephine. 'I'm sure you could do with a rest after such a long day, and I need to be at the theatre on time or Johnny will be a bag of nerves throughout the entire first act. You'd think he'd be used to it by now.' She flashed a winning smile at Elspeth, and picked up Josephine's travelling case. 'Is the rest of your luggage being sent on?' she asked.

At the mention of luggage, a look of panic crossed Elspeth's face. 'I don't believe it,' she cried. 'After all that fuss, I've left my bag on the train. I must go back and get it, then I'd better find my uncle. My mother's entire new range is in there,' she explained, gesturing towards the mountain of hat boxes that an unlucky porter had felt obliged to transfer from the luggage car to a platform trolley, 'and she'll kill us if we don't get it safely delivered to Lillibet's.' Hugging Josephine tightly and promising to look her up at the theatre, Elspeth vanished back into the carriage from which she had so thoroughly emerged, too concerned about her bag to notice that the feather had become dislodged from her hat and now lay on the platform floor. Josephine bent down to pick it up.

'Keep it – it'll suit you,' teased Lydia, looking half-admiringly, half-sympathetically at her friend. 'You really do have the patience of Job. I don't know anyone else who could spend a day with all that enthusiasm and still look sane at the end of it.'

Josephine smiled. 'Much to my surprise, it's been a pleasure. I must give it back to her, though,' she said, turning towards the train.' She'd be so sad not to have it when she meets her young man.'

Lydia caught her arm. 'We really must go, Josephine – I can't be late. Give it to her when she comes to see you at the theatre. My guess is that it won't be long.'

Josephine hesitated. 'No, you're right. I'll probably see her tomorrow. Let's go and find Marta – I'm dying to meet her.'

'Yes, and you can tell me whether this novel that she's writing is any good or not. She's far too divine for me to have any way of telling. She could jot down the shipping forecast and I'd think it was pure Daviot!' Laughing, the two women walked out into the street, too engrossed in their conversation to notice the figure now moving towards the train.

Back on board, Elspeth saw with relief that her bag was still on the floor where she had left it. The train seemed almost deserted, the only noise coming from further down the car where staff were presumably preparing for the next journey. Looking down at the magazine, which now held two precious signatures, she smiled to herself and placed it carefully in the bag's side pocket, thinking with excitement of the pleasure she would get from watching the next performance now that she knew two of the people involved.

As she buttoned the pocket securely and made sure this time that the rest of the bag was fastened, she heard a noise at the door behind her. Turning to explain to the guard that she had forgotten something and was just about to leave, she stared with recognition, then confusion, at a face which she had not expected to see on the train. Instinctively, before she had a chance to consider the strangeness of the moment, she took the gift that was held out to her with a smile and looked down at the doll in her hands, a souvenir of her beloved play and something she had longed to own. When her companion took the 'Do Not Disturb' sign from its hook and hung it outside the door, then stepped quickly over to the window to pull down the blind, Elspeth opened her mouth to protest, but the words were too slow to save her.

An arm reached out towards her, drawing her into a deadly embrace which seemed to mock the physical affection she had so recently come to know. There was no time to scream. The hand that gripped the back of her neck, holding her close, was swift and sure, and by now no strength was needed. Surprise had given way to a paralysing horror and she had no more control over her limbs than the doll which fell to the floor and lay staring upwards, an indifferent witness to her final moments. She tried to breathe normally, to stay calm, but her face was pressed into her assailant's chest and panic welled up in her as she realised that this must surely be death. Please God, no, she thought, not now, not when I'm so happy.

When the lethal point punctured her skin, she felt nothing more than a sharp blow beneath her ribs but there was no chance to be thankful for the lack of pain, nor to wonder that her body should surrender itself with so little ceremony. In that briefest of moments, somewhere between waking and oblivion, between life and death, she was aware of all she would miss but the longing was soon over, replaced as she fell to her knees by a lasting, if premature, peace.

Two

Detective Inspector Archie Penrose could never travel in the King's Cross area without feeling instantly depressed. North London was the city at its most forbidding and, despite the widening of the streets, its most claustrophobic. He drove down an uninspiring thoroughfare bordered with drab houses, few of which had ever been decorated or even cleaned, and past the straggling shabbiness of Euston Station. Then there was King's Cross itself; he always thought that the station's facade – two main arches separated by a clock tower of dreadful yellow brick, turned black with the dirt of ages – looked more like the entrance to a gaol than the gateway to a capital. Certainly it did nothing to help a man on his way to a murder investigation.

A sizeable crowd had gathered at the head of Platform Eight, obscuring his view of the train in which the girl's body had been discovered less than an hour ago by a young railway employee. According to Penrose's colleague, Sergeant Fallowfield, the boy was now in a state of shock. Fallowfield, who had been handling an incident round the corner in Judd Street when the call came in and was first on the scene, approached him now, pushing his way through the on-lookers with very little patience for their ghoulish curiosity.

'You'd think they'd have something better to do on a Friday night, wouldn't you, Sir? Bloody vultures, the lot of 'em.'

The comment was uncharacteristic of his sergeant, who usually had a more positive view of human nature despite years of experience to the contrary. Whatever he had seen on the train had clearly got to him. 'Poor kid, she can't be more than twenty,' Fallowfield said, as if reading his thoughts. 'Hardly had a chance to start her life, let alone live it.'

'Do we know who she is?' Penrose asked.

'Assuming it's her bag in the carriage, her name's Elspeth Simmons and she's from Berwick-on-Tweed – at least, that's where she got on the train, and it's a return ticket. It's a nasty one, this, Sir – as spiteful as anything I've seen. I reckon we've got a sick bastard on our hands.'

When he saw what awaited him in the sealed-off carriage, Penrose could only agree. The dead girl sat – or rather seemed to have been composed – on the middle of the three seats to the right of the compartment, an ornate and deadly hatpin protruding from under her breastbone. Her hands had been clasped together in front of her in a mockery of applause at the scene which someone had created for her benefit in the vacant space opposite. There, a pair of dolls – one male and one female – had been carefully arranged on the seat like actors on a stage. They stood together in a half embrace, and he noticed that the woman's left hand – the one that bore her wedding ring – had been broken off and lay on its own in front of the couple like a sinister prop from a horror film. Close to them on the seat was a hand-written note on expensive-looking paper: 'Lilies are more fashionable,' it said, but the flower that lay on the floor was not a lily but an iris.

It was immediately obvious to him that this was not a random or spontaneous killing but a carefully thought-out, and probably deeply personal, act of violence. Not for a second did he think that the murderer wished to be quickly identified, but there could be little doubt that a message could be traced in every object that he – or she – had been so careful to leave on and around the body. It was a crime that had required considerable nerve.

'Were the blinds up or down when she was found?' he asked.

'Both down, Sir. The boy says he pulled that one up as soon as he came in.'

Even so, Penrose thought, the scene must have taken a few minutes to arrange once the murder had been committed, and that would mean a greater risk of discovery than most people could countenance. That was the point, though: in a symbolic killing such as this, they were not dealing with the fears and doubts of a normal person but with the arrogance and sense of invulnerability that invariably accompanied evil.

'And is this exactly how she was found?'

'Yes, or so he says. Forrester's his name and he's obviously frightened out of his wits. Maybrick's had the waiting room cleared and taken him there with a cup of tea. Poor little sod – I'm not surprised he's scared: I wouldn't have liked to walk in on something like this at his age. Those dolls are enough to put the wind up anybody, and they gave him a right start – as much as finding the body.'

Penrose turned to look at them. The dolls were each about a foot high and elaborately clothed in fringed cloaks and old-fashioned head-dresses. Intrigued, he moved slightly closer, marvelling at the detail with which the faces had been modelled, appearing perversely life-like in a place of death. 'They're not just any dolls, Bill. I wonder if they were hers or if the killer brought them? They're souvenirs from a play that's on in the West End at the moment – *Richard of Bordeaux*; it's a historical piece about Richard II. Those dolls have been made specially to look like the characters in it. And that piece of paper,' he continued, pointing to the note on the seat, 'that's a quotation from it: "Lilies are more fashionable." I think it's the Queen who says it at some point.'

Fallowfield had never heard of the play, but it came as no surprise to him that his superior should know all about it. Apart from policing, theatre was Penrose's great passion and he had an exhaustive knowledge of the subject as well as a few friends and relatives in the business. 'I just thought the note was a funny sort of love letter,' Fallowfield said.

'I suppose in a way it is,' Penrose replied. 'The question is – who's it from? And is the sender going to be devastated when we break the news that Miss Simmons is dead?'

'Or does he know already, you mean?' Fallowfield finished the line of thought. 'Bit of an obvious calling card, that, don't you think, Sir? I mean, we're going to find out if she was courting and if it really is a boyfriend who did it, he might as well have left his address and saved us some time.'

'Yes, I suppose so, but I don't think for a minute it's going to be as simple as all that. For a start, we've no guarantee that it is a love letter and, judging by everything else that's been put here for a reason, I'd say there's a much deeper meaning than some kind of clumsy romantic gesture. And apart from all this extra paraphernalia, don't you think that hatpin's an odd sort of weapon to choose? Not a very masculine sort of killing. It's straight out of Agatha Christie: *Murder on the Royal Highlander* in fifteen easy chapters.'

'Perhaps they all did it then, Sir. And there's only nine chapters, by the way,' Fallowfield said with unconscious irony, betraying an *au fait*-ness with current detective fiction that always surprised Penrose. He suddenly had an image of his down-to-earth sergeant rushing home from the Yard every night to devour the latest thriller by his fireside. Better still, perhaps he was actually writing one of his own. The thought of Miss Dorothy L. Sayers turning out to be a portly, moustached officer of the law in his early fifties was priceless, and he made a mental note to mention it to Josephine when he saw her tomorrow night.

Except now, of course, he would have to see her earlier than planned and there would be no joy in the meeting. For whatever reason, this girl's murder was linked to her play and, no matter how innocent the explanation, he could not conceal that fact from her and neither would she want him to. He wished he could dilute the shock by promising the sort of tidy solution with which she had concluded her first detective story, but he couldn't insult her intelligence in that way and wouldn't get away with it if he tried. He might long for the sort of luck that his fictional counterpart, Inspector Alan Grant, had enjoyed on his debut outing, but he and Josephine both knew that the reality of death was different, that murder brought with it a contagious messiness, a stain of grief, horror and disruption which refused to be contained within the pages of a novel.

He realised with embarrassment that Fallowfield had continued the conversation beyond his erudite knowledge of the works of Mrs Christie, but he had no idea what the man had been saying. The Sergeant, who was used to Penrose's tendency to allow his mind to wander, patiently repeated himself. 'I was just saying about the hatpin, Sir. Turns out that millinery was her job. So perhaps it was just convenient to stab her with that.'

Penrose glanced at the hat which lay scuffed and crumpled on the floor close to the body, a casualty of the violence that had taken place. 'Yes, perhaps.' He looked at the girl intently, trying to see beyond features which had been dulled by death, to imagine what she had been like just a few hours ago and pinpoint what would have struck him about her had he passed her in the street. With any murder investigation, he insisted on giving the dead a dignity and individuality which he could not always assume they had been afforded in life. The old adage was true: there were only a few genuine reasons for murder – love, greed and revenge topped the list – but each victim was different, and each had the right to be treated as if theirs were a unique death. He moved over to the body, close enough to notice a bloodstain on her collar. The mark indicated a cut to the neck but it was so small that it would have been easy to miss it. The victim's head was tipped to one side and slightly forward, and he could see that a small patch of hair had been shaved off at the back. It had been roughly done – obviously the murderer had been in too much of a hurry to worry about breaking the skin – and a few strands of hair still lay on the girl's left shoulder. Such an odd thing to do, he thought – so insignificant, and yet somehow so humiliating.

The air in the compartment was heavy and oppressive, and Penrose was glad to step outside into the corridor. 'Where is the luggage, by the way?' he asked Fallowfield. 'Was it being sent on or was she planning to take it with her?'

'I've had it locked in one of the guards' rooms, Sir. There were no instructions for it to be sent anywhere.'

'Then someone must have been coming to meet her. You'd better go and see who you can find in that crowd, Sergeant. Whoever it is will be worried sick by now – unless they've got something to hide, of course. We'll leave the scene to the boys, but tell them I want photographs of the lot – every small detail, particularly that cut on her neck. And we'll need to start working through the passenger list, so the sooner you can get hold of that and a list of staff on duty, the better. I'll go and see if Forrester can tell us anything we don't already know – I could do with a cup of Maybrick's tea myself, now you mention it – but if you find that anyone's been waiting for her, I want to be told straight away. Have you gone through her bag yet?'

'I've had a quick look, Sir. A few papers and a couple of weeklies, and this was in the side pocket with her train ticket,' said Fallowfield, holding out a magazine. 'Look at page fourteen.'

Penrose did as he was told. When he saw the dated inscription, his heart sank: 'To dear Elspeth, with thanks for an unforgettable trip. I hope we'll meet again! Much love, Josephine (Gordon).' So she had known her as well, and could have been one of the last people to see her alive. Suddenly he needed something a little stronger than Maybrick's tea.

When he saw the closest thing he had to a witness sitting in the waiting room clutching a full cup of tea that must have been cold for some time, Penrose realised he was unlikely to hear anything of great use. Fallowfield had been accurate in his assessment of Forrester's fear, and it was hardly surprising. Most people were fortunate enough to reach a comfortable middle age before an awareness of the transience of life began to weigh heavily on them, but that was a luxury which had been denied to his own generation and he was all too experienced in recognising the moment when someone first came face to face with his own mortality.

For Penrose, that moment had come before he really had a chance to find anything out about himself, to know who he might have become if the world had turned out differently. He could still remember that week in early September – a month or so short of his return to Cambridge for the final year of his medical degree – when the war had begun, but before it had gathered any real momentum. In Cornwall it had been intensely hot for the time of year, and he was making the most of his last days at home. The village had decided to continue as planned with the Harvest Festival in defiance of the stresses and strains of war, so he had joined the rest of the family in a walk to the cliff-top church on the edge of his grandfather's estate to listen while his uncle, the rector of the parish, thanked God for a magnificent harvest and the unbroken weather which had allowed it to be gathered in.

As soon as he saw the great Union Jack which had replaced the usual hanging at the front of the pulpit, Penrose realised that God's representative – a sanctimonious bigot at the best of times, even if he was family – had changed his agenda. After preaching a terrifying sermon on the glories of battle, sanctifying maiming, slaughter and bloodshed with the blessing of a higher authority, the rector had urged all the young men to join the army, to sate the country's appetite for soldiers who would defend the justice of the war. What he had failed to mention was that it was a cause for which thousands of them would be asked to give their lives, but his harvest sermon had done the trick: by the end of the year, every eligible man in the village had signed up to Kitchener's new army, an exodus which was replicated all over the country, swelling the ranks by nearly a million in the space of just four months. Some expected garrison service at home while the real soldiers went off to do the real soldiering; most believed the papers when they said it would be a short war, over by Christmas at the outside. All had been wrong, and he was still sickened to the stomach when he thought of that call from the altar for young men to offer themselves for the glory of God and eight shillings and nine pence a week.

In his darker moments, when a connection to life was harder to find, he wondered if that was perhaps what kept him in this job – not an abstract desire for justice or a belief that he could do anything to stem the evil which ran inherently through some men's hearts, but a desperate need to contain the sense of guilt which he had carried since those days. Sometimes it worked, and the natural course of an investigation in which the humanity of an individual was paramount dispelled the sense of waste that came from seeing death on such a massive scale – but those moments were rare, and the anger that had been a part of him since the war only seemed to grow deeper with time.

'Let's go back to before you found Miss Simmons in the compartment,' he said to the boy gently.

'Is that her name, then?'

'Yes, she was called Elspeth. What were you doing in that carriage?'

'I was only in there to make sure it was clean and tidy, ready for the next journey.'

'But that wasn't your job, was it? You're a waiter, not a porter.'

Tommy took one look at the Inspector's face and knew instantly that it would be pointless to string him along by pretending any great diligence in his work. 'There was this girl, see? In the restaurant car – she kept giving me the eye, so I asked one of the other blokes if I could have a go at checking some carriages because I knew she'd be there somewhere. I thought I could catch her before she got off and see if she fancied a bite to eat later on. There wasn't any harm in it,' he finished defiantly.

'And did you?'

'Did I what?'

'Catch her before she left the train.'

'I did, as it happens. I was supposed to meet her outside the station when I knocked off. I expect she's given up by now,' Tommy said, with a wistful glance in the direction of the door.

'Does this girl have a name?'

'Ivy. I don't know what her other name is. We hadn't got that far.'

'You're sure you didn't really go looking for Miss Simmons in that compartment?'

Penrose's voice had taken on a harder edge and it suddenly dawned on Tommy that his quest for a date might have brought him a little more trouble than he'd bargained for. 'You don't think it was me, do you?' he cried in horror. 'I know I flirted with her in the restaurant, but I was only being friendly and I'm like that with everyone. I'd never hurt a girl and anyway, I thought she was already off the train – I saw her on the platform while I was talking to Ivy.'

'All right, calm down.' Penrose sent Maybrick out to see if the elusive Ivy had anything better to do than hang around outside a railway station waiting for her meal ticket, then turned his attention back to Tommy. 'No, actually I don't think you had anything to do with it, but I need you to be honest with me about exactly what you saw and when. You say you noticed Miss Simmons on the platform, but surely there were a lot of people milling around? What made her stand out?'

'Her hat for a start,' Tommy replied. 'You couldn't miss that. And her luggage – she had loads of it. I remember being glad that I didn't have to unload that lot.' He paused for a moment, then fell back on the criteria that made most sense in his world. 'She wasn't a bad-looking girl, either. Not in the same class as Ivy, obviously, but you wouldn't mind being seen walking out with her.'

'And how long after seeing Miss Simmons on the platform did you find her body?'

'I don't know – about ten or fifteen minutes, I suppose. I caught up with Ivy just as she was about to get off the train – I think she'd been hanging about, hoping I'd come and find her – and we talked just outside the carriage door for a few minutes. That's when I noticed the girl. She was a bit further down the platform, talking to a couple of other women. Then I saw Mr Folkard – he's the boss – coming towards me, so I had to fix something up quick with Ivy and scarper before he asked me what I was doing. It only took me a few minutes to look in on the other compartments to make sure nothing had been left behind – and then I got to that one.'

'Did you notice anybody hanging about?'

'I didn't *see* anybody, no.'

'But?'

'Well, when I got to that compartment, the "Do Not Disturb" notice was hanging on the door so I just knocked and told them to hurry up, then I went on to the next one.'

'How did you know there was someone in there? Wasn't it more likely that the notice had just been left on the door?'

'I could hear someone moving about.' Tommy looked down, embarrassed. 'I thought they were having a bit of . . . well, you know. So I left them to get themselves sorted out and came back a couple of minutes later, after I'd heard someone shut the door and leave.'

'Exactly what did you hear inside the compartment?'

'Just a bit of shuffling.' He looked up at Penrose, suddenly more aggressive. 'You don't think I'd have left her if I'd known what was going on, do you? How was I supposed to guess that there was a bleeding psychopath on board?'

So that was why the boy was so defensive. It wasn't just shock at discovering a body that had so affected him, but the realisation of how close he had come to the murder and a sense of guilt at having failed to stop it. Penrose continued more gently.

'What did you see when you first went into the compartment?'

'It was nearly dark because the blinds were down, but I could see someone was still in there. I thought they must be asleep, so I went over and lifted the blind at the window. When I turned round, I saw the girl, and some funny dolls on the other seat.'

'How long were you in there?'

'It can only have been a minute or two but it felt like ages. I wouldn't have stayed that long but I suddenly thought – what if whoever did it was still about? Then that flower fell off the seat and I just legged it. It sounds stupid, I know, but I couldn't bear it any longer.'

'Did you touch anything?'

'Only the blind when I first went in. It was too dark to tidy up, you see.'

'And the women Miss Simmons was talking to – did you recognise them from the train?'

'One of them, the taller one with the dark hair and the smart suit. She'd been on since Edinburgh and they had lunch together in the restaurant car. Spent a lot of time talking, they did.'

'So they seemed to know each other well?'

'I don't know about that, but they were definitely getting on like a house on fire.'

'What about the other woman?'

'I don't think I'd seen her before, but there are a lot of meals served on that journey – I might not have noticed. But she certainly wasn't eating with the other two.'

'What did she look like?'

'Nice-looking, I suppose, for her age – she must have been in her forties. Long hair, but that's about all I remember.'

Penrose had heard enough to confirm that Elspeth's companions matched the signatures in her magazine. 'Were they still with Miss Simmons when she got back on the train?' he asked, trying to keep the sinking feeling out of his voice.

'I told you – I don't know. They'd all disappeared by the time I looked again and I just assumed they'd left. I didn't see anybody get back on, but you know what it's like when there's people getting off and luggage everywhere – it's far too busy to keep an eye on everything that's going on.'

'All right, we'll let it go now but it's vital that you don't tell anyone what you saw in the train – do you understand?' he asked sternly, without any real hope of his words being heeded. The boy was bound to talk to someone because, as Penrose knew from his own experience, there was nothing worse than the twisted intimacy of being the first to look upon a dead body. The loneliness of it was unbearable.

Maybrick re-entered the room and gave a brief nod. 'Well Tommy,' Penrose said, 'it looks like your Ivy might be keener than you thought. She's confirmed what you've told us, so tell the Constable where we can get hold of you if we need to and you can be on your way. Better not keep the girl waiting any longer but remember what I said – no details to anyone.'

'To be honest, I haven't really got the stomach for courting now,' Tommy said despondently as Maybrick handed him a pencil to write down his address, 'but I suppose I shouldn't disappoint her.'

As Penrose left the waiting room to look for his sergeant, he saw Fallowfield already approaching and knew instantly that the man at his side had come to King's Cross to meet Elspeth Simmons. Her father, he guessed, or perhaps an uncle – too old, in any case, to be a boyfriend. But whatever connection he had had to the girl, the news of her death seemed to have devastated him: his walk, his shoulders, the constant movement of his hands and the blank expression on his face – all signalled the stubborn disbelief of the violently bereaved.

'This is Frank Simmons, Sir,' said Fallowfield. 'He's Miss Simmons's uncle.'

Archie held out his hand, knowing from experience that the habitual formalities of everyday life could, in their very familiarity, act as a small but reassuring prop to those whose world had just been snatched from under them. 'Detective Inspector Penrose,' he said, and then simply, 'I'm so very sorry.'

The man nodded in acknowledgement. 'It's all my fault, you see,' he said, in response to an accusation which came not from the policemen but from a voice inside his head. 'I was so late to meet her. If only I'd just stayed where I was, she'd be all right now.'

Penrose let him talk, making whatever confession he thought necessary, until he had been led gently to a seat in the waiting room. 'This is going to be difficult for you, I know, but it's important that I ask you some questions now about Elspeth and any arrangements that had been made with her for this evening. What did you mean when you said you should have stayed where you were?'

Simmons rubbed his forehead with his fingers, as if the pressure would help him to discipline his thoughts. 'I came to meet her in the van like I always do,' he began, 'but when I got here one of the guards told me that the train was late and wouldn't get in for an hour and a half or so. I often have to wait and usually I just kick my heels on the platform or have a cup of tea round the corner, but today I hadn't finished my round and I thought an hour would give me just about enough time to drop off the last order and still be back here to meet Elspeth. That way, we could go straight home and there'd be plenty of room in the back for the new stock she was bringing down. There's always hell to pay with Betty – that's my wife – if anything gets squashed.'

By now, Penrose was lagging some way behind in the conversation. 'What were you delivering?' he asked.

'Tea mostly, and coffee, but the Coventry Street shop needed some new equipment and that's what was taking up the room.' As the Inspector continued to look questioningly at him, he expanded a little on his explanation. 'I'm a driver for Lyons. I've been with them ever since I left the regiment. It's not the most exciting of jobs, but you get to know your way around. That's why I was sure that a few short cuts would get me there and back in no time, but something had gone on in Judd Street. I was stuck there for ages before I could get through and make the delivery, and then I couldn't find anywhere to park at the station. By the time I got back to the platform, you lot were crawling all over the place and I knew something had happened.'

Fallowfield opened his mouth to speak but Penrose, anticipating what he was going to say, shook his head. There would be a time to ask Frank Simmons to prove that he was away from King's Cross when the train had pulled in, but this was not it; all the life had already been kicked out of him and there was worse still to come. Saving any further questioning for the next day, he concentrated solely on what could not be avoided. 'I'm afraid I'll have to ask you to identify Elspeth's body,' he said quietly. 'Her next of kin must be told, of course. Is that her parents?'

'Yes. Well, her mother at any rate – that's my sister-in-law. My brother died last year. Elspeth was adopted, though. They couldn't have kids of their own so she meant everything to them – to all of us, really. I don't know how Alice would have got through these last few months if it hadn't been for her. Elspeth kept her smiling.' As the reality of his loss came home to him, Simmons finally lost the self-control to which he had been clinging so doggedly. 'How am I ever going to face Alice knowing that I've taken that away from her?'

Acknowledging the question but realising there was no answer he could give, Penrose said nothing. Instead, he led Simmons gently from the waiting room towards his niece's body, and his worst fears.

Three

When Josephine awoke next morning, it had just gone nine and St Martin's Lane was in full swing. It was Saturday and, even at this early hour, an air of obligatory enjoyment had settled on the weekend inhabitants of the West End. From her window at Number 66, she looked south towards Trafalgar Square, marvelling as she did so at the multitude of human dramas which were unfolding in the street below – far more than could possibly be played out each night in the more artificial realms of London's theatre-land.

She shifted her gaze across the narrow street to the building opposite, and wondered how long it would be before Elspeth looked her up at stage door as she had promised. The New Theatre, where *Richard of Bordeaux* was about to enter its last week, sat imposingly between the Salisbury and the Westminster County Court, the daily necessities of ale and justice and make-believe found in companionable proximity to one another. To say it was the finest theatre in London was as pointless as electing a best church – they all served different creeds, and one was as good as another – but it was magnificent, even to an eye less partial than hers. Built only as an afterthought on a leftover plot of land that backed onto Wyndham's, to which it was still linked by a footbridge, the New was nevertheless a splendid example of classical design, its Portland stone facade, bold ornamentation and giant pilasters giving a dignity and permanence to the elusive trick of entertaining the public.

Number 66 St Martin's Lane would be Josephine's home for the next few days, as it often was when she visited London. It had more than its convenience for the theatre to recommend it: once the workshop in which Thomas Chippendale had created understated furniture for an enthusiastic market, it was now home to another name famous for simplicity and restraint. The Motleys were two talented sisters who had revolutionised theatre design and contributed to some of the greatest successes the West End had seen in recent years. Josephine was the first to admit that the appeal of her own play lay as much in the romance of their costumes and sets as it did in her dialogue and, over the last eighteen months, the three women had become firm friends. She was astonished at how naturally she had found herself slipping into the Motleys' cheerful domestic stage set, and arriving at Number 66 always felt like coming home.

As thoughts of breakfast drew her from her room into the large central studio, she was amused to find that the space was even more chaotic than usual. Exhausted from her journey, she had retired before her hosts arrived home and slept the sleep of the dead, utterly oblivious to the furious burst of activity which had clearly continued long into the night. The walls were now covered in deft costume sketches for a new *Hamlet* which she knew was due to go into production later in the year and, even at this early stage, it was obvious that the Motleys had surpassed themselves. The designs were divided into contrasting sections, each extravagantly styled in a picture of medieval Denmark which could not have been further from the Depression-worn shapes of the current age, and she was instantly captivated by their ingenuity. On the floor, work had already begun on materials for the costumes: bits of scenery canvas covered in dye and metallic pigments were strewn across the floor, punctuated by squares of thick felt which had been heavily treated with kitchen soap and paint to look uncannily like leather.

She was pleased to see that the architect of this glorious disorder was, as usual, on the telephone and centre-stage in her own creation. Veronique Motley – or Ronnie, as she was more often called – had inherited her mother's beauty and her father's disregard for convention. Reclining on a peacock-blue chaise-longue which the sisters had dyed themselves, and covered by an enormous bearskin cloak as if in deference to the cold Scandinavian climate in which she had spent the night, Ronnie was in full flight.

'My dear, we're only just recovering from the shame,' she purred into the handset. 'We should have known from the minute they brought the monkey in that the whole production was going to be a fiasco from start to finish. The creature bit everybody at the dress rehearsal and we were all absolutely terrified. Hephzibar threw out her arms in such a fright that her stitching gave up and we had to sew her back in. She still isn't at all herself. And don't even ask about the cost – we'd spent four thousand pounds before the curtain went up, and still the whole thing looked more like the Trocadero on a Friday night. Never mind the *Dream*, it was our bloody nightmare!'

Catching Josephine's bemused expression, she made a face of studied *ennui* and hurriedly brought the call to an end. 'Anyway, dear, I must go. We're seeing Johnny soon and you know what he's like – he'll want to go straight to Ophelia's death-scene and we haven't even got a costume for the poor girl to live in yet.'

'Were the Crummles in town for the gala week, then?' Josephine asked wryly as Ronnie replaced the receiver and picked her way through mounds of upholstery cloth and calico to wrap her friend in a hug.

'Something like that,' Ronnie said, laughing and leading her over to the breakfast table. 'It *is* lovely to see you, you know. Lettice and I were saying only the other day that you've spent too long up in dry old Inverness this time.'

Smiling, Josephine heaped sugar into her coffee. 'It's good to be here,' she said. 'At least in London I don't feel I need to apologise constantly for having a hit. The English are much more generous-minded than the Scots.'

'Oh, all small towns are the same, dear. It doesn't really bother you, does it?'

'Honestly? Yes, I suppose it does a little. It's all this "grocer's daughter made good" business, as if I've no right to a life down here with different friends and a different outlook. For them, it'll always be barrow first and pen second.'

'Hang the lot of them, then. Any more trouble and Lettice and I will come and sort them out. They won't know what's hit them.'

'Don't make rash promises – I haven't told you about the woman who runs the post office yet.'

'Talking of formidable women,' Ronnie said, still laughing, 'I feel I should warn you that the Snipe is in a foul temper today and not exactly on her best form. We used the advance from *Hamlet* to treat her to a new gas cooker because she's always complaining that she misses her old Eagle, but she hasn't quite taken control of the regulo yet. God knows what we'll get for breakfast.'

A curse of confirmation emanated from the small back room that the Motleys had transformed into a makeshift kitchen and the door crashed open to reveal a stout woman of indeterminate age who had obviously already used up what little patience she allowed herself each day. Employment in a household which thrived on colour and changing fashions had cut no ice with Mrs Snipe: her uniform – black alpaca dress, bibbed apron, worsted stockings and house slippers – was as familiar up and down the country as that of a policeman or nurse and, apart from the length of her skirt, she could easily have been serving toast to a Victorian household.

'If you were hoping for kidneys, you can forget it,' Mrs Snipe announced in what would, at any normal volume, have been a west country burr. 'It's cockled 'em with the heat. I expect you wanted fish, Miss Josephine, but the fact is there isn't any, so it'll have to be bacon and eggs, and you'll be lucky to get those by the time that thing's finished with 'em.'

Josephine was not easily intimidated, but there was something about Dora Snipe which turned the normal guest and housekeeper relationship on its head, so she smiled and nodded and accepted what was on offer. Her familiarity with Number 66 had not made her any less wary of the Motleys' cook. The sisters had never known life without her, yet Mrs Snipe had remained an enigma throughout the thirty-odd years that she had been with the family, first in Cornwall and now in London, where she 'did' for Ronnie and Lettice and was housekeeper to their cousin, Archie, to whom she was devoted. As she banged a rack of perfectly browned toast down on the table and returned to the kitchen to beat her new arrival into submission, the front door slammed and there was a squeal of joy from the hall. 'Darling, how absolutely gorgeous to see you! We've been so looking forward to your visit, and don't you look well!'

Josephine smiled as Lettice blew into the room towards her, dragging in her wake her long-suffering fiancé, George, and four large carrier bags. 'Trust you to bring a mystery with you,' Lettice said cryptically as she hugged her friend and threw the morning paper onto a chair, where it soon disappeared under a pile of shopping. 'Life's always so much more exciting when you're south of the border. I'm sorry we weren't here to welcome you properly this morning, but it's the Selfridges shoe sale today and you have to get there early if you're to stand any chance of finding a pair.'

'Don't they sell them in pairs, then?' Josephine asked, exchanging an amused and sympathetic wink with George as he poured himself a cup of coffee.

'Oh no, dear, that would take all the fun out of it,' said Ronnie, who was born with her tongue in her cheek. 'It's a shilling a shoe but you're not so much paying for footwear as for the chance to spend a morning as some sort of modern-day Cinderella.'

'Except that this Prince Charming usually ends up having to carry home enough leather for the entire pantomime,' George chipped in good-naturedly.

As always, Lettice took the teasing with good grace and found refuge in her breakfast. Buttering her toast thickly on both sides but, with uncharacteristic self-denial, confining the Silver Shred to the top, she looked cheerfully at her sister. 'You'll be smirking on the other side of that ravishing face of yours when Lydia's got through her third pair of brogues in the first week. You know how clumsy she can be if she has to dance.' Turning to Josephine, she added: 'We called in at the theatre to pick up the mail. A letter each for Ronnie and I, but that whole bag is yours.'

Josephine groaned and walked over to the sack of correspondence that Lettice had jabbed at with her toast. 'You know, I hardly have to read them these days,' she said, taking a handful of letters off the top of the pile. 'I can tell from the handwriting on the envelope which category they're going to fall into: complimentary and undemanding – they're the ones I always answer; pedantic and smug – usually with suggestions as to how I might strive for greater historical accuracy next time; and worst of all, the invitations – they're what I use to save on coal. God help me when the Mary Stuart brigade springs into action.'

'How is the casting going for *Queen of Scots?*' Ronnie asked. 'Have they found Lydia her Bothwell yet?'

'No. Lydia and I both think Lewis Fleming would be perfect, but I gather there's another pretty face on the horizon whom Johnny would prefer,' Josephine replied, 'and we all know what that means. Swinburne, his name is, but the only thing I know about him is that he's made quite an impression at Wyndham's recently. Anyway, that's one of the things on the agenda this afternoon. Johnny's asked Fleming to stand in as Richard for the matinee so we can go over and thrash it all out with Aubrey. After all, it's his money. They're hoping to open in June, but now that Johnny's got it into his head to try for a film of *Richard*, it's all a bit up in the air. And I don't know how he thinks he's going to direct *Queen of Scots*, work on a film and tour as well. Even our young meteor can't be in three places at once.'

'He told me the other day that he was hoping to get out of the tour by persuading Aubrey to send Fleming instead,' said George who, as an actor himself and the Motleys' self-appointed manager, was no stranger to dealing with egos considerably more fragile than his own, and with characters much less placid and kindly. 'But there isn't a chance in hell that he's going to get out of that contract: *Bordeaux* in the provinces is a licence to print money but, just for once, Johnny's underestimated the value of his name on the bill. The public recognises only one Richard and it wants the real thing, not the reluctant Pretender.'

'You're getting your historical dramas a bit muddled, darling,' said Lettice. 'But it sounds like Josephine's in for a ghastly afternoon. All those boys do when they get together is bitch and squabble and talk about money.'

'Trust me – I'm more than a match for them with the bitching and squabbling as long as we get to the money eventually,' Josephine laughed. 'By the way, what did you mean about my bringing a mystery with me?'

'Oh, there was some nasty business at the railway station last night,' said Lettice, whose grasp of real-life tragedy was never quite as acute as her ability to bring it to the fore on stage. 'The papers are beautifully melodramatic about it this morning, but we don't want that to ruin our breakfast. What I'm dying to know,' she continued, casting a sly glance at Ronnie, 'is what you thought of Lydia's new find. You're always such a marvellous judge of character, and I expect she came to meet you? The two of them are practically inseparable at the moment – we've never seen anything like it. I gave it three weeks before Lydia started sniffing round somewhere else and Ronnie said a fortnight. George, bless him, reckoned a couple of months but men have no idea how gloriously fickle we can be when we're bored. Anyway, as far as we can make out, we're all wrong: she doesn't seem to have even thought about anyone else. At times I'd have said she was almost happy!'

Josephine agreed. 'I wasn't with them for very long, but Lydia *did* seem happy. And it wasn't that sickly new-love happiness, either. I have to admit, coming down on the train I was dreading that – it's always so embarrassing when you're stuck in the middle of it. It was contentment as much as happiness and I've never seen that in Lydia before – she's always been too restless.'

'And Marta?' Lettice asked again, determined to have her verdict.

'Well, she's another beauty, certainly. And she seems very nice,' she finished, conscious of delivering the sort of anti-climax which would never stand up to the Motleys' relentless gaze.

'Nice? What sort of word is that for a writer?' demanded Ronnie indignantly. 'We know she's nice, we can see that for ourselves, but we rely on you for something a little more sophisticated. What do those big dark eyes tell you?'

'That she's got big dark eyes,' Josephine said, with a native matter-of-factness that even the Motleys could not penetrate. 'You surely don't believe all that nonsense about reading character in the face, do you? I only ever use that when I've got myself into a bit of a hole with the plot and need to move things along. To be honest, she really didn't say very much at all and that in itself is a good thing, if you want my opinion. But what she did say seemed awfully – well, nice.'

'Talking of the strong but silent type, our dear cousin telephoned at the crack of dawn to make sure you were all right and to say he was coming over this morning,' said Ronnie, realising that any further probing would get her nowhere. 'He sounded a bit out of sorts, actually. When I told him that Lettice and I hadn't thought for one moment that he'd be able to wait until dinner to see you, he quite snapped my head off. That's the trouble with policemen: they've got no sense of humour.'

In perfectly timed acknowledgement of Ronnie's observation, there was an impatient knocking at the front door. 'I expect that'll be him now,' she said, as Mrs Snipe glided past to admit the caller with all the momentum of a galleon in full sail. 'We'd better stop having such a nice time or he'll arrest the lot of us.'

When the housekeeper returned, the man who followed her did seem distinctly at odds with merriment. Certainly, he bore scant resemblance to the Archie Penrose who, in spite of his cousin's unjust reproach, usually left his job firmly behind when he came to call on the Motleys and blended beautifully into the chic eccentricity of their studio.

'Good God, Archie, you look absolutely awful,' said Ronnie, who excelled at speaking her mind, while Lettice responded with the greatest solace she knew: 'Is Mrs Snipe getting you something to eat?' she asked, pushing the toast rack, now a shadow of its former self, towards the empty place at the breakfast table.

Josephine shared the Motleys' concern at Archie's mood, but not their surprise. During a friendship that had spanned almost twenty years, she had come to realise that there were two sides to this complex individual: the handsome, gregarious entertainer, whose warmth and intelligence made people from all walks of life instantly comfortable in his company and who was genuinely interested in everyone he met; and the detached, serious observer, whose liking for his fellow man did not blind him to the baser motivations of the human mind or to the pain which underpinned more relationships than most people cared to acknowledge. While she enjoyed and admired the former, Josephine's emotional affinities were instinctively towards the latter and, although Archie protested that these were qualities which Scotland Yard demanded of him, the truth of the matter was that in his work he found a natural outlet for a view of the world which had already taken root in his soul.

Penrose waved away all offers of food but gratefully accepted a cup of coffee. 'I need to talk to Josephine,' he said, looking at her for the first time. 'In private, if you don't mind.'

'Oh, don't worry about us – we only live here,' muttered Ronnie as Lettice poked her hard in the shoulder and sent George to gather up the shoes.

'Just ignore her, darling, we've got to go out anyway. Lydia needs a few alterations done in time for this afternoon. In spite of the plague, it would appear that Anne of Bohemia is putting on weight. Some people just have no self-discipline when it comes to food.'

Right on cue, Mrs Snipe reappeared and, ignoring Archie's protestations, placed in front of him a plateful of perfectly cooked kidneys and something that looked suspiciously like a kipper. As the Motleys bustled round, fetching coats and scarves and the various bits of costume that they needed for the afternoon, Josephine looked questioningly at Archie. 'What's wrong?' she asked quietly.

'In a minute,' he said, waiting for the sisters to leave. She carried on opening her mail, glad to have something to do, but her attention kept straying back to Archie. She watched as he ran his fingers idly up and down the handle of his coffee cup, lost in his own thoughts and, for a moment, the gesture took her back to the summer of 1919, when they had met for the first time after the war and his face had expressed the same concentrated sadness as it did now. By that time, the initial bond between them – her lover and Archie's closest friend – had been dead for almost three years, killed helping another officer at the Somme, and Archie had finally come to see her in Scotland. She would never forget the pain in his voice as he described to her how, in the midst of that senseless slaughter, all for the sake of a few yards of mud, Jack Mackenzie, a young private from the 2nd Gordon Highlanders, had responded to a cry from no man's land. There, another soldier, who had lain motionless near the German wire for nigh on two days and was believed by the British troops to be beyond all aid, had, in defiance of nature, regained consciousness and called for help. Following all the instincts of his training – which was medical, not military – Jack had left his trench and walked the short distance to where the man lay. Armed only with a handkerchief, which he waved in the direction of the higher ground held by the enemy, he arrived unscathed and was allowed to dress the wounds as best he could, giving the soldier a drink and reassurance that a stretcher party would be sent to gather him safely in under the cover of darkness. His mission accomplished, Jack turned to go back to his own trench and was shot in the back by a German sniper before he had taken half a dozen steps.

They said he had died instantly, but of course they always said that and she had no way of knowing if it was the truth or if there were things she had never been told which explained why Archie had avoided her for so long, even though he knew she was desperate to hear about Jack's death from someone who had cared about him. She didn't blame Archie, but he had failed her: in dealing with his own grief for Jack, he had been unable to face hers and, although their friendship had lasted, there remained – on both sides – a sense of regret. Now, the girl she had been prior to Jack's death was almost unrecognisable to her: it was hard to believe herself capable of that kind of love.

After Jack was killed, and having seen such tragedies repeated over and over again, Archie gave up all hope of continuing on the path he had once chosen for himself – medicine was no career for someone who had lost faith in his ability to outplay death. But if he was no longer surprised when death arrived ahead of its time, he never shook off a sense of anger at its indifference – and that had proved an excellent foundation for the career to which he eventually turned.

Now, Archie's inability to do anything about the inherent cruelty of the world seemed temporarily to exclude everything else from his life, and Josephine was relieved when the girls were finally ready to go out and leave them in peace to talk.

'You two take as long as you like,' Lettice reiterated, absent-mindedly picking up the last slice of toast. 'We'll be at the theatre all afternoon and dinner's booked for six-thirty, so don't be late. I do so hate to have to rush dessert.'

'And perhaps you'll have cheered up by then.' Ronnie's parting shot was followed by the slamming of the front door, then all was quiet.

'I love them dearly, but it's so nice when it stops,' Josephine said. 'This isn't a social call, is it?'

'I wish it were, but I'm afraid it's about what happened at King's Cross last night. Have you seen the papers yet this morning?'

'No. Lettice mentioned that something had gone on at the station, but she wasn't very specific. What's it got to do with me?'

'You signed an autograph for a young woman yesterday. How well did you know her?'

At his use of the past tense, Josephine's heart went cold. 'Hardly at all. She recognised me on the train coming down and we had lunch together. She loves the theatre and wanted to know all about *Richard*, so we spent most of the time talking about that. I introduced her to Lydia when we got here and invited her to come and find me at the theatre if she wanted to, and that was that. Why? What's happened to her?'

Archie saw no point in delivering anything but the simple truth. 'She's been killed,' he said. 'I'm sorry there's no gentler way of telling you, but it wasn't an accident and it seems that you and Lydia were among the last people to see her alive.'

'You mean she was murdered? Who on earth would want to hurt her?'

'We don't know yet, but I have to ask you this: how did you part?'

41

Josephine stared at him in disbelief. 'We just said goodbye on the platform. She was so excited at meeting Lydia that she'd left her bag on the train and had to go back for it.'

'You never saw her after that?'

'No. The train was late getting in, so we were in a hurry. Marta – that's Lydia's lover – was waiting for us outside with a taxi and Lydia had to get to the theatre. I left them at stage door and came straight here.'

'And you didn't go out again?'

'Of course not – I was exhausted. What am I supposed to have done, Archie? Stalked the poor girl and strangled her with my scarf? For God's sake, I thought I was the one with the vivid imagination.' Archie remained silent as Josephine got up and walked to the window. 'How did she die, or as a suspect aren't I allowed to know?' she asked sarcastically.

'She was stabbed in the compartment of the train,' he replied, ignoring the bait. 'It must have happened quite soon after you left her.'

'If only I *had* gone after her,' she said, her anger disappearing as suddenly as it had come.

'What do you mean?'

'She dropped the feather from her hat on the platform and I wanted to give it back to her, but Lydia was late and there wasn't time.'

'You couldn't have saved her,' he said, gently. 'Whoever did this was hell-bent on violence, so thank God you didn't get in the way.'

Josephine's face was still turned to the window, but he could tell from her voice that any counsel against self-reproach was futile. 'You know, just an hour ago I was looking across at the theatre, half expecting to see her in the queue already,' she said, sadly. 'And I found myself rather looking forward to it. It's funny, isn't it, how quickly some people make an impression on you? Yesterday was the first time I'd ever set eyes on the girl, but I could probably tell you more about her than people I've known for years. The important stuff, anyway – what she was like, what she cared about.'

'And what was she like?'

'She was that quiet sort which always gets overlooked. I don't mean quiet in the literal sense, but most people would probably have thought her quite inconsequential. If she were at a party, she'd be the person you spoke to until you found someone more important. I think she'd got so used to people looking past her that she didn't even notice any more. She certainly didn't seem to mind, because there wasn't an ounce of self-pity about her.'

'Not an obvious murder victim, then. She doesn't sound the sort to inspire that sort of extreme emotion.'

'No, not a victim in any sense of the word. It's a cliché, but she made the best of what life dealt her, and that somehow makes all this even worse. I can't help feeling that when you've worked hard to come to terms with how you entered the world, you ought to have a bit more say over how you leave it – but I don't have to tell you that. You know she was adopted, I suppose?'

'Yes, we spoke to her uncle. He came to the station to meet her.'

'Poor man. From what she said, they were very close.'

'What else did she tell you about herself?'

'Well, her adoptive parents are from Berwick-upon-Tweed – that's where she got on the train – but her father died quite recently. She worked with her mother – I expect you'll have found the hats they made by now. It wasn't unusual for her to be coming to London: her aunt and uncle have a shop here and she always brings the new season's stock down and helps out a bit. The uncle – Fred, I think his name is, or Frank?'

'Frank – he's a driver for Lyons.'

'Frank, yes – he loves theatre as well, so when she was here they spent a lot of time together. Although I suppose that must have changed now that she'd met her young man.'

'So she was definitely seeing someone? Did she mention his name?'

'No, I don't think she did. She just blushed a lot. Romance was new to her, you see, and it goes back to what I said about her not being used to attention. She seemed quite astonished that anyone should want to pick her out, almost as if she didn't deserve it. The only thing I can tell you about him is that he works in theatre. She said he was taking her to see *Richard* tonight and we laughed about it being a busman's holiday.'

No matter how hard he tried to keep an open mind, everything kept coming back to that play. 'Isn't this all a bit coincidental?' he asked. He tried to choose his next words carefully so as not to alarm her, but there was a limit to how far he could skirt around the issue. 'Your biggest fan is on the same train and just happens to recognise you. And then she's killed.'

'It was theatre in general she loved, not just me. I know I'm not exactly a household face, but anyone who read as much about the stage as Elspeth did is bound to have seen a picture somewhere,' said Josephine impatiently, suddenly conscious that this was the first time she had been able to bring herself to use the dead girl's name. 'Anyway,' she continued wryly, 'the only people who don't believe in coincidence are the ones who read detective novels – and policemen. These things happen, Archie, even if we're not sup-posed to use them in books.'

Archie nodded and conceded defeat as he often did with Josephine, although his mind was still terribly uneasy about the relevance of her play to the murder and her close proximity to what had taken place. He looked at his watch, wondering exactly how much he should tell her about the scene which had been cre-ated to mark Elspeth's death. 'It's time I went. I'm seeing the pathologist in twenty minutes, then I'll have to visit the family to see what else they can tell me. Perhaps they can shed some light on the boyfriend. There's one last thing before I go, though: those souvenir dolls from the play – did Elspeth have any with her?'

'There could have been something in her bag without my notic-ing. I doubt it, though, because most of the contents ended up on the floor at one point. Hideous things – I can't imagine why any-body would want one, but it's the sort of thing she might have owned and she had an awful lot of other luggage. Why on earth do you want to know?' He said nothing, but looked more preoccu-pied than ever. 'What's the matter, Archie?' asked Josephine, puz-zled to see her own sadness reflected in someone who had no personal connection with the events he was now investigating. 'You're no stranger to death. You've seen what people can do to each other time and again. Of course you can't let yourself become immune to it, but I've never known you to feel like this about a stranger.'

'That's the trouble. It's not a stranger I'm worried about. I can't tell you the details but, from the way the body was left, I have to assume a connection to *Richard of Bordeaux*,' Archie said, deciding that, no matter how unpalatable, honesty was his best option. 'Now, that could simply be because the victim was obsessed with the play; it could be that the boyfriend did it in a fit of jealousy and – one of your coincidences – he just happens to work in the theatre. On the other hand, because Elspeth doesn't seem the type to have enemies, it could be that someone wants to hurt you, either by damaging your reputation or, God forbid, by actually harming you.'

The implications of what Archie was saying were not lost on Josephine, although he might have guessed that she would interpret them differently: the danger which he was trying to warn her against was all but lost in her sorrow for Elspeth. 'So, one way or another, she died because of me,' she said.

It was not a question but Archie protested nonetheless. 'That's not what I meant. I'm saying that because a girl has been killed, you are bound to suffer – it's not the same thing. At best, you'll have your name dragged through the papers again because the association is certain to get out; at worst – and I need you to take this seriously – your life could be in danger. There was nothing spontaneous about Elspeth's murder and if it turns out that the killer got the wrong person, you can put money on the fact that he or she will try again. Don't waste your time on feeling guilty about something that's not your fault. If you must worry, then worry about yourself.'

'Oh Archie, don't be so bloody naive. How can I not blame myself when the very last time that you and I stood together in this room was after an inquest into another death that would never have happened had it not been for that wretched play?'

'We've been over this a thousand times. Elliott Vintner killed himself because he was a ruined man. He got lucky with one novel and spent the next ten years trying to do it again. When he found he simply didn't have the talent, he tried to take advantage of yours. Nobody in their right mind would accuse someone of plagiarism over a piece of history – let's face it, if that were a viable legal argument, Shakespeare would have spent his whole life in the dock. Vintner gambled by taking you to court, and he lost – end of story. If his life was so miserable that he had nothing else worth living for, that can hardly be laid at your door. By all means mourn for a girl you liked who died too young, but don't waste a minute on that bastard's memory.'

'I know you're right, but it doesn't alter the fact that this afternoon I'm supposed to be signing a contract to license a tour of *Richard*, and perhaps even to make a film, when I really feel like putting a stop to the whole thing before anybody else gets hurt. I know it's making everybody rich and famous, but I'm beginning to believe that the play is cursed and I don't see why we need to inflict that on theatres all around the country. God, they'd be safer with *Macbeth*. Perhaps all doomed dramas come out of Scotland. It's still not too late to pull out and knock this nonsense on the head once and for all. Everyone will be furious, of course, but there are more important things than taking two thousand pounds and half a dozen curtain-calls in Morecambe.'

'Do whatever you need to about the play – that doesn't matter. It's you I care about.'

'I know, and I'm grateful – even if it doesn't always sound like it. But you surely can't believe – if everything was as carefully planned as you say it was – that the murderer would have overlooked the small matter of getting the right victim?' Archie said nothing, acknowledging the logic of Josephine's reasoning but unable to let it overcome his instincts as she continued, more gently this time. 'You don't need to waste time worrying about me but I will be careful, I promise. And there is something else you can do to make me feel better.'

'And that is?'

46

'I'd like to see Elspeth's family. Can I come with you this after-noon?'

'What about your meeting with the boys?'

'Like I said, there are more important things and I need to decide once and for all what I'm going to do before I see them. I'm sure Ronnie and Lettice would go for me if I asked them to, so at least I'll know what happens. Look, I know it's not normal proce-dure and I don't want to be in the way, but I'd like to talk about Elspeth to someone who knew her, and it might help her family, too.'

Archie stood up, ready to leave. 'I'll pick you up at two.' He kissed her briefly at the door. 'It's nice to see you,' he said, smiling for the first time that morning.

Four

It was turning into the sort of day that made even the most faithful of Londoners question their devotion to the city. An unyielding stretch of cloud settled heavily over the rooftops, draining the colour from everything it touched before dissolving, at street level, into a half-hearted, depressing mist. Even so, as he left the house in Queen Anne's Gate, Bernard Aubrey savoured the rush of freedom that accompanied any departure from the four walls which were, but rarely felt like, home. This picturesque relic of Georgian London, built in the eighteenth century by the founder of the Bank of England, was an appropriate reflection of the aesthetic taste and sound financial judgement which had made Aubrey one of the West End's most prosperous and influential theatrical managers. Like its neighbours, from which it differed only in the pattern of a curtain or the choice of flowers in a vase, the house breathed success. It was a smugness which he shook off like an unwanted chaperone every time he shut the door.

With an amiable nod to the statue that gave the square its name, Aubrey turned his back on her mannered serenity and headed for the more worldly stimulus of St Martin's Lane. He loved his work and was diligent in its undertaking, spending most of his waking hours in the two theatres which his parents had built and entrusted to him, theatres which he had developed beyond even their wildest hopes through an addiction to the challenge of balancing art with money. It was a business founded on risk and he was not infallible, but his errors of judgement were few and far between, and he had been blessed with a talent for anticipating what the public would look for next, as well as with the financial means to provide it. The considerable fortune which he had amassed along the way had been wisely reinvested and his instincts were underpinned by a tireless energy: he spent as many nights in the theatre as any actor and, on Sundays, when the stage was empty in deference to the pulpit and the family table, he was invariably to be found at his desk, taking advantage of the lull in one achievement to plan for the next. To actors and playwrights unused to such commitment, he was a self-effacing benefactor; privately, he knew that his ability to make or break a career overnight was little more than a by-product in a quest to prove something to himself, a quest which was nothing short of an obsession. It had been that way for as long as he could remember. Looking back, he could not honestly say if his bond with his wife and child had been sacrificed because of it or whether, in sensing that the emotional commitment required for family life was not his to give, he had instinctively thrown his energies into something he was more certain to be good at. Driven by pride rather than by ambition or greed, Aubrey was not the sort of man who contemplated failure easily, or who liked to be anything other than a few steps ahead.

Today, as usual, he rejected the convenient option of a ten-minute journey to work courtesy of the city's underground railway and set off on foot. The peculiar atmosphere evoked by London's tunnels was not for him, and he never failed to wonder at the willingness with which people now accepted darkness and confinement as a natural part of their day-to-day existence. For Aubrey, the lingering, acrid smell of those subterranean passageways brought back ghosts from a past he tried in vain to forget. Too old at forty-five to take part in the trench war but with a distinguished military record behind him, he had spent those terrible years as a tunneller in the guts of the French earth and had no wish to return to its horrors in his waking hours as well as in his nightmares. A tunneller's war required a different sort of heroism to the fighting above ground, and if the strength and bravery involved had been psychological rather than physical, the sacrifice was often the same. Thousands of miners had been killed underground in explosions which made the water in the tunnels run with blood, and which rendered the precious air thick with the stench of death.

Four years of battling with earth and suffocation as well as with an unseen enemy played lasting tricks on the mind, and the fear and anxiety of those years had haunted Aubrey ever since. On one occasion, not long after the war had ended, his wife had endeavoured to free him of his crippling claustrophobia by persuading him to try the underground at Piccadilly Circus. Before he was halfway down the steps, he could smell burning hair once again, and the pounding of his heart sounded in his head like the muffled thud of a miner's pick. Giving in to the panic which he had always managed to suppress when it mattered, he emerged choking and sobbing into a crowd of embarrassed shoppers. A cure had never been spoken of again, and his illness had only worsened with time: to mix with the crush of bodies in a confined space – even in a theatre bar or foyer – demanded from him the strictest self-control. A vast underground city had opened up beneath London's pavements, expanding further as its open-air counterpart grew, but he was more than happy for it to remain out of bounds.

Pulling his hat further down against the rain which had begun to fall more steadily, and cursing the umbrella that was still in its rack in the hallway, Aubrey strode past the government offices in Great George Street and into Parliament Square, one of the wide open spaces that he blessed the city for preserving. Not even the shabby row of houses to the west of the square could mar the grandeur over which so many of the faces from the past presided. As he walked on, he looked up to see if a regular occupant of one of those dust-dimmed windows was sitting in her usual place. He was not disappointed: there she was, as still and indistinct as ever, but framed this morning in an oblong of yellow light which she had switched on to counteract the gloom of the day. In the last few weeks, this figure had become as much a part of his daily walk as the impassive statues in the square. Every morning, no matter how early the hour, she sat at that window with such reliability that he had begun to question whether she, too, were a statue, until one day he had seen her get up and move back into the room. He wondered at the life she led in that faded building, too near the top to be the lady of the house and not high enough to be the maid – although this was the sort of house in which a maid's services were no longer required. There must be thousands of women like her in London now, widowed or single and long past the age at which marriage would be a realistic prospect, living in reduced circumstances in a bed-sitting-room, staring out at life rather than taking part.

He considered waving but decided, on reflection, that a greeting from a stranger, particularly a well-dressed and affluent stranger, might be regarded as impudent or condescending, so he moved on. A quick glance at his watch confirmed that there was plenty of time to make a detour to Westminster Bridge for a view of which he never tired, no matter what the weather. For once he was in no hurry to reach the New Theatre, where a long and no doubt argumentative day awaited him. That afternoon, he was due to make the final arrangements for the provincial tour of one of his longest-running productions and to discuss the West End staging of its author's new play. He normally looked forward to such meetings, sure of his decisions and confident that those involved would trust his experience, but trouble was brewing with *Richard of Bordeaux*. Admittedly, none of the problems were insurmountable: his leading actor, who fancied himself – with some justification – as lord of the London stage, had changed his mind about the lure of the provinces in favour of the silver screen and wanted out of his contract, but Aubrey had no intention of releasing him; he would consider financing the film, perhaps, but only after John Terry had graced the likes of Manchester with his royal presence. As for Josephine Tey, she was far too principled to be easy to deal with, although he admired and respected her writing and could see its long-term potential. In a reversal of his difficulties with Terry, the issue with Tey was getting her *into* the public eye, and that wretched trial had not helped. Not for the first time, he cursed himself for allowing it to happen. Knowing Vintner, he should have seen it coming.

In fact, those newer to the taste of success than Aubrey seemed to have been transformed by their sudden notoriety – and not always for the better, in his opinion. The entire cast seemed to think that one hit play was enough to keep them in work for the rest of their professional lives, and all the bickering and tension was beginning to tire him; after all, he could usually find that at home. He knew he was perfectly capable of putting a stop to it, yet he felt uneasy about the confrontations ahead. If he had been a superstitious man, he might have said that to plan the play's future before its current run was finished was to tempt fate, but he was far too old to start pandering to the more ridiculous notions of his profession. Having said that, perhaps tonight was the wrong time to indulge in a tradition of his own making. Whenever a play under his management entered its final week, it was customary for him to make a cameo appearance on stage, and tonight he was due to walk on as a guard in the final scene. The moment was supposed to be a celebration, the only part of the limelight that he ever allowed himself, and the idea – thought up in a frivolous moment by his favourite St Joan – had always amused him. Today, it felt more like a curse.

His mood lifted briefly the minute he set foot on Westminster Bridge. He was by no means a fan of Romantic poetry, but he was willing to settle his differences with Wordsworth and concede that the earth had nothing fairer to show than this stretch of the river. It had, of course, changed considerably since those words were written, but its beauty had not diminished: the view of the Houses of Parliament and Victoria Tower, with the majestic sweep of buildings which now lined Millbank as far as Lambeth Bridge, was truly splendid. Turning to look down-river, he admired in a different way the tall, grey outline of Victoria Embankment, dominated by a startling new clock tower and punctuated by the Savoy's reassuring civility. His gaze fell on Somerset House in the background, and he was reminded that he really must track down the information he needed. The matter was becoming urgent.

As he stood there, Aubrey noticed how many people slowed their steps to appreciate the view. One young couple in particular drew his attention. They stood close together, holding hands under the cover of their coats and clinging on to an old umbrella as they leaned over the edge to stare intently into the waters below. They spoke little, but when they did it was of hopes for the future; small things, perhaps, but the joy with which they looked forward to a life of intimacy was so unlike anything Aubrey had ever known that he felt the contrast physically, as a rebuke, and wanted that ordinary miracle so badly that he had to look away. His own marriage had never been the shared adventure of discovery that he had hoped for; neither had he and his wife settled into the easy companionship of middle age which often compensated for the boredom of earlier years. Left at home while he went to war or to work, she had had plenty of time to wonder why they were married, although she was far too well mannered ever to have asked the question aloud. Perhaps she hated to be wrong or was simply afraid of having to acknowledge that he was lonely too. Either way, the moment for second chances was gone, and a sense of waste had hovered between them for years. Worst of all, it seemed to have tainted the next generation. As far as he could tell from their sporadic and awkward communications, his son's marriage was no more fulfilling than his own.

Maybe it was the gloom of the winter months, but he was frequently overwhelmed now by the feeling that his life had finally caught up with him, that the darkness which he had held at bay with the colour of stage artifice had, through that very medium, begun to return. This time, he sensed, the darkness would not be denied. Regret had long been the emotion with which he was best acquainted, but recently he had felt more than that: recently, he had felt afraid. How much of that fear was of his own making he was reluctant to admit but deep down he knew that he had risked too much, that the end could not always justify the means. In those tunnels he had seen damnation too often in the faces of others not to recognise it instantly when it stared back at him from the mirror.

He could stand the cold no longer, so retraced his footsteps along Bridge Street and turned into Parliament Street and Whitehall, where the morning was moving leisurely towards noon. Before him, in the centre of the road and at the heart of a country's grief, stood Lutyens's extraordinary monument to the dead –

quiet, dominant and bearing witness to the greatest emotion that England had ever felt. It was fifteen years and more since the last shot was fired – long enough for the memory to become lazy – but cars still slowed as they passed, men on buses continued to bare their heads, and parents brought their children to stand quietly at the monument's flower-covered foot, transferring a muted sorrow to the next generation. Forgetting for a moment his worries about the future, Aubrey took the deep purple iris from the inside of his raincoat and placed it gently on the steps, removing the dying flower that he had left there a week before. After a minute or two's reflection, he moved purposefully off towards the thin, dark figure of Nelson's Column.

London could be hard on the lonely, thought Esme McCracken as she sat at her window and looked down into the square below. Thank God she had never been susceptible to the pointless melancholy that a solitary existence so often tried to justify. If she were, she would scarcely have lasted long in this run-down, worn-out hole, where the inhabitants of the other rooms seemed to have given up on life at roughly the same time as the wallpaper. At night, when she eventually climbed the narrow stairs to the third floor and crawled into an uninviting single bed, she lay awake until the early hours, attempting to restore its faded pattern in her mind's eye as an antidote to the scenes and conversations that raced in her head and warded off sleep. It was the only time she really paid any attention to her surroundings: the sparseness of the room, the deficiencies of the furniture – a sagging armchair, put under further stress by piles of newspapers and books, and an ugly, fourth-hand table, scratched beyond the endeavours of any polish – never bothered her. Why should they? She had her eye and her thoughts trained firmly on the future.

It was the cold that she most resented, bitter and raw at this time of year. The bars on her small electric fire, inadequate at the best of times, had not glowed for many days now, as every spare penny she earned was spent on words rather than heat. Each morning, on her way to work at the New Theatre, she would steal into the second-hand bookshops to pore greedily over the shelves of new arrivals. Sometimes she was lucky, and managed to slide a slim volume of Ibsen or Chekhov under her coat while the shop assistant's attention was taken by another customer. Reading the book later, as she sat at prompt corner, she felt no remorse over such small acts of theft, knowing herself to be a worthy recipient of the ideas contained in those pages. Better that they should fall into her hands than be wasted on people with full pockets but empty minds, or left, forgotten, to gather dust.

People seemed determined to shelter from life these days, she thought, to resist its joys and its pain in favour of a bland contentment. There was certainly no place in the West End for any play with a soul. She despised the romantic nonsense that everyone seemed so taken with. If she were only given the chance, she knew she could make them understand what they were missing. But, as things stood, Daviot – and others like her – sat smugly in the auditorium, revelling in a success which was undeserved and planning another pointless fairy-tale to sedate the crowds, while she was taken for granted backstage, working long hours just to ensure that fame ran smoothly.

The harsh roar of a motorcycle cut through the air beneath her window as she got up to switch on the light. The gloom of the morning made the bulb's efforts to illuminate the room less feeble than usual, but there was still precious little cheer to be had. Shivering, she took the blanket off the bed and draped it round her shoulders before picking her way across a carpet of discarded paper and returning to the battered trunk that functioned as a makeshift desk. Her typewriter – a Good Companion, bought for twelve precious guineas – looked out of place in that tawdry room, but it was more real to her than anything else there and it had served her well: she was finally ready. Looking up from the page, she smiled bitterly at the sight of Bernard Aubrey, strolling into view as if in response to one of her perfectly timed cues. It amused her to think that he should take the trouble to notice her here, in this anonymous room, when at the theatre he passed her every day without even bothering to remember her name. It had always seemed her fate to go through life unnoticed or easily forgotten, but he would recognise her soon enough. She sealed the envelope and picked up her coat, slamming the door on her way out.

Rafe Swinburne slid quickly and silently from tangled sheets with the ease born of long practice, and saw with relief that the slender young redhead whom he left behind – Sybille, he thought she had called herself, or Sylvia – remained fast asleep. In bed and out, she had proved to be more entertaining than most of the young women who hung around Wyndham's stage door at the end of every performance, waiting for young actors like him to emerge, but he had no wish to continue the relationship into a second day. There was, he had discovered, a seemingly inexhaustible supply of sweet young things who expected him to live up to his stage role as caddish young lover, and he was more than happy to oblige. Acting had many more advantages than a salary of thirty pounds a week and he had always been the ambitious type, as greedy for adoration off stage as on. Last night, he had been adored until well into the early hours.

He dressed quietly in the bathroom, examining his mirror-image over a shelf crammed with creams and powders. Mercifully, his reflection confirmed that he needed nothing more than a splash of cold water to make himself presentable. He was, as he well knew, a strikingly handsome young man, tall and dark with lean features that were softened to just the right degree by hair worn slightly longer than was considered fashionable. Had his eyes held something warmer than their habitual cynical indifference, Swinburne would have been beautiful; nevertheless, he had about him an unmistakable air of self-possession that caught the eye of both sexes.

Carrying his shoes until it was safe to make a noise, he took a pre-written postcard from the pocket of his coat and left it on the hall table – a nice touch, he always thought, and one guaranteed to ease the disappointment of an early departure. Gently, he opened the front door and, with his exit assured, slipped down the stairs. Ignoring the rain and kneeling to tie his laces, he glanced around to get his bearings and was surprised to find himself in Hammersmith. The journey from the West End to these rented rooms had not seemed very far last night, but then he had been racing through London with a pretty girl's arms around his waist and his mind on little else but a craving for sex which did not distinguish between postal districts. In the cold light of day, he wished fate had coupled him with someone a little closer to home. It was already gone noon and there was nowhere near enough time before the matinee to go back to his own rooms on the south side of the river and change, let alone to drop in on John Terry as he had hoped – no, as he needed – to do before this afternoon's meeting. Swinburne rather enjoyed the reputation he had for being late, but he was not prepared to push his last-minute appearances to impossible limits and risk missing his first entrance. He would have to make do with a telephone call en route to the theatre.

He had found to his great relief that his prized motorcycle – a 1932 Ariel Square Four – was still at the end of the passage where he had hurriedly left it just after midnight. Long before it became such a fashionable leisure activity, Swinburne had loved motorcycling with a passion. As a child, his father had driven him all over the countryside on the sturdy Scott model that he had kept when he was invalided out of the war, perching his young son on the special stand at the front which once sported a machine gun but which had been cleverly adapted into the most thrilling of vantage points for a tiny boy. His earliest memories were of the excitement he felt as he swung round with the handlebars, confident in his father's deft handling of the machine. Never again had he felt so close to danger, and yet so safe. By then, it was just the two of them – he had lost his mother during the war and had to rely on his father's stories for most of what he knew of her – and the bond was unbreakable. Many years later, when his father died, he had ridden the Ariel for hours, not caring where he went but desperate to escape the most powerful grief he had ever known. It proved to be unshakeable, though, and it had travelled with him ever since.

Several kicks were needed to fire the reluctant engine into life in such unpleasant weather, but he felt the pressures of the day lift as soon as he moved out into the traffic, weaving effortlessly between the cars and making better time than he could have hoped. When he reached the King's Road, he slackened his pace and pulled over by Chelsea Town Hall, leaving the motorcycle where he could keep an eye on it and waiting impatiently outside the telephone box while a lanky man with a ruddy face and an enormous rain-coat finished his call. An unpleasant odour of rain mixed with sweat and tobacco bore down on him in the confined space, offending his natural fastidiousness, and he was relieved when a voice at the other end of the line demanded his attention.

'Yes?' The musical quality for which Terry's delivery was so lauded by the critics could not have been more absent from this clipped greeting. It was obviously a bad moment, but beggars could not be choosers and a beggar was essentially what Swinburne was about to become.

'It's Swinburne. I wanted to talk to you before this afternoon. Do you have any idea which way Aubrey's going to jump?'

Although not yet thirty, John Terry was beginning to wonder if he had already enjoyed the greatest success of his career. He had known as soon as he opened the manuscript of *Richard of Bordeaux*, with its neat pages carefully typed in blue ink, that he was looking at a gift from heaven. Reading it in his dressing room during a matinee of *The Good Companions*, he had almost missed his cue, so taken was he with its charm and humour, with the modern dialogue which turned a king into a man of the people. He learned later that the play had been inspired by his performance as Richard II at the Old Vic a number of years ago, but he knew nothing of the author at the time. He had not needed to, because the script spoke for itself. Aubrey had required no persuading to back a commercial run and their instincts had soon been rewarded. A clash with another opening night had meant a sub-dued first performance but, at ten minutes past one on the follow-ing day, the telephone began to ring at the box office and had not stopped since. For fourteen months, there had rarely been an empty seat in the house, and some people had seen the play thirty or forty times.

At first, he had been pleased by the adulation. Supper at the Savoy was a novelty which he had never before been able to afford, and he enjoyed being recognised in the street. But pleasure turned to embarrassment, embarrassment to boredom, and now he was utterly sick of Richard. He had been photographed, caricatured and painted, and had had everything from dolls to bronze sculptures fashioned in his image. White harts – the King's emblem – rained upon him in every conceivable form, embroidered on handkerchiefs and stamped on cigarette boxes. Young girls followed him from the theatre to his flat; others turned up unannounced in the middle of the night; and he had lost count of the times he answered the telephone only to be greeted by adolescent giggles and the click of the receiver as the callers lost their nerve before speaking.

But worse than all of that was the knowledge that his performances had lost their sincerity, that he was becoming mannered and exaggerated in an attempt to keep alive his interest in the role. A year ago, exhaustion had forced him to take a short holiday but, unable to keep away, he had returned early from the west country for the pleasure of slipping into a box and watching his understudy on stage. Back then, the play had moved him to tears; now, he often asked someone else to stand in simply because he could not face going through it all again himself. He bitterly regretted the early enthusiasm that had contracted him to the role both in London and on tour, but he could see no way out other than to make Aubrey change his mind, and he knew hell would freeze over before that happened.

He looked around the small, unpretentiously furnished flat in the hope that the familiar surroundings might outmanoeuvre a new emotion which he recognised as despair. His gaze rested on the toy theatre that his mother had given him for Christmas when he was just seven years old: its cream and gold pillars had become chipped and scratched over the years, the plush red velvet curtains were now faded and worn, but he still saw in it the endless possibilities that had absorbed him throughout his childhood. As a boy, he had existed in an intense fantasy world, unaware of all that went on around him, and this miniature stage was at its centre. When he was introduced to the real thing he knew he was lost completely, less to the carefree attractions of make-believe than to what he revelled in as a complete sensual experience: the colour and the lights, the textures of the spoken word, the physical presence of the crowds, the exhilarating taste of success and, as its understudy, the pungent whiff of failure. He had become the biggest star of his day, but recently he had found himself hankering after that toy theatre and a world which had also seemed to be of a more manageable scale. It had to stop. He needed a new challenge before his ambition and his desire faded away into comfortable certainties. He had to hold his nerve with Aubrey and get out of this rut once and for all.

A tall, gauntly handsome young man appeared at the bedroom door, rubbing his eyes and running his fingers through thinning fair hair. 'Who was that on the telephone?' he asked, and the soft, Irish inflection made the question seem more casual than it really was. 'Let me guess: there's a problem with a play and only you can sort it out. Am I right or am I right?'

Without much hope of success, Terry attempted to defuse another fruitless round of bickering before it started. 'It was only Rafe Swinburne adding one more demand to the list for this afternoon. If Aubrey's not in the right mood, we'll all find ourselves carrying spears in Morecambe before the month's out.' It was a feeble effort at lightness, he knew, and the only response it brought was a wearily raised eyebrow.

'Would that be such a bad thing? At least you might come home occasionally.'

'Don't be so fucking sanctimonious – it doesn't suit you,' said Terry, his frustration quickly getting the better of him. 'I'm not sleeping with him, if that's what this is about, so you can stop worrying.'

'You really don't understand, do you? If it were about sex I'd almost be relieved, but it's more than that. I might stand a chance against another man, but I can't take on the whole of the West End. You're obsessed.'

'You used to say that was sexy.'

'That was before I lived with you. Then you had to make an effort to see me; now I'm just an inconvenient interruption to the working day. The actors, the writers, the boy that sweeps the stage – they always come first, whether you want to sleep with them or not. How do you think that makes me feel?'

There was no answer to that. Acting was his life, his work and his play and, if he were honest, his only love; without it, he cared about nothing. Aware of the sadness his silence was causing but too selfishly honest to lie, Terry walked past his lover to dress for the theatre.

By the time Lewis Fleming arrived, the nursing home was almost always in darkness. He walked quietly down sour-smelling corridors which opened onto uniform rooms, nodding to nurses who tip-toed across polished floors and conscious of sleepless eyes watching him pass, glad of any focus to distract them from the darkness and loneliness to which evening abandoned them. For the ill and the desperate – and this plain red-brick building on Gray's Inn Road was the last haven of hope for both – night was the hardest time and sleep the most elusive companion, so he went to cushion her from that hell, sitting wide awake by her bed and letting her sleep safely in the knowledge that, for a few hours at least, she was not alone. Resting on the stark white sheets, her hand felt cool in his.

Surrounded by the murmurs and the restlessness which reached him through paper-thin walls, Fleming had plenty of time to worry about what would happen if he could not manage to support his wife through her illness. Acting was a precarious way to make a living; he had been lucky to land a part in a play which had run for over a year, but it was coming to an end now and his future was uncertain. As the clock across the road struck the hour and then the half, he felt as though his life were passing twice as slowly as everybody else's, while hers threatened to be over so soon. Pain had begun to leave lines around her eyes that even sleep could not entirely smooth away, but she still looked young compared to the home's other inhabitants, who had at least reached the vulnerable middle-age on which this unforgiving disease fed. Her face still held its beauty and its strength, and the blankets did much to belie the wasting of her body but, as he looked at her arms which were the colour of unbleached wax and tellingly thin, he was overwhelmed by the bitter sense of injustice that had been with him since the day the cancer was diagnosed. He remembered the mixture of courage and terror with which she had told him the news, and the stubborn disbelief with which he had received it. Could that really have been only three months ago?

At the first grey streak of dawn, when the rooms began to stir into life, he would kiss her gently awake as she had made him promise to do and slip away from her bed, past the seared faces and broken lives and down the steps into the street. A twenty-minute walk took him home, where he would fall exhausted into their bed and sleep until early afternoon; by three o'clock, he was back for the more conventional visiting period, and took his place among the ranks of husbands and wives armed with flowers, practised cheerfulness and carefully rehearsed homecoming plans, and with a resolve which crumpled the moment the visitor was out of reach of the searching eyes in the bed. On matinee days, he was spared this collective ritual and dared not go home, either, for fear that he would sleep through the afternoon and on into the night. He knew that his exhaustion was affecting his performance – Aubrey had already made that clear – but he had told no one of his situation, terrified that his livelihood would be taken away from him, and with it that thin sliver of hope that he could get them through this, that money could buy time, perhaps even a cure. The doctors had said it was not out of the question: that small chance and his wife's constant faith in him were the only things that kept him on his feet.

On Thursdays and Saturdays, he crawled gratefully into an eating-house near the theatre, using its smoky fug to shake off the scent of flowers and drugs and pity that hung perpetually around him. He drank endless mugs of strong, hot coffee in the hope that it would see him through two performances on stage and a third at his wife's bedside, but ate little, conscious that every penny had to be saved. Today, as usual, the room was full of people for whom every shilling counted, but a woman at the next table stood out from the crowd, not least because she looked as tired and as worried as he felt. She was familiar to him from the theatre, and he had noticed her in particular because she reminded him of his wife. She looked up as the waitress removed an empty cup from her table and glanced in his direction, offering a half-smile of recognition. Embarrassed at having been caught watching her so intently, he returned the greeting in kind and quickly finished his coffee.

It was still raining when he left the eating-house to make his way to the theatre. During the lunch-time period on a Saturday, the area between Charing Cross and St Martin's Lane was invariably full of itinerant young actors heading towards performances in which they enjoyed varying degrees of success, and he nodded to a few of the usual faces as he passed. Then, across the street, he saw Terry emerge from the saddlery shop which occupied the same building as his flat and walk quickly off in the direction of the New. A few seconds later another man, whom Lewis recognised as the actor's latest lover, followed in his footsteps, catching him easily with just a few long strides. He grabbed Terry by the arm and the two seemed to argue for a minute before, in a display of affection which was foolhardy in such a public place, the taller man grabbed a flower from a stall and thrust it melodramatically towards Terry, who could not help but laugh. The tension between them fell away instantly, and Terry continued his journey alone, the flower now adorning his buttonhole.

Fleming felt a sudden stab of anger that God should allow these people to parade their filthy, fickle love in the street while seeming to punish him and his wife for their devotion. If he were to lose the only woman he had ever spoken to of love, the only woman he had taken to his bed, he knew he could never replace her with another. In that instant, he felt vindicated for the decision he had taken during one of those long nocturnal vigils, a decision which went entirely against his character – or at least what his character had once been. Cancer had a habit of eroding morally as well as physically, and everything he loved was under threat. He should not be ashamed of his actions. After all, what had he left to lose?

The dressing room smelt of scent and an electric fire. Outside, a steady stream of traffic passed along the corridor and, whenever the door opened, Lydia could hear the muffled tramp of scene shifters up above and catch a faint whiff of size from the paint dock. Apart from a small chintz sofa, its extent carefully chosen to limit the number of admirers who could be comfortably accommodated at any one sitting, the room contained very little unnecessary furniture but, after fourteen months of occupation, it felt as much like home as her rented lodgings down the road. However perfectly she rehearsed the lines about professional challenges and resisting complacency, no actress was immune to the advantages of a long run: praise and financial security were its obvious accessories, but just as valuable was the sense of belonging. In becoming someone else for more than six weeks at a time, she had discovered that she was also better at being herself.

The layers of familiarity had built up gradually during the many hours spent at the New, manifesting themselves in hundreds of letters and personal items which formed a living scrapbook of the present moment, a flamboyant index of everything that was most precious in her life. One wall was now completely covered in press cuttings, in pages from *Theatre World*'s photographic celebration of the play and in the hundreds of reviews which had offered virtually every positive adjective in the book to her performance. Along another, a rail held the three attractive costumes and numerous accessories which transformed her simply and elegantly into Richard II's consort: the gold dress with peaspod collar and garland of lilies – so strange and exotic when she had first put them on, even to an actress used to playing historical roles – now felt as natural a part of her wardrobe as anything she could find in Kensington.

Her dressing table was reserved for more intimate things: pictures of her father at the height of his musical career before it was ruined by illness and depression; long and loving letters from her mother, with whom she corresponded weekly; and a rare photograph of Marta, taken on a bracing Sunday walk through Regent's Park not long after they had met. Her normally camera-shy lover looked out from the picture through tears of laughter, much to the astonishment of a young man who stood in the background of the photograph, watching as Marta tried and failed not to be amused by the misfortunes of an elderly couple who had taken boldly to the boating lake. She smiled now at the blurred image, remembering how she, too, had been laughing too helplessly to hold the camera steady.

Idly, Lydia removed another chocolate from the box of Prestat which Marta – along with some innuendo about taking sweets from the lap of the Queen – had playfully arranged under the skirts of the lifelike souvenir doll that stood at the back of the dressing table. It was odd, she thought, that the only thing in the room which did not now carry a comfortable sense of the familiar was the face looking back at her from the mirror. She had not yet grown accustomed to the subtle lines of age that were beginning their inevitable dance around her eyes and mouth, nor to the implications that they carried for her career. At forty-three, as Bernard Aubrey had made abundantly clear to her less than a fortnight ago, she was fast approaching the age dreaded by all actresses, those difficult mid-life years which were played out to the tune of too old for Ophelia, too young for Gertrude. She had been lucky with Anne, and was fortunate to have persuaded Josephine to immortalise for her the tiresome, glamorous Queen of Scots but, after that, she was well aware that there could be some lean years ahead, that the cushion of Aubrey's approval might not always rest with her.

Lost in her thoughts, Lydia did not notice that the dressing-room door had opened until she caught sight of Marta's reflection in the glass. Such visits were rare, as Marta preferred to keep out of a theatre circle which she regarded as Lydia's world, and the actress smiled with pleasure, her fears instantly forgotten. 'How long have you been there?' she asked.

'Long enough to know you've got chocolate on your lips,' said Marta, laughing as she bent down to kiss the back of Lydia's neck where it had been authentically shaved to accommodate Anne's elaborate headwear.

'I don't mind if you don't.' Lydia turned round in the chair and took Marta's face in her hands, tasting the coffee on her mouth as she drew her into a long, intense kiss. 'Do you feel any better?'

'I think I've drunk enough coffee to kill or cure the headache once and for all, but this place is hardly likely to lift a girl's spirits. That Lewis chap was in the Corner House looking as miserable as sin, John Terry's upstairs at the stage door shouting at someone, and that young boy who does all the work while your Chekhovian stage manager scribbles away at her next masterpiece nearly jumped out of his skin when I said hello to him. I can see why I don't venture down here very often.'

'Don't take it personally. Hedley's in terrible trouble with Bernard over something; he's been summoned to his office after the matinee for a dressing down. And Lewis has been miserable for weeks now. Rumour has it that his wife's left him and Johnny says he's hit the bottle, but he and Lewis have always hated each other so that might just be the bitch in him talking. Who was Johnny shouting at, anyway?'

'I don't know – he was on the telephone. Just one of the many unfortunates who are less godlike than him, I suppose. But I didn't come here to talk about them,' Marta said, dropping her sarcasm and sliding her hand inside Lydia's silk robe. 'How quickly can you get from here to the stage these days?'

Suddenly the door was thrown open and Ronnie appeared, staggering under the weight of an extraordinary horned head-dress. 'Oh we *are* interrupting something, I hope,' she said wickedly. 'We've come to let out your seams, although a little more exercise before each show might save us the trouble.' The twinkle in her eye brought a deep flush to Marta's face and a pink tinge to Lydia's, and elicited a long-suffering smile of apology from Lettice, who followed closely on her heels. 'Where would you like us to start?'

*

Normally, Hedley White would have been looking forward to his night off but, as he placed the furniture for the opening scene and moved to the side of the stage to run through the list of properties for each successive change, his mind was otherwise occupied. He knew he had behaved frightfully, and cursed himself again for such a rash act of stupidity, one that no amount of wishing or hoping could undo. The deed was done; Aubrey knew about it; and later he would face the consequences when he was called to the producer's office.

Although he had only worked for him for six months, Hedley already looked up to Aubrey as the father he had never known, respecting him as someone who, through sheer hard work, had made a practical success of a profession which liked to make itself as esoteric as possible. Hedley was well aware that working-class boys like himself did not naturally enter the theatre but, in offering him a job as an assistant stage manager, Aubrey had dispelled all notions of Masonic exclusion by showing him that there was an alternative to universities and drama schools and being born into the right family, an alternative which made use of his talents and gave him the experience he craved. Working at both Wyndham's and the New, he spent his days making tea, painting flats, sweeping the stage and walking around sets while electricians focused lamps. It was hard work, physically, which suited his strength and energy, and extra responsibilities built his confidence faster than he would have believed possible. If anybody had told him this time last year that he would be taking walk-on parts in front of hundreds of people and enjoying it, he would have laughed in their face.

Like all outsiders who are suddenly welcomed into a club to which they doubt their right to belong, Hedley was well versed in the peculiar language of theatre and revered its traditions and rituals. Each night, he took great pleasure in carefully preparing the ground for the Ricardians, an exclusive group, established in the early days of the production, whose membership was restricted to the three actors left on stage towards the end of *Richard of Bordeaux*. The rules of the club were strictly observed after all shows except matinees, and it was Hedley's job – or McCracken's in his absence – to place a small table and three chairs in the wings during the final act. Lewis Fleming, as Bolingbroke, was the first of the group to make his final exit, and would open a waiting bottle of claret, the quality of which had improved dramatically as the play's success grew; the actor who played the King's loyal servant was next off and would dutifully pour the wine into the waiting glasses while John Terry paused on stage to make the most of the bitterness and regret contained in Richard's closing lines. As the play finished, Terry joined the other two for a toast to the next performance and, after the cast took its many curtain-calls, all three Ricardians returned to savour the rest of the bottle.

Tonight, when Aubrey took to the stage for his customary cameo appearance as the guard – a role that Hedley often played himself – the club's membership would be extended to four and, as the producer drank nothing but Scotch, it was the junior stage hand's task to ensure that a single malt was added to the inventory before he went off duty after the matinee. The sense of having thrown away his place in this little world haunted Hedley even more than the prospect of being handed over to the police, and he was entirely at Aubrey's mercy. He would kill for a second chance, he thought, as he placed the decanter on the shelf next to the claret, ready for the evening performance.

Five

Penrose sat at his desk on the third floor of New Scotland Yard and stared at the collection of bleak photographs laid out in front of him. Fallowfield must have conveyed his instructions to the letter, because the photographer had been relentless in his thoroughness: in stark black and white, the camera's handiwork offered death from every angle, challenging him to erase the question marks which were all over that small railway carriage, and preserving the scene for those who might need to comment later on whatever answers he came up with. As detailed as the pictures were, his own memory really needed no material reminders of what he was dealing with: it would be a long time before a far more intense image of this particular death was erased from his memory. In his head, he heard his superior's familiar words of warning: 'You only see what you look for, and you only look for what is already in your mind.' The trouble was, his mind was a blank. Rarely had he been so without inspiration in a new case, lacking any instinct other than a sense that things would get worse before they got better.

He turned now to the carefully labelled personal effects which, if he only knew how to read them, told the story of the last few hours in Elspeth Simmons's life. Taken out of context and placed in uniform evidence bags, her things conveyed little of the warmth and animation which, according to Josephine, had characterised the girl in life. There was a handkerchief, a powder compact and comb, a packet of Symington's Jelly Crystals and another of Mackintosh Toffees, a purse and a small pile of loose change, made up of two half-crowns, two sixpences, a shilling, four pen-

71

nies and a halfpenny, and the magazine that had linked Elspeth to Josephine on the day she died – all the paraphernalia of a young woman on the move and, with hindsight, touching in its normality. What he found more interesting, though, were the note and the flower which hinted at a promise of affection, even love. He looked at the iris, with its striking triad of dark purple petals, and wondered what it had meant to her or to the person who sent it. How did she feel when she received it? And how would she have felt if it was her lover's face she had looked into as the life drained out of her? He hoped to put a name to that face when he questioned Frank Simmons and his wife in a couple of hours' time.

There was nothing out of the ordinary about the bag itself, except that the contents scarcely seemed to justify its outlandish size. Perhaps the dolls were the answer. It certainly made more sense for them to have been hers rather than carried by a killer for whom speed and invisibility were of the essence; the fingerprint report would at least tell him whether or not she had handled them. He looked at the miniature king and queen, less lifelike now in their forensic wrapping, and gave an involuntary shudder. There was something unnerving about the violence with which the female doll's hand had been broken off and discarded, but perhaps the gesture was nothing more than spite towards the victim, a scorning of Elspeth's love for the artificial passions of the stage rather than a sinister strike against Josephine herself. As much as he felt for the dead girl, a lovers' quarrel in which the dolls simply represented a mockery of her relationship would be a welcome explanation for her murder.

A brusque knock at the door interrupted his thoughts and, without waiting for a response, Sir Bernard Spilsbury came into the room. Others might have been surprised to see the celebrated Home Office Pathologist at the Yard on a Saturday but, to all intents and purposes, he was also a member of CID and behaved like any other hard-working member of the team. At fifty-seven, he often spoke of retirement but was actually busier than ever, driven hard by the police at his own insistence. In all the years Penrose had worked alongside Spilsbury, he had never known him to refuse a call. His reports were not quite as prompt as they used to be, and age had made him a little excessive in his thoroughness, but Penrose was always prepared to wait a little longer to hear opinions from a man for whom he held tremendous respect. Although by no means infallible, Spilsbury had proved to him on countless occasions that medicine had its value even in the face of death, that it was a path to truth even when life had been outwitted by evil – and that justice could prevail if someone paved the way for it with diligence and care.

'Sorry I'm late, Archie, but the traffic down Gower Street was diabolical. Of course, if the Metropolitan Police thought it worthwhile to catch up with the rest of the civilised world and build a laboratory of its own, then you'd have had your report by now and you might even be halfway to getting another killer off the streets. But who am I to criticise?'

Penrose smiled at the rebuke, which was invariably the first thing Spilsbury uttered when he arrived at Scotland Yard. The pathologist's opinion that Britain lagged behind other countries when it came to a commitment to forensic evidence was well known and, Penrose believed, fully justified. Among many of his colleagues there was still a prejudice against importing too much science into an investigation even though most were coming to rely on such developments as a matter of course; the analysis of dust in a suspect's pockets or mud on his boots was all very well, they would say if asked, but there was still a preference for direct rather than scientific methods of proving guilt and, even if the force as a whole could be persuaded that forensics were an aid to rather than replacement for observation and patience, the argument that English judges and juries were inclined to be distrustful of laboratory evidence had yet to be overcome. If anybody could change that, though, Spilsbury could; no name was more closely associated with violent or mysterious death. He had a quiet authority and a core of steel, yet it would have been hard to imagine a more affable and sympathetic character. Penrose had never known anyone get the better of him in cross-examination, although privately he wondered whether the

73

unquestioned influence that Spilsbury's opinion carried always contributed to justice.

The charm and the steel were both evident today as he sat down and took his report out of the vast bag which he took everywhere. 'It's a nasty one, this,' he said, without wasting any more time on social niceties and, as he always did, affording Penrose the respect of a fellow medic. 'The cause of death is fairly straightforward – internal haemorrhage as a result of sharp trauma to the heart from a penetrating injury originating just below the breast bone. From the angle of the wound, I'd say that she was standing up when the weapon entered her body and that the injury was made with an upward stab – you don't often see that – by someone a few inches taller and right-handed.'

'Man or woman?'

'Could be either, I'm afraid. The victim was only a couple of inches over five feet, so the height issue doesn't help us. If she'd been wearing something a little more robust, I'd have said quite confidently that the assailant was a man, but her coat was undone and a sharp point would have gone through that dress very easily. The tissues are quite soft, you know, and a reasonably fit woman, particularly an angry one, could have done it without a problem as long as the weapon was keen enough – which it most certainly was.'

'Have you ever come across a hatpin used as a murder weapon before?'

'No, Archie, and I still haven't; that's where it gets interesting. The weapon you found in her body wasn't the one that killed her – that much I can be sure of.'

Even with all the possibilities Penrose had been considering, that one had not occurred to him. One of the few things he believed he could take for granted was suddenly removed and he felt the foundations of the case shift again beneath his feet. A feeble 'How do you know?' was the best he could come up with.

'Because of the blood. No hatpin would have caused such massive internal blood loss. It wasn't obvious immediately because there was virtually no bruising to the puncture point and no obvi-

74

ous external haemorrhage, but inside it's a different story. There was a huge amount of blood in the pleural cavity and in the area around the heart, and some had passed into the abdominal cavity along the line of penetration. Yes, it's conceivable that a hatpin could cause enough damage to be fatal, but it would be a much slower death than was the case here and you certainly couldn't rely on it. Once you know you're looking at two different entries, you can see that the hatpin has taken a slightly different route from the initial thrust with the blade, but it's only marginal and the swapping of one for the other had very little effect on the external wound itself.'

'So what sort of weapon are we looking for?'

'Something narrow – like I said, very little blood found its way out from the entry point – and fairly long; it would need to be at least six inches to reach the heart through the liver and diaphragm. A nice paper knife would work, for example, if it were sharp enough – and that's the key: there's no drag on the tissues at the edges of the wound, so it went in and came out cleanly.'

'How much did she suffer?' Penrose asked, conscious that he was soon to see Elspeth's family.

'It would have been very quick and it's doubtful that she knew much about it. From the damage to the wall of the heart, I'd say the assailant moved the knife around in the body once the initial wound was made, and that will have speeded up the process even more. The blood in the pericardium will have prevented the heart from pumping effectively and her blood pressure will have dropped almost instantly, before the impact of a hard and fast stab really registered. It's likely that the shock of what had happened, together with the rapid loss of blood pressure, would override any behavioural pain response in the victim and I should think she was unconscious within a minute, perhaps less. So, depending on your point of view, this particular weapon did a lovely job. It always amazes me that more of our villains don't favour the knife, you know. It's a much better bet than a poker or a piece of lead piping, and so much more imaginative. And that's something there's no shortage of here – imagination.'

Penrose agreed. Flicking through the post-mortem report, he found the section that dealt with the shaving of the girl's neck, a seemingly purposeless act of defilement which, bizarrely, he found more disturbing than the fatal injury. For once, Spilsbury's conclusions told him little; the tiny amount of blood indicated that the cut had been made very shortly after death had occurred, but he had already suspected that. It was pointless to ask the pathologist to speculate on its meaning, so he turned his attentions back to more material evidence. 'Can you tell me anything else about the killer? A name would be nice, but I'll settle for hair or clothes.'

Spilsbury smiled. 'Well, he – let's say he for convenience's sake – certainly wasn't covered in his victim's blood when he left the train, so you can rule out that appeal to the public. There may have been a little on his hand but not enough to make him stand out from the crowd, and there was no blood or skin under the girl's fingernails to indicate any injuries that might arouse suspicion. The shock would have stopped her putting up much of a fight, even if he'd given her the chance to struggle. And there were no prints on the hatpin other than hers. On a more positive note,' he continued as Penrose looked increasingly despondent, 'there were some fibres under her nails and more in her mouth which don't appear to match anything she was wearing so, when we've done more tests, I might be able to tell you what his coat or jumper was made of. My guess is that the killer pulled her towards him with his left hand – there's a mark on the back of her neck to support that – and muffled any noises she might have made by holding her face against his chest as the knife went in. There was a lot of dust on the skirt of her dress but that's consistent with what was on the floor of the carriage, so it tells us very little except that it's certainly not the cleaning you pay for in first class. She must have fallen forward onto her knees when she lost consciousness, and then been lifted onto the seat where she was found: easier for a man to do that, of course, but again not impossible for a woman. There are some pulls in her stockings and the dress is slightly torn under one arm, which could suggest that she was shifted without much care or ceremony, but it's hardly surprising that it was done in a hurry. This is one of the riskiest crimes I've seen – you'd need to be in and out in a matter of minutes. Anyway, I'll let you know as soon as the tests are done on those fibres. It's not much, but it's all I've got for you at the moment. Just for once, the time of death is certain almost to the minute, but you know as much about that as I do.'

There was silence for a moment while Penrose thought about the information that Spilsbury had given him. 'I can think of two reasons for switching the murder weapon,' he said. 'Either the blade that he used was so distinctive that to leave it behind would be to give himself away; or there's something significant in what he chose to substitute it with. What would you put your money on?'

Years in court had taught Spilsbury never to volunteer his views unless asked – and Penrose asked more often than most of his colleagues – but, when he did offer an opinion, his eye for detail, acute gifts of reasoning and a memory which served as an index to death in all its forms meant that he was always worth listening to. 'This killing is personal – as personal as it gets – but it was also carried out quickly and efficiently, so it's almost certainly premeditated. In which case, the killer would hardly plan to use something that was likely to give him away and then be forced to swap it. No, the method of killing here is about the victim; get to know her, and she will lead you to your man.'

Penrose thanked him more perfunctorily than was characteristic of him, but his mind was playing with an imbalance of questions and answers, the most persistent thought being that it was all very well getting to know the victim if you were sure it was her death which had been intended – but his personal jury had yet to deliver its verdict on that one. There was little to be gained from sharing his doubts with the pathologist at this stage: he should be gathering information on the murder which had actually been committed rather than trying to investigate one which existed only in his worst fears.

'I'll let you know if I come up with anything else,' Spilsbury said. 'And good luck – I think you'll need it.'

Looking at the clock and realising he was late to pick up Josephine, Penrose went to find Fallowfield to give him the glad tidings: firstly, that the murder weapon was devoid of any prints other than the victim's; secondly, that it was not actually the murder weapon at all. There was really only one way for their luck to turn.

Six

Josephine was already waiting on the pavement when Penrose's car turned into St Martin's Lane, and he imagined she had been there for some time. Looking at the anxiety etched on her face, he questioned for a moment the wisdom of allowing her to accompany him in what must surely be a painful interview for all concerned but he knew that, had he refused, she would merely have passed a long afternoon alone, grieving for a situation which she believed to be partly her fault, or embroiled unnecessarily in the tangle of raw egos and ruffled feathers that lay in wait at the theatre. Less philanthropically, his instincts told him that Josephine would be a useful string to his bow when it came to questioning the Simmonses. Undoubtedly, there was important information to be had from the encounter and a mildly spoken woman with a natural curiosity and gentle eyes was likely to get much closer to the heart of the matter than either Fallowfield or himself, particularly if she held a certain celebrity status in the eyes of half her audience. When he had telephoned ahead to make sure there was no objection to Josephine's inclusion in the appointment, Frank Simmons had implied that, on the contrary, it was the one thing that might just make the ordeal bearable.

In all their years together, Penrose had yet to decide if Fallowfield's driving was very good or very bad. Down broad streets and across open countryside, he supposed it might be called exhilarating, but breadth and space were rare commodities in London and the Sergeant never allowed his surroundings to intrude upon his style. Within minutes, the car came to a shuddering halt in front of Josephine, who managed – with considerable pluck, Penrose thought – to take only two hurried steps back.

He kissed her briefly, gave her arm a reassuring squeeze and stood aside to allow her to get in. With a jerk, they moved off and the car was soon proceeding at a terrible rate up Monmouth Street. Resisting the impulse to close her eyes, Josephine smiled at Archie as a fellow passenger on the road to perdition and handed him a solid-looking parcel, wrapped in greaseproof paper. 'The Snipe insisted I bring this for you,' she said. 'It's cheese and tomato with extra pickle. She thinks you need feeding up because you've already left two meals she's put in front of you today, and she specifically asked me to tell you that this is your last chance. Eat these or she's giving you her notice.'

'Three Snipes and you're out then, Sir,' chipped in Fallowfield from the front seat as they shot across Hyde Park Corner, oblivious to the set of traffic lights that had just turned red. 'Mind you, she'll always be welcome at my house if she does give up on you. You can tell her that, Miss Tey, when you see her next,' he continued, winking at Josephine in his rear-view mirror while she watched the road ahead on his behalf. 'Fine figure of a woman, she is, and wasted on you sparrows.'

'She speaks very highly of you, too, Bill,' said Josephine. 'There's a sandwich here for you as well.'

'It's a queer business, this, Miss Tey,' he continued with relish, apparently undeterred by having spent a fruitless morning at King's Cross questioning the station staff and going through a passenger list which threw up nothing whatsoever of interest. One of the many qualities that Penrose admired in his sergeant was an utter immunity to despondency, no matter how many setbacks he came up against. Fallowfield was of that school of policing which had an unshakeable faith in the fact that truth will always out in the end; his optimism, which was no doubt nurtured by the amount of leisure time he spent in the company of fictional detectives for whom luck and inspiration knew no bounds, had been a spur to the more cynical Penrose on more than one occasion, and it lifted his spirits again now. When he had given the Sergeant a succinct account of Spilsbury's report on their way to the car, he had expected Fallowfield to share his disappointment at the lack of evidence, in particular the blow of the absent murder weapon, but that had not been the case. There was nothing the Sergeant enjoyed as much as a puzzle, and here he had plenty to occupy his thoughts.

Josephine, keen to hear more about the 'queer' nature of the case than she had been able to glean earlier from Archie's troubled account, and knowing she would get far more out of his sergeant, made an encouraging murmur of agreement. 'From the start, it reminded me of your book, Miss,' he expanded out of the blue, referring to Josephine's detective novel in which a man had been stabbed in a theatre queue. 'You know, a murder in a busy place and a risky one into the bargain. And then when the Inspector told me that the real weapon was a thin knife and not a hatpin – well, I half expected us to start looking for a Dago with a scar on his left hand, brandishing a stiletto.'

The suggestion was not a serious one, but the similarities had already occurred to Josephine and it struck her as ironic that she of all people should find herself on the periphery of a real murder case, travelling to talk to the victim's family with the policeman upon whom she had based her popular fictional inspector, Alan Grant. Not to look at, of course: Archie's height and dark good looks were a million miles from Grant's slighter build and – for want of a better word – his dapperness; no, a pleasant voice and a well-tailored suit were all they shared physically, but professionally speaking they were a perfect match. She had wanted a hard-working, well-meaning police inspector, a credible detective to stand out among the figures of fantasy and wish-fulfilment found in so many other crime novels, and in Penrose she had the perfect model. He could not quite claim Grant's perfect record of never an unsolved murder to his name, but he was patient, considerate and intelligent, a sensitive individual who cared about people both as a human being and as a policeman. She had added a few passions of her own – Archie had never been known to pick up a fishing rod, for example, whilst she was an expert with a fly – but the essence of Grant, the egalitarian nature of his view on the world, had been inspired for the most part by what she liked about Penrose. Seeing him now, though, preoccupied by thoughts which were out of kilter with Fallowfield's gentle banter, Josephine realised how much he had changed in the five years since the book was written. He had even started to look like a policeman, whereas it was Grant's greatest asset that he did not.

'Do you think you might write another one?' Fallowfield asked as he turned onto the Hammersmith Road, where the smell of chocolate from the enormous Lyons factory on the left-hand side reached them almost immediately, taking Josephine back to her own war years – which she had spent at Cadbury's, teaching physical education – with a sudden intensity that only an unexpected sensory experience could evoke. 'Perhaps all this will spur you on?' he added hopefully.

'I don't know about that, Bill. I only wrote the first one for a bet. A friend of mine swore it would be impossible to murder somebody in a crowd and I begged to differ, but I'm not sure in retrospect that she wasn't right. I had to write it in a fortnight and it nearly killed me, up till all hours every day. I swore I'd never do it again, but I have to admit – I do quite like Grant. He may turn up again if Brisena's willing.'

'Brisena?' Fallowfield looked blank.

'My typewriter. I dedicated the book to her because she worked so hard to finish it. It was all a bit of a joke, really. Making death up does have a knack of taking your mind off the real thing, though, so perhaps you're right – now might be a good time to start.'

As they drove past Cadby Hall, the vast headquarters of Messrs. J. Lyons & Company Limited which took up the entire street frontage between Brook Green and Blythe Road, Josephine noted its air of Saturday peace and fell silent, thinking of the one employee who would certainly not be enjoying his day off. As if reading her thoughts, Archie said: 'I'll be interested to know what you make of Frank Simmons. He seemed genuinely devastated last night, but I want to get an insight into how the family fits together.'

'Elspeth certainly spoke about him with affection,' Josephine said, 'and I didn't get the impression that there was any tension there, but there's no such thing as an uncomplicated family. You and I both know that, and I imagine those complications are even more intense when adoption's involved.' She was quiet for a moment, imagining Elspeth's life at home. 'The father's sickness must have taken its toll on the family, even if they managed to shield Elspeth from the worst of it. It would be nothing short of a miracle if they had less than their fair share of doubts and regret, but that doesn't make the family closet any darker than most, I suppose.' Even so, she thought to herself, the combination of suspicion and grief was bound to make their visit to the family an uncomfortable one.

Suddenly, she and Archie were jerked from their seat as the car drew to an abrupt halt, taking its place in the long line of traffic waiting to cross Hammersmith Broadway. 'Bugger,' said Fallowfield. 'I'd forgotten it was the bloody Boat Race.'

'So had I,' groaned Penrose, who usually took a partisan interest in the event. 'Why do they have to live in Hammersmith, for God's sake? The world and his wife will be here this afternoon.' And indeed they were. From where the Daimler stood, they could see the crowds making their way to Hammersmith Bridge or heading towards the river to get a place on one of the barges that offered the best view as the crews rounded the great bend. It had always been beyond Fallowfield's comprehension that this purely private affair between two universities could draw tens of thousands of Londoners – more than any horse race or football match – but today he took it as a personal slight.

'I don't see how I'm going to get through this lot in a hurry,' he said as they crawled along. 'We're not far off now, but we could be here for hours. You'll get there quicker if you walk, Sir. I'll meet you at the house as soon as I can.'

Penrose turned to Josephine. 'Is that all right with you?' She nodded, and he saw her safely onto the pavement, glad to be doing something more positive than sitting in the back of a car. They set off together in the direction of the river, leaving Fallowfield to swear quietly to himself behind the wheel. He glanced at her as they walked along, wondering how others saw them. To a stranger, they probably looked for all the world like a couple out for a weekend jaunt.

'Where are we going?' shouted Josephine above the bustle of traffic on the Broadway.

'Verbena Gardens,' Archie replied, and smiled as Josephine afforded the name the grimace it deserved. 'Number twenty-six, to be exact. It's just off the Great West Road, about fifteen minutes away.'

In fact, it took them nearly twice as long to negotiate the crowds gathered under the elms which stretched all the way along the Mall. When they found the road they were looking for, Penrose was relieved that, after all, they had arrived on foot. Verbena Gardens was the sort of curtain-twitching street that monitored its comings and goings with infallible diligence, and two reasonably nondescript pedestrians were much less of an intrusion than an unmarked but not unidentifiable police car. Frank and Betty Simmons would be going through enough at the moment without having the curiosity of their neighbours to contend with.

'What an odd place to have a shop,' said Josephine, voicing his own thoughts exactly. 'I suppose I should have expected that, having seen a sample of the Lillibet lines. They could never be described as conventional.' Certainly, number twenty-six had been imaginatively if improbably transformed from its unpromising beginnings as a red-brick terraced house, moderate in size and much like the ones that stood either side. The upper storey had managed to maintain an air of residential normality, but that only served to accentuate the enthusiastic attempts to turn the lower living quarters into a temple of fashion. If you knew where to look, London was actually full of little shops known to a special clientele and run by women who designed and made their own wares. Even so, Josephine could not imagine that there was another boutique quite like this anywhere in the city. The lack of passing trade had not deterred its proprietor from making the same efforts with her window-dressing that characterised the more fortunately placed outlets in Kensington and Regent Street. The harmonies of light and colour, the daringly original ideas were bountifully evident and, if her waxen smile was to be trusted, the figure in the window who beckoned the doubtful to step inside seemed to bear no resentment at being asked to market her goods away from the mainstream. The standard wooden front door which was repeated up and down Verbena Gardens had been replaced here by a glass frontage, onto which the name was elaborately painted in gold. But today the closed sign deterred any prospective shoppers and the blinds at the door, still firmly pulled down, contrasted poignantly with the evening frocks and picture hats that spoke of such gaiety on either side.

With a sigh, Penrose stopped outside and, as a discreet card in the window invited him to do, rang for attention. For a minute or two, the bell brought no response then, as he was about to try again, a light came on at the back of the shop and someone shot the bolts back on the door. When it opened, the wretched night that Frank Simmons had spent was written on his face and in the creases of the clothes which he had worn the previous evening.

'I'm sorry we're a little late, Mr Simmons,' Penrose said. 'We were held up by the Boat Race crowds.'

Simmons looked blankly past him, and Penrose wondered if he expected to see people suddenly thronging into Verbena Gardens. 'The Boat Race? Ah yes, it's today isn't it? Cambridge are favourites, I believe, but they say that both crews are strong this year.' He paused, still looking off down the road. 'Normally we'd have gone down to have a look but we just haven't had time today. There seems so much to do, what with Betty having to go up to Berwick to fetch Alice down. You did say that would be all right, Inspector? She's too upset to travel on her own, and Betty's so good with her. They've always got on well.'

'That's fine, Mr Simmons,' said Penrose gently. 'It's important that she has someone with her at a time like this. But we'd just like to have a chat with the two of you first. May we come inside for a bit?'

'Of course. How stupid of me. Please, come in,' he said and led them into the shop, past the overnight bag which stood packed and waiting by the door and into a tidy, unexpectedly spacious sales area. As they moved towards the back of the shop, where a red velvet curtain was pulled to one side to reveal stairs to the liv-

85

ing quarters above, Penrose made the formal introductions. 'I'm so very sorry for your loss, Mr Simmons,' said Josephine, and her words carried such genuine warmth and regret that Simmons relaxed immediately, forgetting for a moment the presence of an inspector of Scotland Yard. 'Elspeth was a lovely girl,' she continued, 'and I'm only sorry not to have known her better. We talked a great deal on our way down here, though, and she was very excited about her visit. She obviously enjoyed her time in London with you.'

'You've no idea what a comfort that is, Miss Tey,' Simmons replied. 'We had some happy times together at that theatre, Elspeth and me, and many of them were thanks to you. It will have meant a lot to her to have met you at last – she always wanted to. Alice – that's my sister-in-law, Elspeth's mother – she's not so keen on plays as we are, but she asked me to thank you for your kindness. There's not much that can console her at the moment, but when I told her what the Inspector said about you making friends with Elspeth so quickly, that helped a bit, I think.'

At the top of the stairs they were met by a small, birdlike woman, dressed immaculately in a sober but well-cut suit. Comparing her with her husband, Josephine would have considered her to be in her early forties but she had that sort of face which had never been truly young and which had probably changed very little over the years. Never in all her life could she remember seeing anyone quite as neat as Betty Simmons: her clothes, her dark auburn hair, the way she stood were all judged with a careful precision that was reflected in her manner of speech; not a word was out of place in those frugal sentences of welcome. How Elspeth's exuberance had fitted into this small house with its tidy containment, Josephine could not imagine.

She could, however, envisage the pleasure that the girl would have found in the eccentric streak which drove Frank Simmons to acquire every bit of theatrical memorabilia he could lay his hands on. When Elspeth had spoken about the collection on the train, Josephine had imagined it to consist of nothing but pile after pile of theatre programmes and magazines gathering dust in a corner. On the contrary, what drew her attention almost as soon as she entered the Simmonses' sitting room was a vibrant pocket of history which told the story of the stage for the last fifty years or more. All along one wall of the room, in a series of glass-fronted cases originally designed to protect precious books, hundreds of small objects were proudly displayed. While Betty disappeared into a tiny kitchen to make tea, Josephine took advantage of a pause in the formalities to look at them more closely. Each was carefully labelled like an exhibit in a museum, and certainly as valuable to anyone with a passion for theatre: the items were laid out chronologically, beginning with a property book used by Ellen Terry as Portia in 1875 and, next to it, a pair of the invisible spectacles which her leading man, Henry Irving, had worn. On the wall in between the first two cases, the mirror from Herbert Beerbohm Tree's dressing room reflected a wax figurine of Edith Evans as Millamant in *The Way of the World*, but so evocative was the setting that the glass still seemed to hold echoes of the extraordinary character make-up that Beerbohm Tree had created for the likes of Fagin and Falstaff. The new stars of the stage were well represented, too; next to a 1925 edition of *The Sketch*, which showed Noël Coward on the cover breakfasting in bed, there was a flask in the form of a book, one of several which the playwright had given to the cast of his operetta, *Bitter Sweet*, on its opening night.

It really was an extraordinary display and, in spite of the sombre nature of the afternoon, Josephine and Archie could not help but be fascinated. Simmons, gratified by their interest and pleased to grasp at any distraction from the real world, joined them by the cases and showed them the intricate workings of a silver plate cruet in the shape of Grimaldi which came to pieces to reveal salt and pepper pots in his pantaloons and a glass bottle for dressing in his chest; as the goose-heads appearing from his pockets were revealed to be the handles of spoons, Archie momentarily forgot his profession and exclaimed in delight. 'This must have taken you years to build up,' he said. 'Where on earth did you get it all from?'

'It's a labour of love, Sir,' Simmons replied. 'I've been lucky in that an old pal of mine got a stage door job when he came out of the army, and he always keeps his eyes open for me. You'd be amazed at what people chuck away – some of this stuff didn't cost me a penny. And when people start to know you collect something, they get in touch with you if they've got something of interest. Come and look at this – it's too big to keep in here.'

Penrose followed Elspeth's uncle into another room to view the pride and joy of his collection – the drum which Irving had used to create the sound of many a battle at the Lyceum. Josephine, who had never had the remotest inclination to open herself up to strangers, nevertheless admired the natural way in which Archie found a common ground with everyone.

'I still can't believe she's dead,' said Betty Simmons, returning with the tea tray and pouring four neat cups without spilling a drop. 'She just wasn't the sort of girl that things happen to. When she was little, she'd make up stories about herself. Alice used to say it was because she was adopted – there was always something that she couldn't know, so she invented it differently every day. They wondered if they'd done the right thing in telling her, but you can't keep that sort of thing secret forever, can you? The shock of finding it out later might have destroyed her, and it wasn't as if she was unhappy with Alice and Walter. She was such a sweet girl to them, so kind and thoughtful. But not knowing who she really came from made her curious about everything.'

'When was she adopted, Mrs Simmons?' asked Penrose, as he came back into the room and sat down.

'It was just before the war ended. Walter had come back in a dreadful state – not physically, you understand, but it had done terrible things to his mind – and Alice was trying to hold everything together for both of them, working all hours of the day and looking after him as well. We did as much as we could, but they were so far away up there. Alice didn't want to come down to London because all her family were in Berwick and that's where the business was. We thought she was mad at the time to take on a baby as well, but we were wrong. It was what she'd always wanted and she coped beautifully.'

'So it was the Berwick authorities that handled the adoption?'

The Simmonses looked at each other doubtfully. 'It wasn't exactly done through the proper channels, you see,' said Frank after a pause. 'Walter arranged it privately when he was in the army. Someone he served with had a child he couldn't bring up himself – I don't know why – but it seemed like the answer to all Walter's prayers. He and Alice couldn't have any of their own, you see, and being without kids was eating up Alice with grief; she made herself quite ill with it at one stage, and Walter was in despair. They were so in love when they first married; I've never seen a man so happy. He would have done anything for her, and a baby was what she wanted most in all the world. When Elspeth came along, it seemed too good to be true. She couldn't have been more loved if she had been their own.'

'It changed them, though,' his wife added. 'The end of the war and Elspeth's arrival all happened at the same time, so somehow she seemed to get caught up in what the fighting had done to him. He was never the same towards Alice when he came back; she said so herself. But the baby transformed her life. Elspeth was the making of Alice, but sometimes I think she destroyed Walter. They might have got through it if it had been just the two of them.'

'Betty! You can't say that about an innocent little baby.'

'It's true though, Frank, and it's nobody's fault. Don't get me wrong,' she continued, turning back to Josephine and Archie. 'I don't mean that Walter didn't love Elspeth. Of course he did. It wasn't that he resented her or that Alice neglected him. It was just that having a child gave Alice an excuse to put all her emotional energy into the little one. She looked after Walter, but she stopped trying to understand him.'

'It's hard to care for a man you love but don't always recognise,' said Josephine, who knew all too well what sort of psychological props long-term sickness demanded. When her own mother had died suddenly, she had given up her teaching career to return to Inverness and keep house for her father. Her sisters were married by then, and it had seemed the sensible thing to do. For the first few years, she had been happy back in her home town; her father continued to run the grocery store that he owned in the High

Street and she had enjoyed the peace and familiarity of Crown Cottage. Alone in the house during the day, she had time to write and was pleased when her early attempts to be published in various journals and magazines were moderately successful. In time, her poems and short stories led to full-length novels, but what began as pure pleasure soon became an essential facet of her own well-being: when her father's health began to suffer, companionship turned to dependence and she found that she desperately needed another place to lay the emotions which she no longer dare attach to him for fear of how strongly she would feel his death when it eventually came. It took a rare amount of strength to care for someone who was lost to you without putting up those barriers of self-protection, and she refused to judge Alice Simmons harshly for failing to find it. 'I'm sure Elspeth must have felt the weight of that responsibility, too, as she grew older,' she said.

'Yes, she did,' Frank agreed, 'although I think it hit her hardest when Walter died and she had to take care of her mother. She was aware of the change in Alice, you see, because she'd always been so capable; she never knew Walter when he was truly himself. It wasn't all bad. There were times when he tried to pull himself together and be what he'd been before, but it never lasted long.' Simmons paused, looking down at his hands. 'Were you over there, Inspector?' Archie nodded and let him continue. 'After a while, you forget how senseless it all seemed at the time. The more the years went by, the more Walter looked back to the war as the time when he meant something, when people respected him. He thought it would be a new start, coming home to a wife he loved with a child of their own to bring up, but it never worked out that way for him. I kept telling him – it's not the war years that were right, it's the peace years that are wrong, but he never would accept that. None of us really found the land fit for heroes that we were promised but you adjust, don't you? He couldn't.'

'Did he keep in touch with any of his army friends?'

'Not that I know of. I remember him telling me once about a reunion they were having. He couldn't afford to go but some of them clubbed together and paid for his ticket. Even then, he hated every minute of it because he didn't think his clothes were good enough. It's no wonder he was bitter, is it? He went off with crowds throwing flowers at him, and when he came back he couldn't even enjoy a drink with the men he'd fought alongside because he was ashamed of the coat on his back.'

Penrose listened, remembering some of the uncomfortable reunions he had been to himself. At times it had felt much easier to drink to the tragedy of the dead than to look the living in the eye, knowing that many of those men came back to the realisation that the world they had fought so hard for no longer wanted them. 'Did anyone ever make contact with Elspeth's real parents?' he asked.

'No, I don't think so. I'm not sure Alice even knew who they were, and Elspeth certainly didn't. It was almost as if keeping in touch with them would have been tempting fate: they might have changed their minds and wanted her back.'

'But Alice did once mention something that she asked me not to tell anyone.' All eyes turned to Betty Simmons, and her husband looked at her questioningly. 'Every year, on Elspeth's birthday, Walter got a letter with some money in it. The letter was never signed and Walter wouldn't tell her who it was from, although he always denied it was from her parents. One year, when Walter was particularly ill, Alice got to the envelope first and opened it. There were ten five-pound notes inside, and a letter that just said, "You know where I am if you change your mind." Walter was furious when he found out she'd opened it, but he refused to explain what it meant; he just told Alice not to worry, that if she wanted Elspeth to be happy she should forget all about it. That's why she begged me not to say anything,' she added by way of explanation to Frank. 'She was terrified she might lose the child.'

Penrose was quiet for a moment as he considered the implications of Betty Simmons's secret. The most obvious explanation for the money was that it had been sent by Elspeth's real parents to help with the cost of bringing her up, but the message in the note made a nonsense of that: surely if they had wanted her back they could have just taken her, particularly as there was no legal agreement to protect Walter and Alice. 'You're sure the letter said "I" and not "we"?' he asked.

'Yes, at least I'm sure that's what she told me it said,' Betty replied with certainty. 'I remember wondering if one of her parents hadn't really wanted to give her up and was trying to get her back, but I didn't say that to Alice. It would have only worried her even more.'

The same thought had occurred to Penrose, who was developing a growing respect for Mrs Simmons's intelligence. Josephine took advantage of the pause in his questioning. 'When we were having lunch on the train,' she began, 'Elspeth seemed very excited about a young man she'd met quite recently. Do you know who he is?'

'You must mean Hedley,' said Frank. 'Hedley White. He works backstage at Wyndham's and the New. They met a couple of months ago when Elspeth and I were queuing for an autograph. He took her programme to get it signed, and when he came back with it he asked her if she'd like to have tea with him. After that, he took her out whenever she was down here. He's a nice lad, and Elspeth was smitten. Nobody had ever shown much interest in her in that way before, and he always seemed to treat her well. Betty and I never worried when she was out with him.'

'She was seeing him tonight, wasn't she?' Josephine asked.

'Yes, they were going to the theatre together. He'd got top-price seats as a treat because he knew how much she loved your play. She was quite upset when she heard it was going to end, and Hedley wanted her to have the chance to see it again once or twice before it finished. In fact, she wasn't supposed to come down until next week but he got her here early, sent her the train ticket and everything. She was so excited, Alice said. She'd never travelled in first class before. That's what I mean about him treating her well – he was thoughtful. It must have cost him a fortune.'

Yes it must, thought Josephine, who – in spite of her reassuring words to Elspeth – had always thought first-class travel a terrible waste of money. The only time she used it herself was when she was invited to London to discuss her work. For some reason, Bernard Aubrey seemed to think that bringing her down in comfort would soften her up a little before each contract negotiation and she had never had the heart to tell him it made no difference to her which part of the train she sat in. But a first-class ticket on a backstage wage must have made quite a hole in Hedley White's pocket, even if he was in love.

'You'll have to tell him, Frank. He'll be devastated,' Betty said. 'He can't know yet or he'd have been in touch.'

'If you don't mind, Sir, I'd like to do that myself,' Penrose said. 'Was he coming here to pick her up, or had they arranged to meet somewhere else?'

'They were meeting in town later on when Hedley finished his afternoon shift. I was going to drop Elspeth off at the theatre, then they were going to the Corner House in Shaftesbury Avenue to have a bite to eat after the show. You'll tell him gently, Inspector, won't you? He'll blame himself when he knows, just like I do. It won't take him long to realise that if it wasn't for him Elspeth would never have been on that train at all.'

Quite, thought Penrose, who had no intention of being remotely gentle when he caught up with Hedley White. 'Do you mind if I use your telephone, Mr Simmons? I'd like to ask one of my colleagues to get over to the theatre and see if they can find the young man before he leaves work. And perhaps you have a home address for him?'

Betty showed Penrose to the telephone and went to get the information he had requested, leaving Josephine alone with Frank Simmons. 'Try not to blame yourself,' she said quietly. 'Even if you'd been waiting on the platform, there was nothing you could have done. I keep wishing that I hadn't been in such a hurry to get a taxi myself. If I'd kept her talking for longer, perhaps this would never have happened. But we can't know what fate has waiting for us, Frank. All we can do is make the people we love as happy as possible while we've got them, and you did that for Elspeth. She made that clear to me even in the short time I spent with her.'

He smiled at her gratefully. As Penrose returned, the sound of the shop bell reached them from the floor below. 'That'll be my

Sergeant,' he said. 'He's made it through the traffic at last. We'll leave you in peace now, but I'll let you know right away if there's any news.'

'You don't want to speak to me any more?' asked Simmons, who had been dreading a much tougher round of questioning from the Inspector.

'No, Sir, not at the moment. We've checked with the Coventry Street Lyons and the waitress there has confirmed the details of your delivery. I'll need to speak to your sister-in-law when she gets here, but that can wait until you've had some time to be together. Have a safe journey, Mrs Simmons. I've arranged for a car to pick you up in half an hour now the traffic's settled down a bit, but if there's anything else you need just give the Yard a call.'

'Thank you Inspector, you've been very kind,' said Betty. 'I'll tell Alice that I know you'll catch who did this to us. It won't give her Elspeth back, but it'll be some consolation.'

As they took their leave, Penrose wished he shared her confidence. He brought Fallowfield up to date, but the rest of the journey back to St Martin's Lane was made in silence. For once, Fallowfield's optimism fell on deaf ears.

Seven

Theatre is a self-obsessed medium at the best of times, but this was not the best of times. By the time the curtain fell on another packed matinee, news of the murder and its sinister echoes of the play had broken into the little world of the New Theatre, courtesy of young Tommy Forrester and the crisp five-pound note which a far-sighted reporter had seen fit to slip into his pocket. The story reached the auditorium first, as the audience shuffled the lunch-time edition from row to row with a delicious sense of melodrama and no discrimination between fourpenny and shilling seats. Gradually it filtered backstage, where certain members of the company experienced the uncomfortable sensation of talking about something other than themselves. They dealt with the novelty in different ways and according to type: Aubrey acknowledged the tragedy whilst considering the logistics of extending the run by a week or two; Esme McCracken – incensed at yet more notoriety for the play she so despised – slammed her notebook down in the prompt corner and scribbled furiously throughout the final act, while her second-in-charge left ashen-faced for his evening off; Lydia was shocked to the core, while Marta – with all the empathy expected of a lover – found herself equally horrified; and Terry, who had crept into a box to watch his understudy at work before going into battle with Aubrey, swore at Fleming for a lacklustre opening and went upstairs with an arrogance unusual even for him. Meanwhile, in the foyer, the kiosk attendant was recovering from an unexpected rush on souvenir dolls.

As six o'clock approached, Josephine could think of nothing she needed less than food or gossip. Nevertheless, conscious of a guest's obligations and resigned to a hefty helping of both, she dressed for dinner and set out for the restaurant, never once allowing her thoughts to linger on the performance that lay just the other side of the meal. Still a little unsteady after the drive back from Hammersmith, she decided to brave the rain and walk the half mile or so to Percy Street, taking pleasure in the distractions of Saturday-night London. The city was at its good-humoured best, the pavements growing steadily more crowded with a tangle of umbrellas and laughter as people emerged from buses and underground stations, determined to enjoy themselves. Gladly, she allowed herself the luxury of joining them, if only for the time it took her to reach a small, unassuming restaurant just off the Tottenham Court Road. The Motley sisters were by no means the only members of their profession for whom it was a favourite haunt: in fact, it was often said that a bomb hurled randomly through the doors of the Eiffel Tower would instantly dim the lights at half the theatres in the West End. Full of gaiety and chatter, the Tower admitted no sign of the jazz-age sophistication which had driven artists into public houses all over the city, and consequently remained the ultimate spot in which to see and be seen, even to eat and drink.

Lettice and Ronnie were already seated at a corner table when Josephine arrived, and she was touched by the concern that replaced their banter as soon as they saw her. Ronnie, who possessed the covetable knack of dealing with head waiters together with a firm belief that bubbles could console as well as cheer, wasted no time in ordering a bottle of Moet and Chandon, while Lettice looked solicitously at her friend. 'This is hardly the celebration we had planned for you,' she said, as Josephine sat down next to her. 'You must have had an awful day.'

The table was for four but it was a smaller party than planned. Reluctantly, Archie had made his apologies and he and Fallowfield had returned to the Yard. His absence was quickly noted by the Tower's ubiquitous proprietor, Rudolf Stulik, whose expression of desolation was hardly a good advertisement for the Champagne that brought him to the table.

'The Inspector is on his way?' Stulik asked hopefully in the thick Viennese accent which, along with an impressive moustache and even more impressive waistline, made him a walking cartoon of a restaurant proprietor. With the exception of a scant regard for licensing regulations, Stulik was unswerving in his devotion to this rather handsome embodiment of the law, and had been ever since Penrose had uncovered a gang of extortionists who had targeted his restaurant a couple of years back. The adoration – a source of much mirth and mischief to his cousins – was a huge embarrassment to Archie, so much so that only the prospect of Josephine's company would have got him to the restaurant at all.

'No, Rudy, I'm sorry – he can't get away tonight,' said Josephine, managing to keep a straight face. 'But he asked me to apologise and he sends his regards.'

'And he'd like a table for next Wednesday to make up for missing out on tonight.' Ronnie's revenge on Archie's earlier bad humour was merciless. 'Can you fit him in?'

Stulik, who was sadly removing the fourth place setting, brightened a little. 'Of course. I will see to it right away and make sure I'm here to look after him personally.' He bustled away, satisfied that the world was not as cruel a place as it had briefly seemed.

Josephine raised an eyebrow accusingly from behind the menu. 'That was positively wicked, even for you.'

'I know,' said Ronnie, lighting another cigarette. 'Sometimes I surprise even myself.'

Josephine laughed in spite of her day and ordered the turbot, bringing forth a culinary invective from Ronnie about a Scottish life being one perpetual Friday. After Lettice had dallied between the noisettes d'agneau and the caneton à l'orange sufficiently long for Stulik to suggest half a plateful of each, Josephine succinctly brought the Motleys up to date with the bare bones of Elspeth's murder, leaving out the more sensitive points of the investigation but outlining the facts that signalled a connection with *Richard of Bordeaux*, most of which they had already gleaned from the newspaper. The cocoon of the restaurant, with the constant chink of glass and clatter of knives against forks, went a little way towards anaesthetising her audience against some of the more chilling details, but not against the tragedy of a young girl's death. As Josephine gave the victim the flesh and blood which had been missing from the lurid but faceless newspaper account, Lettice and Ronnie realised how involved she felt with the crime, and saw through her impatient dismissal of Archie's concern for her.

'We all know he's ridiculously soft on you and always has been,' said Ronnie with her usual directness, 'but he's also a bloody good policeman, much as it shames me to have one in the family. If he's genuinely worried, then you should take him seriously and be careful. Or, if it suits your pride better, at least humour him until he's proved wrong.'

'It's not a question of pride, just common sense. One afternoon with her relatives gave Archie more than enough time to raise plenty of questions about Elspeth's life. If he finds the answers to those,' she counteracted, unconsciously echoing Spilsbury's advice, 'I have no doubt he'll understand why she died, and catch whoever's responsible. In fact,' she continued, looking at her watch, 'he may have already done so. He was off to track down Elspeth's boyfriend when he left me. You'll know him, I should think. He works backstage at the theatre.'

'Surely you don't mean Hedley?' asked Lettice, so shocked that her fork was temporarily halted in its relentless ascent from the plate. 'He wouldn't hurt a flea – it's just not in him.'

'And even if he did, he certainly wouldn't be clever enough to get away with it,' added Ronnie, for whom kindness was no adequate substitute for wit. 'If the girl had been walking out with McCracken, I could believe in a *crime passionnel* – the woman just oozes spite, and if she's got a murderous streak then none of us are safe. But I can't see Hedley taking up arms, and you know me – happy to see the bad in anyone.'

Long practised at ignoring her sister's asides, Lettice pressed on with her questioning. 'Is it really Hedley's girlfriend who's been killed? None of us ever saw her, but he's blossomed since they met and Lydia says he absolutely worships the ground she walks on. She was teasing him about it just the other day, daring him to show her off to us. He'll be devastated: I can't believe he had anything to do with it.'

'But he was in a very funny mood this afternoon,' Ronnie said. 'And he rushed off like a bat out of hell, although I gather he was due a bollocking from Aubrey over something so you can't blame him for a hasty exit. Well, well – Hedley White. It just shows, doesn't it?' she added inconclusively.

'Don't make me regret telling you that by spreading it around,' said Josephine. 'If he turns out to be completely innocent, he'll have enough to cope with without every Tom, Dick and Harry looking at him as though he should have a noose around his neck. And anyway, I'm not going to start imagining that people are waiting for me in dark corners all over London just to please Archie. Let's face it,' she added caustically, 'the ones we have to deal with in broad daylight are behaving badly enough at the moment.'

Josephine's reference to the bickering amongst cast and crew at the theatre was not lost on the Motleys, who had seen her attitude towards those involved in her play go from excitement to admiration to irritation over the last year. With the exception of Lydia, who was the most established of the cast when the run began and who had remained gracious in the face of its unprecedented success, those who had gained fame and fortune through the play had not impressed its author with their tantrums and jealousies and determination to cash in on every opportunity it offered – and she had made that perfectly clear. Not that she had any moral objections to commercial success – she believed wholeheartedly that the purpose of telling a story was to entertain an audience and the money had given her the freedom to do what she most loved – but its trappings bored her and she simply did not need that many complications, or that many people, in her life. All in all, the experience had made her approach the staging of another work in a very different spirit, one that questioned the sense of doing it at all. The solitary appeal of the novel, which required her to rely on no one but herself and Brisena, grew stronger by the day.

Nothing that the Motleys had to report about the afternoon's meeting was likely to change her mind. 'I know your day wasn't easy,' said Lettice, 'but at least it was less fractious than the one you were supposed to have. Bernard kept us waiting for ages while he made some telephone calls and then, when he finally did call us all in, I've never seen anybody less in the mood to compromise. It'll be a wonder if he has any staff left by curtain-up.'

'I've got better things to do with my life than listen to your childish arrogance,' boomed Ronnie in a passable impression of Aubrey. 'Then he stormed out, giving Johnny no chance to have the full tantrum he'd been planning so carefully. He had it anyway, of course, but without the audience it was meant for.'

'Don't tell me nothing was agreed,' Josephine said impatiently.

'I think it would be more accurate to say decided than agreed,' said Lettice, wiping the contrasting sauces from her plate with the last piece of bread. 'Bernard made it quite clear from the start that any changes to the plans for a tour of *Richard* were quite out of the question. He's insisting that if any money is to be made from it out of London, then it must go now on the back of the momentum it has here and it must go with the cast that people have heard so much about and will pay to see. He said he owed that much to you, if nothing else.'

'There was a time when I would have appreciated that,' said Josephine. 'Now, with everything that's happened, it can't be over too soon for me. But he's right about the timing of a tour, of course. I can see why Johnny needs a change, but this is the moment and Aubrey was never going to let him out of a signed contract. Anyway, it's only eight weeks, for God's sake. Surely he can grin and bear it for that long without ruining his career?'

'You'd think so, although from what he was saying I got the impression that Johnny's worries at the moment have more to do with money than artistic integrity. He's usually so choosy about where he wants to go next, but there was a touch of the desperate about him today. He wants this film for the money, pure and simple. If it comes off, he knows how pathetic a stage salary – even his – will seem by comparison.'

'In the meantime, he'll just have to stay strapped like the rest of us because there's no doubt that your name, *Richard*'s glory and

Johnny's frustration will all be enjoying April in Manchester. The Producer has spoken,' Ronnie summarised neatly, 'and that is the script we'll be using.'

'And a murder doesn't affect his plans?' Josephine asked. 'No, you're right, of course,' she continued, matching Ronnie for sarcasm. 'I suppose the only inconvenience that death seems to be causing is by coming at the end of the run. As a publicity stunt, it really would have been so much more beneficial for those quiet matinees just after Christmas.'

'Although to be fair,' said Lettice, a little more charitably, 'Aubrey doesn't realise it was Hedley's girlfriend. I know we lapped up the drama of it all when we saw the latest account in the paper, but it's turning out to be a lot closer to home than we could have suspected. He's really taken that boy under his wing in the last couple of months, and whether he has to deal with Hedley's guilt or just his grief, it won't be easy for him.'

There was no telling which it would be at this stage, thought Josephine, although she had found it difficult to reconcile either Lettice's opinion of Hedley White or Elspeth's obvious affection for him with the person who possessed enough nerve and malice to carry out the murder which had been described to her. She wondered how Archie and Fallowfield were getting on in their search for the boy: he was all they had to go on at the moment, but she could not believe in her heart that the solution was as simple as a lovers' quarrel. In just one short meeting, it had seemed evident to her that the Simmonses were a complex family in which relationships existed on very fragile foundations. Secrets – between husband and wife, between mother and daughter, between brothers – were in plentiful supply, and she could not forget the hurt in Frank Simmons's eyes when he realised that his wife knew more about Elspeth's past than he did. How had he really felt at the prospect of losing the cherished company of his niece to another man? And a man who so obviously shared her passions and could open the door for her to a living, breathing theatre rather than to one enclosed in a glass case. As fascinating as it was, she could not help but feel that Simmons's extraordinary pocket of nostalgia was a little obsessive, to say the least. She thought again about the alibi that he had given to Archie: was a waitress – run off her feet in a busy coffee shop – really able to put reliable timings on anything, particularly something that was part of an established routine?

Dessert arrived, Stulik needing no further prompting to bring three hot, sweet soufflés to his favourite table. 'It is all in the steel of the nerve and the strength of the hand on the whisk,' he said modestly, shrugging off their admiration and remaining oblivious to Ronnie's smirk.

'I hardly dare ask if the boys got round to discussing *Queen of Scots*,' Josephine asked, when the only evidence that remained of Stulik's mastery with a whisk was a light dusting of icing sugar on Lettice's top lip.

'Oh, they certainly did,' Ronnie replied, passing her napkin across to her sister. 'But that just dealt another blow to any prospect of negotiation. When he couldn't get anywhere with the film, Johnny tried to throw his weight about on the casting for your next play. He demanded that Rafe Swinburne play Bothwell and threatened to walk out if he didn't get his way.'

'That's when Bernard really lost his temper. He said that Swinburne was never getting another job from him, and that he refused to have his theatres used as a . . . as a . . .'

'As an expensive rehearsal for a cheap fuck was the phrase I believe he used,' said Ronnie, gleefully jumping in as her more modest sister faltered. 'Anyway, Aubrey just pointed out that if Lewis Fleming would have been good enough to tour as Richard, then he'd be perfectly fine to stay here as Bothwell.'

'So the stage is set for another triumphant night in the West End,' said Josephine with a heavy dose of irony. 'A happy cast, an untroubled crew and death in the wings – what more could we ask for? But at least it sounds like this film is dead in the water: I can do without that sort of fate-baiting at the moment.'

'Oh no dear, you haven't heard the best bit yet.' Ronnie's pause to look for her lighter had the desired dramatic effect on Josephine, who impatiently offered her own in exchange for the rest of the story. 'Well, I couldn't decide if Aubrey was simply flexing his muscles or if he really thinks it's a good idea,' she said, inhaling deeply, 'but his final move was his deadliest. He calmed down after the cheap fuck exchange, and announced very firmly that he had every intention of financing a film of *Richard*, but he wasn't certain that Johnny was the right man for the role on screen.'

'Darling, you should have seen the look on Johnny's face. I thought he was going to hit him,' Lettice said with feeling before looking questioningly at Ronnie, who nodded slightly. 'And that's not the only disappointment, I'm afraid. He's made it clear that he wants Lillian Gish for Anne of Bohemia, not Lydia. He says she has all the qualities on screen that Lydia has on stage, and that she's a bigger name in the film world. I really don't know what's come over him.'

'And that, my dear, was that,' finished Ronnie with a flourish. 'Aubrey stormed out, muttering something which had "McCracken" and "bitch" in the same sentence, and we were left to mop up what was left of Johnny.'

As they paid the bill, Josephine was speechless. She loathed the extent to which she was losing control of her work, but could see no way out of the tangle of triumph and disillusionment that seemed to be its inevitable companion. Even if she refused to have anything to do with a film of her play, there was nothing to stop Aubrey asking another writer to produce something along the same lines. As she had argued successfully against Vintner in court, there was no copyright on history. And anyway, in a sense the damage had already been done. Film or no film, in a circle as small as this one, there was no way that Lydia could be protected from the knowledge that she had been overlooked – and for a woman who had been at the top of her profession since the age of fifteen, the journey down was bound to be a painful one.

On the way out, they looked for their host to thank him but Stulik's attention had already been diverted to another party, recently arrived and headed by a distinguished elderly gentleman around whom the proprietor clucked like a mother hen.

'Look! It's Sickert,' exclaimed Lettice, less subtly than she could have. 'Thank God Lydia's not here or he'd be all over us. I can't believe she spent all that time alone with him. There's something very shifty about him, don't you think?' she asked with a shiver.

Josephine glanced at the painter, who had recently completed an impressive portrait of Lydia as Queen Isabella of France, falling quite naturally under her spell as he did so. Try as she might, the finely cut, sensitive face and untidy white hair revealed to her none of the evil intent which seemed so obvious to Lettice. Before her friend could place London's most celebrated artist at King's Cross with something more lethal than a paintbrush in his hand, Josephine told her not to be so ridiculous and led the way purposefully to the door.

Eight

The telephone on the dark oak desk in Bernard Aubrey's office rang at exactly seven o'clock. Wearily, he lifted the receiver halfway through the third peal, then brightened as the voice at the other end identified itself.

'There's really no need to explain,' he said, cutting short the apologies with which the caller opened the conversation. 'It's very good of you to bother on Saturday night. Do you have what I'm looking for?'

He listened carefully as the woman on the other end gave a succinct but comprehensive response to his questions, his fingers idly tracing the outline of numbers which had been scribbled on the blotting pad in front of him during the last few days. 'You're sure about that?' he asked when she stopped talking. 'There's no possibility of a mistake?' Reassured by her certainty, he thanked her again and carefully replaced the handset. The whole conversation had lasted barely five minutes, but he had all the details he needed. The only question now was how best to act on them.

Reaching for the bottle of whisky which always stood on his desk, Aubrey noticed how quickly its contents had dwindled. He had never been a heavy drinker, preferring the habitual comforts of tobacco and sufficiently aware of the toll that one addiction had taken on his health to know that the acquisition of another was unwise. But he had long since ceased to care about his own well-being, and the peat-filled warmth of the Scotch soothed him now, taking the edge off the cold that had hovered at the back of his eyes and throat since he awoke that morning and centring his thoughts on the evening ahead: he would get through the performance without allowing his anxiety to distract him, and he would speak to Josephine and Lydia after the show. His recent behaviour towards them both had been so out of character that he needed to make his peace; his fears, in all truth, were not their concern. He must promise Josephine that she would not have to endure again any of the unpleasantness which had plagued her introduction to theatre, that the madness which had begun with Vintner's ludicrous allegations was a one-off occurrence. In any case, he knew instinctively that the distorted success of *Bordeaux* was unlikely to be repeated and certainly not by the play which was soon to go into rehearsal; *Queen of Scots* would do moderately well, but it lacked the charm of its predecessor and would, he was sure, have a looser grip on the public's affections. Lydia would be more difficult to appease, simply because the shadow that he had cast over her future in a moment of unnecessary harshness was genuine: it *was* hard for an actress in her forties, even one as accomplished and versatile as she was, but they were friends and he would find a way to reassure her.

Then there was Hedley to consider. The boy had not come to see him after the show as he had been asked, but he did not think any less of him for that. In love for the first time, he was bound to act out of character but, like anyone who has been given an unexpected chance in life and is anxious to please, he learned his lessons quickly and well: the reprimand he had already received seemed to have hit home, and there would be no need to refer to the subject again. In fact, he had wanted to make amends for his earlier anger by allowing Hedley to take his girl backstage, to show her the dressing rooms and let her walk on the stage with the lights full on; from what he had been told about her, he knew how much that would mean to Elspeth and how pleased Hedley would be to be able to offer it. Never mind – it could wait until next week; she was staying in London for several days. As far as he could see, the couple stood a good chance of making a go of it: neither was particularly used to excessive kindness or affection, but nor had they been trained to distrust it through those scarring acts of cruelty and betrayal. They were surprised when the love which they had seen in the picture houses and read about in magazines happened to them, but not afraid to embrace it wholeheartedly and turn it into something uniquely theirs. Aubrey shuddered when, by contrast, he thought of the poor murdered girl in that train and the passions which the papers were speculatively blaming for her death. There was a lot to be said for a simple life, undistinguished by any extreme emotion. He would help Elspeth and Hedley in any way he could and that would give him a deeper satisfaction, he suspected, than any of the success he had enjoyed up to now, if only because they had never asked for it.

If he had known the weight of responsibility that would follow him through life, he would perhaps have chosen another path. Most men were relied upon by a family and he had provided more than adequately for his, but financial support had proved the easiest to give. Every day at the theatre, and throughout those four long years underground, people had looked to him to make things different, to change their fortunes, to keep them alive; the cost of getting it wrong varied, of course, but the pressure was always there, the emphasis was always on him to provide what was missing, be it money, recognition or simply hope. And now, at sixty-five, he was exhausted, so exhausted that he longed to disappear altogether. Perhaps one day he would just give up and leave, but there was something he needed to do first and tomorrow, when he had the building to himself and his mind was more settled, he would consider the most appropriate path to his own redemption. It had been a long time coming and it would be all too easy to snatch at it in sheer relief, but the stain of damage must not spread. The innocent must not be made to suffer again.

He emptied the bottle and walked over to the bookcase, where a woman in a silver frame looked out at him from a backdrop of Bennett and Walpole. The picture had been taken forty years ago or more and, until death brought its miraculous peace, the face had aged in that time more starkly than he cared to admit, but this was how he always remembered her. 'We're nearly there,' he said, raising his glass in acknowledgement of the silent pact that ran between them. 'We're nearly there.'

*

Hedley White stood across the road from the New Theatre in the rain, trying to understand how his world had fallen apart so quickly and knowing it was all his own fault. He had been there for an hour now, huddled against the iron gates that divided the courtyard of 66 St Martin's Lane from the busy street beyond, and taking advantage of the shadows to watch the comings and goings opposite. Since mid-afternoon, people had been queuing along the draughty passage which ran down one side of the New but there had been no sign of impatience or bad humour, just excitement and the companionship that always characterises a crowd with a shared objective. The queue tailed back as far as he could see, following the passage round past stage door – where he had first set eyes on Elspeth – and on to Wyndham's, eventually emerging into Charing Cross Road. All reservable seats were long gone, and had been since the play's last few days had been announced, but hopefuls still turned out in force for the pit and gallery entrances and, even now, when the doors were thrown open and the lucky frontrunners admitted, there was no indication that the line was anything but infinite.

He had liked Elspeth from the moment he set eyes on her, standing patiently at the stage door with an older man whom he later learned was her uncle, waiting for Rafe Swinburne's autograph. With no thought in his mind other than to be helpful, and knowing that the actor would be occupied for some time with the blonde who had arrived halfway through the second act with a bottle of gin and some maraschino cherries, Hedley offered to take the programme backstage and get it signed for her. 'Is she pretty?' Swinburne had asked, after taking careful note of the name and covering his photograph with the usual flamboyant scrawl. Blushing as he described her, Hedley laid himself open to some merciless teasing. 'You have this one, then,' Swinburne had said, casting a sly glance at the blonde. 'As you can see, I've got my hands full tonight – but don't let me down. Make sure she says yes.' And much to Hedley's astonishment, she had said yes. His tentative request that she might meet him for a cup of tea one day had been met with a smile of disarming pleasure and a blush that matched his own. The last two months had been the happiest he had ever known.

And now he was paying for that happiness with a misery deeper than he could have thought possible. Just for a moment, he allowed himself the foolish luxury of playing out the evening as it should have been: their joyful first glimpse of each other and the endless conversation that always followed an absence; more talk inside the theatre – in all their meetings, he could not remember a single silence – where they would go first to the sweet kiosk so that Elspeth could choose a box of toffees to see them safely through the first half, and then to their seats. He would take her hand the moment the curtain went up and, from then on, would steal secret glances at her, smiling to himself as her lips silently formed the lines she knew by heart and watching as she leaned forward in her seat to anticipate scenes she particularly enjoyed. Then the walk, arm in arm, to the restaurant and dinner, before he saw her safely home. Unable to bear it any longer, Hedley brought the fantasy to an abrupt end and sank to the pavement in despair, bowed by a twin grief because he knew then, in his heart, that he would never want to set foot in a theatre again.

From where he crouched, scarcely noticing how cold and wet the iron railings felt against his back, he saw Lydia walking quickly down the passage towards stage door, arm in arm with the other lady and laughing as the two of them struggled with an umbrella that stubbornly refused to close. If she had been on her own, he might have approached her and asked for her help – she had been kind to him from the moment she found out that he shared her joy in music and old songs – but he was shy in front of her friend. In any case, a gentleman soon sacrificed his place in the queue to force the umbrella into submission and the moment was lost as they disappeared into the theatre. There was no safe haven for him there: Aubrey was furious with him and he, in turn, cursed the older man for his interference, without which Elspeth might still be alive and he would not be standing here with no idea what to do next. With all that the papers had implied, he knew the police would be looking for the dead girl's boyfriend and it would not take them long to find out who he was. They were probably at his digs now, waiting for him to come home, but he would not risk that, no matter how tempting it was to collect a change of clothes and the small amount of money that he had managed to save each week from his wages, carefully stored in a tin under the bed.

A coin fell to the ground in front of him. Instinctively, he picked it up and stood, ready to return it to its owner, to explain that he was not one of the beggars who lined the West End streets on a Saturday night and that the shilling should go to someone who really needed it. Instead, he just watched as the man disappeared into the crowd, suddenly aware that he faced a stark choice: he could give himself up and take what was coming to him, or he could run – and for that he needed money, not a conscience. As the dreaded 'House Full' sign was placed on the pavement outside, the queue began to disperse. Before he could change his mind, Hedley pulled his collar up and strode quickly across the road after a couple who were walking away in disappointment.

'Excuse me,' he said, touching the young man's arm. 'I was supposed to be going to the play tonight with my friend but she . . . she can't be here.' From his coat, he took the tickets that Aubrey had given him, two front-row dress-circle seats, the most expensive that money could buy. 'It'd be a shame to let these go to waste. I'll sell them to you if you like, just for the cost price.'

The boy looked at him in disbelief. 'Are you sure?' he asked. Hedley nodded and took the money, embarrassed as the girl gave him a spontaneous hug. 'We've just got engaged,' she said, smiling in delight, 'and we so wanted to celebrate at the theatre. Everybody's talking about it. You've no idea how much this means to us.'

The money weighed heavy in his pocket as Hedley turned away, knowing more certainly than the couple could have realised exactly just how much it meant.

For an actress in a hit West End play, Saturday was usually the most gratifying day of the week but, by five o'clock, Lydia

Beaumont had had enough. An unsettled air hung over the theatre as the tension which already existed among cast and crew was intensified by the shocking events of the day before; everyone seemed out of sorts because of it, herself and Marta included. As a rule, Lydia enjoyed the occasions when Lewis Fleming stood in for Terry because he brought a strained anger to the role of Richard, a rawness which gave her something different to respond to. This afternoon, however, she felt that both their performances had been distinctly below par and would not have blamed the audience for reflecting this at the end of the show. But matinee crowds were always the easiest to please and the applause was as rapturous as ever. One day they would be found out, but not today.

'Come on, let's go for a walk,' Marta said, watching as Lydia wiped the last of the make-up from her eyes. 'We both need some air and it'll do you good to get away from this lot, if only for an hour. If you're lucky, I'll even buy you a sausage roll from that coffee stall on the Embankment. You need to keep your strength up – the plague can take it out of a girl.'

Lydia smiled and took her coat from the back of the door, needing no further persuasion to indulge in a little normal living before she had to return to the stage to die all over again. 'You know, I'll actually be quite glad to leave this behind after next week and get out into the country for a bit,' she said, as they climbed the narrow stairs to ground level and came out into the scene dock.

'I see, can't wait to get away from me already,' Marta said in mock offence, but her playful tone was not reciprocated as Lydia stopped and looked at her.

'Don't be ridiculous,' she said, gently stroking her hair. 'You know how badly I'll miss you, but I still haven't given up hope of talking you into coming with me, at least for some of the time. What do you say? We could find a little guest house by the sea . . .'

'In Manchester?'

'All right, perhaps you'd better skip that week, but how about Brighton? We can walk on the pier if it's nice or stay in bed all day if it's not, then smile over dinner as the landlady frowns her disapproval on us in spite of the fact that she's only got one set of sheets to wash at the end of the week.' Marta laughed as Lydia warmed to her theme and lapsed into melodrama. 'Then, as the day dwindles, I'll show you all the glamour of life on tour,' she continued. 'Scratchy grey blankets and shared bathrooms with no hot water, smelly dressing rooms, half-empty theatres and restaurants that close five minutes before the performance ends, leaving you no choice but to go home to cocoa from an old chipped mug. Are you really going to let me go through all that on my own? It's tantamount to abuse, particularly for a queen of delicate disposition.'

Marta took her arm as they joined the throng of playgoers in St Martin's Lane and headed south towards the river, taking the sight-seeing circuit which they always enjoyed whenever she met Lydia from the theatre between shows. 'Don't make me doubt my decision on this one,' she said, more seriously this time. 'I could easily be persuaded to come with you because I don't want us to be apart any more than you do, but I'll just be in the way.' She held her fingers to Lydia's lips as they started to protest. 'You know I'm right. It's your world, and I can skate around the edges and drag you up for air occasionally, but it's better for both of us if we keep you and me separate from all that. At least that way you have some sanity to come home to, and thank God nobody's thought of opening the theatres on a Sunday yet: we'll have a lot of time to make up for on your days off.'

Lydia smiled wickedly back at her and, sensing that the crisis had passed, at least for now, Marta changed the subject. 'Talking of delicate queens, has your lord and director found you a Bothwell to return to yet?'

'I don't know for sure but we'll find out from Josephine later – she went to the meeting with them. However, judging by the mood he was in when he came out, I don't think he got his way so we're probably safe in assuming that it'll be Lewis rather than Swinburne.'

'How miserable for you! From what I saw of him at lunchtime, he's not exactly going to be a laugh a minute in rehearsals, and there was a gaggle of adolescent girls panting over the other chap's photograph as I came past Wyndham's. Wouldn't he have been a bigger draw?'

'Possibly, but I'm hardly in a position to argue at the moment. Bernie made it quite clear the other day that I'm lucky to have a job at all at my advanced age, let alone a leading role.'

'Don't be daft. Look at the success you've had this last year – he'd be mad to drop you. You've always said before that he values your opinion. He must have been having an off day.'

'Yes, I know. He has been acting strangely recently and I'm sure he wouldn't normally have been as blunt in the way he put it, but even I have to face up to the fact that what he said is absolutely right. I might be able to talk Josephine into writing me another role or two, but make the most of these weeks of peace without me – you'll be seeing a lot more of me until I'm of character age.'

'Well I'm hardly likely to complain about that,' Marta replied affectionately, opening an umbrella to protect them from the strengthening rain. 'You never know – I may even scribble something for you myself one of these days, and I'm slightly more ancient than you.'

'It's all right for you writers, though: you can start as late as you like and go on until you drop, and no one thinks anything of it. In fact, we don't even chide you for being lazy in not getting around to it sooner. I don't know how you get away with it. I've been doing this since I was fifteen – no wonder I'm exhausted!'

'Oh I started on and off a long time ago but if I read now what I wrote then, I'd probably be horrified. When you're young, you only ever write romantic nonsense.'

'And now you're so cynical and worldly wise, I suppose? How does that tally with the woman whose idea of a first date is to take me tobogganing on Hampstead Heath to seduce me in the snow, or the one who leaves a single flower at stage door before every performance even though I've told her it's bad luck, or . . .'

'All right, all right – you win. I'm a different woman since I met you and I'll probably never write another word because of it. Books aren't built on happiness, but I know what I'd rather have.'

'Then we shall be old and poor and illiterate together,' said Lydia, turning to give her a kiss. 'Now, what about that sausage roll?'

The Salisbury public house was known to its advocates for liveliness and companionship, and to its detractors for noise and interference. Rafe Swinburne was not bothered enough to subscribe to either party, but Terry had suggested the Salisbury as a meeting place convenient for both of them before their evening shows and he had willingly agreed, eager to discover what the future held for him. He bitterly regretted having arrived on the scene too late to make his mark in the biggest success of the year, but his debut in *Sheppey* – which Terry was directing at the same time as he starred in *Richard* – had been moderately praised by the critics and keenly welcomed by the audience, and his hopes for *Queen of Scots*, should he get the part, were high. He had known from the moment he met him that Terry was the future of theatre while Aubrey was the past. Always blessed with a remarkable nose for his own advantage, Swinburne had watched with interest the cooling of their partnership, which – or so rumour had it – had been particularly tense of late. If a parting of the ways was on the horizon, he had decided very early on which horse he was going to back, and what his stage presence could not get him with Terry, he suspected his face could.

He was ten minutes late for his rendezvous, but there was no sign of Terry in the crowds that lined the long, curved bar. The Salisbury's clientele was made up almost exclusively of actors, playwrights and the odd agent or two touting for talent, and a dramatic heritage of sorts could no doubt be traced through the various owners of the heavy pewter tankards that hung from the ceiling. Early evening was always one of the busiest times: as the half approached, glasses would be collectively drained and three-quarters of the trade would disperse to one stage or another, gradually drifting back in twos and threes to resume where they had left off. By last orders, the bar would be full again, triumphs mixing leisurely with disasters amid the warm fog of smoke and beer but, at this earlier hour, with the most important performance of the week still to come, the atmosphere was one of nervy expectation. Swinburne bought a glass of beer and found room on the end of one of the hard, horsehair settees that bordered the room, casually taking in the conversations that came and went around him. He counted seven copies of the evening paper lying around on the brass-topped tables and, for once, none of them were open at the situations vacant pages, but rather at the latest account of the King's Cross killing. It never ceased to amaze him that the murder of a complete stranger could be so tirelessly fascinating to so many. What difference could the loss of some girl they had never met possibly make to the ponderous old man in the corner or the powdery-faced redhead behind the bar? Sensation might be the public face of grief, but Londoners were a fickle bunch: there'd be a new headline along tomorrow and the world would carry on as normal through it all.

As he finished his beer, still on his own, Swinburne began to worry that Terry had been and gone without waiting for him. Perhaps he should go and look for him? If he walked straight to the New Theatre there was no chance of their missing each other, so he gave up his seat to a pretty but excessively grateful young girl who had spotted an agent she needed to charm at his table, and headed out. He arrived at stage door without encountering anyone he knew on the way, gave a cheery greeting to the chap on duty and went downstairs. Even before he reached Terry's dressing room he could hear raised voices behind the closed door. Carefully, he went a little nearer until he was close enough to make out the words beneath the anger. It was Lewis Fleming speaking – there was no mistaking that dour northern bravado – and he listened intently, confident that both men were too absorbed in the row to think about leaving the room. No one in the business would have been surprised to find the actors at each other's throats – their mutual hatred was common knowledge in the West End – but this particular exchange ran deeper than professional differences. Swinburne was loath to tear himself away but, by the time Fleming began to shout again, he had heard enough. He left as quietly as he had arrived, a faint smile playing on his lips.

*

Fleming waited until Terry was on his way out of the theatre before making his move. He was deathly tired, but the rain and the cool evening air that ran through St Martin's Court refreshed him a little and helped to focus his thoughts. It was all for her, he reminded himself, fixing her image – well and happy, as she used to be and as she would be again – firmly in his mind's eye so that by the time the familiar figure emerged from stage door and moved briskly, head down, towards St Martin's Lane, he was ready. When he stepped defiantly in Terry's path, that famously sensitive face looked up at him impatiently, then, at the realisation that he was not merely a clumsy passer-by, the impatience turned to anger. Noticing, in spite of Terry's defiance, that the anger was tinged with fear, Fleming felt a surge of power that sickened him to the stomach, but he continued nonetheless.

'Isn't there a little something you've been meaning to give me?' he asked, refusing to let the other man pass. 'It's a couple of days late, but everyone deserves a second chance.'

Terry looked at him and then beyond him down the passage, as if weighing up his options. 'I told you on the telephone: you've had all there is to have at the moment. You can threaten me as much as you like, but it'll get you nowhere.'

'You don't think so?' Fleming gestured towards the queue which was building steadily behind him. It was just a slight move of the hand but proved enough to break Terry's resolve.

'All right, but come back inside. I don't want to discuss this here.'

The bile rose once more in Fleming's throat as he followed his victim through the backstage area, where McCracken was checking that the dice were in their box ready for the opening scene, and downstairs to the dressing rooms. He thought of his wife again, this time in that narrow bed, fighting silently, and he drew on her strength as an antidote for the conscience which made him so weak. It would be all right, he told himself, she would understand why he was doing this and she would forgive him. Then, when she was well, they would think of a way to make reparation, to Terry at least; God, on the other hand, was a different matter altogether.

As they reached his dressing-room door, Terry played for time by feigning difficulty with the lock. He really had no idea what to do, and the meeting that afternoon had left him without any hope of an immediate solution to his problems, without any easy way to make the sort of money he needed to get Fleming off his back. He cursed Aubrey for his intransigence, but only because it was easier than blaming himself. His private life had always been a discreet matter – it would have been dangerous to allow it to be anything else and, anyway, it was of secondary importance – but he had believed himself to be safe in theatre circles, to be among if not like-minded people, at least tolerant ones. How foolish that now seemed! If Fleming did as he threatened to do, all he had worked for would be lost. He would have let everyone down – his family, his friends, the stage itself. Gossip and chatter would follow him everywhere until the worst was suspected of his most innocent friendships, until even he began to believe his behaviour to be wrong. He held Fleming in precious little esteem but he would be lying to himself if he said he was unaffected by the man's evident loathing of all he was, so how would he feel when those he cared for turned away in disgust? When the police were brought in and he faced an exposure so public, so humiliating? Since Fleming had made that first crude and unforeseen threat, his life had been a continuum of sleepless nights and days full of fear. How was he expected to go on smiling and frisking about the stage as if everything were fine when he really felt wretched and despairing of the years ahead? He had to bring an end to it one way or another: violence he could cope with, but shame was more than he could bear.

Once inside the room, Terry took his crown from the chair and threw it on the floor, sitting to face Fleming with more nonchalance than he felt. 'You've got no proof.'

The other man laughed. 'I've got all I need. And you'd be surprised who'll crawl out of the woodwork once the idea's out in the open. Let's face it – there's no shortage of candidates.'

He was right, of course. Terry knew that no matter how careful he had been, he could not rely on everyone to protect him forever and it would only take one loose mouth to ruin him completely. 'How much do you want this time?' he asked, defeated.

'Oh, I don't know. Another five hundred should do for now. When you've got your new projects underway, we can renegotiate. But hurry up: I haven't got all the time in the world.'

'Then you'd better learn some patience, because there aren't going to be any new projects. At least, not immediately.'

'What? Has Aubrey started to tire of his golden boy at last?' Fleming sneered, his professional jealousy for a moment overcoming his other concerns. 'Dear, dear. Well, you'll just have to find another way because believe me – that little fall from grace will be nothing compared to the one you're heading for if I don't get what I need.'

'Need?' Terry retorted, suddenly raising his voice. 'Are you seriously trying to grace that pathetic habit of yours with some sort of necessity? Look at you! You drink your nights away and turn up here to this stage – my stage – to sleepwalk through another performance, and then you expect me to fund your next . . .'

'What?' Fleming was shouting now, and his fury drowned out any level that Terry could manage. 'You think I'd dirty my soul with your money just for a drink? Christ, you've got no idea what normal people have to live with, have you? Locked up here in your own little world, with nothing to care for but your own ego, nothing to lose but another role, another bit of make-believe.' He picked up the discarded crown and threw it across the room, where it crashed against the dressing-room mirror and shattered Terry's startled reflection. 'It's not just kings, you know. Real people suffer, too, and it would do you good to find out just for once how that feels.' His voice dropped again, but the change in volume brought no respite for Terry. 'So yes,' he continued, 'I do *need* that money, and I do *need* it quickly. And for something much more important than a bottle, which makes things rather more dangerous for you.'

'I can't give you five hundred. Fifty's all I've got – take it or leave it.' He held the money up. 'Anyway, it's Aubrey you should be playing your dirty little games with. You're going to need more than my money when you're out of work.'

'What?'

'Hasn't he told you yet? He's going to sack you at the end of this run. Says he can't rely on you any more, that you've lost whatever it was you had. I could never see it myself, but at least he's come to his senses about something. So that's you out of the running for the next show. You'll have to think again.'

It was a cheap trick to buy himself some space and he knew it was only a matter of time before the lie was revealed. Fleming recovered quickly, but not quickly enough to prevent Terry from realising he had scored a small victory. 'Then we'd better think of a way to make Aubrey change his mind about me, hadn't we?' he snarled, snatching the money and leaning close enough for Terry to feel the spittle on his cheek. 'After all, two murders this weekend would look like recklessness.' He stood up and went over to the door. 'And in the meantime,' he said mockingly, 'we must stop meeting like this. You know how people talk.'

It was always at this time of the evening that Esme McCracken felt most at home in her life. Rather than take a break after the matinee like most of her colleagues, she preferred to stay behind and get the preparations for the evening performance out of the way immediately. Impatiently, she ran through costume and property plots which were automatic to her after more than a year, and made sure that all was in place by seven o'clock at the latest. It was then that she most needed time to herself.

Her one good coat – wool, in a daring blue, cast off by a woman her sister worked for and hardly ever worn – hung on the hook where it was always kept for these occasions. She took it down and put it on as quickly as possible, fastening the buttons firmly to cover a faded black jumper and skirt which felt as worn out and as undistinguished as she did, then slipped out of the stage door and round to the front of the New Theatre, eager to be where she belonged. From where she stood at the top of the steps, just outside those polished timber doors, she could watch the audience arrive without being seen from inside, offering a few words of welcome to any theatregoers who caught her eye and practising an air of gracious humility for the future. As the foyer began to fill with expectation, she wondered what her own audiences would be like when Aubrey finally gave in and put her play into production; more discerning than this, certainly, she thought, looking disparagingly at a man in a drenched-through mackintosh and trilby, although she supposed she would have to settle for smaller numbers, at least in the early days. Never mind: what mattered was that those who did come would value her ideas, and of that she had no doubt.

On the dot of seven-thirty, Bernard Aubrey came down from his office into the foyer as he did every night, clad immaculately in evening dress which he wore with a casual elegance. He took up his usual position by the white marble chimneypiece and, ever the genial host, nodded to his Saturday night regulars, many of whom he knew well after several years of faithful attendance. He was still a handsome man, McCracken thought grudgingly, and the attractive coupling of compassion and determination in his eyes had not been dulled by age.

As she watched, Aubrey's general smile of greeting took on a more personal warmth and she felt a sharp stab of jealousy when she recognised its recipient; in the crush, she had not noticed Josephine Tey arrive, but that was hardly surprising – her looks were as bland as her work. She returned Aubrey's kiss on the cheek, and he lowered his head to allow her to speak privately into his ear, then the two moved slightly to one side, away from the main crowd. McCracken tutted impatiently as her view of the pair was blocked, and risked moving slightly forward; by the time she had them once again in her view, Aubrey's expression had completely changed and Tey had laid a consoling hand on his arm. What was that all about? Perhaps she had told him she was giving up the stage? If so, this could be the moment she'd been waiting for. Her heart lifted briefly, until she saw one of the Motley women – the overweight one – dragging a young couple through the crowd to where Tey and Aubrey were still in solemn conversation. The designer, overdressed as usual and apparently oblivious to their mood, pointed to the engagement ring on the girl's finger and

Tey smiled her congratulations, while Aubrey turned and went back upstairs. McCracken watched as the author signed the programme which was tentatively held out to her. All that cringing self-effacement made her sick – it was so affected – and she knew then that whatever had darkened Aubrey's mood, it wasn't the prospect of having to replace a successful author: this one loved her glory far too much to relinquish it. Trust the smug bitch to spoil even this ritual for her. Already late for the half, McCracken turned round and headed bitterly for the dark anonymity of backstage, pushing the last few stragglers roughly aside as she went.

Josephine was about to take her seat in the royal circle when she felt a tap on the shoulder. She turned round, the practised smile already in place, but took an involuntary step back when she found Frank Simmons looking intently back at her. He was soaked to the skin and, as he removed his hat, the water fell in a steady drip from its brim, creating a patch of deeper crimson in the foyer's carpet.

'Mr Simmons – Frank – what are you doing here?' she asked, torn between sympathy for his grief and unease at seeing him so unexpectedly. 'Are you all right?'

'Yes, miss, I'm fine but I had to get out for a bit. The flat felt so empty with Betty gone up north, and all I could think about was my Elspeth lying alone somewhere, so I came here. I know it sounds strange, but this is where I feel closest to her.'

He looked at the floor, tears threatening to join forces with the rain. Josephine struggled to find something to say which would bring this excruciating scene to an end without sounding too callous or too encouraging, but nothing came to her and she remained locked in an uncomfortable silence with him, conscious that everyone left in the foyer was beginning to stare. When Archie appeared at her side, seemingly out of nowhere, she had never been more pleased to see him.

'It's a terrible night, Sir, can we give you a lift anywhere?' he asked, his natural courtesy tinged with a firmness that was not lost on Simmons, who released Josephine's hand and appeared to get a grip on himself. 'That's very kind of you, Inspector, but a walk does me good and I can't get much wetter than I am already. I just wanted to see Miss Tey again and to thank her for this afternoon,' he said, turning to her, although his voice was so low and uncertain that she could barely make out the words. 'I'll let you go in now – you don't want to miss the start.'

'Oh I think I know how it goes by now,' said Josephine with a nervous laugh, and bid him goodnight. Gratefully, she allowed Archie to lead her away and Simmons watched them go, continuing to stare long after they had disappeared into the auditorium.

Nine

Penrose had not intended to use his ticket for the performance but, with his cousins seated in another part of the theatre and Josephine visibly shaken by her encounter in the foyer, he was reluctant to leave her on her own immediately. Their seats at the side of the royal circle afforded a splendid view of the stage, but neither of them seemed particularly inclined to look in that direction. More often than not, Josephine's gaze was fixed on the relief figures of Music and Peace which hovered optimistically above the proscenium arch, and he doubted that the world in which she was absorbed belonged to the fourteenth century. His own attention, meanwhile, was focused on the auditorium. His eyes followed the line of the three balconies, sinuously curved and decorated with painted panels, lamps and sconces, but nowhere could he see the two empty seats which he had expected to stand out as a poignant reminder of yesterday's events. He would have to check in the rear stalls and balcony, which were currently hidden from his view, but every row seemed full; certainly the coveted top-price seats – of which Hedley White was supposed to have had two – were all taken. So what had happened to those tickets? Had he got rid of them, or asked someone else to do it for him? Is that why Frank Simmons had appeared so unexpectedly downstairs? Or had White never actually bought the tickets, knowing that Elspeth would be dead by the time the performance began?

Impatiently, Penrose glanced at his watch and was frustrated to see that the interval was still half an hour away. Almost as restless as he was, Josephine touched his arm and nodded to the exit, urging him to leave her and get on with what he needed to do, but he shook his head – he hoped reassuringly – and tried to settle back in his seat. It was irrational, this feeling he had that she was in danger, but it carried the force of conviction and he was not prepared to take a chance for the sake of thirty minutes, not when someone had already been killed just yards away from a crowd. Trying not to fidget, he was relieved to note that no one else was likely to be disturbed by his irreverent disregard for the play. Every other head was turned towards the stage and held there as if by force, and the silence in the auditorium was of a quality rarely found in London outside of its sacred spaces. In the last year John Terry had acquired the authority and presence of a truly great actor but tonight there was a nervous brilliance about his performance which surpassed everything he had achieved up to now. The audience, many of whom were regulars and had several performances to compare it to, realised they were watching something special.

Terry was only slight in build but he dominated the stage, determined, it seemed, to prove that it was his. In scene after scene he extracted every ounce of opportunity from Josephine's lightly drawn portrait, seeming to relish the King's strengths and weaknesses in equal measure and moving effortlessly from the airy carelessness of Richard's early scenes to the disillusionment of someone in whom the poison of suspicion has begun to work. Eventually, even Penrose was drawn in and he marvelled at the way in which the actor's movements took on a morbid, feline elegance as he responded to the treachery against him. 'To become an expert in murder', he whispered bitterly to his queen as the first act drew to a close, 'cannot be so difficult,' and the intensity in his voice held the audience – Penrose included – spellbound.

He thought back to the first time he had seen Terry, playing the very same role but in Shakespeare's version at the Old Vic. It was five years ago now, but he remembered it vividly because the production's brief run had coincided with one of Josephine's then rare visits to London. They had gone together and, if he recalled the evening more for the pleasure of her company than the power of Terry's acting, it was no less poignant to him now. It had been one of those hot summer evenings which occasionally graced the city with a leisurely decadence. As they walked back down the Waterloo Road, still laughing at one of the more eccentric patrons, whose cracked but resounding rendition of 'God Save the King' rang out from the front of the gallery at the end of the performance, he had seen in Josephine a willingness to engage with the future which had been absent since Jack's death. Since then, she had often referred to that night as the inspiration for *Richard of Bordeaux*, but it had been less fondly of late and, if he really wanted to torment himself, he could curse the impulse that had made him buy those tickets. Fortunately, before he could dwell too long in the past, the dusty-pink brocade and velvet curtains fell, drawing a jarring air of opulence over the simple lines of the Motleys' stage designs.

Leaving Josephine safely in the bar with Lettice and Ronnie, Penrose walked round to stage door to look for Bernard Aubrey. The rain which had fallen so fiercely in the early part of the evening had finally relented, but it was impossible to avoid the puddles, and the light from the Salisbury's solid Victorian coach lamps blurred and splintered as his feet disturbed its perfect reflection. He had met Aubrey a few times, mostly at opening nights but more recently during that vicious court case, when Elliott Vintner had accused Josephine of plagiarism in the writing of *Richard of Bordeaux*, claiming that it echoed the events of his own novel, *The White Heart*, published twelve years earlier. Aubrey, as the play's producer, had given evidence on Josephine's behalf and Penrose had been impressed with his intelligence and sense of justice. His opinion of White's character would, no doubt, be worth listening to and he might even be able to help the police find the boy. There were men posted wherever White was likely to appear and a description would be out by now in the evening paper, but Elspeth's young man had so far proved elusive and any other suggestions would be gratefully received.

He announced who he was and the stage doorkeeper – a burly, red-faced man in his late fifties – wasted no time in telephoning up to Bernard Aubrey's office and handing over the receiver. Penrose came to the point quickly and discreetly, aware that the doorman was giving a display of nonchalance which would never get him a job on the other side of the footlights.

'Bernard? It's Archie Penrose. I'm sorry to interrupt you on a Saturday night but I need to talk to you, and the sooner the better. Is now convenient? It shouldn't take too long.'

There was a second's pause while Aubrey blew a lungful of smoke into the air, then Penrose heard his voice, thick and guttural from a lifetime's devotion to cigarettes. 'Actually, Archie, it might take longer than you think. I'm glad you're here because there's something I need to talk to you about, as well. I was going to come and see you on Monday, but after this terrible business it can't wait until then. As it is, I've got to live with the fact that I've left it this long.' He exhaled again, then continued. 'I've got to be on stage in the second half and I can't get out of that – there's no one else here to do it – but I'll meet you downstairs as soon as we finish. I'm supposed to be taking everyone for a drink, but we can talk privately first. What I have to say might help you. In any case, it will help me.'

'Then perhaps we could at least make a start now?' Penrose said, but the line was dead even before he had finished the sentence. Frustrated, but daring to hope that he might at last be getting somewhere, he resigned himself to another agonising wait and walked back down St Martin's Court.

The Grand Circle Bar was always packed on a sold-out Saturday night. Ronnie, who never allowed even the densest of crowds to stand between her and a large gin, returned triumphant from the bar and passed two tall glasses to Lettice and Josephine before falling heavily into the third herself. 'Fuck, it's Fitch,' she said, as she came up for air. 'Don't look round.'

But it was too late. 'A hundred thousand in a year at the box office!' cried the critic from the *Evening Standard*, forcing his way over. 'Aubrey can afford to go dark for a month and I dare say Inverness has seen a few corks popped of late?'

'Oh, it's been nothing but fizz and fun since last February,' said Josephine, brushing the comment skilfully aside and trying to hide her dislike. 'I can't thank you enough for all the reviews, and I do so appreciate it when you include a list of criticisms.'

Over Lettice's head, Josephine saw Marta appear at the door and make her way through the crowd, drawing some appreciative glances as she did so. 'I've been sent to offer you the chance of some peace and quiet backstage if you don't want to go back in after the interval,' she said. 'Come down to the dressing room. Once Lydia's died, we can all have a drink.'

Gratefully, Josephine took the lifeline she was offered. 'I'll see you at stage door afterwards,' she called back over her shoulder, and felt a brief stab of guilt as she saw Fitch take a deep breath, ready to continue.

'You came just at the right moment,' she said as they went downstairs. 'Grovelling really doesn't suit me, and it's so hard to fake it well.'

'Tell me about it. The only row I've had with Lydia was when I told her to stop fawning round producers and have faith in her own talent. She looked at me as though I were two days out of a lunatic asylum, then asked me how far that approach had got me in publishing.' She smiled, and her eyes were filled with a warmth which transformed the dark beauty of her face into something more approachable. 'That friend of yours has a *wicked* tongue. It's one of the things I love most about her.'

Wryly, Josephine raised an eyebrow. 'I'm sure she'd say much the same about you. She's right, of course – about the fawning, I mean; I can't speak for the tongue. Actresses live on goodwill.'

By the time they reached the dressing room, Lydia had returned to the wings ready for her brief appearance in the second act but Josephine felt none of the awkwardness that often comes when mutual friends are thrown together in the absence of the common link. In contrast to their first brief meeting, Marta made conversation easily, avoiding the small change to which strangers often limit themselves and talking animatedly about the last couple of months, but her concerns about Lydia's future were never far away and Josephine realised that she was genuinely troubled.

'Is her work a problem for you?' she asked almost brutally, realising that Lydia would be back with them in a few moments' time and the opportunity for confidences would be lost.

'No, it's not that. It's been her life and I'd never ask her to give that up – just the opposite, in fact. What worries me is how she'll cope if – when – it all dries up. She's had a couple of knock-backs lately and the harder she pretends to take it all in her stride, the more I know it's hurting her.'

'She's bound to feel unsettled when something like this comes to an end. Long runs are a luxury, but they lull you into a false sense of security and get you out of the habit of moving on. It'll pass as soon as she gets out on tour and into rehearsals for something new.'

'Perhaps.' Marta looked at her as if assessing how direct she could be. 'Tell me – would you have written a play about Mary Queen of Scots if Lydia hadn't asked you to?'

'No, I don't think I would. I can see why the idea of playing her on stage is attractive, but I've never had any real sympathy for the woman.'

Marta nodded. 'You know, I almost wish you hadn't done it. We all need something to work towards, and the idea that someone could bring that creature to life has been a dream of hers for years. Now it's become a reality and she'll have done it before the year's out, and I'm not sure that leaves her anywhere to go. As it is, I keep catching her looking over her shoulder, thinking that the best is behind her.'

Josephine said nothing, wondering if she should warn Marta that another blow was coming Lydia's way if Aubrey's film ever got off the ground. She decided against it. There was enough unrest for everyone at the moment and it might never happen but, if it did, the more time they had to cement their relationship against outside anxieties the better. 'Of course, Lydia's never had anything meaningful outside the theatre until now,' she said instead. 'Having a life with you must count as something to look forward to, surely?'

'Oh come off it,' Marta said scornfully. 'Women need both – love and work – and these days they can have it. Lydia's got a right to *expect* both. Would you seriously put your pen down if you fell

128

in love?' Josephine was silent, taken aback by the question. 'I'm sorry, I don't mean to be rude and I shouldn't be speaking like this to someone I don't know,' Marta continued, 'but I can see so much sorrow ahead for Lydia and there's nothing I can do to stop it. You won't tell her I'm worried, will you? I've spent all this time being so bloody reassuring.'

'No, I won't say anything. But in answer to your question: yes, I think there are times when I would give all this up for a different life. Or, at least, there are times when having someone in particular would make this life a little less lonely, so don't underestimate what you mean to her.'

Marta was silent, seeming to consider how much of what Josephine said was sincere and how much was designed to make her feel better. 'Maybe you're right,' she said eventually. 'Thank you.'

'And perhaps *you're* right about *Queen of Scots*. I think what you meant but were too polite to say is that my indifference to the woman has made for rather an average play?' Marta blushed a little and Josephine continued. 'It's all right – you can be honest, and it's nothing I don't already know. My affection for Lydia made me say yes when I should have said no. You can't write to order – at least I can't. I neither love nor loathe Mary Stuart, so she's a character rather than a person. The best we can hope for, I suppose, is that she'll be popular.'

'It's funny how our ideas of people change. I was telling Lydia earlier today – the people I valued when I was younger and the stories I wrote about them bear no resemblance to what I feel now.'

'Have you always written, then?'

'On and off. Actually, more off than on until a year or so ago. I started during the war when my husband was away. My mother-in-law was a friend of May Gaskell – have you heard of her?'

'No, I haven't.'

'Well, she started a war library for soldiers abroad. Her son-in-law was wounded in the South African War and she sent him books and magazines in hospital to distract him from the misery of it all. Apparently, it's what got him through, so May decided on

129

the first day of war that British soldiers in France would never be without stories to take their minds off the suffering. She was in her sixties by then, but she was a remarkable woman and well connected enough to make it happen. She persuaded somebody to lend her a house in Marble Arch and turned it into a book warehouse. People sent things in from all over the country. One day we'd get dirty packets of rubbish from Finchley; the next, thirty thousand volumes from a country estate would turn up.'

'How extraordinary! And you worked there?'

'Yes, for a couple of years before the Red Cross took it over. The response was better than May could have hoped for, so she needed volunteers. People were donating entire libraries. On a good day, the vans bringing in the books blocked the traffic all around Marble Arch. We sent them to hospitals all over the world, not just France, but whenever I knew there was a consignment going to my husband's regiment, I'd send stories of my own to make it more personal. You couldn't always rely on their getting to the right person, but it was a way of keeping some sort of connection alive.'

'And your husband?'

'He died.'

'I'm sorry.'

'Don't be. It wasn't the happiest of marriages and it seems a lifetime away now.' The sound of applause drifted down from the stage and Marta stood up to look for a corkscrew. 'Talking of dying, it sounds like she's gone again. That's our cue for a drink.'

By now, Josephine had revised her earlier opinion of Lydia's lover, not dropping the 'nice' which had so disappointed Ronnie but adding some more interesting qualities, passionate and engaging being top of the list. Instead of trying to avoid the subject of Marta's own book, she found herself rather intrigued at the prospect of reading it.

'Lydia says you've finished the first draft of your novel, and she asked me to look at it,' she said, accepting the glass that Marta held out to her. 'There's nothing worse than someone chipping in with helpful advice you don't need, but I'd be happy to read it if you want an outside opinion.'

'That's very sweet of you both but you really don't have to, you know. You must get hundreds of people asking for your time and it's hideous to have to be tactful to someone you know.'

'I wouldn't be. If I didn't like it I'd say so, but even then it would just be the comments of a friend. It's your novel.'

'Yes, it is. For better or worse, it's certainly that.'

There was a rustle of satin from the corridor. 'You know, one night I think I might shock them all and simply refuse to die,' said Lydia as she came into the room and collapsed onto the sofa in a heap of pale pink. 'Can you imagine the look on Johnny's face if I suddenly rallied and stole his best scene? It's almost worth it.' She took an appreciative sip of her wine. 'How is everyone?'

'Fine,' said Marta, laughing as she removed Lydia's flowered head-dress and ran her fingers affectionately through her hair.

'Yes, your plan for us to get to know each other better has worked beautifully,' said Josephine drily. 'In fact, I was just trying to get my hands on this manuscript that I've heard so much and so little about.'

Lydia raised an eyebrow questioningly at Marta, who held up her hands in defeat. 'All right, all right,' she said. 'I'll hand it over. But be gentle – that's all I ask.'

As the final scene got underway, Esme McCracken placed four chairs around a small table which stood in the wings, just to the right of prompt corner. Through the flats, she had a fractured view of the playing area and the first two rows but she did not need to look at the audience to know that it would be gazing, as one, at John Terry as he sat alone downstage, a tray of food untouched beside him. She sighed heavily. God knows why, but this scene, with all its cheap sentiment, did it for them every time. In a minute there would be a stifled sob from the auditorium as Richard's fate in the Tower became too much for someone: she could predict it almost as accurately as she could the knock from the rear of the set which served as a cue for Aubrey's cameo appearance. When it came, he pushed past her, dressed in a guard's suit of string mail, and she caught the scent of alcohol already on his breath, as tangible as the felt from his costume which brushed against her skin. Grumbling to herself, she carefully polished three wine glasses and a whisky tumbler and placed them on the table in readiness for the ridiculous private ritual about to take place. They were like schoolboys, the lot of them: as if she didn't have enough to do without preparing little tableaux to which only the chosen few would be privy. Sneering at the bottle of claret – such expense when she was paid so little – she put it next to the corkscrew. Finally, she lifted the crystal decanter down from the shelf and added it to the tray, where the light from the stage sparkled on the glass and gave a rich, amber colour to the liquid inside. There wasn't much left but, judging by his breath, Aubrey had had quite enough already, although that was no excuse for how beastly he'd been to her earlier. Looking round to make sure that no one was watching, she removed the glass stopper and spat into the decanter.

She moved away from the table just in time. Fleming strode purposefully into the wings from the stage, his character having made his last exit. He tossed a role of parchment – the prop for Richard's abdication – to McCracken, then set about easing the cork soundlessly from its bottle, the first duty in the Ricardian ceremony. Aubrey, as his soldier, followed him offstage, his minor role in the play's climax soon over. As he walked past Fleming, the actor grabbed his arm.

'Not joining us?' he whispered sarcastically. 'But we're such a happy company. It would be a shame not to toast our success, don't you think?'

Aubrey shook him off and seemed about to retaliate, but suddenly stopped himself. McCracken turned round to see what the distraction was and found Lydia just behind her, waiting at the side of the stage to take her share of the applause when the curtain fell. The actress smiled at Aubrey, who appeared to calm down and satisfied himself with a glare at Fleming as he took the lid off his decanter. Meanwhile, the next actor off poured the wine into three glasses, not oblivious to the tension among his colleagues but at a loss to know what had caused it.

Then Terry's distinctive voice cut through the atmosphere. 'How Robert would have laughed,' he said, delivering his famous closing line with a hollow amusement which was all the more powerful for its restraint, and the curtain dropped. As the applause broke out – louder than ever, if that were possible – he left the stage, a glint of triumph in his eyes, and raised his glass for a new toast.

'To memorable exits,' he said, his eyes fixed on Aubrey, and drank the wine in one go. His defiance shocked even McCracken, whose acts of rebellion were always less overt, but Fleming simply laughed and replaced his glass untouched on the tray. As the cast assembled round them, ready for the first of many curtain-calls, McCracken watched Aubrey pour the last of the Scotch into his glass, down it with a grimace and head for the stairs to his office.

Penrose waited impatiently at stage door for Aubrey to keep their appointment, and tried not to show how irritated he was by the doorman's constant chatter. 'I haven't seen fans like this for twenty-five years or more,' he said, looking in wonder at the crowds that had gathered in the passageway outside as though it were his first night on the job. 'Of course, it was different back then – all hansom cabs and evening clothes, bunches of flowers and black canes with silver tops. Now they come dressed as they like and ask for signed photographs. Still, it's almost like the old days. A bit of the old magic's come back, that's for sure.'

While privately wondering what sort of man was happy to do a job that involved sitting in the same chair for years on end, Penrose smiled and nodded. There was no denying the truth of what he said, though: his drone only just carried over the noise outside, where an undisciplined but good-natured crowd of enthusiasts waited for their respective favourites to appear. Terry was the first to brave the adoration, plunging into the noise and noticeably drawing the schoolgirl contingent away from the rest of the bunch. Fleming soon followed, and Penrose was amused to note that his rougher good looks appealed almost uniformly to the housewife market. He must remember to compliment Aubrey on his shrewdness in casting someone for all possible tastes: it must have helped ticket sales tremendously.

'The number of times I've been offered a small fortune just to run downstairs with a note,' the doorman continued, oblivious to any lack of interest on Penrose's part. 'Take Miss Lydia, for example: she's always been popular. When she was here a few years ago, there was one gent who'd come every night and insist on reciting a poem to her. Terrible, they were – even I could tell that – but she smiled through the lot of them. A real lady, she is.'

Not entirely comfortable in a world where an immunity to bad verse was a sign of moral rectitude, Penrose was relieved to be distracted by the sight of his sergeant. Fallowfield pushed his way steadily through the crowds, which were building again as *Sheppey* drew to a close at Wyndham's, the proximity of the two theatres doubling the bustle and confusion in St Martin's Court.

'Give me a nice film any day, Sir,' he said as he moved a couple of gentlemen out of the way to reach the comparative calm inside the building. 'None of this nonsense – just home for a cup of tea.' He greeted the stage doorman politely, then – recognising the type – moved to one side to talk more discreetly to Penrose. 'No sign of White at his digs, Sir. Maybrick called in to say that Simmons got back home about half an hour ago, but he was alone and there's no one else at the house. Any luck here?'

'No, but I'm hoping that might be about to change.' He brought Fallowfield quickly up to date and shared his hopes for the imminent interview with Aubrey. 'It might be nothing to do with this, but he's not the type to make something sound more important than it is. Whatever he's got to say, he seems to have taken White under his wing so it's the most promising thing we've got to go on at the moment.'

A renewed murmuring at the door signalled the end of the wait for the male stragglers in the crowd. Lydia signed all the autographs that were requested of her, graciously accepted more flowers, then collected the handful of letters and cards that had been left with the doorman, while Josephine introduced Marta to Archie and Fallowfield. 'I don't suppose you know if Bernard Aubrey is on his way, do you?' Penrose asked. 'I gather he's meeting you for a drink, but I need to talk to him first.'

'I'll go and hurry him up,' said Lydia, overhearing. 'God knows what he's doing at this time of night, but he always has to be forcibly dragged away from his desk. The man's obsessed with work.' While Marta and Josephine exchanged a look that silently spoke the words pot, kettle and black, the Motleys came in from the passage.

'Sorry we're late but we got stopped in the foyer by that *lovely* young couple who got their tickets outside at the last minute,' Lettice said, unwrapping her last toffee and handing the empty box to the doorman with an apologetic smile. 'I don't think I've ever seen anybody so excited.' She turned to Josephine. 'They asked me to tell you . . .' but she was unceremoniously interrupted by her cousin before she could deliver the message.

'What did you say?' asked Penrose.

Lettice looked at him, surprised. 'Nice to see you, too, Archie. I was just saying that this couple were over the moon to have seen the play at last. They've just got engaged, you see, and . . .'

'No, no – what did you say about the tickets?'

'I said they got them at the last minute. Someone outside was selling two that he couldn't use. His girlfriend was ill or something.'

'Why on earth didn't you tell me that before?' Penrose asked, more than a little unreasonably, and Ronnie glared at him. 'Because we left our crystal ball and our police uniforms at home tonight,' she said tartly. 'If we'd known we were working under-cover, we'd have issued a full statement during the interval.'

Ignoring her, Penrose scowled at Fallowfield. 'I thought Bravo was supposed to be watching out the front?' he barked. 'If I find out he's left his post for a second and missed our prime suspect, I'll personally make him wish he'd never been born.' He turned back to Lettice. 'I'm sorry. Will you take Sergeant Fallowfield back to the front of the theatre and see if you can find this couple?'

'Of course I will,' said Lettice, who always remained admirably untouched by her family's sparring. 'How exciting!'

The Yard's newest recruit had been gone only a moment or two when the others heard footsteps coming quickly down the stairs and Lydia reappeared, paler than she had ever been when dying on stage. She gripped the handrail as if it were the sole thing holding her upright and stared at the small group below, seemingly at a loss to understand how they could all be so calm. It could only have been a matter of seconds but it felt like an age before she spoke, and Penrose had the odd sensation of being cast in a bad melodrama, waiting for the next line to be delivered and knowing only too well what the gist of it would be.

'For God's sake, come quickly,' she cried, confirming his worst fears but soon departing from the expected script. 'He didn't deserve this.'

Ten

Bernard Aubrey's body lay just inside his office and Penrose silently acknowledged the truth of Lydia's words: surely no one deserved this. There was nothing restful about the finality of the moment, no indication that the man at his feet had found in death a peace from which the living could take comfort, and he imagined the absolute horror that Lydia must have felt on encountering the aftermath of such suffering. In truth, despite his years of experience, he was not entirely immune to it himself.

A dress suit was draped over the back of the settee but Aubrey had not had time to change after the performance, and the stage clothes lent an artifice to his death which might have been convincing had his face and neck not been visible, clearly showing the signs of poison which no amount of make-up could simulate. Penrose considered the possibilities. Antimony, perhaps, or mercury; arsenic, of course, and he had seen cases of boric acid which looked similar. The most obvious symptoms in front of him could be attributed to any of these substances, but the post-mortem would provide the answers. Whichever it was, the attractive features that age had not been able to undermine were altered almost beyond recognition by the agony of those final moments. Aubrey's eyes, glazed and unyielding, stared out from sockets which now seemed barely able to contain them and their blank expression, coupled with parted lips and sagging chin, gave the face an ugly stupidity which it had never possessed in life. The upper part of his costume, a tunic of false chain mail made from felt, had been violently torn away from his chest and neck, and his throat was covered in raw scratch marks where he had clawed at his clothes and skin, presumably in a desperate struggle for air. One hand remained clenched at his chest, the other reached towards the door, fingers outstretched and palm upwards, as if begging for a little more time.

The expensive but well-worn Persian rug on which Aubrey had collapsed had been caught up in his convulsions, and Penrose stepped carefully over its rucks and past several books and a small card table which had been knocked to the floor. The force of his struggle with death must have been quite incredible: he was a strong man, tall and heavily built and, even now, his limbs seemed to strain towards life, but he had not been able to withstand whatever had invaded his body. Kneeling at his shoulder, Penrose put his hand lightly against Aubrey's cheek. His skin was cold to the touch, unnaturally so for someone in whom life had only very recently been extinguished, and there was a brownish, salivary substance about his nose which mixed with the vomit around his mouth and ran in narrow lines down his face and onto the carpet. The stench of urine and diarrhoea was unmistakable. Even to Penrose, who had encountered the effects of poison many times, it was sickening, almost intolerably so, and just for a second he had to turn away. Looking back, he was struck by how the squalid physicality of Aubrey's death was made all the more humiliating by the bizarre state of his dress: the false armour might hint at the nobility of a soldier fallen in battle, but there was no dignity here; for all man's emotional and spiritual aspirations, Penrose thought with sadness, it was invariably the body that decided his fate in the end.

'Jesus bloody Christ,' said Fallowfield from the doorway. 'That's ruined our chances of finding anything out from him, Sir.'

It was hardly something that Penrose needed to have spelt out for him and his sergeant had put it a little more bluntly than was tactful, but he shared the sentiment. If he had only insisted on speaking to Aubrey at the interval, he might still be alive; at worst, they would have a clearer understanding of what – if anything – linked this violent, messy death with the less agonising but no less theatrical murder of a young girl in a railway carriage. 'Go back downstairs and call the team in,' he said. 'I don't want the telephone in here touched until it's been dusted. Make it clear I want the works and they're to be here immediately. And it must be Spilsbury.'

'I'll send a car to his house right away, Sir.'

'No, it's Saturday night – he'll be at the Savoy Theatre. Get someone to nip up the road – it'll be quicker. Then have the whole place sealed off. Ask anyone who's here to stay until I've spoken to them, but on no account is anyone else to be let in through either entrance. Make that clear to the fellow at stage door until our lot get here. We'll need Aubrey's home address and a next of kin – can you sort that out?'

'Of course, Sir. Was he married, do you know?'

'Yes, I believe he was, but I remember Josephine saying something once about it not being a particularly happy marriage. We'll go and see his wife as soon as we've finished here. Did you see Miss Beaumont on your way up? She found his body.'

'Yes, Sir, she's still down there with Miss Tey and another lady – and your cousins, of course. They're looking after her, but she's in a terrible state. I can't say I'm surprised,' he said, looking down at the body. 'I gather they were friends.'

'Yes, they were. Will you take them somewhere more comfortable and get them a drink? I'll be down to see them as soon as I can. If they'd rather go across the road to Number 66, that's fine, but I don't want them to be left alone.'

'I'll tell them, Sir. Just one thing before I go, though – we found that couple outside, and it was definitely White they got the tickets off. Fits the description to a tee.'

'Then keep that idiot Bravo out of my sight for his own sake, and have a car go over the area. White might still be nearby if he's had anything to do with this.'

'Right, Sir, and don't worry about Miss Tey and her friends – I'll see they're all right.'

'Thanks, Bill, I appreciate it, but come back up here as quickly as you can.'

Fallowfield went downstairs with his usual calm efficiency and

Penrose was left alone. The building was extraordinarily quiet and he took advantage of the silence to absorb every detail of the scene. As soon as Scotland Yard arrived *en masse*, the operation moved into a different phase with recognised procedures, and something was lost in the relentless progress of it all; not the humanity of the victim – he hoped that was always paramount – but what he could best describe as the personality of the crime. This was the closest he would get to the act which he was trying to unravel, and these minutes alone with the victim were rare and precious. It was vital to make the most of them.

He had expected Aubrey's office to have something of the atmosphere of a gentleman's club about it, but he was wrong. The remnant of many a savoured cigarette hung in the air and the furniture – an assortment of mahogany, oak and leather – could easily have been transported to White's or Boodle's, but that was where the similarity ended. In fact, there were a number of unexpectedly feminine touches to the room: vases of flowers – irises, he noted with interest – were dotted around the shelves and on the mantelpiece, and soft, pale colours had been chosen for the walls and cushions. Clearly, Aubrey had spent a good deal of time here: even without the disarray caused by his death, the room was untidy and littered with books – unpretentious editions of plays and novels, most of which looked well-read – and photograph albums containing informal pictures of actors and actresses next to their professional stage portraits. Two large windows – their curtains still tied back – stretched down to the floor, suggesting that, in the daytime, this was a light and airy space.

Penrose walked over to the huge oak desk which dominated the side of the room nearest the windows, and knew as surely as if her blood were still on it that he was looking at the weapon which had killed Elspeth Simmons. Just to the right of a leather blotter, which took up most of the desk's surface, lay a bayonet of simple design, its polished blade contrasting starkly with the dark wood of the furniture. Although shockingly out of context here, the weapon was a familiar sight to him: knife bayonets like this had been common issue in the war as an infantryman's most important close combat weapon. They were a crucial part of life in the trenches – just as crucial, in fact, as the rectangular brass tin that had been placed next to the knife, something less deadly, perhaps, but no less evocative to anyone who had lived through those times. It was a tobacco tin, a Christmas present sent out to the troops each year of the war to boost their morale. He remembered his own, received during the Christmas of 1915; he still had it – everyone did, if they had returned safely, because there was something inexplicably precious about a small piece of English metal that had not been fashioned to kill. An identical tin was the only thing of Jack's that he had been able to give to Josephine after her lover's death. The tin in front of him now was particularly battered and worn. Its hinged lid was open and he could see a cream card with a red crest at the bottom – good wishes for a victorious new year from the Princess Mary and friends at home – but what interested him more was not standard issue. On top of the card lay a flower head, an iris, which had evidently been preserved for some time. It was fragile and drained of all its colour, but unmistakably the same variety that had been found with Elspeth's body. The shape of the leaves, closed tightly around the flower, mirrored almost precisely the form of the bayonet. They lay parallel, and the direction of the twin blades led his eyes beyond the desk towards a single photograph, not in an album like the others but placed alone on a bookshelf. The woman framed in silver had a pleasant face, but she lacked the glamour and self-consciousness that united the actresses pictured elsewhere in the room; it was certainly no one he recognised. Was she Aubrey's wife, or someone else who had been important in his life? And was he reading too much into the flower and knife by imagining that they pointed towards her? They might easily have been casually placed, but somehow he doubted it.

The other items on and around the desk were less incongruous. A crystal tumbler containing half an inch or so of whisky stood at one corner, the corresponding bottle having been consigned – empty – to a nearby waste paper basket, where it nestled amongst some torn-up envelopes. Next to a well-used ashtray, the telephone receiver dangled uselessly off its hook, but it had obviously been put to good service recently because the blotting paper was covered in half a dozen numbers and initials. Penrose copied them down, then put on his gloves and gently opened the top middle drawer of the desk. It was full of headed note paper, and the drawers to left and right contained a similar assortment of stationery, but the lower levels seemed more revealing. The first one he came to was full of bills and accounts, the second of contracts for those employed in Aubrey's two theatres; they would have to be gone through in detail, but it was personal documents that he hoped to find now, anything that might give more substance to an idea forming in his head as to the link between Elspeth Simmons and Bernard Aubrey. Is that what Aubrey wanted to talk to him about? He began to give up hope as he turned up pile upon pile of business correspondence, then, in the very last drawer, he unearthed something more promising – a collection of letters, all addressed to Aubrey in the same distinctive hand and, judging by the lack of any postmark, all privately delivered. Starting at the top of the heap, he worked his way through them with increasing astonishment: the letters were not what he was looking for, but they certainly offered another line of enquiry. So absorbed was he that Fallowfield had been standing quietly at his side for a couple of minutes, looking at the weapon and the flower, before Penrose even noticed he was there.

'Are you thinking what I'm thinking, Sir?'

'A narrow blade, about nine inches long and as sharp as hell – I think it fits the bill perfectly, don't you? But what on earth is it doing here?'

'You don't think he did it then?'

'No, try as I might, I really can't see Bernard Aubrey sneaking into a railway carriage with this to kill a young girl. Particularly if she was his daughter.'

'His daughter? How do you know that?'

'I don't, but at the moment I'm trying to think of logical connections between the two deaths other than the *Richard of Bordeaux* link – but we'll come to that in a minute. Let's think about it: we know that Elspeth was passed over unofficially between colleagues during the war, so we need to find out from Alice Simmons if Aubrey knew or served with her husband.'

'Aubrey was a tunneller, Sir, I know that much because Miss Beaumont was just talking about it. That's why he went upstairs to change: he could never bear to be underground, not even in his own theatre, because he'd had such a dreadful war. We could ask Frank Simmons if they knew each other – Walter Simmons would probably have talked more about his friends and the war to his brother than his wife, and it'd be quicker than waiting for Mrs Simmons to get here from Berwick.'

'True, but I'd rather not let Frank Simmons know anything about the way we're thinking at the moment. No, we'll talk to her alone as soon as she gets here. I'd also like her to take a look at Aubrey's handwriting: if he sent the letters to Walter each year – and let's face it, he was wealthy enough to send the money – she might recognise it from the one she saw. The claustrophobia's interesting, though. I wonder how many people knew about that?'

'It didn't seem to be any great secret, at least not among the theatre lot. But even if he does turn out to be her father, I don't see why that should get them both killed.'

'Don't you? Aubrey was Hedley White's boss, so the chances are he'll have heard about Elspeth. Perhaps he even met her and realised who she was. What if he wanted to acknowledge her and get to know her better? That won't have gone down well with Frank Simmons if he thought he was losing his niece. It seemed to me this afternoon that the whole family has lived in constant fear of Elspeth's being taken away from them. That's only natural if the adoption was illegal – they built all that love on very shaky foundations, but who knows what they'd do to protect it? And then there's White, of course. Aubrey might not have approved of his daughter dating the stage hand. I agree that the motivation is much stronger for his killing Aubrey than Elspeth, but there's a very fine line between love and ownership, and jealousy can distort where it falls. He wouldn't be the first person to kill his girl rather than lose her to another life.'

'No, I don't suppose he would, and we know he was hanging about here tonight.'

'Yes, both he and Frank Simmons were here just before the show.'

'But Simmons couldn't get up here, whereas White could. No one would think twice about seeing him anywhere in this theatre, even on his night off.'

'Don't forget – Simmons said something about having a mate on stage door who helped him collect his memorabilia. He wouldn't admit it, of course, but the man on tonight might have turned a blind eye if there was something in it for him.'

'Tell me again what he said to you, Sir.'

'Aubrey? He said there was something he wanted to tell me, but the way he said it implied that if he'd talked sooner Elspeth might not have died. It was something like "I've got to live with the fact that I've waited until now."' Archie paused. 'Of course, if I'm right about the connection, I suppose we can't rule out suicide. Josephine said he was upset when she told him who'd been killed and I assumed that was because he felt sorry for Hedley, but it could have been much more than that. If you spend all those years wanting to get to know your child, then have the chance so violently snatched from you, that's bad enough – but if you know you could have saved her, that might prove impossible to live with. It's a terrible way to do it, though. Look at his body, Bill: what must those last moments have been like?'

'You can't imagine, can you, but I think we *can* rule suicide out.' Penrose looked at him questioningly. 'Miss Beaumont says that the door was locked when she got up here – from the outside.'

'What? I noticed the key on the outside but I just assumed that Aubrey had used it to get in and not bothered to take it out of the lock.'

'She says not, Sir. She says she knocked a few times and got no answer, so she unlocked the door herself and found him there on the floor.'

'What else did she say, Bill?'

'That he hadn't made himself very popular lately. Apparently there's been lots of bickering about contracts and tours and who gets what part. Lots of people seem to have held a grudge against him: he'd fallen out with John Terry particularly badly, and – this fits in well with your theory, Sir – she'd heard he'd been furious with Hedley White about something earlier today, although she didn't know what. She'd had arguments with him herself lately, too – she was very honest about that.'

'That's probably what she meant about his not deserving what he got: he'd made himself unpopular but it shouldn't have gone this far. Did she mention anyone called McCracken?'

'Yes, Sir, Esme McCracken – she's the stage manager. Apparently they have some sort of tradition at the end of the play where three of the cast make a toast, and Miss McCracken has to arrange things. Sounds like another excuse for a drink to me, but Miss Beaumont said it was different today because Aubrey was involved and it got nasty.'

'She saw it or just heard about it?'

'Saw it, Sir. It happens just before they all take their bows so she was waiting in the wings.'

Penrose listened intently while Fallowfield recounted Lydia's impression of events backstage. 'And you say McCracken gets all this stuff ready?'

'Her or White, Sir – whoever's on duty. Why did you ask about her?'

Penrose pointed towards the bunch of letters that he had found in Aubrey's desk. 'Those are all from her. From what I can work out, she sees herself as a bit of a playwright. They start off very politely, asking Aubrey if he'd read her work and consider putting it on. Clearly he must have ignored her, because they soon lose their courtesy and start criticising all the work he stages and questioning his judgement. She has a very high opinion of her own talent and not much time for anybody else's, and she's particularly vitriolic about *Richard of Bordeaux* and the money it's making – she accuses Aubrey of having no artistic soul, only a commercial one. It's a wonder he didn't get rid of her: I'm not sure I'd keep someone on the payroll if they sent me this kind of thing on a regular basis. It's obsessive, to say the least.' He handed the letters over. 'They were written over a three-month period, and the latest one's dated today. She loses it completely at the end, throws in a bit of abuse, then says that Aubrey would be wise to take her more seriously. That could be just a rather extreme way of letting him know he's missing out on the theatrical event of the decade, or it could be a threat – and judging by what's happened tonight, I'm inclined to read it as the latter.'

'Blimey,' said Fallowfield, glancing through the pile. 'I see what you mean. She's got to be up there with White and Simmons.'

'Yes, particularly after what you've just told me about the drinks session after work. I'd put money on his having drunk whatever killed him then.'

'Me too, Sir. I had a quick look backstage and it's all still there, the decanter and glass I mean. I've put young Armstrong down there until the rest of the team get here to pack it all up. He's a good lad – always does what he's told. It's a pity we didn't have him outside while White was flogging theatre seats.'

'That's good, Bill, thank you. Of course, the world and his wife have walked past that decanter tonight, but McCracken had plenty of time alone with it.'

'I don't quite see why she'd kill the Simmons girl, though.'

Penrose thought about it for a moment. 'Yes, Aubrey's murder is much easier to understand because he was in a position to make enemies, but Elspeth's death made a mockery of *Richard of Bordeaux* and we have all the evidence we need in those letters that McCracken resented that play and despised Josephine. I think we can also safely say that she's not the most stable of people: I can imagine the person who writes notes like this being so full of spite that it could send her over the edge. There's an arrogance about them, a vanity that we've seen in a lot of criminals. Before this happened, it occurred to me that Elspeth's death might have been a mistake, that whoever did it had meant to kill Josephine. Now, I can't help feeling that what links these murders is more deep-rooted than professional jealousy, but it's still a possibility that whoever is doing this is doing it to destroy the play. But we're getting away from this locked door business. Have you spoken to the stage doorman yet?'

'Yes, and he swears that no one went up or down those stairs except Aubrey, Miss Beaumont and you. By the time the body was found, everyone else – actors and staff alike – had gone out through stage door or were waiting there with you. I gather that's not unusual. He says no one ever hangs around for long and Aubrey is invariably the last person left in the building.'

'Then nobody else should know about the murder, at least. Except one person, of course. So how did that door get locked?'

'Come with me, Sir, and I'll show you.'

Penrose looked bewildered as Fallowfield led him out of Aubrey's office and down the corridor. 'Have you been reading John Dickson Carr again, Bill?' he asked.

Fallowfield smiled. 'It's not as clever as that, Sir, I'm afraid. Have you ever noticed that bridge that runs across St Martin's Court?'

Penrose visualised the passage and immediately realised what Fallowfield was talking about. 'Of course. It links the New to Wyndham's. I'd never thought about it before.'

'Go through that door, Sir, and you'll be on it. Apparently Aubrey had it built as an extra fire exit for both theatres. We'd have found it soon enough – it's no secret – but the stage doorman mentioned it and saved us a bit of time.'

Penrose did as he was told and found himself at one end of a small walkway. Moving to the centre of the bridge, he looked down into St Martin's Court. The rain had started again and the crowds were long gone; stripped of its glitter, the passage that had buzzed with excitement just an hour earlier now looked squalid and depressing. 'So it's possible to get up here from Wyndham's without going anywhere near stage door?'

'Exactly. Not for every Tom, Dick and Harry, of course, because it goes through to private areas in both theatres, so the general public could only use it in an emergency.'

'But the people we're interested in would know about it.'

'Yes they would. McCracken and White and the rest of the stage

147

crew work in both theatres anyway, so they'd be familiar with the layout and people would expect to see them there. But according to matey on stage door, there's a lot of mingling among the actors as well. Aubrey employed both casts and they hang around together a lot, have a drink in each other's dressing rooms – that sort of thing.'

Penrose thought about it. The play at Wyndham's had run for around another fifteen minutes after the curtain fell on *Richard of Bordeaux* so, by the time the staff were leaving the New, the passage would have been at its busiest with audiences spilling out to go home or hanging around for autographs. Nobody would find it easy to get through those crowds, particularly actors waylaid by fans, but he had watched most of the *Richard* cast leave while he was waiting for Aubrey at the stage door, and they had not hung about. It would have been possible for them to get into Wyndham's and up to this bridge, and so to the door of Aubrey's office. Whoever it was stood a chance of being seen through the glass on the walkway, but most people were either looking out for a famous face or walking head-down against the cold; it wasn't much of a risk, compared with everything else. 'God, it's just hopeless,' he said to Fallowfield. 'The list is getting longer rather than shorter, and we can't necessarily eliminate them from Elspeth's murder, either. Her death occurred just before any of them would have been expected at the theatre last night. Lydia met Josephine and got back to the theatre in good time, so any of the people we've got here could feasibly have been at King's Cross and not been missed.'

Fallowfield nodded. 'Any of them could have passed through the scene dock and tampered with the whisky, and any of them could have come up here later on.'

'But why do both, I wonder? If the whisky was in the decanter, from which only Aubrey was going to drink, he was already as good as dead. What would be the point of taking an extra chance to go to his office, assuming that the same person did both?'

'To make sure he couldn't get out and call for help, I suppose, Sir.'

'I would have thought the choice of poison made certain of that. It must have acted immediately on entering his system. From what I've seen of his body, no one could have helped him, even if they'd found him alive.'

'But what else could it be?'

'I would have said to incriminate him with Elspeth's murder weapon if it weren't for the locked door. If somebody wanted to set Aubrey up, that would explain why the knife was swapped for the hatpin but the door instantly undermines the suicide theory and I don't think we're dealing with someone who would have panicked and locked it by mistake. No, those other things on the desk are central. The flower again, and the tin; they're like the dolls in that railway carriage. It's almost as if he or she is leaving an explanation at each scene – a message for us, or some sort of justification.'

'I suppose whoever it was could have come here to fetch something, as well, something that might have been incriminating.'

'Yes, Bill – that could easily be it, in which case McCracken's ruled out because those letters would never have been left in the desk.' He sighed heavily. 'We'd better get back – the lads will have arrived by now. I need to talk to Lydia, and then I'll pay a call on Mrs Aubrey while you bring McCracken in for questioning.' He handed Fallowfield a piece of paper. 'That's a list of the phone numbers from Aubrey's blotter – I want to know who they all are as soon as possible, so get someone back at the Yard onto that right away. And can you have a look at the Wyndham's side of this bridge? Find out exactly where it goes and how easy it is to get to from the other side.'

'Right-o, Sir, I'll do it now. I just hope I don't end up on stage in the middle of a performance.'

'I can't help feeling that the performance has been up here tonight – and we've missed it. I'll see you in a bit.'

Penrose went back down the corridor and found that the disquieting calm of Aubrey's room had been dispelled by forensics at work. By the desk, a couple of officers were carefully packing the empty whisky bottle and tumbler, preserving them for analysis.

Another was perched on a set of steps, leaning out over the body to photograph it from above. Unexpectedly, the flash from the camera illuminated Aubrey's face, and the image of death that it framed in that momentary explosion of light was so intensely familiar and so suddenly thrust upon him that he had to blink to rid himself of it, and to anchor himself firmly in the present.

'Archie – there you are. You know, when I dressed for the theatre tonight this wasn't quite what I had in mind.' Without any further preamble, Spilsbury joined Penrose by the body. 'It's nicotine, without a doubt. You can tell by the brown mucus around the nostrils. I'll expect to find a fairly hefty dose in the stomach and kidneys when we open him up – but you can be certain that's what killed him.'

'Can you say when it was taken?'

'Not long ago. The tiniest measure can cause death in a few minutes. In animals, it has much the same effect as hydrocyanic acid – a quarter of a drop can kill; for a man, one or two drops will be fatal. Exposure to nicotine in small doses through smoking or chewing tobacco can build up a tolerance to the toxic effects, and he obviously was a smoker, but nobody's immune. A lethal amount would be the equivalent of absorbing all the nicotine in three or four cigarettes. That's all, but what was it Goethe said? "There's no such thing as poison – it just depends on the dose."'

'Nicotine is used as an insecticide, isn't it? I remember it as a child. My father swore death to the aphids on his roses, but he used to throw a blue fit if I went within fifty yards of the stuff.'

'Yes, every gardener has some tucked away. It's a fairly simple chemical process to extract the neat stuff from tobacco leaves, but there's no need to go to all that trouble now – it's readily available. You could walk into a shop and buy more than enough to manage this, and the toxicologist will be able to tell us the likely brand. You know, it's becoming an increasingly fashionable way to do yourself in. I've had three times as many suicides from a dose of nicotine over the last twelve months as in the previous year. It's a nasty way to oblivion, but it has the advantage of being a quick one. Is that what you're looking at here? Suicide?'

'I'd be surprised,' he said. 'The door was locked from the outside and, in any case, it doesn't fit with what I know of him. He was intelligent enough to find a less painful way if he wanted to kill himself. He could have taken it without being aware of it, I suppose?'

'Absolutely. I've known several cases of people drinking insecticides by accident. In its natural state, it's a sort of colourless, oily liquid but it soon changes on contact with air and looks remarkably like whisky. Of course, it takes so little to kill you that even if you realised what you'd done it would be too late. One swig would do it. An easy mistake, but an expensive one.'

'In that case, there's a decanter and glass downstairs that he drank from just before he died. It's in the scene dock.'

'Fine, we'll go there next.'

'So it could be murder?'

'Well, it's not a common choice for a planned killing, I have to say. I only know of one other case – a French count who killed his brother-in-law by forcing him to ingest nicotine – but that was nearly a hundred years ago. It's usually self-inflicted or a practical joke gone wrong – snuff in beer, ridiculous amounts of cigars smoked in a row for a bet, that sort of thing. I had a child not long back who blew bubbles for an hour through an old clay pipe and died. There's no reason why it couldn't be murder, but it's unusual.'

'What are the symptoms?'

'He would have collapsed almost immediately. If you're right about that decanter, he did well to make it up the stairs at all. Death would have followed in anything from five to thirty minutes.'

'And in between?'

'Briefly, the nicotine will have acted as a stimulant, but that will have given way to a depression of the central nervous system, lowered blood pressure, slowed heart rate and death from paralysis of the respiratory muscles.'

'So he suffocated? That's the cause of death?'

'Asphyxia, yes. Along the way, he'll have gone through nausea, abdominal pain, heart palpitations and increased salivation; he'll have experienced a burning sensation in the mouth, mental confusion and dizziness. Everyone is affected slightly differently, but you don't need a post-mortem to tell you some of what he went through; it's all too obvious here.'

'And his eyes?'

'I'm impressed, Archie. Yes, nicotine poisoning often affects the eyes – that's true of a heavy smoker, not just these extreme cases. It's known as tobacco blindness – the sudden appearance of a rapidly growing dark patch in the field of vision, not dissimilar to alcohol.'

'There was a lot of it in the trenches.'

'Exactly. It was very common then, mostly because of homegrown or badly cured tobacco. That stuff often has a lower combustion temperature than properly prepared tobacco, so less of the nicotine is destroyed.'

'If I told you that Bernard Aubrey spent his war underground and was clinically claustrophobic as a result, what would you say?'

Spilsbury stepped out of the way as his colleagues prepared to remove Aubrey's body from the room. 'Well, he died not being able to breathe or, in all probability, to see, so with the possible exception of being buried alive – which presents obvious practical difficulties – I'd say he had the worst death imaginable.' He gestured to the desk where the bayonet had been found. 'Are you linking this to the girl on the train?'

Penrose nodded. He had two deaths and two victims which, on the face of it, could not have been more different: a young girl and a man facing old age; a stabbing with relatively little suffering and an agonising, degrading end. But he was starting to see more connections and, although the theatre was the most obvious link, the past seemed to him more significant. Aubrey had died surrounded by reminders of the war – a war which was also the backdrop to an illegal and inevitably painful adoption. And even the causes of death, apparently so contrasting, had in common a spiteful appropriateness to their victim: Elspeth's murder had undermined everything that mattered to her, had scorned her innocence; Aubrey, a man of wealth and authority all his life, had been physically humiliated and had died gasping for air. In both crimes, there was a terrifying lack of humanity, a mockery of the dead which chilled him even more than the loss of life itself.

Eleven

Penrose stood at the door to the Green Room, and was not surprised to see that his cousins' efforts to comfort everyone with tea
and brandy had had very little effect: Lydia was dreadfully pale
and clearly shocked to the core, while Josephine and the woman to
whom he had been introduced earlier were united in solicitous
concern for her. It was Marta who spoke first.

'What the hell has happened, Inspector?' she asked with a flash
of anger which took him by surprise. 'How can you have allowed
her to walk in on something like that? You should have gone to
find him, not Lydia.'

'I'm truly sorry you've had to go through this,' he said to Lydia
with genuine compassion, 'and I don't want to cause anybody any
further distress, but I do need to talk to you briefly about what
happened tonight.' He turned to the others in the room. 'And to
anybody else who saw or spoke to Bernard Aubrey in the last
twenty-four hours.'

Marta was not so easily dismissed. 'Can that really not keep
until the morning? Right now, I'd like to take Lydia home to get
some rest. She's had enough.'

Penrose, who had already missed out on one vital interview that
evening through having been made to wait, had no intention of letting it happen again, but he was saved the discourtesy of insisting.

'It's fine, darling, honestly it is,' said Lydia, taking Marta's hand.
'I'd rather do it now. The sooner I stop having to talk about it, the
sooner I can start trying to get that image out of my head.' She
smiled unconvincingly, as if recognising the naivety of her words,
and turned to Penrose. 'Although somehow I don't think it will be

that easy, do you Archie? Can I still call you Archie, by the way, or does it have to be Inspector now that this is official?'

'Archie's fine. And I won't keep you any longer than I have to.'

'All right, but can I have a minute to pull myself together?' She looked at her reflection in the full-length mirror which ran along one wall. 'I know it's not the time to mention it, but I feel worse now than I ever have on my deathbed. I just need to pop to my dressing room for a moment.'

Penrose nodded, trying not to look too impatient. As soon as Lydia had left the room, accompanied by a seething Marta, Lettice took the seat opposite her cousin.

'Can we tell you about our encounter with Aubrey before they get back,' she whispered, nodding towards the door and glancing conspiratorially at Josephine, who understood immediately what she was getting at. 'Something happened that would only upset Lydia even more, and I'd rather not mention it in front of her tonight.'

'Go on. Josephine told me it wasn't exactly an amicable meeting.'

'No, not at all. In fact, it couldn't have been frostier.' She gave an uncharacteristically succinct account of the afternoon's meeting, missing out many of the more entertaining asides which had been shared with Josephine over dinner, but leaving Penrose in no doubt as to how unpopular Aubrey had made himself.

'So, by the time the meeting was over, Terry was put out, to say the least?'

'Oh, face like a slapped arse, dear,' confirmed Ronnie. 'He was absolutely furious.'

'But powerless to do anything about it, presumably.' And impotence had a habit of making people dangerous, he thought. He had seen that quality in Terry's performance earlier – a barely suppressed anger which had made his portrayal of the increasingly vulnerable Richard all the more convincing. But was it enough to drive him to murder? And did he have it in him to kill so maliciously? Arrogance, yes, he could believe that was in character, but spite? He turned to Josephine. 'How serious do you think it is for Terry to miss out on a film like that?'

She shrugged. 'It's hard to say, really. Artistically, it could take his career in a whole new direction, but I'm not sure he'd want that long-term. He'd be starting at the bottom again, you see, whereas on stage he's so established and highly thought of that he can do virtually what he likes. There are very few people who'd dream of standing in his way in the theatre.' And one of those was now dead, Penrose thought as Josephine continued. 'Financially speaking, though, it's a different matter. There's simply no comparison between the money he could make in a film and what he gets for a stage role. And the girls were saying earlier that he seems more money-driven these days. I don't know why that should be. He's never struck me as the greedy type, except for praise, of course.'

'That's useful to know, but I don't quite see why you were so reluctant to tell me all this in front of Lydia. What does she have to do with Terry?'

'Oh, it's not that,' Lettice said quickly. 'We just didn't want Lydia to find out about Aubrey's plans for her – or rather the lack of them.' She stopped guiltily as the door opened again, but it was only Fallowfield.

'Aubrey's address, Sir,' he said, handing Penrose a piece of paper. 'His wife's expecting you, and there's a car waiting outside.'

'Thanks, Sergeant. How did she take it?'

'Calmly, I'd say, Sir. I don't mean she wasn't shocked, but she didn't strike me as the type to go in for hysterics. She insisted she didn't need anybody to wait with her until you got there, but there's a maid in the house, so she's not on her own.'

'All right. I'll get over there now, but wait here a minute – this is interesting.' He turned back to Lettice. 'Go on, but be as quick as you can.'

'It's only that Lydia isn't in line for a part in the film either, and she'll be devastated when she hears about it. I didn't think she needed that news on top of everything else.'

'Are you absolutely sure she didn't know?'

'Archie, for God's sake!' Josephine looked horrified. 'You surely can't be suggesting that Lydia had anything to do with this? That's not what Lettice meant at all.'

'I'm not suggesting anything,' he said, as Lettice put her finger to her lips and nervously checked the corridor outside. 'I just need to establish who knows what. How about Marta? Could she have got wind of it?'

'No, I really don't think so,' Josephine continued. 'We had a long chat this evening about Lydia and the future, and I'm sure she would have mentioned it if she'd known.'

'I can hear someone coming,' said Lettice from the doorway. 'Time for us to go.' She passed Ronnie her gloves. 'That's all right, isn't it Archie? I thought we'd go back to 66 and get a bit of supper ready for everyone. We all need to keep our strength up.'

'That's fine. You'll get one of my lot to see you over when you're ready to go?' he asked Josephine. She nodded and, although he wouldn't have wished the night's events on anyone, he was pleased to see that she seemed now much less defiant about his concerns for her.

Lettice looked worried as she allowed Fallowfield to help her on with her coat. 'I do hope I haven't landed anyone in it,' she said.

'Don't be silly, dear, of course you haven't. It's Archie's job to make a Judas of us all.' Ronnie's smile was sweet and deadly.

'Judas? I don't like the sound of that.' Lydia had returned looking considerably more composed, and Penrose was relieved to see that she was alone.

'I'm afraid so, dear,' Ronnie said, deliberately ignoring Lettice's frantic attempts to catch her eye. 'Detective Inspector Penrose has been quite ruthless in his interrogations and we've had to snitch on Josephine to save our own skins.' For once, her sarcasm defused the tension in the room. 'Seriously, though, we were just saying that Aubrey's behaviour of late hasn't made him very popular with any of us.'

'That's true enough,' Lydia acknowledged, kissing Ronnie and Lettice goodbye and settling down next to Josephine on the settee. 'And before you have the embarrassment of asking, Archie, that includes me. We had a very frank discussion only the other day in which he made it quite clear that my top billing days were nearly over.' She took a sip from the glass of wine that she had brought in with her. 'It must have been torture for him, mustn't it? I'll never forget his face. All that pain, and no one there to help him. I can't think of anything worse than to leave this world alone like that. How did he die, Archie? Do you know? Can there really have been two murders in two days?'

'We can't be sure of what's happened at the moment,' he said, non-committally, 'but I *am* sorry that it was you who found his body. I know you and Aubrey were close.'

'Yes, we were. He was a good man, you know. But how were you to know what was waiting for me at the top of those stairs? Don't think badly of Marta. I'm sorry she was angry with you but this is the first crisis we've had and you know what that's like in a relationship. She's just being protective.'

'I understand. Where is she now?'

'In self-imposed exile in my dressing room. She said she couldn't trust herself to be civil so she'd wait there until I was free to go.'

Penrose took Lydia gently through the period between the end of the play and the discovery of Aubrey's body, but learned nothing that Fallowfield had not already discovered in his earlier brief conversation with the actress. 'I suppose I should have come to fetch you when I realised that the door was locked,' she said. 'Something was obviously not right, but you do things instinctively, don't you? I just opened it without even thinking what might be on the other side.'

'You're absolutely sure that the door *was* locked, aren't you, and not just stuck or difficult to open?'

'I'm positive. I tried the handle once, turned the key and tried again. The door opened, and I saw him right away. I know it's odd, but that's how it was.'

'Did you go into the room?'

'No more than a couple of steps. It was obvious that I was too late to help him. A part of me couldn't believe what I was seeing, but most of all I just wanted to get away.'

'You told Sergeant Fallowfield about some unpleasantness amongst the cast after the show. What had Aubrey done to upset everyone so much?'

'Well, Esme McCracken has always hated him just for being successful, but it's got worse since he refused to accept her play for production. I don't know about Lewis Fleming; he and Johnny have always hated each other, and that's about rivalry and social background as much as anything, but I've never known Lewis to show Bernie anything other than respect until today. As for Johnny, I think he was simply starting to outgrow what Bernie could offer him. He's always been restless, but he's sick to the back teeth of this play and Bernie is – was – determined to hold him to his contract. And there's the Swinburne issue, of course. Johnny was set on having him – in all senses of the word, probably – for Bothwell in *Queen of Scots*, but Bernie preferred Fleming. At least, I thought he did. Perhaps he'd changed his mind. That might explain Fleming's behaviour, but not Johnny's.'

'Aubrey hadn't changed his mind about Bothwell,' Josephine said. 'Apparently he was still very keen this afternoon on hiring Fleming.'

Lydia gave an involuntary shudder. 'You know, I've just remembered what Johnny said when he made the toast tonight: "To memorable exits." He couldn't have known, could he? Surely he wouldn't . . .' she tailed off, unable to bring herself to say the words.

'I thought you said you wouldn't keep her long, Inspector?' Marta stood in the doorway, calmer now, but no less protective.

Penrose looked up at her and said, politely but firmly, 'There are a couple more questions. Please take a seat, though, I'll be as brief as I can.' Marta moved across to be near Lydia, but remained standing. 'Now, the tray of drinks for this ritual,' Penrose continued, 'who got that ready today?'

'Hedley made sure everything was there before the matinee. At least, that's what usually happens. McCracken was on duty tonight, so she'll have put the drinks in place.'

'And do those two get on? White and Miss McCracken, I mean.'

'I don't think you could honestly say that McCracken gets on with anyone – except Johnny, perhaps. He actually thinks she can write. But Hedley isn't the confrontational type and he has to work with the woman, so he puts up with all her nonsense and just gets on with it. How is Hedley, by the way? I didn't realise until Josephine told me tonight that it was his girlfriend who was killed yesterday. I can't believe I met her at the station and didn't make the connection. He'll be devastated. He was so in love with her, you know, it was really very sweet. And of course Bernie had become like a father to him over the last few months. It'll feel like his whole world has collapsed when he finds out what's happened now.'

'Actually, we're having a bit of trouble getting hold of Mr White,' Penrose said, with an edge in his voice which was lost on neither Lydia nor Marta. 'I don't suppose you have any idea where he might be, do you?'

'I haven't seen him since the matinee,' Lydia said, and Penrose was interested to note that her tone had lost some of its warmth. 'If I had, I'd have no qualms about telling you. He wouldn't do anything wrong, Archie. He's just a boy.'

Fallowfield spoke up for the first time. 'He had done something wrong, though, hadn't he, Miss? The stage doorman says he was supposed to report to Mr Aubrey after the matinee this afternoon for some sort of disciplinary, but he never showed up. Do you know what that was about?'

'I've really no idea, Sergeant, but I can't imagine it was a matter for the police.' She accepted the cigarette that Marta held out to her, and paused while it was lit. 'He shares digs with Rafe Swinburne over the river. If he's not there, I've no idea where you'll find him, but I just hope he's all right.'

'Rafe Swinburne – you mentioned him earlier,' Penrose said. 'Why is Terry so keen on him?'

'Well, partly out of sheer stubbornness. He hates Fleming so much that anyone who has some talent and fits the same sort of roles would be preferable. And Swinburne is talented – he's made quite a success of things in *Sheppey* at Wyndham's, helped along no doubt by his looks. Johnny's a fool for a pretty face.'

At the mention of Wyndham's Theatre, Penrose looked across at Fallowfield. 'And does Rafe Swinburne want to take this role as much as John Terry wants to give it to him?'

'Oh, I don't think there's any doubt about that. He's very ambitious. I've seen him work the room a couple of times now, and he certainly knows how to pull out all the stops.'

Marta made no attempt to disguise the contempt in her voice. 'Has the world really come to that, Inspector? Are we all so shallow now that we'll kill for a part in a play? Whatever happened to the good old-fashioned motives that people used to murder for? At least they were a little more convincing.'

Protective Marta might be, but Penrose was beginning to lose patience with her sarcasm. He stood up, aware that Aubrey's widow would be waiting for him. 'My officers will be in the theatre for the rest of the night,' he said. 'You're all welcome to stay here as long as you want to, but I'd be grateful if you didn't go anywhere else in the building. When you're ready to leave, the constable at stage door will call for a car to take you home.' He reserved a smile for Josephine on his way out of the room, and paused at the door. 'Last year, I had to investigate the murder of a young woman in Pimlico,' he said, looking back at Marta. 'She was a secretary in a large firm of solicitors, and she was strangled because she was allocated a desk that somebody else wanted. Not a very old-fashioned motive, I agree, Miss Fox, but I'm sure it seemed convincing enough to the woman who hanged for it.'

Penrose heard four bolts being shot back from their sockets and the jangle of keys in a lock before a maid opened the front door to admit him to the imposing house on Queen Anne's Gate. What a shame, he thought, that Bernard Aubrey hadn't shown the same concern for security in his theatres as he clearly had at home.

'Mrs Aubrey's upstairs, Sir,' the woman said, with a balance of civility and economy born of many years in domestic service. 'I'll show you to the drawing room, and she'll join you shortly.'

The room in which Penrose was asked to wait was of similar proportions to Aubrey's office at the theatre and showed the same exquisite taste in its décor and furnishings, but the signs of everyday living which had personalised his study were entirely absent from the domestic space that he had shared with his wife. It was, in fact, the sort of room in which no object was permitted to serve the purpose for which it had been created: the sofa – an elegant Chesterfield – was attractive but uninviting; the fireplace was beautifully polished but far too clean to have known much warmth; and the handful of books in a corner cabinet seemed chosen more to offset the light browns of the walnut than to entertain. He had little doubt that, were he to take one down, he would find some of its gilt-edged pages still uncut. The masculine traces of cigarette smoke, so dominant in Aubrey's office, were replaced here by a faint, violet-scented fragrance; by now, he was not surprised to trace its origin to a vase of irises, dark purple and all in full bloom, and so uniform in their display that only their perfume proved them to be the work of nature rather than man.

Just above the flowers hung an oil painting, and Penrose wondered if it had been chosen out of a spontaneous love for its beauty or merely with a shrewd eye to its future value. From what he knew of the man, Aubrey was capable of either. It was a beach scene, centred, he guessed, on one of those French coastal resorts that had become so fashionable in the second half of the last century. The foreground was dominated by men with elaborate bathing paraphernalia and women sporting crinolines and parasols – all very different from the easy-going holidaymakers of his own age – and even the children were dressed in the finest of clothes and hats, with no prospect, it seemed, of venturing into the tame sea beyond. Penrose didn't need to look at the signature to know that the painting was by Eugène Boudin: studying in Cambridge, he had been lucky enough to have the Fitzwilliam's fine collection of Impressionism on his doorstep and he had always been drawn to these small, quietly beautiful paintings, much preferring them to the louder canvases of Boudin's more famous contemporaries.

'Beautiful, isn't it? It was my husband's favourite painting. The beach is at Trouville in Normandy, and he used to spend his summer holidays there as a child. Unfortunately, his more recent memories of France were less happy.'

The words were spoken softly but carried authority, and he

turned to greet a woman whose appearance was in perfect harmony with her voice. Grace Aubrey was tall and elegant, with an intelligence in her face that the lines of age had only served to intensify. Unusually for a woman in her sixties, and perhaps only because of the hour, she wore her hair long and loose, making it easy for Penrose to imagine how she had looked in her youth, before the deep browns were tinged with grey. Without question, she was still beautiful and – despite his professional instinct to question appearances – Penrose found it hard to reconcile the Aubreys' visual compatibility with their reputed marital differences.

'You know, after the war he could hardly bear to look at it any more,' she said, her eyes still on the painting. 'I suppose it's not right to mourn such a thing when so many people didn't come back at all, but it seems to me that the loss of a sense of beauty is as tragic as the loss of life.' She sat down at one end of the settee and invited Penrose to take the other, brushing his condolences efficiently aside.

'This has come as a great shock to me, Inspector, but I'm not going to waste your time by pretending that relations between my husband and I were anything other than habitual. I'm sorry he's dead, of course I am. We all hope for the privilege of hanging on until our last natural moment, and no human being should die as he did – your sergeant was very diligent in his efforts to spare my feelings, by the way, but I can't imagine any poison being painless. That said, it would be ridiculous to claim a grief which I simply don't feel.'

Penrose doubted that anyone had ever had cause to think Grace Aubrey ridiculous. 'When did you last speak to your husband?' he asked, confident now that he would be told everything he needed to know with a frankness which was refreshing, if a little disconcerting.

'This morning, at breakfast. He left for work as usual at about half past nine. I wasn't surprised that he hadn't come home by the time I went to bed. He often stays out late, either working or socialising, so I didn't expect to see him until tomorrow morning.'

'And you didn't speak on the telephone?'

'No. We led very separate lives, Inspector. There was little enough to talk about when we were in each other's company, and certainly nothing important enough to warrant a telephone call.'

'How long had you been married?'

'It would have been forty-one years next month, although we stopped marking anniversaries a lifetime ago.'

'That's a long time to stay together if you were both unhappy.'

'Are you married, Inspector?'

'No.'

'I thought not. The idea that you stay together if you're happy and part if you're not tends to be one held by single people. It wasn't as straightforward as that. I can't speak for Bernard, but I don't remember ever actually being *un*happy. We were both privileged to start off with, and he always worked hard to make sure we stayed that way, so we never wanted for anything, materially speaking. And it wasn't that we didn't get on – it's just that we never created that spark of joy in each other's lives that makes everything else irrelevant. It's a terrible thing to admit, but any of the pleasures that I did take from our life together would not have been lessened had he not been there to share them.' She looked down at her hands, and gently touched her wedding ring. 'I was a little harsh on you just then, Inspector. I'm sorry, and perhaps you're right; perhaps if we had been unhappy rather than merely bored we might have separated and looked for happiness elsewhere. But when you're neither one thing nor the other, time slips away before you realise that there might be something more.'

Guessing that Aubrey's widow would despise any form of prevarication, Penrose decided to make his questions as direct as possible. 'Were you always faithful to each other?'

'Yes, absolutely.'

'You seem very sure. Can you speak so certainly for your husband?'

'I can afford to be sure, if only for the simple reason that I wouldn't have minded if he had strayed. There would have been no need for him to lie about it. I might even have been relieved, although of course you never know when jealousy will strike. No, we were both too lazy to have an affair.' She took a cigarette from the silver box on the table beside her and paused to light it.

'Do you have any children?'

'A son, Joseph. He lives in Gloucestershire. He and Bernard were never very close – they were far too much alike to get on well, and Bernard always resented the fact that Joe didn't want anything to do with his precious theatres. And thank God he didn't, bearing in mind what's happened to his father.'

'Did he have enemies, then?'

'Clearly he did, Inspector. I would have thought that much was obvious.'

'But specifically within the theatre? You seem to blame his work for his death.'

'Bernard was a powerful man. He made careers and he destroyed them. His decisions were invariably right but often ruthless, and he made them with no thought for sentiment or even loyalty. And he was found poisoned in the private area of his theatre. You're the detective, of course, but the evidence does seem to point in that direction.'

Penrose resisted the temptation to return the charge of seeing things too simply. 'I believe your husband's death is connected to another murder which took place on Friday. Does the name Elspeth Simmons mean anything to you?'

She thought for a moment. 'The girl who was killed at King's Cross? I read about it in the paper tonight but I'd never heard of her before that. What makes you think Bernard's death had anything to do with hers?'

'She was involved with one of his employees – a young man named Hedley White. I gather your husband thought a lot of him and was very upset at the news of Miss Simmons's death.'

She shrugged her shoulders. 'I'm sorry – I can't really help you there. He did talk fondly about Hedley – I remember because it's an unusual name – and he was certainly a great believer in giving young people a chance, but I can't be more specific than that.'

'Had you noticed any change in his behaviour recently?' Penrose asked, although he was rapidly coming to believe that Grace

Aubrey knew too little about her husband's life to be able to throw much light on his death. 'At the risk of being too straightforward, had he been unhappy?'

She smiled at him with a growing respect. 'At the risk of being pedantic, I'd say angry rather than unhappy. He always had a short temper, but it was usually soon over. Lately, he often seemed worried or frustrated.'

'Do you have any idea why?'

'When Bernard was angry, it was usually because he couldn't get his own way over something, but don't ask me what.'

'I know it's unlikely, bearing in mind the manner of his death, but can you imagine anything that might have led Bernard to take his own life?'

'No. Absolutely nothing. He had no great faith to prevent him from doing it, but after all he went through in the war and all the lives he saw snatched away before they were ever really begun, he scorned suicide as the coward's way out. That was something he never was – a coward – and he despised it in other people. He had a bleak view of the world and he could be very hard on himself at times, usually because of things he hadn't done that he thought he should have, but he always claimed that the greatest punishment for any sin was to go on living.'

Penrose wondered if the sin for which Bernard Aubrey had felt the need to repent went back as far as the war. He asked as much, and was rewarded once again with a look of approval.

'What makes you think that, I wonder? You're right, though. Bernard had a terrible time, and he came back a very different man. Not broken, you understand, but with a combination of resentment and guilt which ran deeper than the grief we all felt to some extent.' She lit another cigarette but lodged it almost immediately in the ashtray, where it burned steadily down, forgotten. 'He'd been in the war in South Africa and distinguished himself there, so, although he was really too old to fight in France, they begged him to go over and lead the war underground. Lots of older men did the same – they needed the youngsters to do all the digging, but they only had a week's basic training or something ridiculous before they were sent out to that God-forsaken landscape and then expected to do battle with earth and water and charges going off all over the place. People like Bernard, who were experienced and could lead by example, were worth their weight in gold. I know that there was no such thing as an easy war for anyone – you look the right age to vouch for that – but it always seemed to me that tunnelling was a different level of hell. There's something peculiarly unnatural about never seeing daylight. But he was marvellous with those boys, at least at first; he looked after them, taught them how to keep their nerve and anticipate the enemy's next move, and believe me – there was nobody better than my husband at doing that. And they learned quickly – they had to; the slightest noise down there could cost lives and if you gave way to panic, that was it – you lost the confidence of your colleagues and your usefulness was over.'

'And is that what happened to Bernard?'

'No, not at all, although I don't know how he kept it together. He had to spend hours alone in cramped positions, straining every sinew to hear enemy noise. Apparently, sound travels further through solid ground and water than it does through air and it was his job to interpret what he heard, to plot the direction of the tunnels and judge the distances for the charges. There must have been enormous pressure on him, psychologically I mean, knowing how much depended on his decisions and how close he was to the enemy. It would have been easy to let your imagination run away with you in a situation like that.'

Penrose waited, not wanting to hurry her. When she didn't speak for some time, he said, 'It's not surprising that he developed claustrophobia. Surely nobody could leave that behind and come away unscathed?'

'I don't know. He was a strong man, in some ways incredibly so, and I think he'd have been fine if it hadn't been for one particular incident. It was in the spring of 1916 – some of the tunnels ran a third of a mile or so under enemy territory by then, so you can imagine how important the ventilation was. They'd judge it by a candle – forgive me if I'm telling you things you already know –

and if it stayed alight, even if it was only the feeblest of blue flames, it was judged safe to work. With the longest tunnels, there'd be an infantryman above ground working those big black-smith's bellows, pumping air to the face along lines of stove piping. It was real teamwork, and a huge act of faith for the men underground.'

She got up and poured herself a whisky and soda from a decanter next to the flowers, then picked up a second glass and looked at him questioningly. He shook his head, reluctant to accept anything that would make him more tired than he was already, and she resumed her story. 'One day, Bernard was down there with two others, young engineers who were placing charges according to his instructions. They'd nearly finished when they noticed that the air was beginning to deteriorate and it was getting harder to breathe. Obviously they couldn't just call up to see what was happening with the bellows – it was too far and anyway, only sign language was permitted below ground – so Bernard ordered them back up immediately. Fortunately, because their senses were so attuned to the slightest change, they'd noticed in time to make it back to safety, but one of them refused to go.'

'Why?'

'Because he'd nearly finished laying the charge and was determined to get it done. Bernard knew the boy had misjudged how long he could stay down there safely and he tried to drag him away, but he wasn't strong enough to do it on his own – the third man had followed orders immediately and left – and he knew it would be dangerous to make a noise by struggling because it would alert the enemy to their position. He had no choice but to go back and get the bellows working again, and try to save him that way. When he reached the surface, he found his colleague and a few other soldiers wrestling with the piping; apparently the infantryman had been working the bellows constantly, so they realised there must be a blockage somewhere in the system. Of course, Bernard knew there wasn't a chance in hell of locating it before the man below suffocated, so he turned and went back down.'

Penrose was silent, trying to imagine the courage it must have taken for anyone to respond like that, to descend to what must have seemed like certain death. The mental picture of Aubrey's contorted face and outstretched hand, already fixed distressingly in his mind, took on a new horror.

'Needless to say, it was hopeless. The air in the tunnel was all but extinguished and Bernard only got a hundred yards or so in before he was gasping for breath and losing consciousness. He was on his knees, still trying to move forward, when the man he'd sent back caught up with him and dragged him out. It's a miracle that either of them got out alive.'

'And the boy?' Penrose asked, although he knew there could only be one outcome.

'When they got the air circulating again, they found him about a hundred yards from the face, obviously on his way back. What a terrible death it must have been – all that blackness and nothing to breathe, and the sheer terror of being down there alone and knowing you're doomed. He was face down, Bernard said, with his mouth full of soil. They may as well have buried him alive.' She shuddered, and added with a wry bitterness, 'The charge was perfectly laid, however. They used it that evening and I gather it was rather successful.'

'It's impossible for anyone who wasn't there to understand how that must have affected him and I'm sorry if this sounds naive – but I don't quite see why he felt that to be a sin for which he had to be punished. Guilty for not being able to help, perhaps – but not responsible. It was an accident, surely? What more could he have done?'

'Yes, it was an accident, but the boy who died wasn't just anyone: he was Bernard's nephew, Arthur, his sister's only child, and Bernard had made a promise to look after him. That in itself is ridiculous, of course – you can't make promises in war, it doesn't work that way – but he made it all the same and never forgave himself for being unable to keep it, even though his sister certainly never laid the blame at his door.'

For Penrose, a piece of the jigsaw fell at last into place. He had no idea how it got him any closer to finding Aubrey's killer, but somehow he knew it was important. 'Do you happen to have a photograph of her?' he asked.

'Of Nora? Yes, of course. I've got one of her with Arthur, taken not long before his death. Do you want to see it?'

'Yes please, if you don't mind.' She was gone only a couple of minutes and, when she returned, handed him a small photograph in a plain gold frame. The boy in the picture was, he guessed, little more than twenty, and he smiled broadly out from behind the glass, handsome in his new uniform and with a warmth in his eyes which would have made him attractive even if the rest of his features had been less appealing. He had his arm round his mother, who looked up at him proudly but with an apprehension which had been justified all too soon. Her face was in profile and she was older here than when Penrose had last seen her, but it was unmistakably the same woman whose picture looked down from the bookshelf in Aubrey's office, the woman to whom he imagined the bayonet and flower had been pointing. Without really knowing why, he asked: 'The irises – here and in Bernard's office – are they connected at all to his sister?'

She looked at him, completely taken aback. 'I suppose in a way they are, although how you know so much about my husband puzzles me.'

It puzzled Penrose, too, although he had no intention of discussing the scenes – and they were, he realised now, very much like theatrical scenes – which had been created for him both on the train and in Aubrey's office. In truth, almost everything he knew about Aubrey was based on what the killer had told him, so who else, he wondered, was so familiar with the man's past?

Too polite to question him more, Grace Aubrey continued with her explanation. 'Actually, the irises are more linked with Arthur. He was a brilliant young man, you know. When he enlisted, he was two years into an engineering degree at Cambridge, but what he loved most was gardening and he spent virtually all his time in the Botanic Gardens. It was always his intention to go back there after the war. There was a job waiting for him as soon as he graduated.'

Penrose remembered the Gardens; he'd visited them once or twice himself during his university days and, although they lay just on the edge of the town, within easy walking distance of his college, their contrasting landscapes offered a seductive other world. He and Aubrey's nephew must have been in Cambridge at the same time, he realised.

'Arthur got his love of flowers from his mother, although she was a botanical illustrator, not a gardener. He transformed their own garden when he was still just a boy, and their neighbours', then he earned money doing it in his spare time at university. The iris was his favourite flower. After he died, when Bernard came back from the war, he had twenty-one different varieties planted here in the garden, one for each year of Arthur's life. Part of the penance, I think, although he hardly needed flowers to remind him.' She stood, and walked over to the vase below the painting. 'Bernard chose the species to have flowers all year round, so it's just as well I've grown to love them too. See how beautiful they are when you look at them closely.'

He joined her and saw what she meant. The flowers which he had believed to be of a uniform deep lilac with a single splash of yellow were, in fact, a complex blend of tones and colours, each slightly different to the next. 'Did you know it's supposed to be the flower of chivalry?' she asked. 'Three petals – one for faith, one for wisdom, and one for valour. Bernard laid an iris on the Cenotaph for Arthur every week, almost without fail. I shall do the same now for both of them – there's no one else left to remember. Nora died five years ago – she had cancer – and Arthur's father was already long dead when he went to France.'

'Did Arthur have a lover?'

'Not that I know of. Certainly there was no girlfriend at the memorial service we held for him.'

Having believed at first that he would get nothing from Grace Aubrey, Penrose now sensed that the time spent with her had hinted at everything of significance in the case. At a loss for the moment as to how it related back to the theatre and to Elspeth Simmons, he fell back on a more conventional line of enquiry.

'Can I have the name of your husband's solicitor, Mrs Aubrey? I'll need to see the details of his will.'

'It's John Maudelyn at Maudelyn & De Vere. They're in Lancaster Place, but I think I can save you some time. If there was one thing that Bernard and I did discuss, it was our financial affairs.' She left the room, again only briefly. 'This is a copy of his will,' she said, handing Penrose a large ivory-coloured envelope. 'You'll want to check with John, but you certainly won't find him at work on a Sunday so this might help in the meantime. I'd be very surprised if he'd changed it without telling me, and there are none of those startling revelations in here that make things so much easier for detective writers.' She smiled wryly. 'And theatre producers, for that matter. Put simply, the houses, Bernard's stocks and shares and a significant amount of capital go to Joseph and to me; neither of us will ever want for anything, as you'll see.'

'And the theatres?'

'Ownership of the bricks and mortar goes to Joseph, but no executive powers in their management. That falls to John Terry, together with a sizeable share of the profits. Or, I suppose, the losses, although he'd have to be very stupid to whittle away assets of the scale that Bernard has built up over the years. A lump sum has been left to Lydia Beaumont; they were good friends, and he could always fancy himself a little in love with her without the fear of having to do anything about it – I'm sure you know what I mean. The most unusual clause concerns Hedley White – I knew I'd seen the name somewhere. He is to have a job – and a well-paid one – at the New and Wyndham's theatres for as long as he wants one or, should he choose to leave, he will receive a sum of money that should set him up for life.'

Penrose thanked her and held out his hand, ready to leave her in peace, but she walked with him down to the hallway, stopping at the door to another room on the way to point out a second vase of flowers. 'These don't strictly belong to the iris family but I liked them so much that Bernard planted them for me. Ironic, isn't it?' He looked at the velvety brown and green flowers without understanding her meaning. '*Hermodactylus tuberosus*, Inspector. Or, to you and me, the widow iris.' At the door, she offered her hand again and looked gravely up at him. 'Will I be able to see Bernard's body soon? We may not have been in love, but we did always respect each other and the more I see of the world, the rarer I consider that to be. I don't intend to stop now simply because he's dead.'

'Of course. I'll have a car sent for you in the morning. Would midday suit?' She nodded, and Penrose paused at the door. 'I spoke to Bernard very briefly tonight – I wanted to ask him about Hedley White and Elspeth Simmons – and he said there was something he needed to see me about, too. I don't suppose you have any idea what that might have been?'

She shook her head. 'I can't imagine why he would need to talk to the police but I can easily understand why, if he did, he would choose you. Thank you for your courtesy, Inspector, and for your intelligence. I appreciate them both, and I'd be grateful if you could do one thing for me. When you find whoever did this, as I've every confidence you will, I'd like you to make sure that they know what they've done. I don't mean bring them to justice in the courts – that will happen, of course, but I have no faith in capital punishment. Death means different things to different people, and I think Bernard was right when he said it could often be the easy way out. But before they die, I'd like you to try to make sure they understand what they've taken from this world. He was a good man.'

Penrose knew it wasn't his place to question what Grace Aubrey had said about the relationship she shared with her husband, but he couldn't help reflecting that there were many kinds of love. As he left, he could not decide for whom he felt the greater sadness: the man who had died so full of regret; or the woman left alone to deal with a grief which she had sincerely never expected to know.

A walk through London in the early hours of the morning would not have been Josephine's preferred way of dealing with the shock of Aubrey's murder, but she found herself with very little choice. Archie's departure had been followed by an uncomfortable interlude in the Green Room, during which Marta's anger had dissolved into frustration tinged with embarrassment, and things were only made worse when Lydia snapped at her to calm down and stop wrapping her in cotton wool. Josephine's gentle suggestion that they all go home and get some rest met with adamant refusal.

'No, you two go home if you want to,' Lydia said, getting up suddenly, 'but after what I've seen tonight I intend to put off rest for as long as I can – particularly the eternal sort. I need to see a bit of life, so I'm going for a walk. You're welcome to join me, or I'll see you later.'

Marta started to protest but thought better of it and gave Josephine a look which begged for solidarity, so they left together, accepting a police chaperone as far as Number 66 and then, as soon as the constable's back was turned, setting off in the other direction. God help him if any harm came to them, Josephine thought: Archie's fury would be merciless.

The night was cold and damp, but the rain seemed to have cleared permanently now and the air was not unpleasant. All signs of Saturday's revelry were long gone and, as they skirted Covent Garden and crossed the Strand to head down Villiers Street towards the river, there was barely a soul to be seen. It was a little after 3 a.m. and ordinary people – those whose evening had not been interrupted by death – had gone home to bed long ago, leaving London in the care of a very different populace. The coffee stalls – which appeared out of nowhere as the public houses closed, taking up their nocturnal pitches at the foot of bridges and on street corners – were in full swing, a magnet to the sleepless, the lonely, and the fugitive; to anyone, in other words, who could be regarded as a poor relation of the city's daylight hours. Josephine and her friends crossed Victoria Embankment and made for the stall that was tucked against the steps to Hungerford Bridge. The soft yellow glow of its interior was a welcome distraction from the unrelenting blackness of the river, and the pungent aroma of sausages and coffee did its best to be inviting, but Josephine doubted that the affirmation of life which Lydia craved was to be found among its clientele.

'Never let it be said I don't know how to show a girl a good time,' Lydia insisted with a flash of her old humour and walked undaunted to the counter, where a man and a woman stared out into the street as if from a box at the theatre. As the woman pushed three mugs of hot liquid towards Lydia, her wedding ring – sunk almost without trace into the middle-aged plumpness of her fingers – seemed a revealing expression of the extent to which she had given up on life.

They sat down on one of the benches that lined the Embankment, and Lydia was the first to speak. 'It's funny, you know, now I think about it – although it was such a shock to find Bernie tonight, I couldn't honestly say it's a surprise that he ended up like that.'

Josephine was intrigued. 'Why do you say that? I know theatre can be harsh but violent death seems to me a little excessive.'

Lydia was quiet for a moment, trying to put her finger on why she felt the way she did. 'This may sound melodramatic, but he always seemed to live in a darker world than the rest of us – something more sinister than the sad old muddle that most of us will admit to. I remember we got drunk one night during a particularly awful run of the *Dream*. It was Christmas Eve and his wife had gone to visit their son in Cirencester, and Bernie didn't fancy seeing Christmas in on his own so we sat in his office and got smashed on his finest malts.' She drained her mug, staring out across the river. 'It's not the most cheerful of drinks at the best of times,' she continued, 'and it was getting close to the anniversary of my brother's death, so we soon got to talking about the war. It surprised me, his attitude towards it all.'

'In what way?'

'Well, I'd always thought of him as quite a peaceable man, a reluctant soldier if you like, but he was adamant that war was a natural instinct. I can still hear him saying it, in that great booming voice he had when what he was saying came from the heart – that the trenches appealed to those murderous instincts which slumbered close to the surface, and the war had simply smashed this flimsy armour of culture that we all thought was so strong. Up until then, I thought that war was the interlude for him as for all of us –

tragic, unforgettable, but something to leave behind. That night, I realised he carried it with him all the time. All the colour and the joy and the make-believe that he made so real for the rest of us – it had never convinced Bernie.'

Privately, Josephine wasn't sure how many people it had convinced. Lydia lived her roles wholeheartedly – it was one of the great joys of watching her on stage – but she would be the first to admit that she sometimes found it reassuring to continue the performance in her daily life. Like Aubrey, Josephine found it difficult to ignore the contradictions between her personal sense of justice and the single-mindedness which war demanded: one day, if an Englishman killed a German he was hanged; the next he was a patriot, and she remembered how upset she had been to see her friends and neighbours, even her family, scanning the papers for news of enemy slaughter with hopeful eyes, driven by fear for those they loved. She was not yet twenty at the time but, as the years passed, she realised that her revulsion had nothing to do with age: now, with talk of Nazi rallies and worries over Britain's air power, another storm was gathering and, at thirty-seven, her anxiety for people on both sides was as complex as ever. If war broke out again, she knew there would be some difficult years ahead for people who felt as she did.

'I can understand what Bernard meant,' she said. 'Jack was in London at the time of the declaration, and he wrote to me about it. Jack was my lover,' she explained, realising there was no reason why Marta should know anything about her personal history. 'He was killed at the Somme. But he said the crowds in the city as war broke out were really quite terrifying: when the population was united like that in a mob, all the instincts of hatred and prejudice were given a free rein and nobody questioned them. It was as if everyone had reverted to an innate violence, with all reason and mercy just swept away.'

'I didn't know you'd lost someone,' Marta said.

'Haven't we all?' Josephine retorted quickly, then remembered she was talking to a friend and put away the curt matter-of-factness which she habitually used to deflect sympathy. 'He was medically trained, and shot in the back trying to help another soldier – an English one, although I'm sure he would have done the same if he'd come across a German alone and needing help. He found it very hard to reconcile his pacifism with the role he was given. It was one of the things I loved about him. In fact, I based a lot of Richard's character on Jack.' She smiled, remembering Marta's earlier comments about *Queen of Scots*. 'And of course I *did* love him, which is perhaps why people are so convinced by Richard.' Marta took the dig good-naturedly, and Josephine turned back to Lydia. 'I don't see why a dark heart makes Bernard a candidate for murder, though.'

'It's not just that, it's something much more personal he told me that night.' She didn't go on straight away, but now it was not her sense of timing in front of an audience that made her hesitate. 'He made me promise never to mention this to anyone, but I don't suppose it matters now. His nephew died in an accident halfway through the war, but Bernard was convinced he was murdered, and that one of his colleagues had killed him out of spite.'

'But why?' Josephine asked, horrified.

'He didn't say anything more. It was a secret he'd carried with him all that time and I think he regretted telling me almost as soon as he'd opened his mouth. But Bernard was there when it happened, so he must have had his reasons for suspecting foul play.'

'Why didn't he just go to the authorities?' Josephine asked, highly sceptical. 'Even in war, there are laws and systems of redress.'

'I got the impression that he had no proof – either that or he wanted to deal with it himself.'

'You should have told Archie this earlier, you know. If Bernard Aubrey was going around swearing revenge for a twenty-year-old murder, I'm not surprised someone wanted him silenced.'

'It really wasn't like that. Bernard knew how to keep his mouth shut.'

'How can you be so sure? He's dead, Lydia, and there's no point in protecting him now. If you don't want to tell Archie, I will – but either way, he has to know.'

'OK, OK, but there are different ways of making amends, you

know. I'm not sure that Bernard intended revenge. I think one of the reasons he was so soft on Hedley was as a way of making up for what happened to his nephew. Hedley's about the same age, and I think Bernard wanted to give him a start in life, to look after him.'

Perhaps, Josephine thought, remembering how devastated Aubrey had been in the foyer earlier that evening when she had explained that it was Hedley's girlfriend who had been killed; had that really been simply sympathy for a young friend's grief, or was there more to it? She wondered if Archie had made any progress in finding a connection between the two murders. Was there anything she could think of in what Elspeth had told her which might link her to Aubrey, or to what had supposedly happened to his nephew? Or something that might give Hedley White a reason to resent them both?

'I wonder where Hedley is?' Lydia said, as if reading her thoughts. 'He must be shattered by what's happened, and I don't expect he even knows about Bernie yet. That's what I really meant about Bernie's death not being a surprise; you don't expect people like Hedley's girl to be killed, not with all that youth and innocence – why would anyone want to? But Bernie was different – you always got the feeling that he understood violence, even if he didn't have it in him.'

'I have to say, I wouldn't have wanted him as an enemy,' Josephine admitted. 'Without his support, I think I would have found Elliott Vintner's accusations much harder to deal with. He propped me up through that trial with his loyalty and his determination – and that was professional, not personal. I can imagine how ruthless he could be if something really mattered to him, if it were a question of life and death.'

Marta, not having known Aubrey, had taken little part in the conversation but she seemed glad now to have the chance to speak about something other than murder. 'That must have been a difficult time for you – after all that success, to be accused of stealing someone else's story. I remember reading *The White Heart* ages ago – I worked in a hospital for a bit after the war and one of the patients asked for it to be read aloud to him. I liked it, but I remember being so disappointed by the books Vintner wrote later; perhaps I'd just moved on.'

'No, you're right, it was something special and I never questioned its merits – only my reliance on them. But he couldn't repeat the success of that first novel, no matter how hard he tried – the rest were all failures.'

'So he thought he'd get the money from you instead?'

'Yes, and he might have succeeded if it hadn't been for Bernard, an expensive lawyer and a judge who said that if any dues were to be paid, Vintner should first settle his account with Shakespeare. Of course, it turned out that the judge had seen the play five times and was a huge fan. I imagine Bernard treated him to a sixth performance on the house after that.'

'You certainly couldn't fault Bernie's generosity,' Lydia agreed. 'Did you know he's given all the money he made from *Richard of Bordeaux* to the families of those who died in the war?'

'What, you mean he hasn't made a penny out of it himself?' Marta asked, astonished.

'Not one. He said its pacifism was what struck a chord and he wanted to honour that. He really was a remarkable man. I owe my career to him. So does Josephine, in a way. I only wish I could have thanked him.'

'The best way to do that now is to help Archie catch his killer,' said Josephine firmly. 'Tell him what you've just told us, or at least let me tell him.' As Lydia looked doubtful, she added, 'Has it occurred to you that knowing something about Aubrey's secret might put you in danger as well?'

Clearly it hadn't. 'All right,' she conceded at last. 'You talk to Archie, Josephine. If he has any questions, no doubt he'll find me, but I've told you everything I know. I wonder what will happen to Bernie's theatres now? It seems disrespectful to say this so soon but, if *Queen of Scots* falls through, I'll have to look for something else to give me a reason to get up in the morning. Nothing would compensate for a future without work. What else is there? I'd rather lie down and die.'

Josephine saw the hurt in Marta's eyes, and marvelled that

Lydia could concern herself with a dead man's feelings when she had just all but destroyed her lover's hopes that they might have a life together. In the silence that followed, she watched as the coffee woman came out from behind her counter, collecting coins from under the plates and brushing bits of saveloy skin and cigarette ends onto the pavement, and was suddenly overwhelmingly depressed by the ease with which – through carelessness or cruelty – hope could be trampled on and destroyed. Having to look on while Marta attempted to shake off the slap and continue as before did not help her mood.

'You know, with all that's happened tonight I completely forgot to thank you for the flower you left at stage door for me,' she said, brushing Lydia's cheek affectionately. 'It's supposed to be the other way round, but I'm not complaining. Those green and brown petals are extraordinary – almost like velvet.' She got up, and Josephine's heart sank still further: she didn't say anything but she could tell from Lydia's bemused expression that, no matter how extraordinary the flower, it wasn't she who had left it for Marta.

'Are you all right?' Archie's voice was urgent and concerned, and Josephine felt a pang of remorse for not appreciating that of course he would worry when he got the message she had left for him at the Yard, asking him to telephone her as soon as possible. She reassured him, then gave a brief but thorough account of her conversation with Lydia.

'If it's true that Aubrey's nephew was murdered, it would be hard to think of a more appalling crime,' he said, and told her about the boy and how he had died. 'It would have been quite easy to arrange, though. I don't suppose there was any suggestion that Aubrey thought he might have been the intended victim and not his nephew?'

'No, nothing like that, and there was no indication of who would have wanted the nephew dead or why. Apparently, Bernard regretted saying anything at all and refused to explain. It was nearly twenty years ago, though – do you really think the deaths could be connected?'

'I know they are, but until now I couldn't see how one could lead to the other. Aubrey was playing a dangerous game if he was out for revenge, and there must be a reason why it's taken so long to come to anything.'

'How did you know there was a link?'

Confident of Josephine's discretion, Archie repeated what Grace Aubrey had told him about the significance of the flower found with Aubrey's body. 'Apparently, the iris represents chivalry.'

'Yes, I think I knew that. "A sword for its leaf and a lily for its heart" – I can't remember where I read that, but it struck me as an interesting description. It was probably in one of the letters I got when *Richard* opened: apparently, I was wrong to go on about lilies; for medieval writers, fleur-de-lis always meant the iris, and plenty of people wrote politely to tell me so.'

Archie remembered the note in the railway carriage: 'Lilies are more fashionable.' Was there a more sophisticated message there than he had thought? A reference, perhaps, to past mistakes, to things being named incorrectly – to an adoption that should never have taken place?

'Archie? Are you still there?'

'Sorry, yes. I was just thinking about Elspeth Simmons.'

'Was there a flower with her body, too?'

'Yes, an iris again. It occurred to me that she might have been Aubrey's child, but Grace Aubrey convinced me it was unlikely. Still, perhaps Elspeth's death was the catalyst for his. Perhaps when she died she took the reason for nearly twenty years of silence with her. The question is – whose silence? I'm hoping Alice Simmons might be able to help there. Betty telephoned earlier to say they were ready to leave Berwick – Alice wanted to come down straight away to be near Elspeth – so they should be here in a few hours.'

'Perhaps Arthur fathered a child before he died,' Josephine suggested. 'Elspeth could have been related to Bernard that way.'

'Yes, she could,' he agreed. 'Again, Grace claimed not to know of a lover, but they could have kept the relationship quiet. And if the girl was pregnant out of wedlock, she's hardly going to parade the illegitimacy at a memorial service.' He sighed heavily. 'There are so many permutations, but what you've told me tonight helps enormously. Where is Lydia now, by the way?'

'She's gone home with Marta. They got a car to take them, as you instructed,' she added, with no intention of admitting that Lydia's revelations had been made by the side of the Thames in questionable company rather than in the safety of Number 66. 'I think there are some things they need to sort out – personal stuff, nothing to do with this – and they both looked shattered.'

'You must be, too. You should go to bed.'

'I know. I don't suppose there's any point in my telling you to get some rest? You can't go on like this indefinitely.'

'I'll see what I can do,' he promised, 'and I'll speak to you tomorrow – well, later today. I can't say when because God knows what's going to happen next, but I'll try to find time to come and see you. And Josephine?'

'Don't worry, Archie, I will,' she said, anticipating his instructions to take care.

As Archie said goodnight, Fallowfield put his head round the door. 'Miss McCracken's downstairs, Sir. She's older than I expected – it's funny, I always think of the theatre set as packed with sweet young things, but she's no youngster now and I doubt she's ever been sweet. Nasty piece of work, but I suppose she'd have to be to write those letters. And she hasn't stopped talking from the moment I knocked on her door to the moment I put her in the interview room.'

'Anything interesting?'

'Mostly vicious stuff about people she worked with – all except Terry. He seems to share her high opinion of herself. Very nasty about Miss Tey, though, and not a good word to say about Bernard Aubrey.'

'But no indication that she already knew he was dead?'

'No, but she's not stupid, Sir. She wouldn't give herself away.'

'I think we'll let her wait for a bit; our hospitality might calm her down and anyway, I want to bring you up to date.'

Fallowfield listened intently to what Penrose had to say, then added his own news. 'Nothing further on White yet, Sir, but

Seddon's been through the list of numbers on Aubrey's blotter. Most of them aren't very interesting – firms you'd expect him to deal with in theatre – but one is the number for Somerset House and another is a private number down south. There's no answer, but I've told Seddon to keep trying.'

'Somerset House is interesting,' Penrose said. 'I wonder what Aubrey was digging around there for?'

'I don't know yet, Sir, but we're trying to track down a home number for someone who works there. If not, it'll be first thing Monday morning at the latest.'

'Good work, Bill – thanks,' Penrose said. What he needed now was a voice to unlock the past, someone who could help remove the barrier which time had placed between him and that first terrible death. From that, the more immediate answers would follow, he was sure, and he looked forward more than ever to meeting Alice Simmons.

Twelve

The early hours of Sunday morning brought nothing but despair to Hedley White. Last night, buoyed up by the beginnings of a plan and some money in his pocket to carry it out, he had almost convinced himself that running away was a feasible solution; perhaps if he left London behind he could also discard the pain of Elspeth's death, if not the fact of it. He would go to one of the stations – not King's Cross, he couldn't bear that and anyway it would be full of police – and buy a ticket to get himself as far away from the city as he could afford to go. He'd choose a town he liked the name of, maybe somewhere on the coast, where he could keep his head down, work hard and start again.

But as daylight released the life back into Paddington Station, things looked very different. Hedley stood by the station's great memorial to railway staff who had fallen during the war, dwarfed by the statue of a soldier and envious of the huge greatcoat in which it was draped. It wasn't the cold or the rain that had eaten away at his resolve, though; it was the loneliness that had worn him down. All his life, Hedley had known companionship: in a large and close-knit family, in the chaotic but familial world of the theatre and, most recently, in the intimate miracle of love; now, as he gazed over towards the long line of platforms, each leading out to a different version of that second chance he had craved, the isolation of such a life bore down on him with a merciless reality. If Elspeth were with him, he thought, he would be stronger; she always brought out the best in him and he would know what to do for them both. He looked up again at his bronze companion, who held not a weapon but a letter from home, and imagined him to be so engrossed in this reminder of tenderness that the trenches were forgotten. That was nobility, he thought, and Elspeth's absence returned again to mock him. Who was he trying to fool? Who was this decisive and courageous protector that his imagination conjured up so readily? Elspeth was dead, and he was no hero.

By now, the ticket office had opened and Hedley joined the queue, hoping it would force him into making a decision. 'Where to?' the booking clerk snapped when his turn came and tapped a ruler impatiently on the counter. As Hedley hesitated, a policeman came into view. He was just a bobby on an early shift, looking forward to his first hot drink of the day, but Hedley – who had been brought up to believe in the power of authority – saw it as a sign. He recalled a book he had read recently. When he first met Elspeth and discovered her love for *Richard of Bordeaux*, he had borrowed a couple of Josephine Tey's novels from the library to impress her. He couldn't remember the titles but the one he had particularly enjoyed was a mystery which involved the chase and inevitable capture of a suspected murderer. Reliving it now, and finding himself on the wrong side of the story, he knew without any doubt that a life on the run was not for him. Hurriedly, he left the queue. What on earth had he been thinking of? He couldn't spend the rest of his life cowering in the shadows, afraid to show his face, no matter how much trouble he was in. Decisive now, Hedley walked quickly to the nearest public telephone and called the only person he could think of without fear.

Lydia took some time to answer and, when she did, her voice was full of sleep. 'I'm sorry to wake you so early on a Sunday,' he said, 'but I didn't know who else to ring.'

'Hedley? Where on earth are you? Are you all right?'

He explained, and she listened patiently. When she spoke again, all traces of sleep had disappeared and her tone was warm but firm. 'You have to go to the police, darling. You haven't done anything wrong but if you run away they'll have something to hold against you; if you go now, there's nothing to be afraid of.' When he didn't speak immediately, Lydia continued reassuringly.

'Inspector Penrose is a fair man, Hedley, and he'll be on your side as long as you're honest with him. You want them to find who did this to Elspeth, don't you?' He could tell from the sudden forced brightness in her voice that she knew it was a cheap shot, but she was right to guess that nothing would make him see sense more readily.

'You're right and this sounds stupid, but I just can't face having to walk into a police station,' he said. 'I know I've made it worse by waiting till now. Could you speak to Mr Penrose for me? Tell him I'm here?'

There was silence on the line, and Hedley waited for Lydia's answer. 'Look, I'll speak to him now for you but I think it's best if you go back to your digs and he comes to find you there. There'll probably be a policeman waiting, but just explain what's happening. You don't want to have all this out in the middle of Paddington Station.'

Reading between the lines, Hedley realised that she was doing her best to keep his shame as private as possible without saying as much, and he appreciated her efforts while suspecting that they signalled a rough time ahead for him with Inspector Penrose. Still, he had made his decision and he wouldn't go back on it now. 'Thanks for trusting me,' he said.

'Don't be silly, Hedley – of course I trust you. I'm glad you phoned me and I want you to let me know straight away if you need me. It'll be all right, really it will. I'm sure the police will sort it out. And Hedley?'

'Yes?'

'I'm truly sorry about Elspeth. I know how much you loved each other.'

Hedley replaced the receiver without speaking and made for the underground, fighting back tears. He trusted Lydia and knew her advice was sensible, but first there was something he needed to do.

Penrose was unavailable, so Lydia left an urgent message with the constable on the desk and climbed back into bed, shivering as she removed her dressing gown.

'You didn't tell Hedley about Aubrey's death,' Marta said, putting her arms around her.

'No,' said Lydia. 'I just couldn't. I was afraid I'd be able to tell from his voice that he already knew.'

Rafe Swinburne rode over the river and into Blackfriars Road, taking advantage of the straight, broad street and peaceful Sunday morning to reach a satisfying speed which was rarely possible in the city. He passed the entrances to Stamford Street and the Cut before turning right into the network of smaller roads behind Waterloo Station, and was pleased to see that the area in which he always parked his motorcycle – close to his digs, where he could keep an eye on it – was clear of cars. He cut the engine, relieved for once to be home and alone: his nightly diversions were taking their toll, although it was the smiling rather than the sex which wore him out. Perhaps he should have tonight off: it was supposed to be a day of rest, after all.

He took his keys from the ignition and crossed Chaplin Close, heading towards the old three-storey house in which he and Hedley shared rooms. It was shabby, but cheaper than lodgings on the other side of the river and, with his bike or the underground, the West End was only a few minutes away. If all went well, it wouldn't be long before he could afford something better but, in the meantime, this suited him perfectly. The street was quiet and, from Waterloo Road, he could hear the bells of St John's. It must be about nine o'clock, he thought. With a bit of luck, Hedley would still be in bed and he could enjoy a cup of coffee in peace before getting some sleep himself.

He was still three or four doors from home when he heard someone call his name from the other side of the street. Looking over, he was astonished to see his room-mate lurking in the shadows outside a butcher's shop. Hedley was beckoning urgently to him, and it would have been hard to imagine a more complete picture of human misery.

'Jesus Christ, you look terrible,' Swinburne said, going across to him. 'What the hell are you doing out here?'

'Waiting for you. I knew you'd be back soon and there's something I need to ask you before I hand myself in.'

'Hedley, what are you talking about? In where?'

'To the police. They'll be waiting at the house, I expect – that's why I needed to catch you out here first.' As Swinburne looked over his shoulder, bewildered, Hedley explained. 'It's Elspeth. She was the girl who was killed on the train and they think I did it.'

'Fucking hell, mate, that's awful. They're here now, you say?'

'Probably. Lydia said they would be.'

'You've spoken to her about it?'

'I had to. I didn't know what else to do. She told me to give myself up and trust them to be fair.'

Swinburne was sceptical. 'No doubt she means well, Hedley, but are you sure you want to do that? Wouldn't you rather just keep out of sight for a bit until they catch the bastard who really did it?'

'I don't think I could stand it. Anyway, the more time they waste looking for me, the less likely it is they'll get whoever did this to her. And I can't bear the thought of him getting away with it, Rafe – nothing would be worse than that.' Swinburne waited while Hedley pulled himself together. 'I'd like you to do something for me, though. I need an alibi for Friday night before the show. The papers said it happened early evening, so it'll be before I got to the theatre. I didn't kill her, but they'll never believe me, so would you say I was with you?'

It was a risk, Swinburne thought; he didn't want to get himself into trouble. 'Aubrey would vouch for you,' he said. 'He'd know you couldn't have done it.'

Hedley looked down. 'I can't ask him, not now. Anyway, I don't think he would.'

'All right, then. I don't see any reason why I shouldn't say we went for a drink together. Not the Salisbury, though – someone might contradict that. We need somewhere more anonymous. How about the Duncannon? It's always busy on a Friday so nobody could swear we weren't there. We went there together and arrived at about six o'clock. Is that early enough?'

Hedley shrugged. 'I suppose so.'

'OK. We sat upstairs and drank beer – two halves each – until it was time to go to the theatre, then we walked back together as far as stage door. I'd say we got there about an hour before the performance, wouldn't you?'

'Can anybody prove we're lying?'

'I doubt it. I was actually with a girl but she wasn't very memorable, and if I can't remember her name, there's not much chance of anyone else tracking her down. Fortunately, she was quite easy to shake off.' He looked at Hedley's worried face and wondered if it was sensible to ask; in the end, he couldn't resist the question, but tried to make it casual. 'What were you really doing, by the way?'

Hedley hesitated, then seemed to decide that he owed an explanation in return for the favour. 'I was singing,' he said, offering perhaps the one answer that would never have occurred to Swinburne. 'Elspeth wanted one of those dolls from the play so badly but I couldn't afford to buy her one. I thought if I did a quick round of the pit doors, entertaining the queues for a bit at each one, I might make enough money to get her a present.'

Swinburne raised a cynical eyebrow. 'I can see why you want an alibi,' he said, then, as Hedley began to protest, cut him short. 'All right, all right – it's unlikely enough to be true. I'll speak up for you, and you're probably right to assume that the police won't go to the effort of tracing theatre queues to prove you innocent.' He put a hand on Hedley's shoulder. 'Don't worry. You can rely on me.'

'Then will you do one more thing for me?' He reached into the bag he was carrying and took out a doll. 'I got the money,' he said, handing it to Swinburne. 'Actually, I did better than I could have hoped. I bought this in the interval ready to give to Elspeth when I saw her last night. Will you take it to her uncle for me? I'd still like her to have it and he'll know where they've taken her. I've written the address down for you – it's in Hammersmith, but it won't take you long on a Sunday. And will you tell him I'm sorry?'

Swinburne looked down at the doll in his hands, relieved to have something to distract him from the intensity of Hedley's grief.

It was the female character from the play, the Queen, and more a puppet than a doll, really. The figure, which wore a rich green velvet gown and head-dress, was sufficiently pliable to be posed and he raised its left arm, examining the coloured glass in the wedding ring and around the neck of the dress. He had always thought there was something hideous about dolls of any sort and this one was unnervingly realistic. An image of it clutched in a dead girl's hands sprung involuntarily to mind and he shuddered, hoping that Hedley wouldn't notice the horror which his posthumous gift to Elspeth had aroused.

'I'll do it now,' he said quickly, wanting the thing out of his charge and remembering what was waiting for Hedley at home. At least it was a good excuse to be out of the way, he thought: he certainly had no desire to come between the police and their prime suspect.

The lights had gone out one by one as the residents of Verbena Gardens took to their beds and now, several hours later, Frank Simmons watched them come on again in near-perfect reverse order. The night had passed even more slowly than he feared it would; more than once, he got up from his seat at the window to check that the clock on Betty's side of the bed was still working; each time, as he picked it up and held it to his ear, the gentle ticking confirmed that time was determined to move on, even if he had no idea how to move with it.

He hadn't tried to go to bed, knowing that sleep would be impossible and, when Betty was not there with him, reluctant to disturb the tidy counterpane which she smoothed into place each morning. As soon as she had telephoned to say that she and Alice were leaving Berwick, he had turned his chair to face the point where the street joined the main road; he knew it would be an age before they arrived, but the very act of looking out for the car seemed to bring them closer. He would feel safer when Betty was home again. The police had been kind but he knew what they must be thinking in private, and he was mortified whenever he remembered the expression in Josephine Tey's eyes as she had turned to face him at the theatre. No one had ever looked at him in fear before, and he had never imagined that they would have reason to, but Friday night had changed all that.

He tried not to think about Elspeth too much, although that in itself felt like betrayal. He had been lucky to have known her. Betty had never wanted children and, although it was the one great sadness in his life, he had kept his disappointment quietly to himself and learned to cherish instead the time he spent with his niece. After his brother's death, he had vowed that she would not go through life missing a father's concern and had watched over her welfare more diligently than ever before without, he hoped, seeming too heavy-handed about it. He thought back to the notes that Alice and Betty had kept secret from him, the notes that Walter had never mentioned, and it pained him now to realise that there were things in Elspeth's life about which he knew nothing. He'd known their relationship must change as she grew into a young woman and, when she met Hedley, had recognised with sadness that the moment had come for him to relinquish some of the privileges of friendship. But Hedley was a good boy and, more than anything else, Frank wanted Elspeth to be happy. He'd always wanted that.

A motorcycle turned into Verbena Gardens but there was still no sign of a car so, for company, he got up to switch the wireless on in the kitchen. He filled the kettle and stood it on the stove, hoping that an indulgence in the habits of the morning might encourage time to pass more quickly. To his surprise, before he had a chance to light the gas, he heard the doorbell. Surely he hadn't missed the car? He'd only been gone a few seconds and anyway, Betty would let herself in. In the brief time it took him to go downstairs and switch the lights on in the shop, Frank managed to conjure up a hundred different scenarios – road accidents, freak weather conditions, other murders – all of which would leave him wretched and alone in the world. When he lifted the blind he was relieved, if bewildered, to see the actor, Rafe Swinburne, standing on the doorstep, holding what looked like a doll.

'Sorry to disturb you so early,' Swinburne said, although Frank was sure his dishevelled dress and exhausted face must make it painfully obvious that he had not been to bed. 'I'm sorry, too, for your loss. I only met Elspeth once or twice, but she seemed a lovely girl. My name's Swinburne and I'm a friend of Hedley's,' he explained. 'I've brought something for you.'

Frank shook the hand he was offered. 'Yes, I've seen you at the theatre. You'd better come in.' He led the way upstairs and directed his guest into the living room while he returned to the kitchen. 'Would you like a cup of tea?' he called. 'I was just going to have one myself.' There was no answer, so he went through to the other room and found Swinburne staring in disbelief at his collection. Realising he had company, the young man reverted to the expression of polite sympathy which he'd worn on arrival, but not before Frank had had time to see the smirk of amusement on his face as he looked into the glass cases. Suddenly, he saw his labour of love through the actor's eyes – pathetic and ridiculous, and stripped of all its joy now that there was no one to share it with. He felt a surge of anger towards this man who, with his good looks and easy charm, had destroyed years of dedication in a second and, when he spoke, his voice was filled with a resentment which would, in the past, have seemed utterly alien to him.

'What do you want? I'm waiting for my wife to come back and she'll be here any minute.'

Swinburne could hardly have missed the change in tone but he kept his composure. 'Hedley asked me to bring you this,' he said, gesturing with the doll. 'He got it as a present for Elspeth and he was going to give it to her this weekend. He also asked me to tell you that he's sorry.'

'What for? Why hasn't he come to see me himself?' As he uttered the words, Frank marvelled at how quickly the poison of suspicion could take hold. He was appalled by the ease with which he was beginning to doubt those he had instinctively trusted, but he couldn't help himself. Until you experienced it for yourself, he thought, it was impossible to understand how murder continued to corrode the living long after the dead were cold.

'He's with the police. Naturally, they want to speak to him

about Elspeth's death – just to see if he can help them, of course. Nothing more sinister than that.' Frank listened as Swinburne talked about Hedley and Elspeth, and found that he resented the casual way in which words like 'love' and 'belonging' fell from his lips, as if he were delivering another script and had forgotten that the emotions he described belonged to real people. For Frank, these were important words and should be used sparingly, not thrown away in a performance. He doubted that Hedley – shy and inexperienced as he was – would have found it easy to express what he felt for Elspeth, but she would have known anyway, just as she had known how much he had always cared. Wasn't that what love meant?

Eventually, Frank took the doll from Swinburne's hands, wishing the scene to be over. 'Hedley really wants Elspeth to have this and he thought you'd know what to do,' the actor said, and looked again at the cases of theatre souvenirs. 'Although, if you don't think that's appropriate, I'm sure he wouldn't mind if you kept it here.'

Before he could say anything, Frank heard the shop door close and his wife called up the stairs. So he had missed their arrival after all, but at least they were back safely. When Betty came into the room, he was as surprised to see her alone as she was to discover he had company. 'Where's Alice?' he asked.

'She wanted to go to Elspeth straight away, spend some time with her on her own, so the car took her there first. The police have been very kind. She's going there next – she said she had to speak to Inspector Penrose as soon as possible – so we probably won't see her till this afternoon.'

'What does she want to talk to the police about so urgently? Does she know something?'

Betty looked at Swinburne, clearly not wanting to discuss their business in front of strangers. 'Who's this?'

'Sorry, this is Rafe Swinburne.'

'I just came to give my condolences, Mrs Simmons, and to bring something for Elspeth. I can see you need to be alone, though. I'll see myself out.'

Betty removed her hat and went to deal with the kettle, while

Frank listened to the fading sound of a motorcycle engine and waited to hear what Alice had said to his wife.

Dead, then, thought Esme McCracken, trying to come to terms with the news as she sat alone in a poky, depressing room on the ground floor of New Scotland Yard. That would teach him to be so fucking smug.

It was a shame the police had found the letters, though. If she'd thought about it, she could have removed them – she'd had plenty of opportunities – but it never occurred to her that Aubrey would care enough to keep them. She cast her mind back over what she had written, and was pleased to recall nothing to be ashamed of. Admittedly, the threats were unfortunate in hindsight – unfortunate but not unjustifiable, and she certainly didn't regret having made them. No, when somebody did at last have the decency to come and see her, she'd be ready and happy to talk. What was keeping them, she wondered? Surely she must be a priority?

To pass the time, she tried to take in all she could of her surroundings. It was important for writers to make the most of every experience and she often played this game with herself, standing outside life, observing. It was second nature to her, really. Ironically, the one time the trick had failed her was when it mattered most, when her father died and she found herself unable to escape her own heart, torn between grief at his loss and resentment that she had had to postpone her writing to care for him. But that was a while ago now. No cell – or interview room, as they had euphemistically called it – could equal that for a prison. She found it hard to imagine a time when a visit to Scotland Yard would have a place in her work, but she would store it up anyway. If the worst came to the worst, she could always knock off one of those sad little detective stories – God knows, everyone else did and Tey had managed it, so how hard could it be? Not exactly something to be proud of, though. No wonder she didn't want her own name on it. Or on *Richard of bloody Bordeaux* for that matter.

It was outrageous, though, the way they were making her wait. She was just contemplating making a fuss when the door opened and two men entered the room. One was the fat idiot who had brought her in for questioning, the other was clearly his superior – in every possible way, she hoped, if he expected her to talk to him. He introduced himself as Detective Inspector Penrose and, as he spoke, she recognised him from the theatre as the man who occasionally hung around Tey. He was handsome, she had to admit, with a richly textured voice and an intelligence in his eyes that must make him enviable company. What on earth did he see in a second-rate scribbler from Scotland?

Although she was too clever to let it show, Penrose's first question surprised her. 'It's clear from your letters to Bernard Aubrey that you were dissatisfied with how things were run at the New Theatre. Would you be happier if John Terry were in charge?'

She thought for a moment before answering, but saw no reason to lie. 'The issue isn't the running of the building but the philosophy of what's on stage,' she said. 'Theatre is about sharing ideas and expanding people's horizons. It's not about making money. Aubrey had cash, but Terry has vision. So what do you think, Inspector?'

'Does entertainment have a place in *your* vision, Miss McCracken?'

'People make do with what they're given, but they need to be led. How can they be taught to appreciate better things if they're never given a chance to experience them?' Her habit of answering a question with a question was beginning to frustrate him, she could tell, but she was enjoying the chance to act out the debate that she had rehearsed so many times in her head.

'Did anyone else share your views about Aubrey?'

'If you mean was he unpopular, that's hard to say. Wealth tends to distort the boundaries of like and dislike, don't you find? Bernard Aubrey was one of those men who people use. He could do so much for so many, and that's never a recipe for true friendship. Anyway, no relationship is ever what it seems in the theatre: you learn that when you work backstage and see what they're really like. Some alliances are built on very shaky foundations, and a pretty face can turn the most unlikely heads.'

'Would you care to expand on that?'

'Not really. Ask Terry or Fleming or Lydia Beaumont what they really thought of Aubrey. Or of each other, for that matter. I think there'd be a few surprises.'

'I'll do that. In the meantime, where were you on Friday evening between six o'clock and eight o'clock?'

Penrose had changed his approach and, for the first time, McCracken felt at a disadvantage. What did he know, she wondered? 'I was in Charing Cross Road, browsing in the bookshops until they closed. I suppose the last one shut at around six-thirty. Afterwards, I went for a walk round the theatres to see what the queues were like, and got to the New just after seven. I like to be there in plenty of time.'

'Did you buy anything in the bookshops?'

She hesitated. 'No, not this time.'

'I gather you've written a play of your own. What's it about?'

She expected better from him. The question was disappointingly simplistic, and she gave it the contempt it deserved. 'It's not a simple narrative that can be summed up in a couple of sentences, Inspector. If I could sit here and paraphrase it, what would be the point of going to the trouble of writing it at all? It's a play of ideas.' She thought again of Tey, and wondered how much he cared for her. 'But at least they're my own ideas and I haven't had to borrow them from someone else.'

He smiled. 'Well, no doubt we'll find out what they are if the play goes into production.'

McCracken tried to keep her fury in check and was helped by a knock at the door. The Sergeant, who might as well have been struck dumb for all he was contributing to the interview, got up and returned a few seconds later. He whispered something to the Inspector, who closed his file.

'I'm sorry, Miss McCracken, but we'll have to leave it there for now.'

'What do you mean?' she cried indignantly. 'Surely you want to ask me about Aubrey's death?'

'I do indeed, but not at the moment. You won't mind waiting, I'm sure. I'll get the constable to bring you a cup of tea.'

She began to tell him what she thought of his hospitality, but the door closed in her face before the second adjective was uttered.

Despite the brief euphoria of his performance the night before, John Terry knew he would not be happy until he had settled things with Aubrey. Yesterday's meeting had left him restless and frustrated. Now, as he lay in bed, he found reassurance in his lover's presence but knew that this easy solace was only temporary: the fear he had felt during his encounter with Fleming was stronger than ever. He hated confrontation and would go to any lengths to avoid it, but too many things were going wrong in his life; the only way to get back on track was to face his demons one at a time, and he might as well start now. Aubrey was often at work at the weekend, and by now he'd probably have calmed down. Quietly, Terry got up, dressed and left the flat.

Out in St Martin's Lane, he began to feel better. The area was different altogether on a Sunday, with the shops shut and no prospect of life in the theatres, but he still felt at home here and the familiarity brought with it a sense of permanence which made the future less intimidating. Was his position really so bad? He had had fights with Aubrey before – never as serious as this, admittedly – but the two of them had always worked out their differences. Why should this be any different? He had no reason to suppose that Aubrey now doubted his talents or his importance to the stage. There was Fleming, of course, but perhaps he should even come clean to Aubrey about that? After all, it wasn't him doing the blackmailing and he doubted that such a stunt would be looked upon favourably. The lie he had told Fleming in the heat of the moment yesterday might yet prove to be a self-fulfilling prophecy.

His optimism was short-lived. He was surprised to find the stage door open on a Sunday and even more astonished to find it manned by a policeman who refused to let him in or explain his presence. Irritated and a little alarmed, he walked down St Martin's Court and into Charing Cross Road, and stopped at the first telephone box. Unless Aubrey was inside the theatre with the police, he would be at home and would know what was going on.

It was Aubrey's wife who answered, however, and when Terry replaced the receiver five minutes later, he was at a loss to know how to make sense of what she had told him. How could Aubrey be dead? Terry had never known anyone with a greater sense of vitality, a stronger grip on life.

There was a sharp rap on the glass and he looked up to discover that people were waiting to use the telephone. Apologetically, he stepped outside and took none of the usual gratification in noticing how their attitude changed when they recognised him. It had begun to rain again, so he stepped into a doorway to shelter while he tried to come to terms with conflicting emotions: sadness at the loss of a friend and mentor, who had taught him so much and from whom he still had plenty to learn; shock at the brutal reality of another murder following so swiftly on the heels of the one at King's Cross; and relief that, in death, Bernard Aubrey had offered him a way out of the mess he was in. Grace Aubrey had been gracious about her husband's generosity towards him and had wished him well with the future of the theatres. He was more grateful than she could possibly have realised.

Suddenly a whole new world of opportunity opened up in front of him, and Terry felt both exhilarated and terrified at the prospect of having to prove himself without the cushion of Aubrey's backing and judgement. He knew, however, that he would not be able to think about it properly until he had sorted Fleming out, and there was no reason why he shouldn't do that now. He knew where he lived and didn't doubt the truth of Grace Aubrey's words; he had enough money to shut Fleming up once and for all, and the sooner he did it the better. He would offer him a one-off payment for his silence and then have to trust the man to keep to his word; if the sum was large enough, he couldn't see a problem.

It didn't take him long to get to Bloomsbury and find Fleming's street but, as he was looking for the house number, the man himself emerged from a door about a hundred yards ahead of him. The strong build was unmistakable but, even at this distance, Terry could see that he looked awful, hunched into a scruffy old brown coat. Instead of calling out to Fleming, Terry decided to follow him, enjoying for once the role of hunter rather than hunted. In any case, it would be no bad thing to have the discussion in a public place; Fleming's anger yesterday had unnerved him. He looked at his watch and saw it was nearly opening time; the nearest public house was where they were most likely to end up.

But no. Fleming passed three pubs on his way up Guilford Street and into Gray's Inn Road, and didn't give any of them a second glance. Where the hell was he going, Terry wondered? And why, if it was so far, hadn't he taken a bus? Fleming was intent on his destination, so at least he was unlikely to look behind, but Terry was struggling to keep pace with him; then, just as he was about to abandon the chase, Fleming slowed down and took what appeared to be a photograph out of his pocket. He glanced at it briefly, then mounted the steps of a large, red-brick building and disappeared through its doors. When Terry caught him up, he stared in confusion at the discreet notice to the right of the entrance. What could Lewis Fleming possibly be doing in the Edith Kent Nursing Home?

He waited a while, unsure of what to do, but his curiosity eventually got the better of him and he went inside. The entrance hall was small but sparsely and efficiently furnished to make the best possible use of the available space, and a pretty girl in a nurse's uniform sat behind the front desk. She was on the telephone but smiled when she saw him and gestured to a small chair that had been placed in the hollow under the stairs. He took the seat and waited for her to finish her call, impressed by the friendly manner which bore no traces of the stress that a daily battle with sickness and pain must produce. In fact, the whole place spoke of a calm which was invariably found when disparate people were united – often in adversity – by a common end. Remove the life and death elements, he thought ironically, and it was not unlike a theatre company.

'Sorry to keep you,' the nurse said at last. 'How can I help?'

'I'm here as a visitor and this is my first time. I wasn't sure where to go.'

'That's fine. Who have you come to see?'

Terry risked a long shot. 'The name's Fleming.'

'Ah, Mrs Fleming's on the second floor. Her husband's just gone up actually, but you might want to give them a few minutes. She's not too good today.'

'I'm sorry to hear that. She's on the mend, though?'

She looked at him kindly, and he could tell how experienced she must be at channelling blind optimism into something more constructive without giving false hope. 'Cancer's not quite as straightforward as that, I'm afraid. But she's a tough lady and she has the best possible care here. I think it's her husband who's really keeping her going, though. He's been remarkably strong from the moment Ruth was diagnosed, and I don't think he ever sleeps. He's with her every night, even though he works in theatre, and I can't imagine that's an easy job. If anyone deserves to pull through, it's those two.'

'Perhaps I should come back another day, though, if she's not so well.'

'That might be best, but shall I give her your regards?'

'Yes, please do,' he said, and left without giving his name.

On his way down Gray's Inn Road, Terry looked back at the building's facade. Without question, it was one of the finest nursing homes London could offer and places like that didn't come cheap. He knew now why Fleming was desperate for money and understood, too, why he had spat out those words of recrimination so bitterly. No wonder the actor was adamantly opposed to going on tour: how could he leave his wife when he didn't know if she'd still be alive when he got back? Then, with a feeling of absolute horror, Terry recalled the lie he'd told Fleming yesterday. He could have had no idea at the time what it meant to Fleming, but now he realised all too clearly what was at stake. If Aubrey sacked him, that would be the end of his wife's treatment. Now Aubrey was dead. What had that one reckless lie led Fleming to do?

The cold oak of the pew was hard against his forehead and his legs had lost all feeling, but still Lewis Fleming did not get up.

'*There is no soundness in my flesh because of thine anger,*' he prayed. '*Neither is there rest in my bones because of my sin.*'

Never before had he felt beyond forgiveness but neither, in the past, had he pushed God's mercy so far. Today, as his wife screamed in pain, barely aware of his presence, he had known the true meaning of hell. It was the moment he had feared the most, the sudden deterioration of her condition, and he knew that it had come as punishment for his transgression. How else could he interpret it when one seemed to follow so swiftly on the other? What he could not understand, though, was why his sins were being weighed against her suffering, why his inner corruption should be reflected not in his own body but in hers.

There was a noise from the back of the nave, and he looked up to see the beginnings of a congregation for the next service. He must go. This time, his prayers were a private matter between him and God, and not something that should be allowed to taint a public act of worship.

'*For I am ready to halt, and my sorrow is continually before me,*' he whispered, anxious to find some comfort in the familiar words before he left the church. '*I will declare mine iniquity; I will be sorry for my sin.*'

Thirteen

As Penrose left the interview room and walked out to the Derby Street entrance of the Yard, where a car had been brought round for him, he could barely contain his anger. Lydia Beaumont had telephoned with a message about Hedley White but the officer who had taken the call had been so keen to go off duty that he had forgotten to mention it to the day shift, and the news only filtered through when the man posted at White's digs called to see why no back-up had arrived. The mistake could have been disastrous: nearly three hours had passed, and that was more than enough time for a frightened boy to have changed his mind. Penrose cursed the errant constable and, less reasonably, Lydia for not having insisted on speaking to him herself. She must have known how important it was.

'At least tell me it was Bravo,' he muttered to Fallowfield. 'I'd rather have two cock-ups from one idiot than feel like the whole force is turning a blind eye to murderers and felons. Any more of this and I'll think Bravo and White are in it together.'

'If it'll make you feel better, Sir, I'm sure it was Bravo. Shall I drive?'

Penrose was about to retort that they had enough trouble already without throwing a road accident into the mess when he remembered how proud his sergeant was of his driving. Reluctantly, he took the passenger side and tried to concentrate on White. Why had he decided to give himself up, he wondered? Of course, he wasn't to know that the police were nowhere near catching him and he might have thought things would look better for him if he handed himself over first but, even so, it took courage, whether he was innocent or guilty. He tried to fit White into the story of Arthur's death. Obviously he was far too young to have been involved in the war, but he could be a relative of the murderer. A son might kill to protect his father, for example – such a motive might even pass Marta Fox's rigorous criteria – but that was pure speculation. In fact, although he had looked at the deaths again from every angle since his conversation with Josephine, he had to admit that everything was pure speculation.

Sunday morning was an uncluttered time for the city and Fallowfield kept to the main thoroughfares. He had suggested that they send a team to bring White in while he and the Inspector continued with McCracken, but Penrose had been keen to see the boy in his digs, to get a sense of his personality from where he lived. And, in truth, Penrose had wanted to do the job himself; he readily acknowledged that he had a problem with delegation which might one day impede his progress up the force, but he would not be happy until he had White sitting in front of him.

The street was unattractive, a long stretch of dignified but tired bricks and mortar given over almost entirely to boarding houses, and uniformly faded. The door to Number Three was standing slightly ajar, and Penrose and Fallowfield climbed the stairs to the attic rooms which White apparently shared with Swinburne. As he looked back down the stairwell, Penrose saw that they were being watched through a crack of one of the doors on the second-floor landing – a crack which was hurriedly closed when the observer realised he had been spotted. This might not be the most glamorous part of town, but it was still an area unaccustomed to visits by high-ranking policemen; the residents must be wondering what evil lurked unsuspected in their midst.

PC Bartlett was standing outside the room on the left-hand side of the stairs and Penrose could see past him through the open doorway to where his quarry sat on the edge of the bed, his head in his hands. White stood up as soon as he heard them come in and held out his hand half-heartedly, as if uncertain whether it would be grasped in a formal handshake or cuffed to the iron bedstead. Penrose did neither, but simply nodded politely and asked him to resume his place on the bed, then looked round for another seat.

Finding his options somewhat limited, he took a battered old chair with rush seating from the corner of the room and placed it just close enough to the boy to be intimidating rather than threatening. Fallowfield remained standing at the door.

The room was chilly, but not without comfort. Two of the walls were decorated with theatrical posters of recent productions – presumably those on which White had worked at Wyndham's and the New – and the monastic austerity of the single bed had been softened by a couple of cushions and a piece of dark red fabric which served as a cover. The small bedside table held an alarm clock and a photograph, and Penrose was momentarily taken aback to see Elspeth so suddenly and unexpectedly brought to life. The picture showed her standing with White outside the New Theatre, next to the 'House Full' sign, and triumphantly waving two tickets at the camera. It was a moment of unreserved happiness and it brought the tragedy of her death home to him more starkly even than the murder scene or the Simmonses' grief. Next to the photograph, a handful of picture postcards from some of London's tourist attractions had been propped against a water jug full of flowers, and Penrose was relieved at last to find someone whose pocket preferred daffodils to irises; he was beginning to find the more majestic flower a little oppressive. He wondered if the neat domesticity of the room was habitual, or if a special effort had been made for this weekend.

White followed his gaze and anticipated the question before it was asked. 'I got those for Elspeth on Friday,' he said. 'I thought she could look through the postcards and choose where she wanted to go on Sunday, then we could save the rest for another time. And the daffodils – well, if she did happen to come back here, I wanted it to be nice for her.'

Penrose looked round the room again and, with a stab of nostalgia, recognised all the signs of someone hoping to take his first tentative steps towards a physical relationship. The flowers, the window open to air the small space, the best clothes hung ready complete with carefully darned socks – all were part of a universal language spoken by young men regardless of class and geography. Hedley had left nothing to chance. The gas ring on the floor – a typical feature of rented accommodation – held a kettle, and two mugs had been placed next to it, not matching but brightly coloured and welcoming; there was an alternative to tea, too, in the form of a bottle of Guinness and a pair of tumblers, and Penrose was sure that if he were to move a little closer to the bed he would be able to catch the optimistic scent of freshly laundered sheets.

These first impressions of Hedley White were both an affirmation of what he had expected, and a surprise. He had thought of him as a frightened boy and fear was certainly written all over his face – fear, and the relief which Penrose often saw in people who had decided to confront the worst thing that could happen to them. But he had not anticipated someone quite as out of the ordinary as the young man in front of him. Hedley was remarkably good-looking, with the broad shoulders and narrow hips of an athlete and an open, spirited face which was devoid of all vanity and all the more handsome for that. If Penrose didn't steer clear of such adjectives when questioning a suspect, he would have said it was an honest face. There was a strength, too, behind the fear, a resolve in his eyes to stick to the course he had chosen no matter what; whether that was to White's credit or not, Penrose hoped now to find out. 'Was Elspeth fond of daffodils?' he asked.

For a moment, White seemed to think that Penrose was mocking him. When he realised it was a serious question, he just looked bewildered. 'She liked all sorts of flowers.'

'But no particular favourites?'

'Not that I know of. She talked about rose bushes in her garden at home, but I've bought her violets and snowdrops as well as daffodils, and she said she liked them all.'

'Why did you run away, Hedley? You must have known how that would look.'

'Because I was scared,' he said with disarming simplicity. 'The papers were calling it a crime of passion, so I knew you'd be looking for me and I knew you'd think I killed Elspeth. Haven't you ever been so frightened that you just wanted to get as far away as possible, even though you had nothing to hide?'

It was a rhetorical question, although Penrose could have cited several salient examples. 'When did you find out that Elspeth had been killed?' he asked.

'During the matinee. I didn't know straight away that it was Elspeth but everyone backstage was talking about what had happened at King's Cross the night before and how it was connected to the play. Then after the show I saw a newspaper in the Green Room. It didn't give any names or a description or anything, but it said a young girl had been killed and the time, and I just knew it had to be her. I left the theatre at about five o'clock and went to a telephone box, and I kept telephoning her aunt and uncle, hoping they'd say she was with them and all right, but there was no answer. That confirmed something was wrong. They'd never leave the shop on a Saturday.'

'So why did you go to the theatre last night?'

'Because of the Boat Race.' Penrose looked confused, so Hedley continued. 'I suddenly thought that might be why no one was at home. Elspeth had mentioned it in one of her letters – they always go if she's there because they live so close to the river, and I thought they might have stayed on to join in the celebrations after the race. So I waited outside the theatre in case it had all been some horrible mistake, hoping she'd turn up just like we'd arranged. I suppose I knew in my heart it was no good, but I so desperately wanted there to be another explanation.'

'What arrangements had you made for the weekend?'

'We were going to meet at the theatre, an hour or so before the show so we'd have time for a drink. Afterwards, we were going to have dinner at the Lyons on Shaftesbury Avenue. Her uncle works for them and he put in a good word for us. The staff there love Frank, so we knew we'd get a good deal.'

'And afterwards?'

Penrose could see that imagining how the weekend should have gone was painful for Hedley, but the boy was making a big effort to hold himself together and he carried on. 'I would have taken her home. On Sunday, we were going to go out for the day but we hadn't made any definite plans. We thought we'd see what the weather was like.'

'How long did you stay at the theatre on Saturday night?'

'We'd agreed to meet out the front, so I waited across the road. I got there at about a quarter past six, I suppose – Elspeth was always early because she'd get so excited, so I didn't want to miss her. I stayed until the house had gone in and they started to turn the queues away. By that time, I couldn't pretend any more. I knew she wasn't coming, and that I wouldn't need the tickets, so I sold them.'

'Where did you go after that?'

'I walked about for a long time – it must have been hours. I couldn't come home because I knew you'd look for me here, so I went in the opposite direction, round all the parks, and ended up at Paddington. I thought about getting a train and making a run for it.'

'So why didn't you?'

'I didn't know where to go, or what I'd do when I got there. The only person I could think of who would help me was Miss Beaumont, so I telephoned her and she told me to come here. She said if I didn't, I'd be wasting your time when you should be trying to find the person who did this to Elspeth.'

Clever, thought Penrose, or true. 'If you were so excited about the weekend, why didn't you meet her at the station on Friday night? You would have had time before work, even if it was just a quick hello. She must have been looking forward to seeing you.'

'Yes, but her Uncle Frank always met her. She brought loads of luggage down with her which needed his van, and anyway, I liked to give her time to settle in with her family. I didn't want to get in the way, so I went for a drink with a friend before work. Rafe Swinburne – he lives across the landing and he's on at Wyndham's, so we often go in together. We arrived in town at six o'clock, had a beer or two upstairs at the Duncannon, and left there in plenty of time to get to work. You can check with him if you like. He'll probably be home soon.'

'We'll do that,' Penrose said. The alibi had been offered very readily, he thought, and with more detail than was natural. He didn't yet know what to make of Hedley White. He was certain the boy was lying about Friday evening but, if he was capable of killing at all, Penrose doubted that he could do so in such a cold and calculating way. In the heat of the moment, perhaps, but not with the careful planning that both murders had required. Then again, he remembered what Frank Simmons had said about Elspeth's travel plans.

'I understand that Elspeth wasn't supposed to come down until after the weekend, but you brought her visit forward and sent her the train ticket?'

'Yes, although I didn't buy it, of course. I could never have afforded first class. It was a special treat for her. Mr Aubrey helped me sort it out. He knew how much Elspeth loved the play because I'd told him, and he was making arrangements for Miss Tey to come down for the final week, so he suggested getting Elspeth booked on the same train. It was supposed to be a lovely start to the weekend. Mr Aubrey thought it would mean a lot to her to meet her favourite author, and he fixed the seats so they were bound to bump into each other and get talking. Elspeth always found it easy to talk to people – it was one of the things I loved about her.'

So Josephine's encounter with Elspeth had been carefully orchestrated after all. He had never entirely believed in the coincidental meeting, in spite of Josephine's reassurances, and, significantly, the hand behind it all was Bernard Aubrey's. But was it important to the crime that the two had met? Would Elspeth still have been killed if Josephine had not been on the train? There was no doubt that the murders were linked, but how could Josephine have any part to play in Aubrey's past? Whether the explanation was innocent or not, he wished fervently that Aubrey hadn't decided to involve Josephine in something that had ended so tragically, no matter how kind his intentions had been towards Elspeth.

'That was a very generous thing for Bernard Aubrey to do. Had he met Elspeth?'

'No, but he always asked after her. When he found out we were courting, he looked out for us. The train ticket was typical of him –

not just the money but the thoughtfulness. He's always doing small kindnesses for people – well, they're small to him but they mean so much to the people he does them for. He gave me the theatre seats as well – top price for Saturday night.'

Penrose would come to Aubrey's death in a moment, but he was interested to note that there was no giveaway past tense in anything White had said so far. 'Did you send anything else with the train ticket?' he asked.

'Yes, a note and a lily. The lily was from Miss Beaumont's dressing room; she has so many flowers that she's always giving them to us. So I put that in with the train ticket and a note. Well, it was just a line from the play, really – 'Lilies are more fashionable' – but it was one of Elspeth's favourite scenes and I knew she'd recognise it and be thrilled when I told her where the lily came from.'

'Are you sure it was a lily? It couldn't have been another flower?'

'I do know what a lily looks like. I ought to – we have enough of them on stage every night.'

'But nothing else? No magazines or souvenir dolls?'

'No, nothing else.' He looked down at his hands. 'I was going to give Elspeth one of those dolls – she so wanted one – but I hadn't got round to it.'

If Hedley was telling the truth, someone had been very prepared when that train pulled in. Penrose asked if anyone else had known about the arrangements.

'Uncle Frank, of course – I told him all about it. And Mr Aubrey. I told Rafe because I knew he'd be pleased for us – it was him that encouraged me to ask Elspeth out in the first place – and he teased me about keeping the noise down at night, not that he sleeps here that often. Oh, and Miss McCracken knew. She saw me putting the flower and the note in an envelope backstage, and asked me what the poor girl had done to deserve a night out with *Richard of Bordeaux*.'

'When was the last time you spoke to Elspeth, or heard from her?'

'The last time I actually spoke to her was ten days ago. She telephoned me at the theatre as soon as she got the note and ticket, just to say how thrilled she was. Then she phoned again on Thursday, but I was out getting some more candles for the play so I missed her. She left a message at stage door, confirming when she was arriving and saying she couldn't wait to see me.'

'Was the message written down?'

'Yes. I collected it from the pigeon holes when I got back.'

Where anybody could have seen it, presumably. Penrose decided to change tack slightly; he was interested in relations between Hedley and the Simmonses.

'How did her family react when you and Elspeth got together? Were they pleased about the relationship?'

Hedley shrugged. 'They seemed to be. Certainly we never had any problems seeing each other. I've never met her mother, of course. We'd only been together eight weeks and I didn't have enough time off to go up to Berwick. Mrs Simmons never comes down here. Elspeth's Auntie Betty was always perfectly polite, but Uncle Frank's been fabulous, really friendly.' Hedley pointed towards the photograph on the bedside table. 'He took that and got three copies framed, one for each of us and one for himself. He and Elspeth were always really close. I suppose it's because they had so much in common.'

Penrose hadn't seen the photograph anywhere in the Simmonses' flat. He wondered again about the nature of Simmons's feelings for his niece. It wouldn't surprise him if Frank turned out to be Elspeth's real father, although where that left him with Bernard Aubrey and Arthur he couldn't begin to work out.

'What about your own family, Hedley? Tell me about them.'

'I don't see what they've got to do with any of this.'

'Humour me. What does your father do?'

'He died when I was a baby, just before war broke out, but he was a blacksmith. My mother was left on her own with six children, but she remarried a few years later, to a farmer, and we moved in with him. He had three children of his own, but we all got on really well. Still do. Most of my brothers and sisters stayed in or around the village, helping on the farm or teaching at the local school. I missed them when I first left home to come here, but I go back as much as I can. I was planning to go in the summer and take Elspeth to meet them. They would have loved her.'

'Did any of your family serve in the war?'

'No. We were lucky. My dad was already dead, like I said, and none of my brothers were old enough. My stepfather was consumptive, so he was excused military service. It must have been terrible, though. Elspeth talked a lot about her father as we got to know each other better. His illness really upset her.'

'Did she ever talk about what happened to him or anyone else he served with?'

'No, just how bad it got towards the end. I think she and her mother both felt guilty for being so relieved when he died.'

'Let's go back to Saturday, Hedley. It was your night off, but did you get things ready for the evening performance before you went off duty?'

'As much as I could, yes. We re-plotted for the first scene right away, but it doesn't take long now because we're so used to it. Miss McCracken likes to check everything before the evening performance, so I was finished quite quickly.'

'I've heard there's a drinking tradition that goes on after the show. Were you involved in preparing that?'

'It doesn't happen after the matinees, but I put the stuff at the side of the wings ready for the evening.'

'Can you tell me exactly what you did?'

White was beginning to look concerned. 'It was slightly different on Saturday because Mr Aubrey was taking part, so I made sure there was an extra chair. I fetched the decanter from his office, added a tumbler to the other glasses and checked there was a corkscrew for the wine. Then I stood the whole lot on the shelf ready for Miss McCracken to take down at the curtain-call. It gets in the way otherwise.'

'Did you take the lid off the decanter for any reason?'

And now concern had turned to fear. 'Of course not. Why are you asking me about this? Elspeth was dead by then. Has something else happened?'

Penrose ignored the question. 'Are you absolutely sure that you didn't touch the contents of that decanter? Or see anybody else go near it?'

'I swear nobody touched it when I was there. Tell me what's going on!' He was on his feet and shouting now, and there was no doubt in Penrose's mind that he knew nothing about the second death. Gently, he put a hand on Hedley's shoulder and sat him back down.

'I'm sorry, Hedley, but Bernard Aubrey died late last night. We're treating his death as suspicious, and I have to ask you again – apart from Aubrey, did you see anyone near that whisky decanter while it was in your care, or did you touch it yourself?'

Hedley's self-control evaporated at the news of Aubrey's death, and he was unable to suppress his grief any longer. 'How could I be so ungrateful?' he said at last. 'I let him down so badly, and then last night, when I was standing outside the theatre in the rain and I realised that Elspeth wasn't going to turn up, I blamed him for her death. I thought if he hadn't arranged that ticket, she might still be alive. And I hated him. I wished it was him dead and not her. Now they're both gone.'

Penrose looked up and wondered why Fallowfield had slipped quietly from the room. He turned back to Hedley and spoke more sympathetically than ever. 'How had you let Aubrey down, Hedley? Why was he angry with you?'

'I did something really stupid and he found out about it. Elspeth's uncle collects theatre stuff, autographs and all sorts of memorabilia. So I stole some of the props from the play to impress him and Mr Aubrey caught me with them. I don't know why I did it. Frank didn't ask me to and the really daft thing is that Mr Aubrey would have given them to me after the run if I'd just asked, but I wasn't thinking straight. I wanted to make Elspeth happy and I knew I could do that by making her family happy. I was supposed to go and see Mr Aubrey after the matinee, but by that time I was too worried about Elspeth and I just left the building as soon as I could. And I'm sorry, I did lie to you earlier when I said I hadn't taken the lid off the decanter.'

'Go on,' said Penrose encouragingly.

'I took a swig of the whisky during the matinee when nobody was looking. I thought it would give me the courage to face Mr Aubrey later.'

At least that narrowed the timing down a little, Penrose thought. Whoever had doctored the whisky could not have done so until after the matinee. He gave White a moment to compose himself, leaving him in PC Bartlett's care while he went to look for Fallowfield. The Sergeant had not gone far. 'Rafe Swinburne's just turned up, Sir,' he explained, coming out of the room across the landing. 'He says he's only nipped back to change his clothes and then he's going out again, but I've asked him to wait until you've had a chance to speak to him.'

'Thanks, Bill. I'll do it now. You go in with White.'

'He didn't know about Aubrey, did he Sir?'

'No, I don't think he did. And I think he's telling the truth about Elspeth, as well, although I'm not convinced by his alibi. We'll see about that now.'

Swinburne's room was the mirror image of White's but had none of the transforming touches of ownership. Clearly Hedley had been accurate when he said that his friend spent very little time at home. The actor was by the small sink in the corner, shaving with a casual indifference to the presence of Scotland Yard. If he had been at all surprised to find the police in his digs, he did not show it now.

'Good morning, Inspector,' he said, looking at Penrose in the mirror. 'I hope you don't mind if I carry on getting ready while we talk, but I'm on a promise this afternoon and I don't want to keep the lady waiting.'

Instantly irritated, Penrose picked up a towel from the bed and handed it to Swinburne. 'If she's so keen, a few more minutes won't hurt,' he said. 'I'd like you to tell me what you did before work on Friday – say from half past five onwards.'

Swinburne wiped the soap from his face but not the smirk and Penrose, whose tiredness was getting the better of him, experienced an almost overwhelming desire to help it on its way. He was annoyed to see that the actor not only sensed his frustration but

seemed gratified by it. 'Of course, Sir,' Swinburne said with infuri-
ating politeness, 'anything to help,' and proceeded to echo Hedley
White's account of the evening, adding a few details here and
there. The speech was convincingly delivered, so much so that
Penrose wondered if Hedley's suspiciously rehearsed version of the
same story had, after all, been down to nerves.

'What about after the shows? Did you and White come back
here together?'

'No, Inspector. We hardly ever do. I've usually got business elsewhere, if you know what I mean, and Hedley's the faithful type.'
He looked slightly ashamed as he realised the inappropriateness of
his words. 'I'm sorry, that was a bit tasteless bearing in mind
what's happened. How is Hedley?'

'Upset, as you would expect,' Penrose replied curtly, and cut
Swinburne off as he began to vouch for White's good nature. 'Did
your business extend to Saturday night, as well?'

'In a manner of speaking, yes, but the location was different. I
like variety and so far, touch wood, it seems to like me. Speaking
of which, do you mind if I throw a few clothes in a bag while we
chat? I doubt I'll be back here tonight and I need to make sure I
can go straight to the theatre tomorrow if necessary.'

Penrose nodded, and watched as Swinburne transferred two or
three items from a drawer to an empty holdall. 'This variety that
you've been with all weekend – does any of it have a name and a
contact address?'

'First names and districts only, I'm afraid. There's a Sybille in
Hammersmith, or it could be Sylvia, and a Victoria in Bloomsbury.
Sorry I can't be more specific.'

'Hedley tells me you brought him and Elspeth together. Is that
right?'

'I only gave him a shove in the right direction. It was hardly
Cupid at work but it seemed to do the trick. From what I could
tell, they were made for each other.'

'You saw a lot of them, then?'

'No, not at all. I only met her a couple of times in passing, but
he talked about her all the time and he was obviously happy.'

It seemed to Penrose that Swinburne was not the sort to consider other people's happiness very often. 'You weren't interested in her yourself?'

'I do have some scruples, Inspector. She was spoken for and clearly smitten, and I only like to make an effort if I'm sure of the pay-off. Rejection's not good for the soul.'

'I'm sure someone of your experience could limit the chances of that.'

'You're barking up the wrong tree, Inspector. I didn't kill her, and neither did Hedley, so am I free to go?'

'By all means, for now,' Penrose said sweetly, 'but we may need to talk to you again.' At the door, he turned back. 'Just one more thing,' he said casually. 'There's a walkway between Wyndham's and the New. It runs over St Martin's Court. Do you ever use it?'

Swinburne closed the bag and picked up his motorcycle helmet. 'I have done, many times,' he said. 'We all used to have a bit of fun with it, running back and forth during the show and playing poker in the wings, seeing how far we could push it before having to get back to our own theatre. Then somebody missed a cue and Aubrey put his foot down. He doesn't have much of a sense of humour.'

Penrose let him go, angry with himself for not having managed to disguise his dislike of Swinburne during their interview. It had allowed the younger man to take control of the exchange, and that was not something that happened very often. He went back to the other room, where Hedley White was standing at the window, watching as Swinburne left the house.

'Did Rafe tell you about Friday night?' he asked anxiously. Penrose joined him, and watched the actor climb onto his motorbike and move off in the direction of the river. 'Yes, he confirmed your story.'

'So what happens now? Am I under arrest?'

'I'd like you to come back to the station with us so we can take a formal statement and some fingerprints from you. Are you happy with that?'

'Of course, if it will help.'

'Then you're not under arrest. Do you remember what you were wearing on Friday?'

The fear had returned to Hedley's face, but he nodded and reached under the bed for a laundry bag. He handed some trousers and a jumper to Fallowfield, who accepted them and then took the whole bag. 'Go with PC Bartlett, lad,' Fallowfield said, and his tone was not unkind. 'We'll be with you in a minute.'

As Bartlett took White down to the car, Penrose and Fallowfield searched the rest of the room quickly and efficiently, but found nothing of interest. 'I think a quick look round next door, Sergeant, don't you?' Penrose suggested with a wry smile, but the result was the same there. 'You know, Bill, we've got the so-called prime suspect in custody and we're no further forward now than we were an hour ago,' he said, unable to hide his disappointment. 'When are we going to get some help?'

The answer came sooner than he expected. 'Sir,' Bartlett said as Penrose shut the car door, 'there's an Alice Simmons at the station and she wants to talk to you urgently.'

There were two messages waiting for Penrose when he got back to the Yard. One was from Josephine, who had remembered where she read about the iris, but said it would wait until she saw him later; the other was from Maybrick at the theatre, reporting that Terry had tried to get into the building during the morning and had demanded to know what was going on.

'Could be a bluff, Sir,' Fallowfield suggested. 'After all, he had a lot to gain from Aubrey's death. He could be making a public display of ignorance to fool us.'

Penrose was doubtful but not in the mood to rule anything out. 'We'll have to see him later today, but I'm hoping Alice Simmons will point us in the right direction. In the meantime, perhaps you'd be kind enough to telephone Mr Terry and tell him that his first task as boss of two theatres is to cancel all productions until further notice. That won't go down well, I'm sure, but it will keep him busy for a few hours until we can get to speak to him. Then come back here. I want you to see Alice Simmons with me.'

While he was waiting for Fallowfield, Penrose tried to telephone Josephine, but was told her line was engaged. He doubted he'd have time to see her today: there was a lot to do and he wanted to get through as much as possible before he had to report to his super in the morning. And he desperately needed a few hours' sleep. The only time he remembered being this tired was when his regiment had been on the move and he hadn't fully recovered from an injury; they'd had to march for hours at a time and he remembered falling over in the road while others staggered round him, too exhausted to lift their feet high enough to step over him. It wasn't long after Jack's death, and his nights had been sleepless with sadness and worry about Josephine – it was that more than the physical exhaustion which had really affected him. Nothing, it seemed, made him quite as weary as worrying about Josephine, though she wouldn't thank him for it.

A mug of strong, black coffee appeared on the desk in front of him and he smiled gratefully at his sergeant. 'Where do you get your energy from, Bill? Is it all that good Suffolk air you grew up with?'

'I think it's more straightforward than that, Sir. You sent me home for a couple of hours, remember? And as predicted, John Terry has gone up in the air and not come down. I didn't know actors had such a vocabulary, but I've learnt a few words that aren't in any script I know of.'

As they made their way downstairs, Penrose confided his fears to Fallowfield. 'If Alice Simmons can't tell us much about Elspeth's background, we're in an impossible position,' he said. 'We're relying on there being a link between her and Aubrey but it would take an age to trace it by official records, and this killer's going at the rate of one a day. There won't be any room in the mortuary if we don't soon find a shortcut between the past and the present.'

'It's a good sign that she wanted to see you right away, though,' said Fallowfield, as optimistic as ever. 'She must have something to say.'

'She probably wants to know why I haven't found her daughter's killer yet,' Penrose muttered as he opened the door of the interview room. 'I would in her position.'

But the woman seated at the small table in the middle of the room did not look as though she had come to complain to anybody; in fact, she looked like someone with no fight left in her at all. There was no blood relationship between Alice and Betty Simmons so it was silly of Penrose to have assumed a resemblance, but he realised now that he had imagined Elspeth's mother as another version of her aunt. In fact, nothing could have been further from the truth. In her bearing, at least, she had none of the restraint that had been evident in her sister-in-law's every move; in fact, even in the formal surroundings of a police interview room, she looked more relaxed than Betty had been in her own home. She was tall, with attractive silver blonde hair which refused to be contained in its entirety by a plait, and she wore a suit which was sober only in its colouring; no part of the outfit had escaped a few little finishing-off touches and Penrose, who had never realised that black could be so expressive, searched in vain for a square inch of plain material; even the gloves on the table were attached to velvet flowers, while the hat, which was too big to go anywhere else but on the floor beside its keeper, was the most creative item of mourning attire that he had ever seen. What was most remarkable, though, was that Alice Simmons carried it all off with a dignity and composure which few people achieved with straight lines and understated simplicity.

'Thank you for coming here so quickly, Mrs Simmons,' Penrose said, 'but I'm truly sorry for the circumstances that have brought you.'

'Everybody's been very kind,' she said, so quietly that Penrose could barely hear her. 'At the . . . the people who are looking after Elspeth couldn't have been more thoughtful, and Betty said you were all working so hard to find out what happened. I am grateful, you know. Really I am.'

She looked at Penrose for the first time, and it seemed to him that fate had played a cruel trick in deciding that Alice Simmons would share no characteristic, no matter how small, with the daughter she so dearly loved. Her colouring, build and general demeanour were all distinctly at odds with the Elspeth he had seen in Hedley's photograph, and he wondered if the physical disparity had been a painful reminder to both mother and daughter that their relationship was built on a fragile practical arrangement rather than an unassailable natural bond. 'We're doing our best, Mrs Simmons,' he said, and introduced Fallowfield, who took the empty cup from the table and sent the constable at the door off for a refill. 'But I have to admit, we could do with a little help and we're hoping you'll be able to supply it.'

'Of course you need help. How can you be expected to get any-where when you only know half the story?' She took a handker-chief from her bag, a safeguard against what was to come. 'They let me sit with Elspeth for a bit, just the two of us,' she continued. 'I had to tell her I was sorry. She grew up surrounded by so much misery and the only consolation was that she never knew about it – we always managed to keep it at bay. Now this has happened, and she's paid the price after all for something that was never her fault. At a time like this you're supposed to say you can't believe it, aren't you? But that's not true for me. I hoped Walter's death would be the end of it, but I think deep down I always knew there'd be worse to come. That's why I'm here now – to stop it going any further.'

'Do you know who killed Elspeth, Mrs Simmons?' Penrose asked gently, hardly daring to believe that the answer could simply have walked through the door. He glanced at Fallowfield, and saw that he was also finding it hard to control his excitement.

'No, but I can try and explain why it happened. Betty told you that Walter and I couldn't have any children of our own?' Penrose nodded. 'We tried and tried before the war, but it didn't happen and it was ruining our marriage. I couldn't think about anything else except having a baby. All the joy I'd felt in just being with Walter, in knowing how much he loved me, disappeared and I couldn't get it back. Every time I looked at him, all I could see was our failure. It tore him apart inside. There was no pleasure in sex any more. We'd always been really close in that way – he was so tender and loving – but it stopped being an intimate connection between the two of us and became something set apart from our relationship, if you know what I mean. He stopped talking to me, too. I don't think he had any idea what to say, so we ended up in this no man's land; we couldn't turn ourselves into a family, and we couldn't go back to being happy as a couple. I hope you don't mind my telling you all this, but it's important.'

'Of course not,' said Penrose, who was genuinely happy to let her talk. Selfishly, though, he hoped that what had brought her to him was something more than a confession for one side of a bad marriage, and was pleased when Fallowfield gently moved things along.

'So did you suggest adoption to your husband, Mrs Simmons?'

'No, Sergeant, nothing as sensible as that, I'm afraid.' She hesitated. 'I suppose it's ridiculous of me to be ashamed of what I did suggest when so much else came later, but I *am* ashamed. It was so thoughtless, particularly as we didn't know whose fault it was that we couldn't conceive, but I asked Frank if he'd father a child for us. He agreed, but only if Walter and Betty knew about it and were happy with the arrangement. I must have been out of my mind – Walter's own brother! No man could stomach that. He was so angry when I told him. I'd never seen that side of him before – well, I'm not sure it existed until I drove him to it. I don't think Frank ever got round to telling Betty – there was no need, because Walter would never have agreed. Shortly after that, war broke out and Walter couldn't sign up quick enough. Anything rather than stay with me and face that betrayal.'

That explained why Alice never came to London, Penrose thought, and he wondered if Frank Simmons had ever regretted his honesty. Was his interest in Elspeth a way of making up for that missed opportunity to be a father? And what on earth had he been thinking while they sat there yesterday discussing Walter and Alice's marriage? 'Frank told us that Walter arranged Elspeth's adoption with someone in the army,' he said. 'Do you know who Elspeth's real parents are?'

'Yes, at least I know who her father was. I didn't at the time, though – I was so grateful just to have Elspeth that I didn't dare question anything about how I got her. All I knew then was that there was no one to bring her up. She was only a month old when Walter brought her home to me, and the prettiest little thing you could imagine – so good-natured, even at that age. We called her Elspeth – it was Walter's mother's name and I wanted him to have a connection with her as strong as the one I felt. After that, I never looked back. It was only last year, when Walter realised he was dying, that he told me everything he knew.'

'Was her father's name Arthur?'

Alice looked astonished. 'So you know? Yes. He was an engineer in the war. How did you find out?'

'Elspeth's death is connected to another murder which happened shortly afterwards.' Penrose was about to explain further, but Alice interrupted him.

'Is Bernard Aubrey dead?' Now it was the Inspector's turn to look surprised. 'If there's been another killing, it had to be him. Apart from me – and whoever's doing this, obviously – he's the only other person left alive who knew what really happened. Arthur was his nephew. Bernard kept in touch with Walter after the war. He sent us money to help with Elspeth – on her birthday, every year without fail.'

'With a note, asking you to let him know if you changed your mind about the adoption?'

'Oh no. I mean, he did send a note but it wasn't about the adoption. He knew we'd never change our mind about that and he was satisfied that Elspeth was well cared for. No, he wanted Walter's help and Walter wouldn't give it to him – that's what Aubrey wanted him to change his mind about. You see, Inspector, Walter did something terrible to get Elspeth, something he never forgave himself for. He confessed to me, just before he died and it explains everything – why he changed so much, why his love for Elspeth always had a sense of regret about it. I don't think she knew – I hope to God she didn't – but Walter was capable of a much more generous love than he ever showed to her. I know everyone was affected by the war – how could they not be? – and if I'm being honest, it was easy for me to put his behaviour down to that because I couldn't be expected to make it better for him. But there was a much deeper grief. I wish more than anything that he'd told me earlier, because as soon as he did the old Walter came back. I'm making it sound like a sudden confession and it wasn't that – he told me everything gradually, a bit more each day; you could tell it was a terrible strain for him, but it gave me long enough before he died to remember how much I loved him and I'm grateful for that, even though it made his loss so much harder.'

'What did he tell you, Mrs Simmons?' Penrose asked after a long silence, bringing her back from wherever her story had taken her.

'I'm sorry. Of course – you need to get on. Well, Walter was an infantryman and his regiment worked closely with the tunnelling operation. We were hardly speaking when he went away because of what happened with Frank, but he soon began to write – it was so much more terrible out there than he could have imagined, and I think any connection with home helped. The very first thing he had to do was bury people. He'd never seen a dead body before, and there he was – faced with two or three hundred of them. I'll never forget that letter. He told me how they had to pack them in the dirt so that the bottom of the trench was springy like a mattress because of all the bodies underneath. The stench was horrific, he said, but the flies were the worst thing; they lined the trenches like some sort of moving cloth and no matter how many the men killed with their spades, every day was just as bad. He liked the democracy of the trenches, though, the fact that everyone was in the same boat no matter who they'd been in civilian life. That was naive of him, I think, because not everyone saw it that way – it was just a case of getting by however you could, and it soon changed back when peace came. But one of the officers took him on as his batman, and they looked out for each other. Walter mistook that for friendship and he must have opened up to him about the trouble we were going through, because this man – the Captain, Walter always called him – got to know how desperately I wanted a child. As the war went on, I think he saw a weakness in Walter, someone who was willing to follow, and in the end he used it against him.'

'In what way?' Penrose asked gently

'He promised Walter that he'd help him get a child in return for a favour when the time came. Of course, Walter agreed; he never could have guessed what the favour would be.' Penrose thought he could, but waited for Alice to continue. 'One of Walter's tasks was to work the bellows that kept the air supply flowing down in the tunnels. Usually, they worked in pairs and took it in turns but there'd been so many casualties, and so many more men were sick with dysentery, that he was having to do long stints on his own. One day, when there were three men underground laying a charge, a long way from the entrance, the Captain walked over and ordered him to stop pumping.'

How easy it could be to take a life, Archie thought, but what ruthlessness such a crime would require. He had seen some elaborate murders in his career, and plenty of deaths which would have demanded both strength and nerve from the people responsible for them, but nothing as callous as this casual execution. He imagined the cold-heartedness it would take to stand there as the seconds ticked past, knowing what suffocating horror must be going on beneath your feet and yet feel no mercy, no compulsion to pick up those bellows and grant life to three men.

'Walter protested, of course – it went against everything he believed in, everything that was natural. But he wanted that child – wanted it for me – and I honestly think he would have done anything. If he'd had longer to consider what he was doing he might have stuck to what he knew was right, but he had to act quickly and he made the wrong decision. I think the Captain was relying on the speed of the whole thing for his co-operation. Then when Aubrey and one of the others made it back to the surface unexpectedly, he pretended the system was blocked. In the end, only one man died, thank God, but it was the most important one – Aubrey's nephew and Elspeth's father.'

'But why did Arthur have to die? And what gave this man the right to decide what happened to his child?'

'The law gave him the right. You see, Arthur had been having an affair with his wife. It had been going on for some time, while he was away and before Arthur signed up, and the Captain found out about it. I think he intercepted a letter that his wife had written to

224

Arthur – stupid, really: she must have known how they were all living in each other's pockets. The trenches were never renowned for their privacy. But she had written to tell Arthur she was pregnant, and that was that – it sealed his fate, and I don't know if he ever discovered he was going to be a father. Her fate, too, of course. Women had even fewer rights in those days than they do now, and the Captain wasn't the sort to bring up another man's child. As soon as the baby was born, he made his wife give her up.'

'What happened to her? Elspeth's mother, I mean.'

'I don't know. Walter never asked, and I don't think Aubrey could have known either, or he'd have done something about it. Apparently, when we first had Elspeth, Walter kept expecting her mother to turn up out of the blue but she never did. As the years went on, he assumed that the Captain had found a way to get rid of her – after all, someone who did what he did to Arthur was capable of anything. But he didn't want to know. He had enough on his conscience.'

'The man who orchestrated all this – the Captain – do you know his real name?'

'Oh yes. After what he did to my husband, it's hardly likely to be a name I'd forget. And anyway, he achieved a certain notoriety in his later years.' She smiled bitterly and Penrose waited eagerly for her to continue, desperately hoping that what she said would make sense within the context of his investigation. His mind raced through several possibilities, but never in a million years could he have predicted Alice Simmons's next words. 'His name was Elliott Vintner,' she said. 'You probably know him as a novelist. These days, I think of him more as a murderer.'

Penrose was stunned, so much so that Fallowfield had to pick up the questioning. 'Did Bernard Aubrey know all this, Mrs Simmons?'

'Not immediately, no, but he wouldn't let it rest. He was devastated by his nephew's death, of course, and he nearly died himself, but there was no reason to think it was anything other than a tragic accident. He only became suspicious because of the state Walter was in – it just didn't make sense that he should be so traumatised. He'd always been a reliable soldier and he had a reputation for staying calm in the most terrible situations, but he fell apart after that incident. He became ill, and God knows what he must have said in his delirium, but it was enough for Aubrey to realise that something had gone on. When Walter got better, Aubrey begged him to tell the truth about Vintner; he was the only person who could testify, you see, and Aubrey was obsessed with getting justice for his sister's son. He promised Walter absolution if he would only bring the real murderer to trial, but he refused. There was too much at stake with the baby.'

'But Aubrey didn't give up.'

'No, he never gave up, but Walter had made up his mind once and for all. It's funny – he was never as deferential when he came back. I think our men were generally less inclined to take orders after they'd fought so hard, but for him it was personal; he'd taken one order too many. But Aubrey kept trying. He felt responsible, you see, and he'd promised his sister – Arthur's mother – that he'd find out the truth.'

'Did Aubrey ever try to get the baby back?' Penrose asked, surprised that the fatal agreement had been allowed to stand.

'No, I'll give him that. He genuinely wanted what was best for Elspeth, and he put that before his hatred for Vintner. Arthur was gone and his mother wasn't able to raise a child on her own – and he knew how much we loved her. She was happy with Walter and me, you know, in spite of everything. So Aubrey sent the money and the notes, but there was no more pressure than that. He had a deadly patience, Walter once said. In the end, they came to a sort of unspoken agreement: Aubrey wouldn't disrupt Elspeth's childhood by raking up the past before she was old enough to deal with it; and Walter would tell the truth about what happened when he felt the time was right. I don't suppose he thought it would be on his deathbed, but that's how it worked out.'

'So Aubrey got what he wanted?'

'Yes. Walter wrote it all down – it was one of the last things he did. He was so ill by then that I had to help him with it; perhaps that's why he told me, but I prefer to think he did that because he wanted to. Aubrey came to collect it, and he spoke to Walter. I don't know what he said but afterwards it seemed that Walter was happy to die. Like he'd found some peace.'

The existence of such a document could well explain why someone had been willing to take the risk of entering Aubrey's office on the night of his death, Penrose thought; its removal was vital to anyone wanting to protect Vintner's reputation. He wondered how Josephine's ordeal fitted into the pattern of events. 'When did Walter die, Mrs Simmons?' he asked.

'In September last year. It was just after that trial, and of course Vintner committed suicide shortly after that. Everyone assumed it was because he lost in court, but it wasn't that – it was something far deeper. He knew by then that he'd soon be back in the dock. Vintner was stupid to bring that case with Aubrey on the other side, but he thought he was invincible. It was another way to taunt Aubrey for the past, but it backfired on him. He lost, and Aubrey took the opportunity to make it clear that it was only a matter of time before he'd lose far more. Vintner had no idea that Walter and Aubrey had been in contact, you see, but by then it was too late for him to do anything about it – Walter was beyond threats and Aubrey implied that the police had already been told. So Vintner took the coward's way out, but it was Aubrey's taunting that drove him to it.'

So Vintner had simply been using Josephine to get at Aubrey. All the anguish, all the remorse she had suffered after Vintner's suicide was because she had been caught up in a deadly game between two men. No wonder Aubrey had been so loyal in his support for Josephine, but how could he have allowed her to assume responsibility for someone's death when the blood was anywhere but on her hands? Penrose had watched as all the joy had been stripped from Josephine's success. He had sat with her for hours, trying to convince her that she was not to blame for Vintner's decision to take his own life – but nobody could tell you that you weren't responsible for someone's death; you had to feel it in your heart. If anyone understood that, he did.

'I kidded myself that Vintner's suicide would be the end of it,'

Alice Simmons continued, 'but of course it wasn't. Death wasn't enough for Aubrey – at least not if it came at a time of Vintner's choosing. Aubrey wanted his name linked to what he'd done, to expose him as a murderer rather than as some sort of broken man who deserved pity. His plan was to bring everything out in the open as soon as Elspeth turned eighteen. He'd put all the money from *Richard of Bordeaux* in a trust fund for her – I suppose he thought that was some sort of justice with all the trouble that had gone on. She would have come of age next month, but someone was obviously determined that should never happen.'

'Was there anyone else involved in Arthur's murder?'

'No, just Walter and Vintner. No one else knew until Aubrey found out.'

So who on his list could have been close to Vintner? Who would kill to protect his name? In a book, this was the moment when a striking resemblance would suddenly spring to mind, Penrose thought drily, but he would have to do it the hard way, and his heart sank at the thought of tracing endless family trees. Was that why the number for Somerset House was on Aubrey's blotter, he wondered? Had Aubrey been trying to make the link himself before he died? And had he been successful? At least those questions might be answered in the morning when everyone got back to work after the weekend. In the meantime, he must talk to Josephine to see if she had learned anything about Vintner during the trial. And, just as importantly, to give her some sort of freedom from her unwarranted guilt.

Alice Simmons seemed to read his thoughts. 'Betty told me about Miss Tey and her kindness to Elspeth,' she said. 'I'm sorry she went through what she did because of Vintner. I know there's no consolation for that, but it will have meant so much to Elspeth to have met her – she so loved her work. Will you tell her that for me?'

Penrose smiled kindly at her. 'It would be nice if you told her yourself – she'll want to meet you and talk. And knowing Josephine, that's exactly what will console her for what she went through.'

'I'd like to see her. You know, Elspeth always thought I hated theatre but I didn't. I was just afraid of it. It hurt me so much not to be able to share that with her but I was so scared of her being pulled into another life, one that I couldn't compete with. I wonder if all women who adopt worry about their happiness being snatched from them, or if it was just because we didn't do it properly? It was even worse after Walter died and I had to face it on my own, and when Aubrey told me about the trust fund I knew things would never be the same. It would have made her so happy, to be welcomed like that into a world she loved but could only dream of. It's right that she should have had that chance, but I'd be lying if I said I was glad about it. I thought she'd forget about me, and the love we had was the one thing that made what Walter did bearable. If that went, everything would have been in vain. So much loss and pain and evil, all for nothing.' She sighed heavily. 'I knew I'd lose her eventually, but I never expected it to happen like this. I suppose you have to believe in some kind of judgement, though, don't you?'

'I don't think judgement is something we're entitled to pass, Mrs Simmons,' Penrose said softly, 'either on other people or on ourselves. It's too big a word. But if it helps, I don't think there's anything to regret in loving Elspeth or wanting to protect her. I know you feel that Walter did what he did for you, but it was his decision.'

She met his eyes, and Penrose could all but trace every moment of the last forty-eight hours in the lines on her face. 'That's kind, Inspector,' she said. 'The trouble is, if it meant missing out on those years with Elspeth, I wouldn't give that boy his life back even if I could, and that *is* something I'll be judged for when the time comes.'

Fourteen

Peace was an infrequent visitor to 66 St Martin's Lane, but one which Josephine welcomed with open arms whenever it arrived; on a Sunday afternoon, when there was so much for her to think about, it was more eagerly greeted than ever. She looked at her watch, reckoning to have half an hour or so of solitude before she was disturbed – time to collect her thoughts and bring some sort of order to the studio's chaos. The doorbell rang before she had made much headway with either.

'Archie! What a nice surprise! I thought you were Marta.'

'Oh God, are you expecting the redoubtable Miss Fox?' he asked, feigning a look of horror. 'Perhaps I should have brought Bill for back-up after all.'

She laughed, and kissed him. 'I'm afraid she *is* imminent. I telephoned them earlier to see how things were after last night, but Lydia was out. Marta sounded so down that I found myself asking her over for tea. They're having problems, I think, and she said she needed to talk.'

'Do you actually like her? Or is this just support for Lydia through another romantic crisis?'

Amused by his cynicism, Josephine led him through to the studio. 'Don't sound so weary about it. Lydia can't help being a little . . .'

'Flighty?' he suggested provokingly as she paused to find the right word.

'Unsettled,' she countered, smiling. 'And yes, I do like Marta – very much, in fact. I hope they'll work it out, but it would take a remarkable woman to be happy to play second fiddle to Lydia's career. Marta may prove to be remarkable, of course, as well as redoubtable – we'll see. But don't worry – if she turns up while you're still here, I'll look after you. Not that you need protecting – that parting shot you delivered last night was chastening to the point of humiliation. I don't think you'll have any more trouble.' She gave up trying to find an uncluttered space on the room's incongruous collection of chairs. 'Let's sit on the floor, but I'll get you some coffee first. You look shattered.'

'No, don't bother. I need to talk to you and it sounds like we haven't got much time on our own. You are on your own? There's no one lurking in the kitchen?'

'No, the girls have gone out to lunch with George and the Snipe is with her maker – in the temporary sense, I mean. You know how it is on a Sunday.'

'Of course.' Archie laughed but only half-heartedly, and Josephine had an ominous sense of déjà vu. What was he going to tell her now? Surely there was no room left this weekend for yet more tragedy? 'Is this about Hedley White?' she asked. 'I gather you've caught up with him.' Archie raised an eyebrow questioningly, so she explained. 'That's where Marta said Lydia had gone – to the Yard, to see if you'll let her see him. You must have just missed her. Apparently she's worried about him. Are you as convinced as she is that he's done nothing wrong?'

'I certainly don't think he's killed anybody,' Archie said. 'I'm fairly sure he's lying about where he was when Elspeth died and, if so, he's persuaded Rafe Swinburne to give him an alibi, but I don't honestly believe there's anything sinister in that. He wouldn't be the first suspect to assume things would look better for him if he could prove he wasn't on his own. We're doing the usual tests but I don't think he's got anything to fear from the results.' He told her how upset White had seemed at the news of Aubrey's death, and added, 'His troubles won't go away just because we think he's innocent, so I'm pleased Lydia's supporting him. He'll need help to get him through losing two people he loved. But Hedley's not why I'm here – things have moved on since I spoke to him. I got your message about the iris. Was the reference to the flower of chivalry in Vintner's book, by any chance?'

'Yes it was,' she said, surprised. 'I started to read Marta's manuscript this morning and it reminded me of Vintner's novel – not the story, that's modern and completely different – but the style. I know she admired his first book. But how on earth did you guess?'

'Because he's raising his ugly head in the unlikeliest of places, and judging by what I've heard about him in the last couple of hours, irises would have been on his mind when he sat down to write *The White Heart*. Chivalry, on the other hand, wouldn't be something he was qualified to talk about.' He noticed that her face had clouded over as it always did when Vintner's name was mentioned, and the anger he had felt since speaking to Alice Simmons was only partly tempered by the knowledge that he could now dispel Josephine's guilt once and for all. 'I need you to listen carefully to what I'm going to tell you, and to believe me,' he said. 'You are not responsible for Elliott Vintner's death.'

'It doesn't help to keep going over this, Archie,' she said dismissively, and started to get up. 'You and I will always disagree about it and it just makes it worse for me if . . .'

He caught her arm and gently turned her face towards him. 'But this time it's not just my voice. Would you believe it from someone who knew Vintner? Someone who would swear that his suicide was down to something that happened years ago, long before you ever wrote a play or heard his name?'

Josephine looked at him, confused by his words and hardly daring to acknowledge that they hinted at a reprieve for her. 'But he left a note explaining why he did it,' she said. 'It was read out at the inquest. He claimed that losing the court case had ruined him, financially and emotionally, and the papers went to town on it because he blamed me for everything.' Contrary to the advice of all her friends, Archie included, Josephine had attended Vintner's inquest, determined to face her demons. Not even in her worst nightmares could she have predicted how unpleasant it would be, though, and she would never forget the anger she had felt when she first heard the contents of that suicide note. Sitting in a sweltering court room, flanked by Ronnie and Lettice who had insisted on going with her, she had listened as the last words of a dead man accused her of stealing his work, and the law of sanctioning her theft. What frustrated her most, however, was not the smug, self-righteous tone or the unfairness of the charge but the irrational sense of shame which overwhelmed her then and which had dogged her ever since. Afterwards, despite numerous requests from journalists and several newspaper stories which painted her as the villain of the piece, she had adamantly refused to speak out in her own defence, partly from a determination to guard her privacy but mostly from a fear that she would not be very convincing. 'It was a masterly piece of prose, that note,' she added bitterly now. 'Much more affecting than most of his books. He even asked for God's forgiveness on my behalf. He could afford to be benevolent, I suppose, because I'm sure he knew I'd never forgive myself.'

'Exactly. I'm not saying that Vintner didn't resent you. He was a spiteful bastard and I'm sure he took a great deal of pleasure in knowing he could go on hurting you long after he was dead, but that isn't why he killed himself. It was a smokescreen, Josephine. You were caught up in a deadly game between two powerful men and it was convenient for them both to use you, one more maliciously than the other.' He paused to make sure she was taking in what he was saying. 'You see, if Vintner had given the real reason for deciding to take his own life, it would have been a confession to murder.'

She listened, at first incredulous and then shocked, as Archie outlined the connection between Elliott Vintner and Bernard Aubrey. He had not got far before her relief was dispelled by an immense sadness. She had thought nothing could be worse than the burden of responsibility which she carried, but she had reckoned without an act of pure evil that had cut so many lives short and filled others with pain and loss. Now, who could say when this new nightmare would be over? Several minutes passed before she was aware that Archie had stopped talking and was waiting for her response. The truth had been his gift to her, she knew, and he wanted her to be comforted by it, but all she felt was grief – grief for those who had died so suddenly and for the horror which she felt sure was still to come, and a deeper, less tangible sorrow for the fundamental cruelty of the world.

'Are you all right?' Archie asked gently.

'Yes and no,' she said. 'I will be, but all I can think about now is how sorry I feel for Elspeth. I keep remembering something she said about hoping her real family had some theatrical blood in it. Never in her wildest dreams could she have hoped to be related to the father of the West End. She would have been so thrilled, and yet it's the very reason she's dead.'

'Aubrey set up a trust fund for her from the profits of *Richard of Bordeaux*, you know.'

'That makes sense. Lydia said he'd given money to a charity to help families who'd suffered losses in the war. Funny, isn't it, how something that's broadly true can hide so much.'

'Yes. In this case, the charity really did begin at home. Elspeth would have come into the money next month when she turned eighteen – and he planned to tell her everything then, as well. Alice Simmons was terrified of the effect it would have on their relationship. She thought she was going to lose the only thing that mattered to her.'

'I can understand that. It's so hard for anyone on the outside to know how families work, but Elspeth didn't strike me as a girl who'd forget love. There's no doubt she would have embraced a connection to something she was so passionate about, but not at the expense of the life she already had. If anything, knowing where she came from might have settled her and satisfied the restless curiosity that Betty spoke about.' She sighed heavily. 'It hardly feels right to sit here speculating over lives we didn't understand and people we didn't know when there's no future left for any of them. Elspeth didn't make it to eighteen, for God's sake, and I can't even begin to contemplate what hell Alice Simmons is going through. In all of this, I think it's her I feel for most. What a burden that must be to carry. Confession is a very selfish thing, it seems to me. I'm sure Walter felt much better afterwards, but I can't help thinking it would have been kinder of him to take his secret to the grave rather than pass the guilt on to his wife.'

'That's all very well, but are you honestly telling me that if you were in her position you'd rather not be told the truth?'

There was an urgency in his words and Josephine understood that he was asking two questions, only one of which was about Alice Simmons. She thought before answering, realising what was at stake, and said eventually, 'You're right, of course. I would have wanted to know – when the time was right. But I'd rather not have had to wait until one of us was on our deathbed.' Archie had walked over to the window now, and she had no way of knowing if he realised the significance of what she was saying. When he did not speak, she continued, but on safer ground. 'I wonder what happened to Elspeth's real mother? Or how much she knew about what happened to Arthur?'

He turned round, and she was sad to see how relieved he seemed to pull back from the conversation he had tentatively begun. 'I don't know. Alice Simmons thinks Vintner was capable of finding a way to dispose of her, and she could well be right. I was hoping you might be able to help me there. Did you learn anything about Vintner's background during the trial? Anything that might help us link what we know about Arthur's death with the current murders?'

'Well, I wasn't exactly in the mood to be impartial about him, but I remember being surprised by how arrogant and manipulative he was. I know hindsight's a wonderful thing but I can easily see now that he would be capable of murder, and confident of getting away with it. At the time, though, what struck me was how at odds his personality was with the sensibility of his book. It seemed extraordinary that someone so narcissistic – and now, as it turns out, so evil – could have written a novel with such compassion and insight.' She thought about what Marta had said on the subject, and added, 'His later books were much more in character – very masculine, almost to the point of misogyny. But *The White Heart* showed a real understanding of women. He painted the historical relationship between Richard and Anne in very human terms and made them real people. That's supposed to be what I stole from him. There was nothing like that in his other books – they tended to be full of relationships founded on power, even cruelty. I suppose he'd argue now that his wife's betrayal with Arthur changed his view of women.' She considered that for a moment. 'Who's to say what effect it had? But you didn't ask for a literary critique of his work, did you?'

'No, although it's interesting that his outlook changed so radically. I'm sorry to revert to something more superficial, but did he remind you of anybody? Did he look like anyone you know from the theatre?'

She smiled at the thought that someone who prided himself on his intellectual and emotional approach to detection had been forced to fall back on such a storybook line of enquiry. 'Not that I can think of, but you were in court for a while as well. What do you think?'

'I only saw him briefly. You had a chance to study his mannerisms, and I suppose I was hoping for some miraculous moment of revelation when you realised that he scratched his head in exactly the same way as Terry, say, or Fleming.'

Now they were both laughing at the absurdity of his question, and some of the earlier tension between them disappeared. 'Definitely not Johnny,' she said. 'Vintner would never have entertained all that feminine grace. Fleming's dark-haired, I'll give you that, but it's not much to go on.'

'What about Esme McCracken?'

'Who?'

Archie smiled. 'I can't tell you how furious she'd be if she knew you weren't even aware of her existence. She speaks very highly of you. She's the stage manager and about Vintner's age.'

'Oh yes, I know. The pinched woman who writes plays. Johnny says they're actually quite good. I'm afraid I can't recall precisely what she looks like, though, so I can't help you there.'

'What about family? Do you remember any relatives from the trial? Was there anyone there to support him?'

'No, only his lawyer.' She thought for a moment. 'He did have a family, though. I remember now – he played the big sympathy card about having to bring up his son on his own. That's why he started writing, apparently – he needed to stay at home and earn money. But there was no indication of how he lost his wife.'

'And the son wasn't in court?'

'No. I don't think he was even mentioned by name. I certainly don't remember it if he was.'

'Any idea what he does or where he might be?'

'No. There were obituaries after the suicide, of course, but nothing very significant. Vintner's reputation soon dwindled when each book turned out to be a bigger flop than the last. By the time he died, the general feeling was that the most exciting plot development he'd come up with in years was to shoot himself. Still, the papers might tell you something about his family life.'

'Yes, they might. It's a good place to start, at least.'

'Do you know how he found out about the affair?' Josephine asked.

'He read a letter that was meant for Arthur. I remember letters from home getting mixed up all the time – it was a miracle they got there at all. They arrived in one big pile, and there was such a stampede to get to them. You can just imagine it, can't you? Vintner automatically reaches for something in his wife's handwriting and then notices it's not for him; he's hardly likely to put it back on the pile and say nothing. It was a stupid thing to do, really – to send something so damning with no guarantee of its getting to the right person.' There was a sound of footsteps on the stairs. 'That's my cue to get going,' he said. 'The Fox woman's on the prowl.'

'You don't have to rush off,' Josephine said. 'She really isn't as fierce as all that.'

He grinned. 'No, but it sounds like she needs a heart-to-heart without interruptions. Anyway, I've left Bill chasing phone numbers and post-mortem reports, so I ought to see how he's getting on. And I want to have a look for those obituaries. Tracing Vintner's son is vital – he's the obvious candidate if we're looking for someone desperate to protect Vintner's reputation.'

Before he could go any further, though, the front door was flung open with almost indecent vigour. 'Only us,' called Ronnie from the hallway. 'Has anyone else died while we've been at lunch?' She sauntered into the room and collapsed onto the chaise longue, apparently oblivious to the pile of sketches that she was sitting on. 'Shouldn't you be out catching criminals, cousin dearest?'

Archie flashed what Josephine had come to recognise as his Ronnie smile. 'I'm on my way to do just that,' he said. 'I'd hate to think that your exquisite neck was in peril.'

'Oh do stay and have some tea, Archie,' Lettice said on her way through to the kitchen. 'I'm gasping for a hot drink. Guermani's was so crowded today that we ended up on the table next to the Daintrey-Smythes and you know how Angelica gets on my tits. I couldn't possibly stay for coffee – as it was, dessert took endurance beyond all measure. All those loud-but-oh-so-self-effacing references to her double-page spread in *The Sketch* when we know full well what she had to spread to get it. It's enough to make a witch spit.'

Archie had to laugh at this uncharacteristic outburst from his cousin, who normally left vulgar asides to her more experienced sister, but he stuck to his guns about going. His goodbyes were drowned by a squeal from the next room. 'Oh lovely!' Lettice exclaimed, and emerged carrying a vase with a single flower that looked a little the worse for wear. 'You brought something to cheer Josephine up, Archie. How thoughtful. And what an extraordinary colour.'

'Good tactic, dear – move in when she's vulnerable,' piped up Ronnie. 'You may get somewhere at last. A little tip, though – bring one that's alive next time.'

'Stop teasing him,' said Lettice, but Archie just stared at the flower, oblivious to them all.

'Archie didn't bring it,' Josephine said quickly, in case he was feeling awkward. 'I found it tucked in Marta's manuscript. She must have forgotten it was there. She thinks Lydia left it at stage door for her but I know she didn't, so, for harmony's sake, I thought I'd better find a home for it. Another admirer on the scene isn't what their relationship needs right now.'

'Is there trouble, then?' Ronnie asked wickedly, settling in for a good story, but Archie interrupted before Josephine could feel obliged to satisfy her curiosity.

'You say that belongs to Marta?' he asked, looking thoughtful.

'Yes. Why?'

'And Lydia definitely didn't give it to her?'

'No, she just looked bewildered when Marta thanked her for it. Is it important? Why do you look so worried all of a sudden?'

'Because I've already seen one flower like that today, and I don't think it's a coincidence. The first was at Grace Aubrey's – she had a vase of them. Bernard planted them for her, apparently. Its common name is widow iris.'

'All this horticultural chat is fascinating, but I'd rather shoot myself than take up gardening so would you mind telling us what your point is,' Ronnie said, but Josephine understood immediately what Archie meant.

'You think Bernard's killer left it for Marta as some sort of message, don't you?' she said, and Lettice slammed the vase down on the cocktail cabinet and moved hurriedly away from it. 'And if that's the case, the obvious implication is that Lydia's next.'

As Ronnie and Lettice looked at him in disbelief, Archie said, 'I certainly think she could be in danger, and whoever's doing this is capable of anything. It's funny – Lydia's been on the periphery of everything this weekend; she was at the station with you when Elspeth was killed and she found Bernard's body. It's all too close for comfort, but at least she's safely at the Yard now – I think that's the first stroke of luck we've had since this started. I'd better get back straight away and make sure she's still there. Just before I go, though – is there any chance that Lydia could be in some way connected to Aubrey other than through the theatre? This is confidential,' he added, looking pointedly at Ronnie, whose expression implied she had much to teach the Virgin Mary on the subject of innocence, 'but Aubrey left her a considerable lump sum in his will. I just wondered if she could possibly have had any part to play in what happened with Arthur?'

'I really don't think so,' Josephine said. 'I haven't known her that long, of course, but we have talked a lot about our lives and she's never mentioned anything that could possibly fit in. She had a brother who was shot in the trenches, but I'm sure she didn't meet Bernard until long after the war was over.'

'I'm not surprised he wanted to look after her financially,' Lettice added. 'They really were good friends, you know, and he valued her opinion on everything. I think she was closer to him than anyone, and of course he always admired her professionally. He wasn't one to let sentiment interfere with his business, but their personal friendship would have been strong enough to last through any decisions that the actress in Lydia didn't like.'

Josephine agreed. 'Lydia has a talent for friendship, if not for relationships,' she said. 'She was always fiercely loyal to Bernard and I think he prized loyalty above most things. It's not a terribly common currency in theatre.'

'But if the killer suspects they were close enough for Bernard to have confided in her about Arthur, that would be enough to make her a target,' Archie said. 'I'll go and speak to her, and I'll telephone to let you know she's all right. Would you explain the situation to Marta when she gets here? I'm afraid it'll mean coming clean about the flower, but try not to alarm her too much. I could be over-reacting and Lydia could be perfectly safe – let's hope so – but I don't want another death on my hands, so I've got to consider every possibility. I'm happy to look stupid – even in front of Marta Fox – but not negligent.'

'Is Marta coming over?' asked Lettice, casting another suspicious glance at the flower which had so recently enchanted her.

'Yes, in fact she should be here by now.' Josephine looked at the clock, still distracted by what Archie had said. 'I wonder what's keeping her?'

'Perhaps she's sparing a thought for nervous policemen.' Archie smiled and kissed her goodbye. 'Try not to worry about Lydia,' he said reassuringly. 'I won't let anything happen to her, even if I have to keep her under lock and key for her own protection.'

'Thanks, Archie,' Josephine said, walking him to the door. 'And not just for that.' When she returned to the middle studio, she was surprised to see that Ronnie and Lettice had put their coats on. 'Are you going out again already?'

'Apparently so,' said Ronnie peevishly. 'It seems we've got to walk the streets to give you time to reassure Marta in peace.'

'Don't be silly,' Lettice said. 'We can go to George's for an hour or two. It would be better for you if you were on your own with her, wouldn't it?' she asked Josephine. 'You'll be all right?'

'Of course I will. I don't want to drive you out again, but it would make things easier and I'll bring you up to date when you get back. There's an awful lot you don't know yet.'

'Yes, like who the fuck Arthur is for a start,' Ronnie called over her shoulder as they clattered down the stairs. Josephine waited a minute or two, then picked up the telephone. It was more than an hour now since she had spoken to Marta, and Lydia's flat was only a ten-minute walk away. Where on earth could she have got to? Anxiously, she waited for a reply but none came. Perhaps Marta had simply got carried away with something else, but was now on her way? She was about to replace the receiver when the call was answered and she heard Marta's voice, sharp and slightly agitated.

'Hello?'

'It's Josephine. Are you all right?'

'Of course. Why shouldn't I be?' she snapped, then softened. 'I'm sorry, Josephine, I should have telephoned. I can't come over after all – not at the moment, anyway. Perhaps later – but I'll ring first. I need some time on my own. All right?'

It could be her imagination, but it seemed to Josephine that she was being despatched as quickly as possible. Why was that, she wondered? 'That's fine. I hope you and Lydia work it out, but you know where I am if I can help.'

'It was very sweet of you to offer, but I think it's something we need to sort through ourselves.'

As Josephine recalled, it was Marta who had asked rather than she who had offered, but there was no point in splitting hairs. 'Have you heard from Lydia?' she asked.

'No. I told you – she's at the police station. I don't expect her back for a while yet. Now, I really must go. Perhaps I'll see you tomorrow.'

There was no further explanation, and Josephine heard the line go dead long before she had a chance to raise the subject of Lydia's safety. God, Marta was volatile. How could her attitude have changed so much in such a short time? It was like speaking to two different people. She was about to hurry down to the street to stop the girls making themselves scarce unnecessarily, but paused as she passed the ominous flower, incongruously dumped between bottles of Cointreau and crème de menthe. The widow iris. Of course, in her anxiety for Lydia she hadn't thought to tell Archie that Marta was already a widow. Could that be significant? She tried to remember what Marta had actually told her: there was very little to go on – just that the marriage had been unhappy and that her husband had died; at the time, Josephine had assumed she meant during the war but, looking back, she realised that Marta hadn't actually said that. When had the relationship turned sour, she wondered? She reflected on the letters she had received from Lydia, hoping that some of them might have contained information about Marta's background, but the facts were remarkable only in their scarcity. Certainly, though, someone who was unhappily married didn't bother to write stories for her husband and send them to the front; that was an act of love. So what had gone wrong? Unless, of course, those stories had been sent to her husband's regiment but not actually to her husband.

Josephine sat down, still looking at the widow iris. She was used to working back from an unlikely starting point to see if she could build a plausible chain of events, but no scenario she had considered in her fiction could compete with the story now playing in her mind. Could it be that Marta's interest in Elliott Vintner was more personal than that of one writer in another? Surely there were too many objections to the idea that Marta had been Vintner's wife and Arthur's lover? For a start, she didn't seem the type to stand by and do nothing about the crime that had been committed: wouldn't she have created hell about Arthur's death – if she suspected it wasn't an accident, that is? But perhaps that was a little naive:

Josephine was well aware that the independence she had always enjoyed was still the exception rather than the norm, and things would have been very different for a young married woman twenty years ago; she shouldn't underestimate how difficult it would have been for someone shackled to a man like Vintner to stand up for herself, let alone for anyone else. If he showed the sort of violence towards his wife that he was clearly capable of, who could say what abuse she had suffered or what sort of fear she lived in; and because she had been unfaithful, society would have been against her, too. Pregnant with another man's child, she would have been utterly at his mercy and completely alone in the world.

After he died, though, she would no doubt have moved heaven and earth to find her daughter; was that why she was here? Even for Josephine, it was far too much of a coincidence that Marta should happen to turn up in a circle of people who were so connected to the other part of her life – if that's what it was. Had she moved in on Lydia merely as a way to get to Aubrey, and so to Elspeth? Was it Lydia who was being used after all? She remembered the look of pain in Marta's eyes the night before when she had believed herself to be unimportant in her lover's life; that had been genuine, Josephine was sure, but perhaps Marta was dealing with feelings she had not expected to have, feelings which would have complicated things if she had simply been waiting for the right moment to let Aubrey know who she was and to be reintroduced into her daughter's life. With a start, Josephine realised that Marta and Elspeth had come within a whisker of meeting at the station: was that why Marta had disappeared to find a taxi? If she had recognised Elspeth, she wouldn't want to be forced into an introduction on a railway platform.

Josephine was so absorbed by the narrative she was creating that it took her a few moments to spot the obvious flaw. She was being ridiculous, of course; if Marta were Elspeth's mother, she'd be behaving very differently now. She'd seen enough of Marta since Friday night to know if she were grieving for a lost daughter: that wasn't the sort of thing that could be kept hidden. No, she could just about believe that Marta was capable of keeping her composure while Lydia discussed Arthur's murder in front of her, but the tragedy of a daughter's death was not something that could be borne in private. In any case, with Elspeth gone there would be no more need for secrecy.

Nevertheless, there was still something that bothered Josephine about Marta. She might have woven an intricate fantasy around the woman's past, but she had not imagined the echoes of Vintner's first novel in her manuscript, nor her strange behaviour just now on the telephone. Things needed to be clarified and there was only one way to do it. She picked up her gloves from the table in the hall and took her coat from its hook, then – without really knowing why – she went back to fetch the flower. As she walked across the cobbled courtyard and out into St Martin's Lane, she could not quite rid herself of a niggling suspicion that it wasn't Lydia who was in danger after all.

The five-minute journey back to Scotland Yard seemed one of the longest Penrose had ever taken and he was relieved to be back in its long corridors, surrounded by the familiar police-station smell of disinfectant and typewriter ribbons. As he walked through the building to find Fallowfield, he tried to plan – as far as he could – the next few hours of the investigation. Exploring Vintner's background and tracing his son was now a priority, and he needed to bring his sergeant up to date and then talk to Lydia. After that, it was time to call a conference with the whole team to discuss the murders from every angle, review the work done over the weekend and take advantage of all the information that could be gleaned from the Yard's various expert departments. It was the first duty of any detective in charge of a case to co-ordinate this complex web of knowledge, ensuring that every detail – no matter how insignificant it seemed – was available to everyone. He enjoyed his role tremendously: it gave him the chance to test his own thoughts on the case and to gain a full understanding of other lines of enquiry which might come unexpectedly into play. In other words, it satisfied him that he was in control.

He found Fallowfield in the long, pillared CID office, studying a wall of maps which showed every street in the London area. The Sergeant was talking to Seddon, who listened intently to every word, and – not for the first time – Penrose blessed the day he had been given such a competent second-in-charge. He had always respected the way Fallowfield handled the team, giving them friendly encouragement and guidance without ever losing his authority, and he looked now with admiration at the scene in front of him – a room full of men engaged in the methodical and frequently tedious aspects of police work, but tackling it willingly and with great determination.

As soon as he saw Penrose, Fallowfield got up and made his way over to him through a sea of desks and green filing cabinets. His excitement was obvious. 'Good timing, Sir. We've just got the breakthrough we needed. Constable Seddon's got through to the number on Aubrey's desk – the one down south that no one was answering.'

'And?' Penrose asked, glancing approvingly at Seddon.

'The number belongs to a landlady in Brighton, Sir,' Seddon explained after a nod from Fallowfield. 'She runs two boarding houses down there which provide digs for theatre people on tour. Apparently, Bernard Aubrey had been in touch with her recently, asking her to confirm some bookings she had a couple of years ago for the cast of *Hay Fever*. He sent her a programme to look at to see if she recognised any of the actors – and she did. She telephoned Aubrey on Saturday night and told him.'

The boy's excitement was infectious. 'Who was there?' Penrose asked urgently.

'It was someone called Rafe Swinburne, Sir. She recognised his face from Aubrey's programme, but the name confused her. You see, when he was in *Hay Fever* he wasn't listed as Rafe Swinburne. He was listed as Rafe Vintner.'

'Rafe Swinburne? You mean we just stood there and watched Vintner's son walk away?' Penrose was furious with himself. 'That wasn't an overnight bag – he was packing to leave right in front of me.' He could scarcely countenance the nerve it must have taken for Swinburne to answer his questions with such casual arrogance when he knew how much was at stake, but it fitted the audacity of both murders perfectly. 'It's his father's egotism all over again. How could I have been so bloody stupid?'

'To be fair, Sir, you didn't know what we were looking for then,' Fallowfield said, but logic only made Penrose's expression even more thunderous.

'Put the call out right away,' he barked at Seddon, whose sense of triumph was fading fast, 'and get his photograph in the next *Gazette* along with a description of the bike. It's an Ariel Square Four – do you know what that looks like?' Seddon nodded. 'Christ, he could be anywhere by now on that thing. There's no point wasting manpower at the stations. He's not stupid enough to risk public transport, so I want every available car on the main routes out of the city.' Seddon hurried off but Penrose called him back. 'It was good work to keep on that number, Constable,' he said. 'Well done.' He turned to Fallowfield. 'Is Lydia Beaumont still here, Bill?'

'Yes, Sir. She's waiting downstairs to see White.'

'Good.' Penrose brought him quickly up to date. 'If Swinburne – or should I say Vintner – has done a runner, at least she's safe for now, but I still want to talk to her. Will you tell her I'll be down in a minute or two and reassure her about Hedley? Then go and see him again – find out what he knows about Swinburne's background and see if it was Swinburne who put him up to the alibi after all.' If Vintner did turn out to be their man, he thought, how on earth would Hedley feel when he realised he had shared rooms with Elspeth's killer? 'We need to get to the truth about that because at the moment it works for both of them.'

'Right, Sir. Anything else?'

'Yes, just a second.' Penrose picked up the telephone on the nearest desk, but there was no answer from his cousins' studio. If Marta had arrived and they were deep in conversation, perhaps Josephine would ignore the telephone? 'I want someone to keep an eye on 66. Get one of the officers at the theatre to pop over the road and make sure everyone's all right. If Josephine's there, I want someone on duty outside.'

'What shall I tell him to do if she's not?'

Penrose thought for a second. If Marta hadn't turned up, might Josephine have gone to look for her? 'Get Lydia's address – it's somewhere off Drury Lane – and send him there instead. Let me know as soon as you find her.'

Fifteen

Even late on a Sunday afternoon, Longacre seemed too narrow to hold all the traffic that wished to pass through it. Pleased to be on foot, Josephine hurried down the busy thoroughfare, and walked on through the heart of Covent Garden. At the end of the street, she turned right into Drury Lane and was relieved to be within a stone's throw of her destination; what little sun there had been seemed to have given up on the day before its time, but it was more than the gloomy bank of cloud and encroaching cold that made Josephine quicken her pace still further.

Lydia's lodgings were on the first floor of one of the artisan dwellings which had replaced the slums at the southern end of the street. Her rooms were instantly recognisable, even from a distance, thanks to a pair of typically flamboyant window boxes that underlined each sash with red and yellow wood and spilled their contents down towards the floor below. Lydia always joked that they were a way of keeping her hand in for the big house in the country when it finally arrived but, in truth, she had a gift for making a home anywhere; despite her mutterings about the impossibility of putting down roots, her digs were always welcoming, elegant and utterly her, and Josephine usually looked forward to spending time there. But not today. As she crossed the road, uneasy about the reception she would get from Marta, she noticed an elderly woman coming out of the house and recognised her as the occupant of the top-floor rooms. They had met once or twice at Lydia's spur-of-the-moment parties, and now she waved a cheerful greeting.

'I'll save you the bother of ringing, dear,' the woman called, holding the front door open. 'I hope you've got your tin hat with you, though. It didn't sound like a lazy Sunday afternoon when I went past.'

She was gone before Josephine had a chance to ask her what she meant. Perhaps Lydia had come home earlier than expected and they were 'sorting through things' as Marta had put it. If that was the case, it would be tactful to beat a hasty retreat but that didn't solve the problem of Lydia's safety and it didn't answer any of the questions she had for Marta. No, she'd have to brave it, if only briefly.

She had barely climbed half a dozen steps when Marta's voice rang down to meet her. 'If you'd been where you were supposed to be all weekend, we wouldn't be having this conversation,' she shouted. 'I've been trying to get hold of you since last night – where the hell were you? You must have known I'd want to speak to you. And what are you doing here now? I told you never to acknowledge me when I was with Lydia.'

'Make your mind up – either you want to see me or you don't.' The exchange certainly sounded like a lovers' quarrel but it was a man's voice, unfamiliar to Josephine and with a petulant quality which she instantly found disagreeable. Could Marta be having an affair? That might explain her moods and the mysterious flower, but Josephine found it hard to reconcile with what she had seen of Marta's feelings for Lydia. 'Anyway, your sainted Lydia isn't here, is she?' the man continued. 'I watched her leave. She looks a bit peaky, though – it must be the distress of losing a close friend.'

'Oh shut up and act your age – this isn't a game.' Marta's words were defiant, but she sounded upset rather than angry. 'I hate it when you behave like a child. We've got to stop what we're doing – it just doesn't make sense and innocent people are getting hurt. I can't live with it any more – I've got to tell Lydia.'

Even as she reached for the door, Josephine knew that the sensible decision would be to turn around and leave, but it was too late: carried forward by her curiosity and her concern for Lydia, she committed herself to the scene before weighing up the consequences. Inside the room, Marta stood next to Lydia's small piano, talking to a man who reclined on the low divan in front of her. He had his back to Josephine, but she could see his face reflected in a full-length Venetian mirror; he was handsome, although his features were marred by a sulkiness around the mouth which matched his voice, but what struck Josephine most was how unperturbed he seemed. Marta, on the other hand, had clearly been crying, and her tears seemed to bear out the vulnerability hinted at in her exchange with Lydia the night before.

'Josephine! What are you doing here?' she asked, her expression suddenly filled with horror.

Josephine ignored the question. 'What's going on, Marta? What have you got to tell Lydia? And who's this?'

Marta hesitated and tried to compose herself, but the fear in her voice made the attempted casualness of her next words sound absurdly false. 'It's Rafe Swinburne. He's from the theatre.'

Josephine recognised the name of Terry's choice for Bothwell in *Queen of Scots* but, before she could speak, Swinburne leapt to his feet and walked over to her.

'There's no need to be so coy, surely,' he said sarcastically. 'Stage names are for strangers, and Josephine's practically a friend of the family.' He held out his hand. 'I'm Rafe Vintner,' he said. 'I believe you knew my father.' He noticed the flower she was holding and turned back to Marta. 'I left that at stage door for you. I'm quite hurt that you should have given it away already.'

'You left it? Why?' Marta looked astonished, and Josephine could see very clearly who was in control of the alliance – whatever the alliance was. She remembered what Archie had said about Vintner's son, and realised the danger she had put herself in. How could she have been so stupid?

'I don't know why I left it, really,' Vintner was saying. 'Let's call it filial affection, shall we?'

'Rafe, don't – not in front of . . .' but Marta was interrupted before she could finish.

'Oh, the game's up, Mother,' Vintner said. 'It's a shame, I agree – my career was going rather well and I really did want that part in *Queen of Scots*. But it's time we called it a day. You see, I happen to know that a little bird's just flown down from Berwick-upon-Tweed to spoil the fun we've been having. In fact, she's probably doing it as we speak. That's why I'm here now – to tie up a few loose ends.'

Marta looked at her son as though he had gone completely insane, but Josephine was piecing together the most terrible of pictures. When she had considered a connection between Marta and Elliott Vintner, the stumbling block had been Marta's lack of grief for Elspeth; could the explanation for that really be that she was somehow implicated in her murder? Like most people, Josephine was reluctant to believe that a mother was capable of harming her child, and she stared at the woman she thought she had been getting to know in utter disbelief. What sort of monster would conspire with one of her children to destroy the other? Marta looked back in desperation, as if pleading with Josephine not to judge her, but suddenly her expression changed to one of pure fear. Turning round, Josephine saw that Rafe Vintner had placed himself in between her and the door. He had removed a scarf from a battered leather holdall and was now carefully unrolling it. Inside was a gun.

'Don't Rafe, please!' Marta cried, but Vintner was already moving back towards Josephine. Before she had a chance to register what was happening, he had grabbed her arm and turned her roughly round and she felt his breath on the back of her neck. The barrel of the gun was pressed hard into the small of her back and, in that moment, she understood what it meant to know true fear. She had written about it many times and, in the past, had been afraid for others – for Jack, of course, and for her mother as she lay dying – but this blind terror was something altogether different. It was a selfish, humiliating emotion, stronger than anything she had ever known.

'Don't you think it's a little late for such a sudden change of heart, *Mother*?' Vintner said, emphasising the last word in a way which scorned the relationship. For a second or two, he removed the gun from Josephine's back and used its barrel to trace the contours of her face. The steel was cold against her cheek and she tried to fight back the tears of anger and frustration, but in vain.

Vintner laughed quietly. 'So this is the great but elusive Josephine Tey,' he said. 'You know, Mother, she's not at all like the woman you described to me at the railway station when you were trying to tell me who to kill. How could you have got it so wrong? Still, there's always a second chance.' He turned back to Marta. 'You believe in second chances, don't you Mother? That's what this is about, isn't it? Being a family again after all these years. So don't go soft on me now – we started this together and we haven't finished yet.'

This time, the shock served to strengthen Josephine's resolve rather than destroy it. 'You told him to kill me?' she asked, looking incredulously at Marta. 'Why the hell would you want to do that?'

Marta stayed silent. 'Perhaps I was being a little disingenuous there,' Vintner said. 'It was my idea. After what you did to my father, you surely can't wonder why *I* would want to kill you? Mother just offered to help me out. We've been estranged for a while, you see, and she was so pleased to see me that I think she'd have agreed to anything.' Marta opened her mouth to speak but he interrupted her. 'There's no need for secrecy now, not with our little friend here,' he said, gesturing with the gun. 'And I'm sure Josephine would like to know that you weren't exactly opposed to the idea of bumping her off.' He put his mouth closer to Josephine's ear. 'In fact, it was her idea to do it in a crowd – she thought it would be a nice tribute to your little crime novel. And she had her own reasons for wanting you dead. It's a shame you don't have time to talk to her about them.'

'But you killed . . .' Josephine began, but Vintner put his hand quickly over her mouth. 'No, no, no,' he said. 'I see you're a few steps ahead of us, but all in good time. It's a shame to rush a good story – you should know that.' He paused. 'Where was I? Ah yes – your murder. You see, Mother was supposed to point you out to me and make herself scarce. The thing is, she was a little bit hasty in getting out of the way. She didn't wait to meet you properly and confused you with someone else, so she gave me the wrong information. Before you got here just now, she was even blaming Lydia for saying something about a hat.' He shrugged his shoulders and added sarcastically, 'A tragedy.'

With a mixture of horror, incredulity and pity, Josephine realised that Marta had no idea who her son had killed at King's Cross. As if to prove her right, Marta spoke again.

'You're frightening me, Rafe. This is not what the plan was. We're no nearer to finding your sister now than we were when I agreed to help you, and you promised we'd be a family again. I thought you wanted that as much as I do.'

'Aren't I enough for you then?' Vintner spat the words out, and the bitterness in his voice was almost as palpable to Josephine as the gun which rested in her back. She could not see his face, but she could tell from the growing fear in Marta's that the agreement which she had believed to exist between them was gradually being exposed as a lie. 'Do you have to have your bastard daughter to play happy families?' he continued, and Marta flinched as if the blow had been a physical one. 'Anyway, if you want to talk about promises, what about your promises to me? Like the one you made to add a little something to Bernard Aubrey's whisky. Thank God I didn't trust you to carry that off.'

'I couldn't do it – we'd already made one mistake.' Marta was crying again now. 'And he didn't need to die.'

'Oh he did, you know. He was far too close to the truth about everything, so it's just as well I made sure, isn't it? That's one broken promise. Then there are the promises you made to your husband, of course. You didn't keep those for very long, did you?'

'We've been through this time and time again. Your father was an evil man.'

'How the hell would you know? You turned your back on him after five minutes of marriage. He went off to fight for us, to fight for his country – and what do you do? Jump into bed with the gardener. I wasn't even five years old, for God's sake – what sort of effect do you think that had on me?'

'But you didn't know anything about it. I kept you out of the way.'

'Children wander, Mother. They're curious.' Vintner pushed

Josephine over to the divan and made her sit down next to Marta, while he took his place on the piano stool opposite them both. He rested the gun on his knee, and Josephine watched his fingers moving lightly over the trigger as he talked. 'I wonder if you remember my fifth birthday as clearly as I do? You gave me a kaleidoscope, and it was so beautiful I couldn't tear myself away from it. It was hot, and we had all the windows open in the house. You'd left me playing in my room and gone out to the garden for a while, and then suddenly I heard a man's voice and you were laughing. I thought it was Father, come home for my birthday, and I ran down to show him my present. I couldn't see you at first, but then I noticed the summer-house door was open. It was always your favourite place, remember? You went there to write and I was never allowed to go in, but I thought you wouldn't mind on my birthday and I knew you'd want me to come and see Father. Except it wasn't Father, was it? He was still choking on dirt in the trenches while you made other arrangements. One present for me and another for yourself, except your birthday came more than once a year. I remember standing outside the summer house, look- ing in at the window through all those fucking flowers you'd planted, and I was so frightened. That man had you pressed up against the desk and at first I thought he was hurting you, but then you cried out and I knew, even then, that it wasn't a cry of pain. So I ran away. Neither of you saw me, of course – you were too engrossed in each other. I went back upstairs and smashed that kaleidoscope so hard against the floor that it broke. You found me crying not long after, and you thought it was because I'd broken my present, so you put your arms around me – still smelling of him – and promised to get me a new one. You did, as well, I'll give you that, but of course you could never replace the thing that I really lost that day. I thought I was the most important thing in the world to you, and suddenly I realised I wasn't. After that, I noticed how many times you brushed me aside, how often you pretended to listen to what I was saying when you were really thinking about something else. And how often you went to the summer house, of course.'

'I'm so sorry, Rafe, but you don't understand what it was like for me.'

'Oh, I understand all right. Father sat me down and explained it to me. When he finally came back on leave, he wanted to know why I was so upset and I told him what I'd seen. I thought if he got rid of the other man you'd spend time with me, just like you used to. He didn't say anything at first, and then he made me repeat it to him, over and over again, every detail, asking about things I didn't understand. But he did nothing about it – not straight away, anyway. Eventually, he explained that he'd had to send you away and I thought that was my fault. I suppose, in a way, it was. After you'd gone, he'd sit in that summer house and brood for hours on end. It was your special place.' He seemed to make a conscious effort to drag himself back into the present, away from his memories. 'Still, I don't think you'd like it as much these days. The décor leaves a lot to be desired since Father blew his brains out there.'

Josephine knew her presence had been all but forgotten in the recriminations between mother and son. She looked at Marta, and was surprised to see that she seemed to be growing calmer as the exchange went on. Now, she leaned forward and put her hand on Vintner's shoulder. 'I wanted to take you with me more than anything in the world, but your father put me away and made sure I couldn't see you,' she said. 'You'll never know how it destroyed me to lose you, and I swear I'll make it up to you, but we need to stop this now. There's been enough violence.'

Vintner shook her off. 'You could never make it up to me. We could spend every day together for the rest of our lives and it wouldn't make up for those years of not having you. There was a time when I longed for you to reach out and touch me, but not any more.' He met her eyes, his own filled with hatred. 'As it happens, though, I have kept my promise to you. I've managed to trace your daughter. In fact, I've known who she is for some time. I was with her just the other day.'

Josephine would have given anything not to have noticed the small flicker of hope that passed across Marta's face before she walked into the trap her son had set for her. 'Why didn't you say? Where?'

'She was on a train,' Vintner said and sat back, waiting for the horrific truth to sink in.

Marta had gone a shade of white which Josephine had always believed to exist only for the dead. Her own sense of grievance had, she realised, all but disappeared in the face of this torture: whatever Marta had done, she did not deserve to be played with like this. Josephine reached out and took her hand. She was convinced the two of them were going to die very shortly anyway, so what danger was there in a little compassion? 'The girl who died on the train was called Elspeth Simmons,' she said and then, when Marta showed no sign of recognition, 'She was your daughter. Yours and Arthur's.'

As she uttered the words, she saw shock transform itself into the adamant disbelief which so often delayed the onset of grief. 'Don't be ridiculous,' Marta said, shaking her off. 'You just want to hurt me for what I tried to do to you. That couldn't possibly be true.'

'I'm afraid it is, Mother,' Vintner said, and there was a hardness in his voice which signalled to Josephine that his deadly game was reaching its conclusion. 'You see, what I haven't told you is that Father gave me a few instructions before he died. You don't think that pathetic note he left on his desk was his final word, do you? That was just something to be read out at the inquest for Tey's benefit.' He glanced at her for a second and then turned back to his mother. 'No – Elliott Vintner was capable of something far more creative than that. The very last thing he wrote was actually a letter to me. I've got it here, in fact.' He rested the pistol on the piano and took a sheet of paper – worn and dirty from repeated handling – out of the pocket of his corduroy trousers. Josephine recognised the scrawl of dark red ink from correspondence she had had by the same hand. 'Shall I share it with you?' He did not wait for an answer but unfolded the paper and started to read. 'To become an expert in murder cannot be so difficult,' he began, then paused and looked again at Josephine. 'You'll recognise that bit, of course, but guess what? It's actually true.'

He continued and Josephine knew that she was watching a performance, as carefully rehearsed as anything he had ever spoken on stage. She listened while the letter was read out, and Rafe Vintner's voice was replaced in her head by his father's, that low, confident drawl which had tried and failed to destroy her in court. These words, however, were far deadlier; the argument, more emotionally charged: '"We have always been close, Rafe, bound not just by our love for each other but by your mother's betrayal of us both. If that love means anything to you, you can keep it alive, even after I'm gone, but only if all traces of that betrayal are destroyed. I can tell you *how* to do that, but you must search within your heart to decide if I'm asking too much. If the answer to that is yes, then forgive me for asking and go on with your life as best you can; if, however, the answer is no, if you share any of the pain and resentment that has led me to ask such a thing of my son, then this is what you must do to protect my name and to lighten the burden which you will carry alone after I'm gone."' Rafe Vintner's voice was filled with emotion as he read on, outlining instructions from a dead man which had sealed the fates of Elspeth Simmons and Bernard Aubrey, and now seemed certain to do the same for Marta and for her. Josephine only had to look at Marta to know that Elliott Vintner's final wish – that she should be made to suffer beyond all measure before she died – was a *fait accompli*: she could see that Aubrey's relationship to Arthur had been as much a revelation to Marta as the identity of the girl on the train, and the combination would surely destroy her. 'That's the gist of it, anyway.' Vintner folded the letter carefully and put it back in his pocket before picking up the gun again. 'I won't bore you with the practical details at the end except to say that they were very thorough.'

There was silence in the room and Josephine wondered if his arrogance was such that he expected applause. When Marta eventually spoke, her voice was barely audible but surprisingly steady. 'So it wasn't a mistake at all. When we met at the theatre afterwards, you already knew exactly what you'd done.' It was a statement, not a question, but her son was eager to explain further.

'Oh yes. I had no intention whatsoever of killing Tey – not then, at least. I was going to *pretend* I'd misunderstood your description of her, but then you told me to go for the woman in the hat – so it ended up being your mistake. Never in my wildest dreams could I have hoped for that. It's the ultimate irony, don't you think? You instructed me to kill your own daughter. How Father would have laughed,' he said, turning to Josephine, 'to paraphrase your *splendid* play.'

'And then you tricked me into agreeing to kill Aubrey by making me panic,' Marta continued, 'knowing all along that, if I did, I'd be killing the last link with Arthur.'

'Yes. Neat isn't it? Two down, one to go.'

Josephine knew it was only a matter of time before Vintner carried out his father's instructions to the letter and added her to the tally as a bonus. Playing for time, and understanding that he was the type to enjoy talking about his cruelty, she said, 'How could you have known that Elspeth was going to be on that train? Or anywhere near me? We met by chance.'

'Not exactly. I gather from poor Hedley – he's a friend of mine, you know – that Bernard Aubrey arranged the tickets as a treat for his soon-to-be-acknowledged great-niece. In fact, Hedley saved me a lot of trouble all round. I knew who Elspeth was and what she was interested in – Father could tell me that much because he'd made it his business to keep an eye on things after he'd given her away. I knew I could arrange to bump into her, either at the theatre or at that ridiculous shop, but I thought I was going to have to seduce her myself to get her where I wanted. As it happened, Hedley did my dirty work for me and there was no need to venture into those murky waters, so I suppose I have to own up to a bit of help there. I couldn't believe my luck when Hedley came downstairs one night after the show and asked for an autograph for Elspeth Simmons. It only took a bit of gentle encouragement to get them together and, after that, I could always find out where she was. It was embarrassingly easy, really. He was so excited about her coming down this weekend that he never stopped talking about it and how thrilled she'd be that his precious Mr Aubrey had arranged for her to meet her favourite author. It was pathetic.'

Now Marta spoke up. Unlike Josephine, however, she was not trying to distract Vintner but to understand him. 'How could you have so much hate in you for someone you've never known?' she asked. 'She did nothing to you. She didn't even know you existed, for God's sake. That girl – your sister – was just as much a victim in all of this as you are. More so. And yet you took her life away just because your father told you to. What sort of puppet are you?'

'She was my half-sister, actually. Get it right, Mother. I did have my doubts, I admit, but you soon dispelled those for me. If I was ever remotely tempted to ignore Father and just settle for having a mother again, you put me off that straight away. Do you know how desperate you sounded when I came to see you in that pathetic place and offered to reunite you with your daughter? I thought Father was wrong about what you'd agree to do, but you actually wanted her – your piece of the gardener – so badly that you were prepared to kill. There was a time when I wanted you to love me that much but you never did, so I thought I might as well cut my losses and go ahead with Father's plan. He did love me, you see, so I thought I'd make one parent proud of me, at least.'

'Oh, he'd certainly be proud. You're in a class of your own.' Marta's defiance was surely a symptom of shock but it seemed to unsettle Vintner a little. Whatever reaction he had expected from her – horror, despair, grief – it had not been this and, for the first time, Josephine sensed that he had underestimated his mother. His response, though, was to continue to taunt her.

'So what if I did do it because Father asked me to?' he shouted. 'I loved him, and that doesn't make me a puppet. You destroyed him by what you did all those years ago, and what do you think my childhood was like after that? Believe me, I'm more than happy to do as he asked because his memory is worth protecting. What memories do I have of my mother to look back on? Oh yes, the one of you playing Lady Chatterley and fucking someone who wasn't fit to lick his boots. So yes, I killed for him and yes, I enjoyed it. I found your apology for a daughter in that railway carriage and I stabbed her with Father's bayonet. It's a shame she didn't know her own father, of course, but I left an iris with her in his memory – I thought you'd appreciate that. Aubrey had one, too, except his was an original. Your gardener kept a flower head in his tobacco tin – sent by you from our garden, presumably. Father found it on his body when he was dragged out of the dirt, and he kept it in case it came in useful.'

Marta was on her feet by now and Josephine recognised someone who had long ceased to care whether she lived or died. Vintner took a couple of steps towards her, tightening his hold on the pistol. 'And I did something in your honour, too, Mother. I shaved her head. That's what they do in asylums, isn't it? I would have made a better job of it but I was interrupted. Still, it's the thought that counts, and it was the least I could do for you. You said you always wondered if she looked like you. Well, she didn't really so I thought I'd make sure you had something in common. I'd hate for her to have been a disappointment after all these years.'

'For God's sake, you don't know anything about Elspeth – either of you.' Josephine's fear was quite forgotten in her indignation on Elspeth's behalf. 'You destroyed everything she had,' she shouted. 'Her childhood and her family, her sense of who she was and who she could be, and now even her life. Leave her some respect, at least.'

She had spoken without considering the impact of her words, but they served both to distract Vintner and to break Marta's self-control. Vintner only turned to Josephine for a matter of seconds, but it was long enough for his mother to hurl herself at him in fury with no thought for the danger she was in. It occurred to Josephine that Marta may have wanted him to fire and put her out of her misery but, if that was indeed the case, she was unlucky. The gun went off as she knocked him off balance but the only casualty was a small alabaster idol, given to Lydia as a present and kept on the mantelpiece. Vintner fell to the floor, dragging Marta down with him, and Josephine scoured the room frantically for something she could use as a weapon, but there was no need; as he went down, Vintner's head smashed into the corner of the piano stool and he lay still on the carpet, the gun a few inches from his hand.

Marta did not move immediately and Josephine began to wonder if she, too, was hurt, but eventually she raised herself onto her knees and looked at her son, then put her hand to his neck. 'He's still alive,' she said, and Josephine stepped across to pick up the pistol, but she was too slow. Marta got there first, and Josephine felt a resurgence of her earlier fear; no matter how much sympathy she had for Marta's grief, the woman had tried to kill her and here she was with a far more straightforward opportunity. But that was not what Marta had in mind. She stood staring down at her son, the gun levelled at his chest, and Josephine could not even begin to imagine the emotions that ran through her head as she held the life of her child in the balance. For a second or two, she thought Marta was actually going to pull the trigger but, in the end, the battle in her heart came out on the side of mercy. Instead, she held the gun out to Josephine.

'Here, take this,' she said wearily. 'I hope you won't need it, but just in case. Will you get him some help?'

Josephine took the weapon from her. It was the first time in her life that she had held something whose only purpose was to kill, and she was disconcerted by how natural it seemed, by how comfortably the weight of the gun rested in her hand. 'Where are you going?' she asked, although she thought she already knew the answer.

'To finish what he started. Or perhaps I should say to finish what I started all those years ago. I know I'm not in a position to ask for anything from you, but I'd like to end it in my own way. No one could punish me more than I can punish myself.'

'Marta, please, you don't have to do that,' Josephine said, and tentatively raised the gun.

'That would be such an easy way out for me, but not for you,' Marta said, gently lowering Josephine's hand. 'It's impossible to live with someone's blood on your hands – I should know – so I wouldn't want you to do it even if you were capable.' She knelt beside her son and lightly ran her fingers over his cheek. 'He's so like his father, you know. I don't know why I couldn't see it.' Quickly she stood up to leave the room but turned back as she got to the door. 'You can't possibly justify to someone why you tried to take their life, but I am sorry, Josephine. I really am.'

Then she was gone, and Josephine waited for the front door to close. Keeping her eyes on Elliott Vintner's son, she moved over to the telephone to call Archie.

As it happened, Scotland Yard arrived rather sooner than Josephine expected in the shape of a bewildered young constable who seemed more frightened of Rafe Vintner than she was; God help them if Vintner had been conscious, she thought. Minutes later, Archie's car screeched to a halt outside, flanked by an ambulance and a marked police vehicle.

'It really is the Flying Squad, isn't it?' she said when he appeared at the door, but Penrose was in no mood to joke.

'What the hell do you think you're doing coming here alone?' he yelled at her. 'Do you realise what could have happened to you?'

'I've spent the last hour trapped in a room by a madman with a gun, so I think I've got a fair idea,' she said sharply, then softened when she saw the panic in his eyes. 'But nothing did happen to me, Archie. I'm all right – honestly.'

As Vintner was lifted onto a stretcher and taken from the room, Josephine explained exactly what had happened. 'God, it's like something out of a Greek tragedy,' Penrose said when she had finished, and looked at Fallowfield, who was packing away the gun ready to remove it from the scene. 'We need to circulate Marta Fox's description immediately. If she leaves London we might never find her.'

Josephine signalled to Fallowfield to wait a moment. 'Will she hang for what she's done?' she asked.

Penrose considered. 'Probably not,' he said. 'She hasn't actually killed anyone and, from what you tell me, a good barrister could argue that she wasn't of sound mind when she agreed to help Vintner. She's been through so much and, ironically, the fact that she's been committed to an asylum will work in her favour in court.'

'Then I think I can tell you where she'll be, Archie. There's only one place she'd want to go now. But you have to let me speak to her.'

'Absolutely not,' he said. 'Never in a million years would I let you go near that woman after what's happened. She wants you dead, and she nearly got her wish.'

'If she still wanted to kill me, she could have done it easily just now,' Josephine argued. 'She gave me the gun, Archie – there's no danger for me any more. But there is for her. She's determined to die, you know, but I might be able to change her mind. Are you really going to stop me trying?'

Penrose hesitated, but Fallowfield backed her up. 'If anyone can get her to give herself up, Sir, Miss Tey can. And we can stay close by to make sure nothing happens to her.'

'All right,' Penrose said, making his mind up. 'But I'm not going to let you out of my sight this time.'

King's Cross was not as crowded as it had been when Josephine was last there, but the station still had an air of efficient busyness about it. The stable-yard clock over the entrance chimed six o'clock as she passed underneath it, and she walked quickly over to the huge boards that indicated arrivals and departures. As agreed, she left Penrose and Fallowfield to wait there and turned purposefully towards the trains.

Marta was standing a little way down the platform, between two trains preparing to depart and just yards from where the daughter she never knew had died. Josephine walked towards her, and sat down on a nearby bench. Certain her approach had been noted, she waited for Marta to speak.

'You were absolutely right, Josephine,' she said, turning round at last. 'I didn't know anything about my daughter, not even her name. What was she like?'

'She was a joy,' Josephine said simply. 'The sort of girl who could lighten your heart without ever realising she'd done it. There was nothing self-conscious about her, you see. She was warm and honest, and she didn't try to be anything she wasn't – and that's so rare. She had an innocence about her – and I do mean innocence rather than naivety. Life had been difficult for her at times; she found not knowing where she'd come from hard to accept, and there were problems in her adoptive family, but a lot of love, too, and she seemed blessed with a talent for happiness. Very few of us can claim that.' Sadly, she remembered Elspeth's sudden shyness about her new romance. 'She was at a crossroads in her life, as well; she'd just found love with Hedley and that seemed to have given her a new confidence, a real excitement about the future. You would have been pleased, I think, and so would she.'

Marta joined her on the bench. 'One of the things I loved about Arthur was that he could always find something to be fascinated by. He was so very special, you know. Whenever I was with him, all I knew was joy – and after being married to Elliott, you can imagine what a surprise that was. That talent for happiness you mentioned – that was so much a part of him. I'm glad it lived on through his daughter, if only briefly.'

'There are a few people in life you feel privileged to have known,' Josephine said, thinking about Jack. 'Elspeth was one of them, although she would have laughed at the idea. I'd have loved the chance to get to know her better.' She looked at Marta. 'I'd like the chance to get to know her mother better. I can't be sure, but I suspect Rafe was wrong when he said she wasn't like you. Before all this happened, I imagine you were rather different.'

Marta nodded. 'So much so that it feels like another life. I don't recognise myself any more. The woman Arthur loved hated violence and revenge and mistrust – all those things that men go to war for. She would have found murder abhorrent.'

'And craved peace and beauty? She sounds very much like the Anne of Bohemia that Vintner wrote about.' Marta's sharp glance was not lost on Josephine. 'You don't have to explain why you wanted to kill me, Marta,' she said. 'You hated me for the same reasons that Elliott Vintner did. But he didn't write *The White Heart*, did he? You did. It was your work I was supposed to have stolen, not his.'

'I shouldn't have given another writer the new book if I wanted to keep that a secret, should I? Yes, I wrote the novel that made

Elliott Vintner's name. I sent the manuscript to Arthur in one of the consignments that went out from May Gaskell's war library. Elliott must have either intercepted it or found it in Arthur's things after he died. The next time I came across it was in the hospital that my husband sent me to. There it was on somebody's bed, a published book with Elliott Vintner's name plastered all over the cover. All that fuss he made and everything he put you through, and it was never his to lay claim to, never his privilege to feel wronged.'

'Why didn't you say something?'

'I had no proof. The manuscript was long gone and anyway, I had no fight left in me. I was so afraid of him, Josephine. I never wanted to marry him, but outwardly he was the perfect match – wealthy, a little older than me, an academic – and my parents took it for granted that I'd accept him. I was too young and too naive to argue. He turned out to be very different behind closed doors, of course.'

'Did he hurt you?' Josephine asked.

Marta gave a bitter laugh. 'Oh yes, but not by doing anything as straightforward as hitting me. No, he was far too clever to do anything that I could talk about without being ashamed. He was hateful in bed – truly hateful. He used to pride himself on thinking up new and inventive ways to humiliate me. One day, he found a stash of short stories I'd written, and he was so scornful about his little writer wife. After that, whenever he'd finished with me in bed – and he was insatiable in his cruelty – he'd make me write about what we'd done and read it out to him. I had to relive the shame of it over and over again. It was his bid for immortality, I think, and he knew it kept him in my head when he couldn't be inside my body. He used to give me marks out of ten for the prose.'

Josephine was shocked. 'No wonder you turned to Arthur,' she said. 'It's a miracle you could be with anyone after that.'

'Yes, but Elliott knew exactly how to destroy me for what I'd done, and the world made it easy for him. Women like me – pregnant with a child that wasn't my husband's – were outcasts, fallen and in need of salvation. What's terrible is that you start to believe it yourself when you've been in there for a while, and the people who ran that place went to great lengths to keep you ignorant of the fact that things might be changing a little for the better in the world outside. The worst thing was the way that they stamped on any solidarity between the women; it would have been bearable if we could have helped each other through it, but we were constantly separated and played off against one another, and God help you if you got into what they so charmingly called a "particular friendship".' She took a cigarette out of the case in her bag. Josephine lit it for her and waited as she used the distraction to rein in her emotions. 'I was lucky, I suppose,' she continued at last. 'Some people spent decades there, detained for life. You could always tell which ones they were because they were obsessed with sin and religion; it didn't matter if they were prostitutes, victims of incest or rape, or just feeble-minded – they'd all been taught to despise themselves.'

'And you were there until Rafe came to find you? You must have been desperate to get out for years.'

'Yes and no. Arthur had died and both my children had been taken away from me, so there didn't seem much to get out for. Depression is the cruellest of things, you know. It deadens everything – there's no pleasure left in life, no colour or sensual enjoyment. Just an absence. I don't think I'd have felt any different if I'd been in a place I loved, seeing things that used to bring me joy every day. In fact, that probably would have been worse, so I welcomed being somewhere that turned me into no one.' The cigarette had been smoked quickly, and she threw the end down onto the track. 'Elliott took everything from me – my children, my book, my creativity in every sense of the word.'

'And your talent for happiness.'

Marta nodded. 'Exactly. It's hard to put into words how that felt. I remember being with Arthur in Cambridge just after Elliott had gone to war. He took me to a museum, just along the road from where he worked at the Botanic Gardens, because it had a collection of paintings that he loved. There was a whole wall of Impressionists and we stood for ages looking at an extraordinary

Renoir landscape – it was so sensual that I couldn't take my eyes off it. Next to it were two smaller paintings of women, one dancing and one playing a guitar. I was surprised at how awful they were by comparison – you could hardly believe they were by the same artist – but Arthur said that, if anything, he liked them better because they'd been painted late in Renoir's life when his hands were crippled with arthritis, and he thought there was something very noble about someone being so determined to create beauty in spite of the pain. I've never forgotten that, and I suppose it's how I felt, emotionally. I knew there was still so much that was beautiful in the world and I wanted so badly to write about it but, after Arthur died and I lost everything, I just couldn't. Books and art – they should all have a beauty about them, even if they begin with a scream, but it was as though someone had put a pen in my hand and frozen it. Does that make sense?'

'Yes, it does,' Josephine said. 'More than you could know.' Marta looked questioningly at her but there was no time to go into her own darkness as well as Marta's; even from this distance, she imagined she could feel Archie's growing impatience.

'Then Rafe turned up and suddenly there was a glimmer of hope,' Marta continued. 'How does that speech of Lydia's go in your play? "When joy is killed it dies forever, but happiness one can grow again." I always loved that line because it's exactly how I felt. I knew the joy had gone with Arthur, but I thought if I could get my children back, I might at least be able to rediscover the happiness. I would have done anything to make up for those lost years.' She fell silent and Josephine resisted the temptation to prompt her, sensing there was more to come. 'I knew that what he was suggesting was evil, of course I did, but at the time I didn't care. And yes, I did hate you but never because I thought you'd stolen my work. It was more complicated than that. You see, the only thing that kept me alive in that place was the thought that I might one day be able to have revenge on Elliott, to hurt him so badly for what he'd done to me. But you beat me to it. You won that court case and drove him to take his own life before I could make him suffer, and you've no idea how much I resented you for that.'

Josephine did not contradict her, but asked instead, 'Did you really intend to kill Aubrey?'

'Yes, at first. I had no idea he was related to Arthur, of course. I was in such a state on Friday. When you turned up at the taxi with Lydia, I realised what a mistake I'd made in pointing out the wrong person. I went to see Rafe at Wyndham's as soon as Lydia was on stage, and when he told me he'd gone through with it I was horrified. Then he said that Aubrey suspected something and was on to us, and I panicked. I knew I'd never be with my children again if we were caught, and that was all I wanted. Rafe assured me that we could salvage things if we acted quickly, and at first I went along with what he suggested. But when the moment came I just couldn't go through with it. Aubrey didn't know anything, though, did he? Rafe just used that to get me to do his dirty work.'

'He knew something, Marta,' Josephine said quietly. 'But not who you were or what you'd done.' Marta listened in disbelief as she repeated Alice Simmons's account of Arthur's murder and Walter's pact with Vintner, and Josephine wished that it had not fallen to her to shatter this woman's world all over again. 'So Vintner's suicide had nothing to do with *Richard of Bordeaux* or the court case,' she added. 'He killed himself because he was about to be exposed as a murderer. Arthur's murderer.'

Marta was silent for a long time, then said, 'So that's what Lydia was talking about last night. I sat there listening to her discuss a murder and had no idea it was Arthur. Did Rafe know his father was a killer?'

'I think so, yes. Archie's convinced that this has all been about protecting his father's reputation. Bernard Aubrey had been look-ing for proof for nearly twenty years to get justice for his nephew and he finally had what he needed. It was all to come out on Elspeth's eighteenth birthday.'

The platform was beginning to fill with passengers waiting to board the two departing trains, some bound for the Midlands, others further north, but Marta seemed oblivious to everyone but the dead. 'So many lies,' she said at last, so softly that Josephine had to lean closer to hear her above the bustle. 'So many people who just couldn't let the dust settle and turn their back on the evil. Arthur would have been horrified to know what he and I set in motion all those years ago. We've all magnified Elliott's violence in our own way. If I'd refused to help Rafe or if Aubrey had been strong enough to let it go, Elspeth would still be alive.'

'He couldn't let it go – he wasn't that sort of man. Bernard had a very clear sense of right and wrong, and it wouldn't have occurred to him that bringing Elliott Vintner to justice would open more wounds than it healed. He always felt responsible for Arthur's death, and he loved his sister and her son. According to his wife, Bernard planted irises in his memory all year round.'

Marta had, Josephine thought, remained remarkably composed throughout the exchange but this simple act of homage broke her in a way that more shocking revelations had failed to do. Josephine waited, unable to do anything but hold her until the tears had subsided. 'It was the first flower he planted for me,' Marta explained, turning her face away in embarrassment as she noticed a porter further down the platform staring at the two women in astonishment. 'He put it all round the summer house because its name meant "eye of heaven" and it was supposed to be the Egyptian symbol of eloquence; it was to help me with my writing, he said. And he made me promise to include a flower with the letter whenever I wrote to him in France, because Iris was Zeus' messenger and he was sure she'd get it there safely.' She smiled sadly. 'She failed me with *The White Heart*, though. It was my love letter to him, and I don't even know if he read it or not. It's silly, but sometimes that makes me more miserable than anything.'

'Then take this. At least it will answer one of your questions.' Josephine took a sheaf of papers out of her bag and handed them to Marta, who looked down in astonishment. 'While I was waiting for the police, I looked through the holdall that Rafe was carrying and found this. He must have got them from his father. It's not the whole manuscript, but most of it's there and there are some notes in the margins. I'm afraid I was curious enough to read some of them – only a few, but enough to know that whoever wrote them was very much in love with the author.' Marta was lost for a moment in the pages. 'That is Arthur's handwriting?'

Marta nodded, then looked gratefully at Josephine. 'I think you know how much this means to me,' she said, 'so there's no point in trying to thank you – it could never be enough. I can't believe what I've done, you know. I shouldn't have trusted Rafe. I should have known what growing up with that man would have done to him. I knew how wrong I'd been when I listened to you and Lydia talking about Aubrey last night – that wasn't the man Rafe described to me at all, just as you're not the woman he said you must be.' She sat up and looked back towards the main station building. 'It's time to put an end to all this. I take it you didn't come here on your own?'

'No. Archie's here with his sergeant and I expect there'll be reinforcements outside by now. He promised to give me time to talk to you, although I don't know how much longer he'll wait. But he'll be fair, Marta, and so will the courts. You've suffered so much – they won't ignore that.'

'You mean they won't hang me?' Her wry smile softened the harshness of the words which Josephine had been trying to avoid. 'The trouble is, the last thing I want is to live. That would be the brave way, to carry this through the years, but I'm not brave, Josephine. I want to die, but I need to do it my way, in a place that's special to me. And I want to say goodbye to Arthur first. I'm afraid I have no faith in the idea that I might be about to see him again. I'm begging you – please let me get on a train and simply disappear.'

'It doesn't have to come to that, Marta. Rafe will live and be made to face what he's done in court. Let that be the end to it, not this. You haven't killed anyone, after all.'

'Haven't I? You of all people don't think I could live with what's happened, do you? There was a rope around my neck from the moment that Elliott sat down to write that letter to Rafe. What does it matter if I do it myself? If they take me in now, I shall plead guilty to Aubrey's murder. I picked up the decanter to do it, so my prints will be all over it, and Rafe's hardly going to argue, is he?

271

We both have to face what we deserve, but this way is kinder and not just to me – surely you can see that. I don't want Lydia to go through a trial and an execution. As it is, I'll never forgive myself for allowing her to find Aubrey's body. Because I couldn't bring myself to kill him, though, I didn't expect there to be a body to find.'

'Isn't Lydia worth living for?'

'Do you really believe I'd come first over her work?' Josephine could not honestly give the answer that Marta wanted, so she stayed quiet. 'You have to come first with each other, Josephine. Do you remember what you said about having someone to make the work less lonely? I know exactly what you meant, but Lydia's never lonely when she's at work. She'd be happy to be cast as "woman with vegetables" for the rest of her life as long as she could be on that stage.' They both smiled, acknowledging the truth of Marta's words. 'Look after Lydia for me, won't you? She'll have to know what I've done, but I want her to understand why and you're the only person who can explain.'

'Does she know anything about what happened to you before you met her?'

'We scratched the surface, but that's all and she obviously doesn't know who else was involved. It's funny what ends up being important, isn't it? I don't mind her knowing I'm a potential murderer, but I do need her to understand that I wasn't just using her. It started out like that: we needed access to the theatre and she was close to you. And she had a certain reputation, of course. But I genuinely loved her. Please make her understand that.'

'Isn't there anything I can say to change your mind?'

Marta smiled sadly and Josephine wondered what she was thinking. She seemed about to speak, but changed her mind and instead took Josephine's hand. 'There might have been once, but too much has happened now, even for that.' She stood up. 'Shouldn't you go and find your policeman? The train will be leaving in a few minutes.'

Josephine tried desperately to think of something that would make Marta change her mind. She had honestly believed that she would be able to stop her, either with reason or by resorting to emotional arguments, but what could you say to someone who was so determined to die? Would Archie and the courts have more success after all? Perhaps if Marta were forced to live long enough, she would feel differently.

Marta sensed her dilemma. 'While you decide what's best, can I ask you to do something else? Will you go to Elspeth's funeral? Say goodbye to her for me. Hello and goodbye.'

With mixed feelings, Josephine agreed. She wanted to pay her own respects, too, of course, but she had always hated the trappings of professional mourning and resented having to say goodbye to those she loved in such an atmosphere.

'And make sure the new book gets published – under my name this time. Give the money to a charity that cares for women. Cares for them in this life, I mean, not one that just redeems their souls for the next. That's if it sells, of course.'

'Of course it will sell. You don't need me to tell you how good it is.' She paused, then gave it her final shot. 'The third novel would be even better, though.'

It was a straw, she knew, but in spite of everything Marta seemed gratified by Josephine's regard for her work. 'At least I know the manuscript's in good hands this time,' she said. 'And I've always hankered after a foreword by someone famous if you have time on your hands.' She held up the papers in her hand, the manuscript of the book that had started so much trouble. 'Seriously, Josephine, whatever happens to me I want you to put the record straight about this. Write a foreword that explains everything, and make sure people get to read it.'

A crowd of well-wishers was gathering to see loved ones safely on their various journeys, and Marta looked back at the carriages. As a trail of steam from the engine signalled the promise of departure, Josephine finally made up her mind. 'No, Marta, write it yourself and send it to me from wherever you are,' she said, pushing her quickly towards the train. 'I'll make sure it's read, but promise me you'll do that before you even think of doing anything else.'

Marta turned and looked at her for a long time. 'I promise,' she said. 'Thank you, Josephine.'

'And think about what you do after that. Please.' They kissed as if the journey heralded nothing more than a week at the seaside, then Marta got on board without looking back and Josephine lost sight of her. She waited until the train was pulling out, then turned back to face Archie's fury. In the end, it was she who had broken her promise, not him, and there was also the small matter of tampering with evidence to own up to. Before she had taken half a dozen steps, however, she heard her name called and looked up in surprise to find Fallowfield coming towards her. He was alone and she looked questioningly at him, wondering where Archie had gone. Shrugging as apologetically as a policeman could, Fallowfield nodded towards the train, which by now had almost disappeared from view.

So Archie had been one step ahead of her after all. She should have known. Her anger and frustration threatened to get the better of her and, on the verge of tears, she brushed aside Fallowfield's arm and walked back up the platform, desperate for a few moments alone. It was the other train's turn to depart now, and she had to move several yards further on to get some peace from the hustle and bustle. Shivering from the cold, she looked sadly back at the carriages, remembering the journey down with Elspeth and wondering what would happen when Archie caught up with Marta. Her attention was caught by the lamps going on in the final compartment, and she watched as a mother and daughter settled themselves by the window. How different things could have been, she thought, and was about to turn away when another woman slid back the carriage door and settled into one of the vacant seats. She stared in astonishment, but Marta simply put her finger to her lips. From a distance, it was difficult to be sure but Josephine could have sworn she was smiling as the train moved slowly out into the evening.

Sixteen

In the early hours of Monday morning, St Martin's Lane was still reluctant to engage with a new day. Lydia slipped quietly from the Motleys' studio and out into the deserted street, confident that the soft click of the front door would not be noticed: everyone inside was exhausted, and unlikely to stir for at least another hour or two. Unable to face going back to her digs the night before, she had been glad of company – but sleep was out of the question. In fact, feeling as she did now, she wondered if she would ever manage to sleep again.

Across the road, the New Theatre seemed strangely untouched by the violence: its walls were as solid as ever; its steps as polished; and the photographs on the boards outside – apart from being half-covered with a 'Final Week' announcement – promised the familiar glimpse of romance and excitement. How extraordinary that this glamorous world of make-believe should still exist in the face of such horror, she thought, but exist it did – and the play would indeed go on. Archie had confirmed that performances could begin again as normal on Tuesday and, although Johnny had offered to put an understudy on for Lydia or to cancel the rest of the week as a mark of respect, she had refused both options, knowing that work would get her through as nothing else could and that Bernard would not want Terry's first week in charge to be dark. She had little doubt that Johnny would make a success of what had been left to him, but what his reign would mean for her she could not say.

She crossed the street and sat down outside the theatre, watching as the light grew stronger over the city. Was Marta somewhere waiting for the day to start, or had she already taken that last, terrible step? Lydia had been furious with Josephine for letting her go, but she knew in her heart that it was a selfish reaction which stemmed in part from jealousy: those vital moments had created a bond between her lover and her friend from which she was excluded and, in her grief, she found that hard to accept. She wanted to believe that she could have succeeded where Josephine had failed, but was too honest to ignore the truth for long. Now, her anger replaced by helplessness and regret, she was left to reflect on what she could have done to make Marta want to live. Could she have put work second for Marta's sake? Smiling sadly, she was brave enough to acknowledge both the answer and the guilt that came with it. She had loved her, certainly, but that had not been enough – for either of them.

Just for a moment, Lydia saw herself in ten years' time – grateful for insignificant parts that kept her on the stage; enduring long, second-rate tours in bleak lodgings with poor company; and trailing a string of broken relationships. She was grateful to Aubrey for having left her financially comfortable and she had always longed for a house in the country, a place to retreat to when she was not on the stage, but perhaps she should consider more permanent changes?

A van turned into St Martin's Lane and idled its way up the street, stopping just a few yards away. The milkman got out to place a couple of cans on the Salisbury's doorstep, and looked surprised to see someone sitting outside the theatre at the wrong end of the day. Then he recognised her, raised his cap politely and returned to his van. Instead of driving on, though, he poured a glass of milk and brought it over with a piece of paper.

'Early rehearsal, Miss?' he joked, and handed her the milk. 'This'll keep you going till they let you in. I've been to the show a couple of times myself, but the wife practically lives here. No disrespect, but thank God it's finishing or I'd be bankrupt.'

Lydia laughed, and nodded at the paper. 'Would you like me to sign that for her?' she asked, taking the stubby pencil that was offered and chatting graciously until the milkman felt obliged to get on his way. How easily the mask came down, she thought, when he had gone. A new career? Who was she trying to fool? Tired of her own company, Lydia stood up and walked back across the road, hoping that by now someone might be up and about, ready to keep her from herself.

As soon as the police had finished questioning him about Swinburne, Hedley White asked to see Elspeth. Sergeant Fallowfield looked at him kindly, but with concern. 'Are you sure that's a good idea, lad? Mortuaries are terrible places, even for people who are used to them. Wouldn't you rather wait until we take her somewhere else? It'll be any time now.'

But Hedley had insisted, unable to bear the thought of Elspeth all alone, and he sat now in a poky room off Gower Street, waiting for someone to fetch him. The door opened and a lady came in, but she was not the member of staff he had been expecting: her dress and the circles around her eyes made it obvious that her relationship with death was anything but a professional one. Not recognising her, he was surprised when she spoke his name.

'I'm Alice Simmons,' she added, and waited for him to respond.

So this was Elspeth's mother – the mother who had brought her up, anyway, and of whom Elspeth spoke so fondly. He stood and held out his hand, nervously wiping it on his trousers first. She looked at him for a long time, assessing the boy who had earned her daughter's love, and he wondered what she saw and how it tallied with anything that Elspeth might have told her about him.

'This isn't the sort of place that a mother dreams of meeting her daughter's boyfriend,' she said eventually, 'but I *am* pleased to meet you and I'm glad you're here. The more company Elspeth has, the better, don't you think?'

Hedley nodded, and they sat down. Mrs Simmons made the sort of small-talk that any potential mother-in-law might resort to, and Hedley sensed that she was as reluctant as he was to refer to the evil that had brought them here.

'What will you do now?' she asked, and he was touched to see genuine concern in her face, but had no idea what the answer was. He had vowed never to enter a theatre again, and had meant it. His whole love of the stage had been guided by Elspeth's enthusiasm and Aubrey's belief in him, and it would never be the same now that they were both gone. Lydia always joked that he had a job with her looking after the elusive house in the country, but who could say if that would ever be a reality? Even so, he knew he could be sure of Lydia's friendship: they had always got on, but were bound now by a mutual sense of loss for a daughter and her mother, a victim and . . . well, he didn't quite know how he felt about Marta Fox but, for Lydia's sake, he would try to focus on sympathy rather than on the bitterness that sprang more readily to mind. As for Swinburne, he would be outside the gaol to hear the clock strike nine on the morning that bastard was hanged.

'Anyway, you'll come and stay with us at Frank and Betty's, I hope, for now?' she said. 'They've asked me to say you'll be more than welcome. There's not much room, I know, but it'll be good for us all to have each other.'

Hedley accepted, grateful to have his next steps marked out for him. When a woman came to fetch them at last, they went in to see Elspeth together.

The manuscript of Marta's new novel lay on the table, untouched since Josephine had left it there the day before. She had not felt able to look at it again, but she had read enough to know that its subject was a fictional account of Marta's marriage, powerful in its own right and not in the least self-indulgent, but poignantly auto-biographical nonetheless. Josephine could already imagine a publisher rubbing his hands together with glee. What sort of ending had Marta written for herself, she wondered? She would find out in time, but not yet. At the moment, the manuscript was too strong a reminder of her own doubts and fears. She had felt certain yesterday that she was doing the right thing, but now she questioned her decision.

Archie had been white with rage when he caught up with her at the Yard. It had not taken him long to realise his mistake, but the other train had stopped at three stations before he was able to have it searched, giving Marta plenty of time to disappear. God knows what would happen to her now: Archie had vowed to find her if it was the last thing he did and Josephine had never seen him so angry; he had even threatened to arrest her for aiding and abetting Marta's escape. In part, his fury was with himself: he had acted rashly in underestimating Marta Fox, and he would regard that as inexcusable. But Josephine also understood that she had betrayed his trust and undermined his integrity, and he might find that hard to forgive, no matter how much he loved her. Yesterday, when he accused her of taking justice into her own hands just like Vintner and Marta and Aubrey, the truth of his words had stung.

For something to do, she went through to the small kitchen to make breakfast and found some bacon in the refrigerator. She took it out, then put it straight back and settled for a pot of tea instead. Food was more than she could face.

'Is there enough in that pot for two?' Lydia spoke hesitantly, as if wondering what sort of reception she would get.

'There's plenty,' Josephine said, delighted to see her. 'But I'm afraid it's proper tea, not the scented apology for a hot drink that you prefer.'

'I'll slum it, just this once.' Lydia smiled, sharing Josephine's relief, and found some cups and saucers in the cupboard. 'I'm sorry, Josephine,' she said, suddenly serious. 'It was much easier to blame you for letting Marta go than to think about how I might have let her down. Who knows, if I'd taken more time to listen to her and read between the lines, she might have felt strong enough to rebuild her life another way. I miss her so much, but I was a cow to blame you because she's not here any more.'

Josephine took her hand. 'I'm sorry, too,' she said. 'I really thought I was doing what was right, but then so did Marta and Bernard, and even Vintner in his way, and look where that got them. I might just have made it worse. But she does love you, you know. She wanted you to be sure of that.'

Lydia had not missed the present tense. 'Do you think there's any chance she might change her mind now that she's away from everything?'

'I really don't know,' Josephine said, conscious of the irony that, if Marta did have a change of heart, it would be her work that kept her alive. 'I hoped she would and I asked her to, but I'm honestly not sure if I could live with what she knows.' She poured the hot water into the pot and looked at Lydia. 'And Archie's determined to track her down. It's become a battle of wills between those two since they first clashed swords. He's probably staking Cambridge out as we speak.'

'Is that where she went, do you think?'

Josephine considered. 'It would be my first guess, although I purposely didn't ask – I wouldn't have been able to lie to Archie in the mood he was in. It's where Marta met Arthur so, in spite of Vintner, she was happy there. If she has gone to Cambridge, though, I don't think she'll be able to keep it a secret. It's a small place, and Archie knows it well.'

'Has all this caused problems between the two of you?'

'It certainly hasn't made things any easier, but then my relationship with Archie has never been easy.'

'Why is that? Because he loves you and knows you don't feel the same way?'

'It's more complicated than that. It goes back twenty years.'

'Doesn't everything?' Lydia raised an eyebrow wryly. 'We don't have to talk about it if you don't want to.'

'It's not that. It just feels disloyal to Archie.'

'Then you should speak to each other – get it all out in the open. Look what secrets can do to you.'

Josephine nodded, knowing that Lydia was right. After what had happened in the last couple of days, she was reluctant to let old grudges continue to fester. 'I'll talk to him when I get the chance,' she said.

Voices drifted through to the kitchen from the central studio, confirming that Ronnie and Lettice were finally awake, so she added two more cups to the tray before carrying it in. Lettice thumped down onto the sofa next to Lydia and gave her an enormous hug. 'Look on the bright side, darling – you hated that alabaster statue from the moment Hephzibar gave it to you.'

Lydia had to smile, as Ronnie leaned forward and poked her sister in the shoulder. 'What did I tell you?' she said triumphantly. 'Everything that Hephzibar touches is cursed.' Then the smugness disappeared. 'She hasn't ever given us anything, has she?'

'Don't be ridiculous,' Lettice snapped, but Josephine was amused to see her glance nervously at a small Buddha by the door. 'Listen,' she continued, 'with all the fuss, we forgot to tell you that Johnny telephoned last night. He wants to talk to you about adding a week to the tour and finishing in Hammersmith as a tribute to Hedley's girl – he thought of dedicating the week's performances to her. Do you think the family would like that, or is it too soon?'

'I think they'd be very touched,' Josephine said. 'If it can be made to work, it's a wonderful idea.'

'Good. He's going to see if people are free. It might mean delaying rehearsals for *Queen of Scots* by a week or so, though.'

'I'm sure no one will mind,' Josephine said, adding privately to herself that the longer she could put off going through another play, the better.

'Actually, we were a bit bewildered by the rest of the conversation,' Lettice added. 'It scarcely sounded like the real Johnny. Apparently, he's given Fleming three months off on full pay to sort out some personal problems. I don't know what's come over him. We half-wondered if we should do a few sketches for *A Christmas Carol*.'

There was an abrupt knock at the door and Ronnie got up to answer it. 'Archie, dear,' she said, letting him in. 'Where are you going today? I believe you can get season tickets if you intend to make a habit of rail travel.'

Josephine was relieved to see that Archie's wrath had been replaced by composure tinged with embarrassment. 'Is there any news of Marta?' Lydia asked as soon as she saw him.

'I'm afraid not,' he said, sitting down and accepting some tea. 'I really am sorry, Lydia. I know that whatever professional duty I have to find her, it's nothing compared to how much you must long for news. I promise I'll tell you as soon as I know anything. And I owe you an apology, too, Josephine.' He looked at her a little sheepishly, but a smile hovered at the corners of his mouth. 'So I've decided not to arrest you after all.' He drank his tea, and continued more earnestly. 'We've checked the hospital records, though, and they confirm what Marta told Josephine about her time there. In fact, she didn't tell you how bad it was.' He glanced at Lydia.

'Go on, Archie,' she said. 'Don't worry about me.'

'Well, I managed to speak to someone who was a young nurse there at the time – she's moved on now – and she remembers Marta very clearly. The depression was severe, it seems, and this nurse didn't mince her words about how Marta was treated by those in charge. Apparently, she made a couple of attempts to take her own life just after Elspeth was born, then simply resigned herself to her fate.'

'It's hard to imagine how she got through it at all,' Josephine said.

'Yes, but that's not everything. The reason this woman remembers Marta so clearly is because of what happened when the baby was taken away from her a few weeks later. Her husband came to fetch it, she says, and he brought a young boy of about five or six with him. Marta clung to the baby, desperate not to let her go, but of course it was no use. When the husband – Vintner – had Elspeth in his arms, he turned to the young boy and told him to go and give Mummy her present. The child went over to Marta and, when she bent down to him, he spat in her face. The sisters just stood by and watched. The woman I spoke to left the hospital the very next day – she said she couldn't bear such cruelty.'

Lydia was pale by now, and even Ronnie and Lettice were too shocked to speak. 'Have you spoken to Rafe Vintner yet?' Josephine asked at last. 'It seems that everyone's a victim in this. I can't imagine how being filled with so much hatred must have affected him at that age.'

'Yes, and I couldn't begin to tell you how it's grown over the years. I've only spoken to him briefly because he's still in hospital and fairly weak from that knock on the head, but I don't think I've ever seen so little remorse. He's trying to blame his mother for everything, but that doesn't surprise me.'

'He won't get away with it, surely?' Josephine was horrified.

'Oh no, if only because he can't resist making it clear how clever he's been, even as he tries to push all the responsibility onto Marta. He's his own worst counsel – so keen to make sure I've appreciated all the little signs he's left along the way. You know, I still think that's the most chilling part of these murders for me – the extent to which each scene was designed to humiliate his victims.'

'Were the dolls his?' Josephine asked.

'We'll find out when we can interview him properly, but I'm sure they were. Now we know what we know, the doll with the broken hand and the wedding ring was clearly a reference to Marta's infidelity. The iris was a jibe at Arthur, and the more I think about it, the more I'm convinced that the choice of nicotine was, too. It's used by gardeners, don't forget, and I'm sure the irony wasn't lost on him when he was planning the worst possible death for Bernard Aubrey.'

'And the locked door?' The question was from Lydia, and Archie could imagine how the memory of that terrible discovery had stayed with her.

'I'm not certain yet, but there's no doubt Swinburne used the bridge between the two theatres to get to Bernard's office that night and leave the bayonet on the desk,' he said. 'I wouldn't be surprised if he expected the room to be empty – nicotine would have killed most people long before they got up those stairs – and, if so, he'll have had the shock of his life to find Bernard there, alive or dead. Perhaps he just panicked and locked the door without thinking – everybody makes a mistake eventually. Whatever happened, we'll get to the bottom of it.' He thought for a second, remembering his promise to Grace Aubrey. 'Vintner and I have a lot to talk about, so the sooner he's fit enough, the better I'll like it.'

'But will there be enough evidence to convict him?' Lydia asked, an urgency in her voice.

Archie looked at her reassuringly. 'Yes, we've got a very good case, and Walter's confession was lodged with Aubrey's solicitor, which helps tremendously.' He turned apprehensively to Josephine. 'I'm afraid you'll have to testify against him, though. We can't risk it without you.'

'In court against one Vintner is misfortune, but two looks like carelessness.' Josephine spoke lightly, but the prospect of another trial filled her with dismay. This time, if she were successful, she really would be sending a Vintner to his death. Would it never be over?

Archie looked at his watch. 'I'm sorry, but I've got to go now – Bill's expecting me back at the station. Will you see me out?' he asked, and Josephine nodded.

'Actually, I'll walk with you,' she said. 'I could do with some fresh air.'

Traffic coiled around Trafalgar Square as Josephine and Archie made their way towards Whitehall, and news vendors were just starting to emerge, ready to catch the lunch-hour trade. 'They're going to have a field day when this comes out,' Archie said. 'I just hope we can find Marta before she has her life story splashed all over the front pages. I didn't want to tell you in front of Lydia, but Bill and I are going to Somerset House this afternoon. Apparently, Aubrey telephoned there on Friday to make an appointment. I'm not certain yet, but I'd say he was about to go through the records to find out who Elspeth's mother was. If only he'd done it sooner.'

Once again, Josephine considered how differently things might have turned out – for Marta and for Elspeth. 'I'm glad you didn't mention it,' she said. 'Lydia's had about as much as she can take for now – I think everyone has. She spoke to Hedley last night, and said he was absolutely inconsolable.'

'At least he needn't be on his own – the Simmonses have said he can stay with them if he wants to.'

'Have you been to see them yet?'

'Yes, first thing this morning. When I got there, Frank Simmons was out the back burning the doll that Hedley had sent. He said he couldn't bear the thought of anything Vintner had touched going near Elspeth, and he's already packed away all his theatre stuff, ready to sell to another collector. He and Betty seemed to be getting on better, though; there was a warmth between them today that I didn't see the last time we were there. Strange how people can be brought closer together by the death of someone they love.'

'Or driven further apart.' She stopped, and looked at Archie. 'Why have you never told me?'

'Told you what?' he asked, but she could tell from the way he hesitated that he knew what she meant.

'The soldier Jack saved – the man he died for – it was you, wasn't it?' She waited for him to say something, half hoping that he would deny it, but he simply looked at her with a mixture of shock and relief. 'It's the only thing that makes any sense,' she continued. 'I know you were wounded at around that time, and it explains why you avoided me for so long after Jack died. God knows, I've had long enough to think about it.' His silence was making her angry now. 'How could you let me go on wondering year after year? You've made it impossible for us to have any sort of truthful relationship, and you can't even speak to me about it now.'

'I didn't know you had any idea,' he said at last. 'I suppose that's why I haven't said anything – because I didn't want it to affect our friendship.'

The excuse sounded feeble, even to him; to Josephine, it was insufferable. 'And you don't think it has been affected?' she said scornfully. 'For Christ's sake, Archie, there's always this sadness about you when you're with me. I thought at first it was because I reminded you of Jack, but you've had years to get over that, and if I can manage it, you should be able to. I watch you with other people, and there's a spark in you. But not with me. You're so bloody careful around me all the time. You know, it was quite gratifying yesterday when you were furious with me – at least it felt honest.'

'Oh, don't talk to me about honesty,' he said, relief giving way to resentment. 'Why didn't you say something? If you wanted this so-called truthful relationship, you could have made it easier for me to talk to you. But no – instead, you have to piece it all together like some sort of cheap detective story, building your evidence out of my feelings and my silence. Do you have any idea how cold that is?'

Afraid of what he might say next, Archie turned to walk on but Josephine caught his arm. 'All right, I should have done things differently, too. I know that, and I'm angry with myself as much as with you. But I needed to feel you *could* tell me – don't you understand that?'

'But I couldn't,' he said. 'Facing up to it with you would have meant dealing with it myself, and that was too much to ask.' He paused, wondering how he could ever give Josephine the explanation she wanted when he barely understood it himself. 'You see, I didn't know much about it at the time. I was unconscious for days, and it was a long time before anyone thought I was well enough to talk about it. I don't know if they'd ever have told me exactly what had happened if I hadn't started to remember bits and pieces, and to ask questions about Jack. When I heard the whole story, it was as if it had happened to someone else. I don't know if it was some sort of defence mechanism or just cowardice, but I distanced myself from the whole thing, acted as though I hadn't been there. I'd talk about that soldier in the third person, as if he were a complete stranger. Eventually, I came to some sort of peace with myself – well, acceptance rather than peace – but I could never find that with you. All I could think about was that last summer when I went to stay with Jack in Scotland, and I'd watch the two of you together and marvel at how happy you were. So no, I couldn't own up to what I'd taken from you, and the longer I left it, the more impossible it became ever to say anything.'

'Did it never occur to you that it might be easier for me to know Jack died for someone I care about?' As soon as the words were out, she realised how selfish they seemed. Archie smiled, but there was no reassurance in it.

'That's a nice sentiment, but I doubt it's true, however much you care. It's not to my credit to be jealous of a dead man, especially one I loved, but if you'd had the chance to play God back then, it wouldn't be me you'd have allowed to live.'

Now it was Josephine's turn to pull away. 'Listen to yourself,

Archie,' she said, oblivious to the scene they were making. 'How can you talk about playing God after all that's happened? You know, I'm sick and tired of people making decisions for me, telling me how I would and wouldn't feel. First I'm caught up in a private war between Vintner and Aubrey, and now you've manoeuvred me into some sort of no man's land between you and Jack.'

'Don't be ridiculous,' he said, stunned. 'It isn't the same thing at all.'

'Isn't it? You're manipulating me because of your own guilt, and from where I'm standing that's exactly the same thing. How dare you tell me how I'd have felt when you never gave me the chance to find out? Yes, I was in love with Jack, but it was young love and it didn't ask for very much. It might have grown, of course – I assumed it would at the time – but I would have looked for something more sooner or later. I'm not going to live my whole life according to the options I had when I was nineteen. So don't think you know what's best for me, because you don't.'

'And when exactly is this sooner or later going to arrive? You were let off the hook in deciding whether or not to commit to Jack, and ever since, you've used his death as an excuse not to commit to anyone. Instead, you just throw yourself into your work, living with people who don't exist and never will.' He stopped, and turned away, unable to trust himself not to go any further and suspecting that he had already said more than he would be forgiven for.

Josephine let him walk away. Shaken by the truth in his parting shot, she sat down on the cold, stone steps of one of the government buildings that lined the street and watched him stride angrily down Whitehall. He stopped by the Cenotaph, and bent down to pick something up from the foot of the memorial. As he stood there, looking at it, she wondered what was going through his head, and realised sadly that she would never truly know: no matter how hard she tried to put herself in his position, or how strong the instinct for forgiveness and reconciliation, understanding was one of the casualties of the war; even now, there was an unbearable void between those who had fought it and those who had not, a stifling of emotion which was not so different from the deadening of joy that Marta had talked about. How many generations would it last, she wondered? And what would the future have held for Elspeth if those who loved her had not been so crippled by the past? In the distance, Archie replaced whatever he had taken up and walked on towards Derby Gate. Before he could move too far out of reach, she got up and went after him.

Author's Note

To write fiction about historic fact is very nearly impermissible.

Gordon Daviot, *The Privateer*

An Expert in Murder is a work of fiction, inspired by real lives and events.

Gordon Daviot was one of two pseudonyms created by Elizabeth Mackintosh (1896–1952) during a versatile career as playwright and novelist; the other, Josephine Tey, was taken from her Suffolk great-great-grandmother and did not actually appear until 1936, with the publication of *A Shilling for Candles*. It was reserved for detective fiction, and is the name by which we know her best today.

By 1934, she had written a mystery and two other novels as Daviot, but it was *Richard of Bordeaux* which made her name and led to a number of important friendships and professional relationships. Mackintosh divided her time between London and her hometown, Inverness, where she looked after her father, and, when she died, she left the bulk of her considerable estate to the National Trust for England. The Josephine Tey who appears in *An Expert in Murder* mixes what we know about Elizabeth Mackintosh with the personality which emerges so strongly from her eight crime novels – novels which are loved for their warmth and originality by those who have discovered them, but which are still vastly underrated in comparison with the work of her contemporaries.

Richard of Bordeaux ran for 463 performances at the New Theatre (now the Noël Coward Theatre) in St Martin's Lane, closing on 24 March 1934. It took more than £100,000 at the box office under the management of Howard Wyndham and Bronson Albery (who lived to enjoy the success), and acquired the sort of popularity that films enjoy today: hundreds of Elspeths went thirty or forty times to see it; the cast took part in high-profile publicity stunts; commemorative portrait dolls were produced; and it turned its leading man, John Gielgud, from a brilliant young actor into a celebrity overnight. The beauty of the set and costumes, designed by 'Motley' (Margaret and Sophia Harris and Elizabeth Montgomery), was vital to the play's success, as was Gwen Ffrangcon-Davies's performance as Anne. *Bordeaux* toured provincial theatres and was produced on Broadway, but the over-all experience was not entirely positive for its author: fame was unwelcome, particularly in Inverness, and, according to Gielgud, she was subject to unfair accusations of plagiarism which hurt her deeply. Gielgud's own hopes for a film starring himself and Lillian Gish were never realised.

Daviot wrote many other plays – *The Laughing Woman* and *Queen of Scots* were produced at the New later in 1934 – but none were as successful as *Bordeaux*, whose humanity and romanticism struck a powerful chord in an audience haunted by one war and threatened by another. The war's significance in the public response was a surprise even to the author: what she thought of as a tale of revenge, she admitted later, turned out to be a play about pacifism.

For an author who wrote several historical plays and novels, Elizabeth Mackintosh took a dim view of mixing fact and fiction – but she allowed it if the writer stated where the truth could be found, and if invention did not falsify the general picture. Readers wanting to know more about the real people involved in *Richard of Bordeaux* should consult Gielgud's autobiographical writings, the biographies by Sheridan Morley and Jonathan Croall, and Michael Mullin's *Design by Motley*. Murder, of course, does rather distort the general picture, but I hope that it won't entirely eclipse a unique moment of theatrical history and the true beginning of a remarkable writing career.

Acknowledgements

An Expert in Murder was part of the 2005–6 Escalator Literature Awards Programme and funded by Arts Council England, and I am especially grateful to the New Writing Partnership and Michelle Spring, and to all at Arts Council England, East, for their support.

The book is a tribute to the people whose hard work and achievements created such a special world during the 1930s – particularly to Sir John Gielgud and Margaret Harris of Motley, both of whom were kind enough to talk to me at length about the theatre of the period, and, of course, to Josephine Tey, whose work is at the heart of the novel.

Many other people have helped – wittingly or unwittingly – and I owe particular thanks to Karolina Sutton, Jennifer Joel, Laura Sampson and ICM for wonderful advice and encouragement; to Claire Wachtel, Jonathan Burnham and Heather Drucker for their passion for the novel; to Peter Mendelsohn, Cindy Achar, Roni Axelrod and Julia Novitch at HarperCollins for their care and vision in its production; to Walter Donohue for his magic at the beginning; to Dr Peter Fordyce and Stewart P. Evans for their expertise in very different areas of unpleasantness; to Richard Reynolds for his enthusiasm and knowledge of detective fiction; to Jane Munro and the Fitzwilliam Museum, Cambridge, for influencing Archie's taste in art so beautifully; to Helen Grime and Margaret Westwood for their great interest and help with the project; to Josceline Dimbleby for the story of May Gaskell in her book *A Profound Secret*; to Virginia Nicholson for the wealth of information in *Among the Bohemians*; to Ian Ross, for the time to make a start; to H.W. for additional typing; and to Sir Donald Sinden, Frith Banbury, Dulcie Gray and the late Michael Denison for their generosity in sharing recollections and stories with me.

Love and thanks go, as always, to my parents and family – for much, much more than their enthusiasm for this novel.

And to Mandy, who has been so instrumental in every moment – from the original idea and wild beginnings to the fine detail and finished book – the joy of this is all down to you.